P9-CSE-958

THE STRANGER'S MAGIC

ALSO BY MAX FREI

The Stranger:
The Labyrinths of Echo—Book One

The Stranger's Woes
The Labyrinths of Echo—Book Two

THE LABYRINTHS OF ECHO: BOOK THREE

THE STRANGER'S MAGIC

MAX FREI

Translated from the Russian by Polly Gannon and Ast A. Moore

THE OVERLOOK PRESS
New York, NY

This edition first published in hardcover in the United States in 2012 by
The Overlook Press, Peter Mayer Publishers, Inc.
141 Wooster Street
New York, NY 10012
www.overlookpress.com
For bulk and special sales, please contact sales@overlookny.com

Cataloging-in-Publication Data is available from the Library of Congress

Book design and type formatting by Bernard Schleifer
Manufactured in the United States of America
ISBN 978-1-59020-479-5
FIRST EDITION
1 3 5 7 9 10 8 6 4 2

CONTENTS

Previously in the THE LABYRINTHS OF ECHO . . .

MAX FREI was once a loser. He's a big sleeper (during the day, that is; at night he can't sleep a wink). A hardened smoker, an uncomplicated glutton, and a loafer, one day he gets lucky. He discovers a parallel world where magic is commonplace, and where he fits right in. This is the city of Echo of the Unified Kingdom, a land where a social outcast like Max can be remade as "the unequaled Sir Max."

In this upside-down universe, Sir Max's deadpan humor and new-found talent for magic soon earn him a place in the secret police—night shift only, of course. As Nocturnal Representative of the Most Venerable Head of the Minor Secret Investigative Force of the City of Echo, Max's job is to investigate cases of illegal magic and battle trespassing monsters from other worlds. With his occupation comes an unusual band of colleagues—the omniscient Sir Juffin Hully, the buoyant Sir Melifaro, the death-dealing Sir Shurf Lonli-Lokli, bon vivant and master of disguise Sir Kofa Yox, the angelic Tekki, and the captivating sleuth Lady Melamori Blimm.

Plunging back into the threatening and absurd realm first portrayed in *The Stranger*, Book One of the Labyrinths of Echo series, and *The Stranger's Woes*, Book Two, *The Stranger's Magic* follows the new adventures and misadventures of Sir Max and his friends in this enchanted and enchanting world.

ONE

GUGIMAGON'S SHADOW

I MUST ADMIT THAT THE WEATHER WAS NOT ENTIRELY SUITABLE FOR A PLEASure ride on the motorboat—or, rather, on the water amobiler, which looked very similar to a regular four-seat pleasure boat.

The fierce river wind—too cold for the mild Uguland autumn—whipped up the waters of the Xuron so that the first ride I took down one of the finest rivers of the Unified Kingdom on my own was more like riding on the back of a giant kangaroo. The ride wasn't just bumpy; I was shaking so much that I kept kicking my chin with my knees. The ice-cold wind brought tears to my eyes. They flowed down my cheeks, mixing with splashes of river water and tiny droplets of drizzling rain. No idiot but me would willingly submit himself to such torture, especially at the very beginning of the Day of Freedom from Care, which Magic had bestowed upon me.

I was completely happy.

I had been meaning to get the hang of the local water transportation. From the very beginning, my reckless driving of regular land amobilers had become one of the capital's most cherished subjects of gossip. I never thought that I deserved that fame, though: any countryman of mine who could more or less manage to drive a four-wheeled buggy with an engine would be a celebrity here. I had been meaning to get behind the lever of the water amobiler for quite some time, partly because in my previous life I had never driven a motorboat. Nevertheless, I had mustered my courage and taken a few lessons from old Kimpa. I wasn't too keen on losing my authority in the eyes of the junior employees of the Ministry of Perfect Public Order, and Sir Juffin Hully's butler had been looking after me back in those days when I couldn't even manage unfamiliar cutlery.

Now I was gliding headlong down the dark waters of the Xuron in my own motorboat in complete solitude, soaking wet but very happy. The fact that I had managed to pick the only day of bad weather in the late sunny autumn just added fuel to the fire of my new passion: the riot of the elements turned the innocent pleasure ride into a small local apocalypse—exactly what I needed.

I had needed a good shake-up: the preparations for my accession to the throne of Fanghaxra were underway. My humble abode, the Furry House, former library of the Royal University, had once stood derelict, dusty, and somewhat mysterious. Now it was quickly turning into a vulgar bulwark of luxury and bliss. Even the floor of the small watchtower at the very top had been decorated with horrible carpeting that clashed with my taste. I had to enter it from time to time, if only to indulge Gurig, whose servants had wasted a great deal of money and time remodeling my would-be residence. At these moments, the reality that I had barely begun to get used to started feeling like another strange dream—not a nightmare, mind you, but a rather tiresome dream. The only thing I took solace in was that His Majesty Gurig VIII had sworn up and down that not a single dratted high official would ever make me stay there between the receptions when I granted audiences to my subjects, which, according to my calculations, would not happen more than a few times a year and would last no more than a couple of hours. His Majesty had given me his word, and one must believe the word of a king.

Yet while I was riding my flimsy vessel over the frothy waters of the Xuron, jumping over the crests of springy dark waves, those problems simply didn't exist. I was not remembering anything, nor was I making plans for the future. There was only here and now, and the here and now were too wet and too cold for my liking.

Are you busy right now? The polite voice of Sir Shurf Lonli-Lokli's Silent Speech rang in my head. It was so sudden that I came to an abrupt stop. The tiny water amobiler tossed about helplessly on the waves of the Xuron.

I guess you could say no. Has anything happened? I answered.

I don't think so. Still, I would like to discuss one peculiar event with you. It has to do more with my private life than our duties.

All the better, I said. In any case, I need to change into something dry and try to get warm. Just drop by Tekki's, I will be there soon.

I am very sorry, Max. You know how much I love the Armstrong & Ella, but I would rather not discuss my problems in the presence of Lady Shekk. Matters of this kind call for confidentiality. Would it really disappoint you if I suggested we meet at some other place?

A hole in the heavens above you, Shurf! You know that I love mysteries. Then come to my place on the Street of Yellow Stones. If you get there first, just come right in. The door is unlocked; no one would dare break into my house of his own volition. Oh, could you also order a whole tray full of various hot stuff from the Fat Turkey?

I quickly steered my new toy to the Makuri Pier, where I had had my own mooring since yesterday. A phlegmatic, mustached old man came out of his shed, seemingly annoyed, to help me tie up my nifty little water transport. He looked at me with almost superstitious horror, not because he had recognized the "horrible Sir Max"—after all, I wasn't wearing my Mantle of Death—but simply because any human being bold enough to take a pleasure ride down the river in this weather deserved to be viewed with nothing less than superstitious horror, at the very least, if not to be locked away in the nearest Refuge for the Mad.

I gave the doddering old fellow a crown, which probably made him doubt my mental state once and for all: the pay was far too high for such a small service. Such incongruity threatened to destroy his notion of the world—the dismal yet precious result of several hundred years of life. Yet the old man was a diehard: he batted his eyes, discolored over the years, mumbled the few words of gratitude that we've all known since childhood and save for such occasions, and hurried back inside his little hut, where I am sure a brazier with hot kamra was waiting for him.

I followed his stooping back with an envious gaze: a short but unpleasant trip back to the New City lay ahead of me. My freezing looxi would slap relentlessly on my back like a cruel wet bed sheet.

I climbed inside the amobiler and sped off as if an entire family of hungry werewolves were chasing me. Two minutes later, I dashed inside my living room on the Street of Yellow Stones.

Lonli-Lokli was already there. He sat motionless in the middle of the room. I wouldn't have been surprised to learn that he had carefully measured the room to calculate its exact center. I couldn't help but admire my friend. His snow-white looxi flickered mysteriously in the dark; his death-dealing hands in their protective gloves lay on his knees. He looked more like the Angel of Death than a human being.

"You beat me to it," I said with sincere respect.

"This is not surprising: I sent you the call when I was on the Street of Forgotten Dreams. I thought I would find you in the Armstrong & Ella. I could not imagine that you had gone for a walk in this weather."

"That's me all right: mysterious and unpredictable," I said, laughing. "Would you be so kind as to wait a few more moments? If I don't change right away, I will definitely catch a cold, and I don't even want to begin to remember what that is."

"Of course you need to change. And if I were you, I would also consider a hot bath."

"I have already considered that. It won't take more than a few minutes. You know that I do everything fast."

"Yes, I know," Shurf said with a nod. "Perhaps I should send a call to the owner of the Fat Turkey and ask him to add something stronger to my order."

"That won't be necessary," I said as I ran down the narrow winding stairs. "It's not so bad. I don't have to get smashed."

"My experience suggests that intoxication brings more pleasure and goes away faster than a cold, and you can trust my experience," said this magnificent fellow.

I returned to the living room in the best of spirits. I had thawed out, put on a warm house looxi, and accepted a petition from my stomach claiming that it was fit enough to digest an entire herd of elephants, if need be.

The dinner table was chock-full of trays and jugs. For starters, I poured myself a full mug of hot kamra.

"Now I'm back," I said after a few cautious sips.

"If you say so, it must be true. Well, this is not bad news at all," said Lonli-Lokli.

I took a good look at his serious face, trying to catch the traces of a fast disappearing smirk. This game of catch, however, was not mine to win. As usual.

"By the way, at my place you can safely remove your gloves," I said, pulling my plates closer. "Or do you prefer to keep them on in case I start telling stupid jokes so you can make me shut up once and for all? I'm going to have to disappoint you: some people say that my chatterbox mouth won't close even after my death. So killing me is not the solution."

"What a strange idea! I do not consider your life to be so meaningless as to require snuffing out due to such trifles. There is another reason for me to keep the gloves on."

"Are you sensing danger?" I stopped eating and attempted to pull a serious face. Danger that threatens Lonli-Lokli himself definitely deserves to be taken seriously.

"No, Max, I am not sensing any danger. At least, not here and not now. I'm not taking off the gloves because I left the box I keep them in back in my office in the House by the Bridge. Did you really think that a weapon such as my gloves could simply be kept in my pocket?"

"I guess that would be against all safety codes," I said, laughing. "All right, to Magicians with your horrifying mittens. Tell me what happened to your 'private life.' I'm dying to know."

"Nothing really happened," said Shurf. "Nothing that one should confide about to strangers. Nothing that people should worry about. Yet I feel somewhat uneasy about it. Max, do you remember how you once took me into your dream?"

"Of course I do. It was when we were on our way to Kettari. We had to sleep in a really small bed, and you offered me 'the possibility of using your sleep,' to borrow your own bombastic expression."

"That is correct," said Shurf, nodding. "Yet that was not what happened. Instead, we traveled to some amazing places from your dreams. Frankly, what happened didn't look like an ordinary dream. I have always suspected that the nature of your dreams deserved a most thorough study. But I digress. Do you remember that among other visions there were endless sandy beaches at the shore of some strange motionless sea? Quite a hostile place, although in your company I enjoyed the trip very much."

"Sure, I remember that. But how come you're bringing this up now?"

"Simply because the time has come to bring this up," said Shurf. "Recently I have been dreaming about that place too often. Without your intervention, as far as I can tell. And I no longer think that it is a place I enjoy visiting, be it in a dream or otherwise."

"Definitely without my intervention," I said. "For one thing, you and I sleep on different pillows."

"Well, in theory, the distance between the heads of the sleepers only plays a role for such novices in these matters as myself. And if my estimation of your abilities is correct, you are quite capable of making me contemplate your dreams remotely. I am certain, however, that this was not your doing. I would have felt your presence had they been your dreams I was dreaming. Yet never once have I felt your presence in them, of that I am sure. I have always felt someone else, however. Someone whom I can never see. I do not like his presence, even though it is barely noticeable. What's more, I think I know him."

"Well, I'm outraged," I said. "Some strangers have been wandering around in my favorite dream without my knowing it. I'm glad that you have reported the situation to me. Trust me, I would never intentionally drag you into my dreams, even if I could. And I can't. At least I've never tried. I haven't seen these beaches in my dreams for a long time myself. The last time I walked along those beaches was when I spent the night in the bedroom of Sir Melifaro's grandfather. To be frank with you, I even began to forget about them. It's not entirely surprising though. I forget about things that are much more important than dreams on a regular basis."

"You are underestimating the situation, Max. Nothing is more important than certain dreams. I am surprised that I have to tell this to a man who gains his power from dreams," said Lonli-Lokli, shaking his head in disapproval.

"You're right," I said, ashamed. "It's just that recently reality has been playing a lot of practical jokes on me. In any case, what you're saying is exactly what I have suspected all along."

"I wanted to find out whether something similar was happening to you," said Lonli-Lokli. "Apparently nothing is happening to you. Tell me, before, when you dreamed about those beaches, did you ever meet anyone there? Or perhaps you, too, felt someone's ominous presence there?"

"No, I never felt anything like that. I'm very fond of that place, and have always thought that it belonged to me and me alone. You know how you sometimes have a strange, vague feeling of being absolutely sure about something, which is not based on anything concrete?"

"Absolutely," said Lonli-Lokli. "In my view, one should trust such a feeling. Oh well, I guess you are of no help in this matter then."

"What do you mean 'no help'?" I said. "I'm the one who lured you into that unwholesome spot. Naturally I had no idea what I was doing and all that, but it doesn't relieve me of responsibility for the possible consequences. After all, it's my dream. Who else is supposed to take care of it but me?"

"And how are you going to 'take care of' the dream that you stopped seeing a long, long time ago?"

"I have to think about it."

I put aside the plate, which was now empty, and gave a loud, resonant sneeze. The cold was definitely standing on my trace. It was licking its lips, anticipating how it would gobble me up.

"Perhaps you should put aside your childish belief in your invincibility and have a glass of hot wine. It is a tried-and-true method," said Lonli-Lokli in the tone of a lecturer. "Authors of numerous books on medicine support the common notion that this beverage has a positive effect on those who have fallen victim to exposure to cold."

Without waiting for an answer, he put the jug of wine on the hot plate.

"Well, perhaps from your holey cup. Do you have it on you?" I said. "Maybe this magic ritual will not just rid me of my cold but also help me collect my thoughts."

"This is quite possible," said Shurf, producing his ancient bottomless cup from the folds of his looxi. "This ritual will be no less effective on you than it was on the former members of my Order. It certainly won't make matters worse."

"They can't get any worse," I said as I discovered that I had become the proud owner of a few tons of fresh snot. "A hole in the heavens above my nose! This cold sure isn't wasting any time."

"Here you go." Lonli-Lokli, his hand in the enormous protective glove covered in old runes, handed me the cup, one quarter full of hot wine. "I think this should be enough."

"I sure hope so," I said, snuffling, and carefully accepted the holey vessel.

I was worried that it wouldn't work this time. When you have a cold, it's difficult to maintain faith in your own powers. The powers were still with me, though: the liquid remained in the holey vessel as if I had spent half of my life as a novice at the Order of the Holey Cup, side by side with my magnificent colleague.

I drained the hot wine with one gulp and almost swooned with relief. I still had the cold, but it didn't matter. Nothing really mattered: I felt so light on my feet and indifferent that even more serious inconveniences wouldn't have mattered.

I returned the magic cup to its owner and became very still, listening to the special broadcast coming from within the depths of my body. The cold retreated first. A slight but persistent pain in my throat increased momentarily and then abandoned me for good. Finally I coughed, but the bout was gone as soon as it had started. It turned out that I had come down with a cold, but this existential experience lasted little more than a minute rather than your usual dozen days or so.

"Well, I'll be," I said when I regained the ability to speak again. "That was awesome, Shurf! Your holey cup works a little differently every time. It's as if it knows what I need from it. Now you and I won't have to rummage through my house looking for a handkerchief, which I've never had to begin with. Instead, we can take on the case of the empty beaches."

"Are you really willing to get down to the bottom of my dreams?" said Lonli-Lokli. "I am very honored to receive your magnanimity—although, knowing you, I will be so bold as to surmise that your primary motive is curiosity."

"That's as good a reason as any to begin an investigation," I said, embarrassed.

"What is it that you're going to do? Perhaps I should offer to share my dream with you again as I did when we were on our way to Kettari. But in this case we might lose a great deal of time, as I do not dream of your beaches every single day. The last time it happened was, in fact, last night. Who knows how long we will have to wait for the next opportunity? Three days? Five? A dozen? Besides, you still work nights, which complicates the task at hand even further."

"Normally I work around the clock, praise be Sir Juffin Hully. There's never a dull moment with him," I said with a sigh. "You know what I think, Shurf? I think for starters I should pay a visit to the Melifaro homestead. It's a piece of cake to control one's dreams in the bedroom of his grandfather. Tell you what, I'm going there today. Not sure if the trip will turn out to be useful, but there's no doubt that it's going to be pleasurable. Darn, I sure know how to seize an opportunity, don't I?"

"Do you have any reason to believe that my problem requires immediate action?" said Shurf.

"Do ants in my pants count as a reason? Just yesterday, Juffin was needling me about why the heck I demanded two Days of Freedom from Chores instead of one. He insists that R & R is not my area of expertise. According to him, I have absolutely no talent for it. As far as I'm concerned, our boss is right. It's not even sunset and I'm already moonlighting, if you'll pardon the pun. Speaking of the boss, why haven't you told Juffin about your terrifying dreams? He is old and wise and knows almost everything there is to know about the dark side of life. I know that those dreams are something I dream from time to time, but everything else about them is beyond my ken."

"That is an amusing way of putting it," said Shurf, approvingly.

And that's just quintessential Shurf. You never know which one of the silly things I say is going to fly in one of his ears and out the other, and which one he will jot down in his notebook.

"As for Sir Juffin Hully," said Shurf, putting his terrifying notebook back under the fold of his looxi, "you see, Max, this matter concerns your dreams, not mine. If a third party is to learn about them, you should be the one to divulge this information. In theory, every person has the right to keep private secrets. It says so in the Code of Krember."

"It says a lot of things," I said, smirking. "I'm afraid Juffin knows more about my 'private secrets' than I do myself. But you're right, let's not pester the boss with trifles. Maybe I'll be able to figure out what's wrong with my empty beaches on my own, and then we'll see. I'm sure Melifaro will be on cloud nine if I take him to his parents' estate on the spur of the moment. At least some good will come out of our undertaking."

"I admire your determination, Max," said Lonli-Lokli. He placed the empty cup on the table and stood up. "Thank you. I hope you will not be offended if I tell you that I have some other unfinished business."

"I have been told more than once that hope is a darn-fool feeling. On the other hand, being offended is also a darn-fool feeling, an even greater one. And so I'm not offended. If you give me a few moments, I can change and give you a lift to Headquarters. Does this unfinished business of yours glumly hang around outside the doors of your office, by any chance?"

"Thank you, but that will not be necessary. My business usually hangs around in other places," said Lonli-Lokli, nodding. "I must hand it to you, sometimes you combine words in a very eloquent manner. Good night, and please keep me posted."

As he was heading toward the exit, I admired his upright stance. People as tall as he have a natural inclination to stoop. But Sir Shurf Lonli-Lokli broke the laws of gravity, as well as other laws of nature.

"Thanks for dumping your troubles on me," I said to his back. "Compared to my recent enthronement, this sure smells like a good adventure."

"I would like it very much if it didn't smell like anything of the sort," said Shurf, turning around. "But as Sir Aloxto Allirox used to say, there are very few creatures in this World whose desires really matter. He was a particularly observant person, that sad Arvaroxian war chief, don't you think?"

Without waiting for my answer, Sir Lonli-Lokli went out the door, leaving me with the lightest imaginable load on my chest. I shrugged it off, kicked it as far as it would go, put on the first warm looxi I could find, and left for the Armstrong & Ella.

On my way there I sent a call to Melifaro.

You might like my plans for tonight.

Have you finally decided to open an imperial brothel? said Melifaro. It's high time that you did.

After my colleagues—at the cunning suggestion of Sir Juffin—had watched Caligula with Malcolm McDowell and had more or less recovered from mild culture shock, they wouldn't get off my back. They said that now they knew exactly what methods I was going to employ to enforce the policies of the Unified Kingdom in the poor Lands of Fanghaxra. Little by little, I had begun to feel that they were going a bit too far with this. I had even resorted to threatening that I would send the video collection they had grown so fond of back into the bowels of the place from whence it had come. Alas, no one fell for my empty threat.

Actually, I was thinking of starting small and practicing in the company of your venerable folks, I said. Would you care to join me, buddy? You're going to love it, I promise.

What royal impudence! said Melifaro. What disrespect for the private lives of ordinary citizens! This nutcase of a barbarian king is going to introduce my folks to the inhumane customs of his boundless steppes. Verily, you are a great man, O Fanghaxra!

Quit being such a show off. As if I have nothing better to do than listen to your Silent Speech. It makes my head swell. What if it gets too big for my crown? I'm going to be in trouble. Just meet me at

Tekki's. Once you have thoroughly licked my boots, I will condescend to take you to your parents' house. Then, in the morning, I will deposit you back at the House by the Bridge. And here's the best part: this whole thing is not going to cost you a penny. Now who's going to make you a better offer?

No one, said Melifaro. But you could've just swallowed your pride and admitted that you were dying to curl up in a dark corner of the mysterious bedroom of my legendary grandfather. All right, all right. I'm coming. But you owe me one, mister.

Over and out, I said. But if you're not here in thirty minutes, I'm going to draw and quarter you.

It was a good time to end our silent conversation. I had just arrived at the Armstrong & Ella.

"My goodness, Max! You were supposed to be soaking wet and miserable, yet here you are, dry and smiling from ear to ear. Pretty suspicious, if you ask me." Tekki did her best to try and look fierce. Still, if there was anyone smiling from ear to ear, it was none other than Tekki.

"What are you so surprised about? After all, I am a powerful sorcerer. All it takes is the nine hundred ninety-ninth degree of Purple Magic, and a miserable, soaking-wet person becomes dry and happy in an instant."

"Why Purple?" said Tekki.

"I don't know. It's a pretty color. You can't limit yourself to just Black and White Magic. It's so conservative."

"Sir Shurf dropped by," said Tekki. "I told him that you had gone to take a pleasure ride down the Xuron, but I think he thought I was joking. In any case, he honestly tried to smile. By the end of the third minute, he had almost succeeded."

"Consider yourself lucky—that is a rare feat. On second thought, maybe not that rare, at least not recently. He's tried to pull it off a couple of times today. I already saw him. On top of that, I also managed to take a bath, change my wet clothes, have lunch, get a cold, get rid of the cold, go insane, offer Sir Melifaro an all-night trip to the country, and get him to agree to it. Would you say that I lead an eventful life?"

"You can say that again," said Tekki. "Are you serious about that night trip with Melifaro?"

"Sure. By the way, you don't have to take such candid delight in the prospect. I am a wicked man, and I would like to think that my absence makes you unhappy."

"If you stayed, I'd have to babble on for hours about how I hate to walk around town in this weather. Besides, just this morning, Sir Juffin told me that he had dug up some incredible movie from your collection," said Tekki with downcast eyes. "He says I'm definitely going to like it even though it's full of 'nonsense.' You know, the usual deal with him."

"Oh, what's the name of it?" I said. I had to know what movie that scoundrel Juffin had recommended to my girlfriend. After all, one could expect anything from him.

"It has a very strange name: Played Runner."

I almost choked on my hot kamra. The title had been garbled almost beyond recognition, and Blade Runner was one of my favorites.

"Juffin's right. It's a great movie," I said. "No objections to that. By the way, you didn't have to take such a gloomy view of your prospects for the evening. I'm no monster."

"Sometimes you're worse," said Tekki with a dreamy smile.

"Right you are."

I have no idea when that son of a gun Melifaro had appeared behind my back. Lucky for him, it had taken him less than thirty minutes, so I didn't have to draw and quarter him.

"You are a monster," Melifaro began his old refrain. "Dragging me off somewhere in the middle of the night. I was going to take your girlfriend to your place to see a movie tonight. We could have been making out in the dark, with just a bit of light flickering from that funny box with moving pictures. Am I right, Tekki?"

"Sure. The only other light would have been Sir Juffin's fangs gleaming in the dark. He's recently been known to grow them occasionally. I'm sure he saw them in one of those movies. It even scared me."

"He's just flirting with you," said Melifaro. "Well, that's too bad. Looks like he's not going to let us make out in peace. He's such a meanie. Although, compared to this monster"—he made a mocking bow in my direction—"Juffin is as mild-mannered as a saint."

Having discussed me and Juffin, they started picking on other mutual friends. According to them the entire city of Echo was full of evildoers and villains. The only true angel was Melifaro himself. And Tekki, too, of course, what with her being the daughter of Loiso Pondoxo—although I couldn't agree more with that last opinion.

"All right, let's go," I said half an hour later when I realized that those two could mock and scoff till the cows came home if nobody stopped them. "As I understand it, Tekki, you've already decided about your plans for tonight. I mean, it would be useless for me to crawl at your feet, choking on my own tears, and beg you to come with us, right?"

"Choking on your own tears, huh? Tempting, very tempting," said Tekki. "But I think we can put this orgy off until some other time. There is no hurry. Keep in mind, though, that in the morning I'll begin to miss you. Don't make me regret the chance I let slip, okay?"

"Never, my love," I said. "In any case, early in the morning I'm going to have to take your spurned lover to work. So please try not to entertain too many naked men in my house, and generally be a good girl."

"All right," said Tekki, giving me a hug. "I'll bring over just a few naked men, if it matters so much to you. Just five or six. I want you to be happy. Will you be happy?"

"I will."

"Sinning Magicians, it takes so little to make some people happy," said Melifaro, laughing.

"Yep, I've always been an ascetic," I said.

When we arrived at Melifaro's family estate, we were still in high spirits. I had almost forgotten why we were taking the trip in the first place. I was about to inquire of Melifaro why he had invited me to visit his parents, but thankfully I remembered why we were there myself.

In the spacious den of the mansion, we found an idyllic, unworldly scene: Sir Manga, quite content, was sitting comfortably in a large armchair. His better half was braiding his long red hair. She had just managed to finish half the braid when we arrived. She had a lot of work ahead of her.

"Sinning Magicians, what a surprise!" said Lady Melifaro.

"This is no surprise. It's just our son and Sir Max," said Sir Manga. "These gentlemen will live to see far scarier things, so do go on please."

"I'd rather you had a harem," his wife said, sighing. "At least I'd have someone to do all the dirty work for me."

"A hundred and fifty years ago, dear, you had a completely different opinion on this matter. That you have changed it now is not my fault. Boys, will you excuse me if we skip the passionate embraces this time?"

"If you were to rush up and gave me a passionate embrace, Dad, I'd cry bitter tears and haul you off to the nearest Refuge for the Mad," said Melifaro.

"Do you get so lonely there that you need company?" said Sir Manga. "But never mind. I think you'd better put something in your mouth and start munching right away. Otherwise I'll never be able to look Sir Max in the eye, after all the nonsense we've been spewing out in his presence."

"Frankly, I don't see how you can look me in the eye after spewing out this nonsense, once upon a time," I said, pointing my finger at Melifaro Junior. "However did you manage that, Sir Manga?"

"For your information, I wasn't home at the time. Kindly address your complaints to my wonderful wife," said Sir Manga, giving his wife a scornful look. "What can you say in your own defense?"

"Mom, don't listen to these ridiculous people," said Melifaro. "You did a great job. In any case, I'm very happy with the results."

"At least someone is," his mother said. "All this notwithstanding, your father's offer still stands: you should have something to eat. It's not often that such brilliant thoughts occur in Manga's head."

"You're quite wrong there, my dear. Thoughts about food occur to me on average six or seven times a day," said Sir Manga. "How's my hair coming along, by the way?"

"You'll know that it's done when you hear a loud sigh of relief escape my lungs," said his wife.

I was enjoying the scene. The more members of the Melifaro family gather in one place, the more kicks I get from it.

"Where has my brother Baxba disappeared to?" my colleague said, sitting at the table.

"Magicians only know," said Sir Manga. "If I recall correctly, in the morning he mumbled something about a trip to Landaland. He said he was going to the fair in Numban to buy some household junk, but frankly I wasn't paying much attention."

I imagined the gigantic Baxba "mumbling something" and couldn't contain a smile. The Melifaros would make a great soap opera that should air around the clock. It's too bad that none of the many powerful Grand Magicians who have inhabited Echo since the foundation of the Unified Kingdom have thought to invent television.

My indefatigable colleague was the first to turn in that evening. Muttering something about his working schedule for the coming day, he deserted us and retreated into his bedroom.

"Oh, dear, dear me!" his mother said. "It was no more than a hundred years ago that my little boy swore he would refuse to sleep when he grew up."

"Ah, so he's also a perjurer," I said. "What a nice young man."

"It runs in the family," said Sir Manga with pride. "Granted, Anchifa is the crowning glory of my upbringing methods. The first real pirate in the family. That's quite something, I'll tell you."

"If I understand correctly, he's already left?" I said.

"Of course. Anchifa has never stayed home for more than a couple dozen days."

"Good for him," I said in a dreamy voice. "You know, I sometimes think I should quit my job and ask him to hire me as a regular sailor on his ship."

"I'd advise you not to. A shikka isn't exactly a resort for a sailor: a barbarian Ukumbian contraption, no magic, and—as a result—too much work for everyone, including the captain. And I wouldn't say the passengers fare much better: the vessel is subject to violent rocking. Yet my son wouldn't hear of buying a new ship, even though he could easily afford one, and then some. The boy tries to imitate his mentors in every possible way. This is a case of typical Ukumbian bravado. The local pirates believe that a man can only be considered a true captain if he has sailed the same shikka for no less than five dozen years."

"What's a shikka? A kind of a ship?"

"Indeed. The swiftest and most maneuverable there is, and not quite what one would consider a pleasure boat, believe me. I once had the misfortune of hiring a Ukumbian shikka, and I lived to rue the day I decided to go on an around-the-world journey. If I hadn't managed to transfer to a regular three-mast karuna equipped with several magic crystals when we reached the next port, this World would have lost four of the eight volumes of my sinning encyclopedia, and myself to boot."

"All right then. I guess I won't try to hire myself out as a sailor to your Anchifa after all," I said. "Thanks for warning me. I think I'll go to sleep instead. After all, it's the cheapest way to travel in comfort."

"If you are referring to the bedroom of my prodigal father, Filo, you couldn't be more correct. As for the other bedrooms, I'm not so sure. Do you remember where it is, or do you want me to show you the way?"

"Do you think my feeble intellect would suffice to find anything in the endless labyrinth you call your house? You're flattering me, Sir Manga."

"Oh, but of course I am," the greatest encyclopedist of the World said with a yawn. "All right then. Let's try to find that sinning door together, shall we?"

For some time, we wandered through the spacious hallways of the mansion. Sir Manga did his best to play the part of a lost child. It wasn't very believable, but I was noble enough to play along, insofar as my humble acting abilities allowed.

At last I was alone in the small dark bedroom I was already so fond of. When I'm there, I always think that Filo Melifaro, the famous grandfather of my colleague and one of the powerful Elder Magicians of the Order of the Secret Grass, had me in mind when he built his wonder-working bedroom. He somehow knew that his efforts would benefit more than just his own kin. Hey, if you think about it, it's quite possible that such a great man could sniff out in advance my eventual presence on his territory. For instance, I could have appeared to him in a dream. Why not? People are known to have all kinds of nightmares from time to time.

But none of this really mattered. It was just another fairy tale, the kind it's nice to tell yourself before you fall asleep while staring, enchanted, at the ancient crisscrossing beams of the ceiling somewhere above your head in the darkness of the room.

This time I crossed the border between reality and dreamland so slowly that I probably could have marked the path I traversed with white pebbles, like Hansel and Gretel. In this dream, however, I didn't have any white pebbles with me.

First I wandered around in a few blissful dreams, not fully understanding who I was or what I was doing there. Only when I ended up on the barren sandy beach—which, after all, was the goal of this journey—did I begin to remember myself as I was in real life. This was not as easy as one might think, but in certain fundamental dreams, recurring dreams I've had since childhood, it always happens in the end—of its own accord, without any apparent effort from me.

The difference this time around was that I was returning to myself very slowly and painfully, as though I were trying to recall what I had done while drunk. I was able to recollect the evening I had spent in the company of Melifaro's parents, the trip through the twilit countryside, Tekki's "promise" to bring home naked men, and then, finally and very unclearly, the conversation with Shurf Lonli-Lokli that had worried me. Then I looked down and saw footprints in the sand.

The footprints, somewhat akin to those of sneakers, had been left by someone wearing soft Uguland shoes. I concentrated, and it suddenly dawned on me that the footprints belonged to Sir Shurf himself. I didn't guess or deduce it by any clues—I simply felt it. I knew it in my heart (and it was clear which one of the two). This had happened to me more than once in real life, too. Recently I had noticed a kind of one-way connection between my colleagues and myself, the nature of which I did not fully comprehend. Moments before one of them appeared, I would begin to detect a faint scent only emitted by that particular person. And if I happened to enter a room where one of my crew had just been, I would know without the shadow of a doubt who had been there. Maybe that's how loyal dogs anticipate their master's return, I explained to myself. No, that's ridiculous. Dogs use their sense of smell, and I was using . . . I was using . . . Gosh, I had no idea what it was.

Neither had I the time to think about man's best friends. My head began to spin. No wonder: my mind had just gotten a good kick. In my dream, I had just found actual footprints of another person who had recently seen this very dream. It looked as though we had both walked along the sand somewhere on the shore of a very real, wet, and salty sea, each of us following the footsteps of the other.

I decided that the best thing to do would be to scream and wake up—the sooner the better. It was all too much for me.

"Shut up," I said to myself. "After all, you're here on business. You can have a tantrum in the morning in Sir Manga's bathroom if you so choose."

My stupid habit of talking to myself often proves to be very helpful. Having yelled at myself, I realized that I was quite capable of putting off my hysterics until later. Not until morning—in the morning I would still behave myself. I would hold off on my hysterics until I was in Juffin's presence. The boss would probably bestow upon me two or three of his highly theoretical yet thoroughly pacifying explanations. I would then pretend that I understood them, and I would feel great.

I found the courage not to wake up. Instead I walked for a long time up and down the barren beach, trying to find any trace of the presence of the evil stranger Shurf had been talking about. I had found nothing and I was already dead tired. Each step required an enormous amount of effort. I don't recall ever experiencing anything more dispiriting in any of my dreams than what I felt on this walk.

Having expended all my energy, I woke up. Peace and quiet reigned in the cozy bedroom built by the magical hands of Filo Melifaro. Outside everything was dark and quiet—even the birds hadn't woken up yet. The runes on the beams in the ceiling were doing their magic: it took them only a few seconds to calm down my restless hearts, and then a few minutes more to lull me to sleep. This time, the switchman angels that watch over dreamers as they arrive at their destinations took mercy: I dreamed some meaningless but very sweet nonsense. I couldn't ask for more.

I woke up at dawn, happy and content. Unsolved mysteries did not spoil my mood. It was even pleasant to think that the barren sandy beaches that I had grown to love did indeed exist, and that I might have the chance to see them in real life one day. Something similar had once happened to me: while walking around the mountains near Kettari, I discovered the town from my childhood dreams. It turned out that the sandy beach was good news rather than bad—that is, if the news was ever amenable to such primitive terms, and the usual morning grogginess notwithstanding.

"Sir Filo," I said in a tender voice, addressing the ceiling, "I adore you. I don't know what I would do without you, and so on and so forth. Just keep me in mind when you begin recruiting new grandchildren."

Naturally, the ceiling was silent, yet after this insane tirade, my mood improved even more. I had to go down the narrow stairs leading to the bathroom sideways—otherwise my smile wouldn't fit.

Moments later, I was flying down to the dining room. I had the rare opportunity to have breakfast alone, then wake up my colleague and observe his suffering, deriving a sadistic pleasure out of it. Generally, Sir Melifaro Junior was no keener to get up in the morning than I had been as a schoolboy. That was strange, though, considering he was going to be spending another great day in the House by the Bridge rather than meeting the principal.

Today, however, my colleague had gotten up all by himself and was feeling not too bad, to put it mildly. I had the presence of mind not to be upset about it.

"Well, does everything please Your Majesty?" he said when he entered the dining room.

"Yeah, I think I'm not going to execute you this year," I said. "After that, we'll see about it."

"Dream on. I'm not one of your subjects yet, praise be the Magicians."

"We'll see what tune you're singing when my boys are galloping down the streets of Echo on their antlered nags. I'll let you in on a big secret: my personal plan for the unification of the Barren Lands and the Unified Kingdom differs somewhat from the official one. I figured it'd be better if I annexed the lands of His Majesty Gurig VIII to mine rather than the other way around."

"Is that so?" said Melifaro, shoving an enormous sandwich in his mouth. "I think I'm going to denounce you then, if that's okay with you. I've never done this before, but better late than never, I guess."

"Please don't. I'll make you my prime minister."

"Tempting, very tempting. Fine, give me a ride on your amobiler for starters, mister. Then I'll think about it."

"Can do. At your service, sir."

"This has been the dream of my miserable life—to make you my personal chauffeur," said Melifaro with a sigh. "You should give this lengthy consideration. It's the only talent you have that's worthy of the name, anyway."

"Thanks, but no thanks," I said, snorting. "I know how much a chauffeur makes. I've already been poor once, and didn't like it one bit."

"You? Poor? When?" said Melifaro. "All right, let's go. I'm really running late for work now."

"That's what I thought," I said. "In case you haven't noticed, I've been standing in the doorway shuffling my feet for thirty minutes already."

We were tearing along toward Echo through the sleepy suburbs on this gloomy morning. Melifaro, who loved sunny weather, looked visibly downcast. At one point, he demanded that I entertain him, but I said I had to keep my eyes on the road. He calmed down and even began to doze off from boredom.

I was completely entranced by the beautiful gloomy morning.

Each raindrop on the windshield looked like a tiny inimitable wonder. Just recently, I had noticed that even rain in this World was different from the usual precipitation I had spent my first thirty years soaking in. Sure, it was just water, but the sweet scent of the pollen, the barely noticeable purple tint of the streaks of rains, the . . .

It was nice to remember that I still was a newcomer in this beautiful World. Deep inside, I hoped that this feeling would stay with me a lot longer. So many new ways to get myself in trouble, so many opportunities to be amazed over trivial things. The latter—the blissful opportunities to be amazed over trivial things—filled my life so fully that I could almost afford not to wish for anything else. Frankly, that morning, I didn't wish for anything else.

Once I had dropped off my daytime half by the House by the Bridge, I decided it was a good idea to drop by myself. I had to tell Juffin the mysterious story of my silly dreams.

Sir Juffin had not yet arrived. I guessed that at that time of the day I could probably find him on the Street of Old Coins: he still hadn't sated his craving for late-night movie screenings. I carefully weighed the options and decided that Shurf's (and, by extension, my own) problem could wait until the evening—unlike Tekki, who had probably begun tossing and turning by now. Yesterday she had said she might regret the chance she had let slip. I couldn't allow my beautiful lady to fall so low. From time to time, I discover that I have principles that I simply cannot forego.

I returned to the House by the Bridge only an hour before sunset and went straight to the office that I shared with Juffin. Kurush was the only occupant. He sat on the back of the armchair with an all-important look.

"Where's the boss, O wise one?" I said.

"I don't know," said the bird. "He came and went, came and went. People, as you know, are known to be somewhat restless."

"That we are," I said, sighing, and sent Juffin a call.

It's the second time I've come to the Headquarters today and not found you here.

It's your own fault. You should work on your sense of timing, said Juffin. It's high time that you learned to come exactly when I'm in. More to the point, however: What on earth are you doing there? As I recall, I gave you two days off—at your own persistent request, may I remind you. What happened? Couldn't bear the life of a loafer?

Nah, loafing wasn't the problem. It's my absentmindedness—I thought it had already been two days, I said. Then I added with a sigh, Juffin, to be honest, I have a few questions that you're the one most likely to have the answers to.

Well, I've had a rough day, so if your confession can wait, let's put it off until tomorrow, said Juffin. Otherwise, you can come to the Street of Old Coins tonight. You'll definitely find me here. It won't even matter if your sense of timing is off.

Thank you, Juffin. I'll do that.

Good. Now get out of my office. I know you all too well. First you'll drink two or three mugs of kamra, and then you're going to say that you had to work overtime.

Hey, it's my office, too! I said. All right, all right. I'm gone already.

Liar!

You can't fool the boss, I thought. I gave a loud, deep sigh, rose from the armchair where I had just curled up, and went to the Hall of Common Labor. Shurf Lonli-Lokli wasn't there, so I decided to take my chances and look for him in his lair.

He wasn't in his huge, almost empty, and sterile office either, but I sensed that he would show up any minute now. I had gotten so used to trusting my instincts that I didn't bother to burden myself with Silent Speech. Instead, I grabbed a random book from a small white bookshelf over his desk, sat on the only (and very hard) chair in the room, and prepared to wait.

The book was The Pendulum of Immortality. I had seen Shurf reading it many times already. I didn't have the chance to dip into this literary monument, however. Moments later, the door at the far end of the office opened with a quiet creak. I'm a fast reader, all right, but not that fast.

"You came even sooner than I expected," I said, getting up from the owner's chair. I rushed to put the book back on the shelf—I knew what a pain in the neck Shurf was.

"I am happy to see you, Max," said Lonli-Lokli. His stone face looked almost friendly. "But I should be very much obliged if you returned the book to the place you took it from."

"Wait, what did I just do?"

"You put it on the shelf—you didn't return it. The book was the third from the right, and now it is the rightmost item on the shelf. Do not get me wrong, Max. I am all for changes in general, yet untimely changes do not facilitate a good mood."

I submitted without a murmur and returned the book to its original place. Then I couldn't contain myself and laughed. "Oh, this is just brilliant, Shurf! Sometimes I think that the World stands on your back."

"It may well be true," said this wonderful fellow in an indifferent tone. "Do you have any news for me, or have you just decided to pay a visit?"

"Yes and yes. But my news requires a more intimate setting: a candlelit dinner and whatnot. Got a minute?"

"Must it be candlelit?" said Lonli-Lokli. "There are not many taverns in Echo that use candles, you know. Illuminating gas is much more practical."

"Fine, we'll do away with the candles," I said in the tone of a person who was willing to sacrifice the most sacred principles in the interests of business. "To be perfectly straight, we can do away with the dinner, too. I don't have much in terms of news. I just like to combine business with pleasure."

"So do I," said Shurf, grinning. "And since you mentioned candles, we could go to the Vampire's Dinner. Their cuisine is not bad, and I think they still don't have too many customers there. They even have candles. Would this be agreeable to you?"

"The Vampire's Dinner is a marvelous place. I had no idea you ever went there."

"At one time, it was one of my favorite taverns, and I still find it pleasant. I used to dine there almost every day."

"'Used to'? Was it during your Merry Fishmonger days, by any chance?" I said.

"Oh, no. Much, much later. Incidentally, it was there that I met my wife. She caught my fancy by ordering precisely the dishes that I found virtually inedible. I thought that studying that woman would grant me access to a new side of human life that hitherto had been unknown to me. A side that does not find the taste of Kuankulex wine or Loxrian xatta revolting."

I shook my head, bewildered. This fellow baffled me every now and then. Sometimes I thought he did it on purpose, and not entirely without ulterior motives. I'm sure he keeps a special notebook at home where he writes down how many times a day he has baffled me. He then rubs his hands together in his fancy laced gloves and chortles when nobody can see him.

The interior of the Vampire's Dinner was as dramatic as its name: candles, semidarkness, and tabletops with splashes of red paint suggesting blood. A large but friendly fellow was dozing off behind the bar. He had gone through the trouble of putting on some evening makeup, whitening his face, blackening his eyebrows, and painting some fluorescent formula around his eyes. Gobs of red lipstick were supposed to create the impression that this nice guy had just quenched his thirst with a few glasses of blood from his innocent victims.

I shook my head in amusement. The first time I had walked into the Vampire's Dinner had not been the best day of my life. Yet even then, the place had lifted my spirits. Now, when I was feeling so wonderful and so complete, I couldn't have asked for a better place to be.

Shurf and I were the only visitors in the tavern. We sat down at the table farthest from the door. The proprietor, happy with the sudden arrival of customers, promptly brought us the menu. He was friendly and courteous. Neither the protective gloves covering the death-dealing hands of Sir Lonli-Lokli, nor my Mantle of Death—both well known in the Capital—seemed to bother him. On the contrary, they seemed to complement the mood of the place.

"I remember once having a Breath of Evil here," I said. "An excellent treat, I must say, Shurf. I highly recommend it."

"Strange. I do not recall seeing it on the menu before."

"That's because you used to come here back in the unpalatable times right after the ratification of the Code of Krember. I came here in the good old days when every chef was ordered to wear the Earring of Oxalla and allowed to cook whatever he wanted."

"Oh, I see. It's one of the dishes of the old cuisine. Indeed, I have not come here at all since Sir Juffin solicited a relaxation of restrictions for the chefs. Still, Max, you are exaggerating, as usual. Last time I was here was not more than four years ago—not a hundred and seventeen, as one might assume based on your unreasonable assertion. Well, I should not pass up the chance of becoming acquainted with the dish you have recommended. Perhaps I should try the Breath of Evil."

Shurf spoke in such a serious tone that it sounded as though he was talking about choosing a weapon that would (or wouldn't) save our lives.

After the small pieces of cake on our plates had "blown up" like popcorn on a hotplate, and Sir Shurf Lonli-Lokli had deigned to approve my choice of dish, I decided it was time to talk business.

"I was there last night, Shurf," I said. Shurf raised his eyebrows in perplexity, so I had to clarify. "In our dream—yours and mine. I went to sleep in Filo Melifaro's bedroom and found myself on that sinning beach. I didn't find any strangers there, though. The beach can still hold the title of Most Desolate Place in the Universe. What I did find there, however, was your footprints in the sand. Frankly, it shook me to the core."

"It did, did it not?" said Shurf. "Are you sure those were my footprints and not someone else's?"

"Positive. If I weren't, I'd have told you that I found footprints that could be yours, but I'm absolutely certain those were your footprints. By the way, the footprints were made by boots. Do you keep them on while sleeping?"

"That is nonsense. Naturally I take my footwear off before I go to sleep. Yet in my dream, I was wearing boots, that is true. Hold on a moment, Max. Are you saying that you always walk in your dreams naked?"

"Uh, no, of course not," I said, taken aback. "But this dream . . . See, Shurf, this beach isn't just a dream—it's a real place. I'm sure of it now. I wish I knew which World it was in. Also, you know what I think? I think there are no people there. Not just people—there is no living soul at all. I've had dreams of empty places before, but not so empty that they gave me the willies. The other places had some kind of fathomable 'human' emptiness, so to speak. I mean, the assumption was that there was someone there, just somewhere far, far away. And let me tell you, I was pretty happy in those dreams. So I thought that my desolate beach was someplace like that—abandoned, but fathomable and safe."

"And you do not think that anymore?" said Lonli-Lokli.

I shook my head. "I'm telling you: for starters, it's real. It isn't just part of some kind of dream you can discard and forget while you're brushing your teeth. Second, that place is absolutely empty now. And it wasn't before. See, before, I wasn't scared of that place—I liked it. I'm not such a complicated person that I love something I fear. Long story short, I don't want you to go there anymore, Shurf. But it's not up to you, if I understand it correctly?"

"It is true. I, unfortunately, have no control over the situation," said Shurf. "What are you going to do about it? I have studied you long enough to know that you are not going to leave this alone. Am I right?"

"I wish I could just leave it alone," I said, sighing. "I just don't think I can."

"Then I guess I am lucky," said Lonli-Lokli with a barely noticeable hint of doubt in his voice. "I presume you are going to discuss this with Sir Juffin."

"Of course I am. Even if you didn't approve of it, I'd have to. All my problems have something to do with or somehow affect Juffin. I think it's just one of Nature's laws. And at this point, it's the only thing I can do. I don't know where to begin such an investigation. Maybe he knows."

Shurf carefully picked up a small cup of kamra, took a sip, and put it back on the table. I still can't figure out how he manages to do this without taking off his massive protective gloves. I guess I never will.

"Maybe he does, maybe he doesn't. Why, by the way, did you think I might not approve of it?" he said.

"I don't know. Just a thought. In any case, you're a free man and you have the right to have personal secrets. And I'm not the one to pry into them. Then again, I'm not too eager to obtain your permission to do so either."

Lonli-Lokli gave me a long, piercing look. His gray eyes, which usually radiated icy calm, lit up with such blinding fury that I almost choked on the air I was inhaling.

"I am not a free man. I am the Master Who Snuffs Out Unnecessary Lives. 'Death in the Service of the King,' as you put it. Therefore

I have no right to personal secrets. Such luxuries may come at too high a price for those who have no obligation to pay for me."

The oratorical fury of my ferocious friend extinguished itself as suddenly as it had ignited. His eyes dropped, and he continued in a quiet voice. "I am telling you this only because you and I are in the same situation. We should not entertain meaningless illusions about our freedom and 'right to have personal secrets.' This is not a tragedy—simply a certain period in our lives. Perhaps one day it will end, but for the time being we must play by the rules. It is imperative that you tell Juffin this story, no matter what I think about it."

"Has something happened, Shurf?" I said, taken aback. "Is this conversation bothering you? I've never heard you speak with such passion before. Even the Mad Fishmonger that I had the pleasure of meeting in Kettari wasn't such a passionate speaker."

"Something has happened," said Lonli-Lokli, nodding. "And the sooner I find out what it is, the better. This conversation is indeed bothering me because there is a part of me that does not want you to talk to Juffin. So I was talking to myself, rather than to you. It would pain me deeply if I learned that I had offended you."

"Hey, I don't take offense that easily, Shurf. But you got me worried. All for the better, I guess. Now I'm going to dive right into this."

"Very well," said Lonli-Lokli. "The sooner you do it, the better. You know, I have a feeling that I will indeed require your help, even though I cannot put into words why. It is a rather peculiar feeling: I am not used to needing or relying on someone else's help. I prefer to think of myself as the only living creature in the Universe, neither requiring nor expecting anyone else to help me. Such a conviction does not make life more comfortable, but it gives me steadily good, practical results."

"You yourself have said on more than one occasion that one should not dismiss an opportunity to gain new experience," I said, laughing. "All right. Let's have one last shot of the blood of innocent babes and head out into the open air. You, I'm sure, want to get back home, and I'm going to spoil our boss's placid serenity with my incomprehensible monologue about the mysterious nature of my precious dreams."

"What do you call the 'blood of innocent babes'?" said Shurf. "I do not recall seeing anything like that on the menu. Is this a new house beverage?"

"Nah," I said. "But considering our reputation, any drink that we order can be considered to be the blood of innocent babes, don't you think?"

"I am sorry, but I do not find this funny," said Shurf in an injured tone.

"Yeah, well, you're not alone there," I said. "I don't find it very funny either. The joke was more along the lines of Sir Melifaro Junior. Too bad he's loafing around somewhere instead of hanging on my every word around here."

I ended up demanding another cup of kamra, which, alas, was not the best kamra in Echo. On the other hand, I had reason to believe that it wouldn't be the last cup in my life, and in this respect, I was quite satisfied with it. Shurf, upon considering the matter for a short time, ordered himself a glass of some dark wine.

"Aren't you going to pour it into your holey cup?" I said, disappointed, watching as my colleague brought the glass to his lips. "I was just going to ask for a sip. I like to stick my nose into other people's business, as you know."

"Presently, I do not feel the need to call upon the power of the holey cup. I do not consider the day I have lived to have been particularly difficult. Besides, I am feeling somewhat excited. I believe that your conviction that the barren beach is a real place has affected me."

"Let me tell you, it's nothing compared to how it's affected me," I said. "But I've resigned myself to it and tried to think about doing something else. It's one of my little rules: whenever a situation gets out of hand, I try to think about doing something else. You can always do something else; the tricky part is to start. Anything that distracts you from an unsolvable problem will do fine. Because when you try to control something beyond your capacities, the world can explode into a million pieces in your hands."

"This is one of the strangest lines of reasoning that I have ever heard," said Shurf, nodding in approval. "Still, I do not think that such an extraordinary piece of advice will be of use to anyone but yourself."

"I guess you're right," I said. "I sometimes need a piece of good advice, too, though. Say, Shurf, do you think I can borrow your cup? I have this premonition that I simply must not pass up the chance of drinking out of your magic vessel."

"Must you?" said Lonli-Lokli. "You are beginning to behave like a true former Magician of our Order, Max. It is quite funny. Why, you should get your own holey cup."

"Oh, yeah? But how? I don't know any of your rituals."

"You have the most peculiar notions about magic," said Shurf. "What rituals? Either a man has the power to hold liquids in a bottomless vessel or he does not. Rituals are for scaring novices with—well, to instill a certain mood in them, rather."

"But I am a novice. No need to scare me, but a 'certain mood' is just the thing for me."

"No," said Shurf. "You can already do away with rituals." He produced his famous bottomless cup from somewhere in the folds of his snow-white looxi and handed it over to me. "What are you going to drink from it?"

"Well, how about this kamra?" I said. Then I poured the contents of my cup into Lonli-Lokli's holey cup and drained the now almost cold beverage in one gulp.

"Are you feeling anything?" my friend said, surprised. "You see, kamra is not exactly the drink that helps achieve the best effect."

"Really? I think that I'm about to lift off. Seriously! Like any second now."

"It does not in truth matter what you think. The power assists one to fly in actuality, not simply to enjoy the illusion of flying. I hope I will have an opportunity to explain certain aspects of the ways of the Order of the Holey Cup to you, if you wish. But I already know that you will: curiosity has always been one of your strengths. We should go now. It is getting late, and as you know, I live in the New City. I even intend to ask you to give me a ride: unlike the drivers of the Ministry of Perfect Public Order, you drive very fast. It would take me at least an hour if I chose to use one of the official amobilers."

"Jeepers! Of course I'll give you a lift. I'll get you home in less than a dozen minutes."

"I should be very grateful to you for this. My wife prefers to spend evenings in my company whenever possible. Frankly, I am quite surprised: I am not sure I am a very good interlocutor."

"Well, I'm not surprised at all. It's safe around you, Shurf. While you're around, one doesn't have to worry that this wonderful World might come to an end."

"A most peculiar thought," said Lonli-Lokli, frowning. "Well, in any case, it is time to go."

We paid our bill to the cute "monster" in makeup still dozing off at the bar and went outside. The dim orange light from the streetlights was doing a poor job of dispersing the darkness. The moon that night refused to take part in illuminating the streets: the sky was covered in clouds so thick they seemed to have been made by some pedant like Sir Shurf Lonli-Lokli. I could easily imagine Shurf, in all seriousness, distributing thick, dense patches of autumnal clouds across the sky. Just the job for him.

I sat behind the lever of the amobiler. Shurf sat next to me, and I took off as fast as I could. Kamra may not be the right beverage for drinking out of a holey cup, but I enjoyed the strange lightness that was pouring into me like champagne pouring into a glass: it might start overflowing any moment.

"Look, Shurf, I have another question for you," I said. Frankly, I didn't think the question I had in mind was that important. I just wanted to chat a little more. "About our mutual dreams . . . I don't quite follow how you manage to sense the presence of that hypothetical stranger. You told me yourself that you never got to see him. Then, at the same time, you're sure he's there, and you're almost sure you don't know him. So it appears that something's going on between you two. Does he talk to you, or what?"

"I am not sure that he talks to me," said Lonli-Lokli. His voice lacked the usual confidence. "But anything is possible. You know, Max, for some reason it is hard for me to focus when I try to remember what happens in these dreams. I remember the barren beaches, I remember my conviction that someone else is there, and I remember the threat emanating from that someone. When it comes to remembering what happens between him and me, I draw a complete blank. I am truly sorry."

"Hey, that's all right, Shurf. You know, when I want to remember my dreams, I close my eyes and try to doze off. Not to fall asleep for real but just to doze off, to enter the border state between reality and dreamland. This is important. It's not going to help you now—it only works right after you wake up—but you should definitely try it next time."

"Are you sure you want me to remember?"

I was a little unnerved at the unfamiliar sarcasm in Shurf's voice, but I wasn't surprised. All evening he had been a little too uptight—well, to the degree that the imperturbable Sir Shurf Lonli-Lokli could be uptight. Besides, I was focusing on the road: I was flying down the narrow streets of the Old City at such speed that I couldn't afford to relax even for a split second.

"I think it makes sense to try to remember everything that happens to you, even in your dreams," I said, smiling, and turned my head to my colleague.

I rotated it just slightly, just enough to adhere to my own standards of courtesy while keeping my eyes on the road. That courteous, barely detectable movement was enough for me to be able to notice something unusual—no, not just unusual, something that went against everything I knew to be within the realm of possibility. Shurf had just finished taking off the protective glove from his left hand. His death-dealing inner glove—the former hand of the dead Magician Kiba Attsax—shone in the twilight of the evening, cutting through the orange mist of the street lamps with its dangerous whiteness.

If I had allowed myself even a second to evaluate the situation, if I had wasted any time on doubt, reflection, or even panic, death—my indefatigable companion—would definitely have caught up with me that night. Yet I didn't even bother to assess the situation. Praise be the Magicians, I didn't waste time trying to understand something that could not be understood. Sir Shurf Lonli-Lokli, my most predictable and reliable friend, who, according to my naive, childish notions, held the World on his shoulders, was about to kill me there and then without elaborating on the details of his eccentric intention, to put it mildly.

I hit the brakes, and the amobiler stopped as abruptly as it could. Even lucky boys like me rarely get away with a trick like that, but I was spared. Something cracked in my right wrist, which had been squeezing the lever, but unlike the face of my passenger, mine didn't hit the windshield. He hadn't expected such a turn of events, so he catapulted out of his seat. Instinctively, he threw his left hand with the death-dealing glove forward, to protect his head. The windshield died a quick and painless death, leaving only a pile of silvery ashes behind. Barely realizing what I was doing, I picked up the protective glove from the floor of the amobiler, grabbed the arm with the lethal hand just below the elbow joint, and yanked the protective glove onto it. I think I acted faster than was humanly possible: the entire operation took less, much less, than a second.

"Quit it with your stunts, you reptile!" the creature hissed.

What else would you call it? That voice didn't belong to my friend Shurf. No way. Not in a million years.

It had taken the creature an instant to recover; it was spoiling for a fight. I was surprised I had managed to pull anything off at all, but I didn't have time to be puzzled. I didn't have much time for anything.

Completely on their own, the fingers of my left hand snapped a short, dry snap, producing a tiny green fireball, a Lethal Sphere. None other than Shurf Lonli-Lokli himself had taught me this trick way back when. It hadn't occurred to me that he'd ever run me through a test that would cost me my life if I failed it.

"What a load of crap! All your tricks are useless, you snake. You haven't learned a thing," my colleague said, laughing, and he caught my Lethal Sphere with his right hand, in the protective glove covered in runes.

The green glow wobbled and disappeared. At the same time, Lonli-Lokli's left arm dislodged itself from my grip without any visible effort. I had never been a strong guy and didn't stand a chance against Lonli-Lokli himself.

I had to admit he was telling the truth. I didn't have too many tricks in my arsenal—at least none that could stand up to the Master Who Snuffs Out Unnecessary Lives, a veritable killing machine whose "skillful hands" many an ancient Grand Magician had failed to escape. Maybe I could shrink him and hide him between my thumb and my index finger?

I was sure, however, that my favorite trick would be tantamount to suicide: however small Sir Shurf might be, nothing was going to prevent him from exposing his death-dealing hands even while he was curled up in my fist. And then I'd be dead. Very, very dead.

Spit at him! Spit at him now, you idiot! my mind was yelling, but this uninvited adviser had to stuff it. I wasn't going to waste precious time on experiments, the results of which were already obvious to me.

My logic was approximately as follows: Sir Shurf was my colleague, my comrade in arms, my partner in many perilous adventures—my mentor, one could say. Since he himself had taught me a great deal of magic, he knew what to expect from me. Moreover, one would assume, he was prepared for everything, as well. For example, I was sure he had some kind of protection from my venomous spit. To get out of this alive, my primary objective was to forget all of my old tricks and pull off something absolutely unimaginable, something that shattered all his preconceptions of me and, indeed, my own preconceptions of myself.

I had nothing to lose—I was virtually a dead man. Sir Shurf was already taking off his left protective glove. Fortunately, he was doing it slowly and carefully, which was a usual safety measure. Unfortunately, however slowly he was fiddling with his gloves, I still didn't have a chance in hell for survival.

All I could do was try to have a good time dying, and to go out in style. Why not? My scant but sad postmortem experience suggested that I wouldn't have much time for it after the fact.

I laughed like a madman and jumped onto my feet, not quite realizing why I was doing it. Was I going to challenge my friend Shurf to play a game of chase? Then again, knowing me . . .

The next thing I knew, my feet were no longer touching the ground. The wonderful lightness that had poured into me after the ritual with the holey cup had finally overflowed. A moment later I was contemplating the spiky rooftops of the Old City with surprise. The street lamps were glowing somewhere down there. I hadn't merely levitated; I had shot up into the sky: a merry lightweight force had jolted me, then launched me upward like a cork from a bottle of champagne.

I was still laughing like crazy. Maybe I was crazy. What else would happen to a man if his most trustworthy and predictable friend was going to kill him? The fact that I was hovering above the Echo night like Winnie-the-Pooh at the end of his balloon complemented the crazy events of the evening very nicely.

A piercing white flash somewhere down below brought me to my senses. Until that moment, I had had no idea of the range of Lonli-Lokli's deadly left hand. For a moment, I thought it was curtains for me. Yet I was about to learn some good news: the distance to the target mattered. The snow-white lightning flashed and fizzled out somewhere above the roofs of the Old City. I was much higher and, apparently, completely beyond reach.

Gotta see Juffin right now, I thought. What I really need now is to curl up and shelter under Sir Juffin Hully's wings. I don't think I can solve this problem myself.

I clutched at this thought like a drowning man grasping hold of someone else's lifebelt. For a few moments, I thought only about how desperate I was to see Juffin: I rehearsed my performance, imagined the boss's possible reaction, and prayed to the indifferent heavens to arrange this meeting for me. When I finally forced my mind to shut up and made myself look down, I saw that the ground was much closer than it had been before. If Sir Lonli-Lokli wanted to give his long-range shooting experiment another go, he had a very good chance—a hundred percent chance, rather—to complete it and tuck it under his belt as the crowning glory of his brilliant career.

Then I realized that neither Lonli-Lokli nor the remains of my favorite amobiler were anywhere to be seen. This was a different street. I was just a few blocks away from the Ministry of Perfect Public Order, and it was in my best interests to be on the ground—the sooner the better.

No sooner had I thought about it than my feet touched the sidewalk. I didn't even try to understand how I had managed first to defeat gravity and then to join the Greater Pedestrian Community as though nothing had happened. I dashed to the House by the Bridge. Quite possibly, I beat the sprint record that night, however meaningless it was under the circumstances. Fortunately, my heart, though indignant at the inexcusable overexertion, hadn't blown up in my chest, although I have to admit it tried to the best of its ability. My other heart—the mysterious one—simply ignored the situation, which was either below its dignity, beyond its comprehension, or simply out of its jurisdiction.

When I crossed the finish line on the Street of Copper Pots, I remembered that the boss's shift had long been over, so I didn't bother going inside Headquarters and instead sank into the driver's seat of one of the company amobilers. Praise be the Magicians, I didn't have to explain anything to the driver. The fellow had probably gone off to have a cup of kamra in the company of his colleagues. That was very wise (and timely) of him: I could not possibly have uttered a single comprehensible word at that moment. I'd no doubt have scared him to death if I tried.

I grabbed the lever and tore along to the Street of Old Coins: Juffin had said that I could find him there tonight. I really hoped I would. I seriously doubted that I could use Silent Speech: it would have been as difficult as making a phone call under general anesthesia.

I hit the brakes by the door of my old apartment on the Street of Old Coins almost as hard as I had a few minutes before when I had to save my own precious skin. Well, maybe not quite that hard.

I didn't have to get out of the amobiler: Juffin was standing in the doorway. I nearly died from relief when I saw him. I was so happy, I was about to demonstrate a mixture of hysterics and a swoon, but I got a grip on myself just in time.

It's not over yet, I said to myself. Far from it. If you think about it, it's just the beginning.

"Someone tried to kill you," said Juffin. He didn't ask—he stated it.

I nodded. I still couldn't speak: I needed a little more time to come to my senses. Praise be the Magicians, I could use the breathing exercises that—oh, the irony—Lonli-Lokli had taught me.

Juffin watched me very calmly, and I think I even detected a hint of curiosity in his gaze. He noticed the effort I was making to calm down and recover, nodded in approval, and got into the amobiler beside me.

"Let's go to the House by the Bridge," he said. "It's the best place to solve any problem. Actually, that's what it was built for."

I nodded again, and we drove back. Now I was driving at a normal, human speed, maybe even a little slower than usual: Sir Juffin Hully's presence, along with the breathing exercises, had a most salutary effect on me.

The boss was lost in thought all the way back. He spoke only when we were already in the hallway leading to our office: "I still don't understand who was trying to kill you."

"Shurf," I said in a wooden tone. Then again, a wooden tone is better than none.

"I see. Are you certain it was him?"

"If there's anything I've ever been really certain about, it's that it was him when we left the Vampire's Dinner. And it was him sitting next to me in the front seat of the amobiler. And then the person sitting next to me in the amobiler tried to kill me. Logic suggests that it was Shurf who tried to kill me. There was no one else there. Yet I refuse to accept this kind of logic," I said, sinking into my armchair.

"So do I," said Juffin. "All the more since this is not the only kind of logic known to me. Just the most primitive. I'm afraid that the fellow is in even deeper trouble than you are, if being in deeper trouble is even possible."

"It is," I said, shuddering at the thought of what might have happened to my friend. "After all, I'm still alive, as far as I can tell. I'm even sitting here talking to you. I wish Shurf could say the same about himself."

Juffin nodded a slow, thoughtful nod and stared somewhere behind me with a motionless gaze.

"I have good news," he said suddenly. "Sir Shurf can say the same about himself—or, more precisely, will be able to very soon. He just sent me a call and will join us in a few minutes."

My body tensed up in an unnatural way, and then I felt the already familiar sensation of supernatural lightness. I had to exert an enormous amount of effort not to float up toward the ceiling. The only thing that stopped me was the fear of piercing the roof of the House by the Bridge with my tender head.

Juffin contemplated my inner struggle with visible pleasure. "Come on, Max. Everything is all right," he said. "It is Sir Shurf Lonli-Lokli and not some crazed channeler. And do you really think I couldn't put a stop to anything untoward that might happen in my presence?"

"Sure you can. Maybe. It's just that it's a bit too much for me."

"Oh, shush. Stop your whining," said Juffin. "'Too much for me.' You'd be surprised if I told you how many surprises you could gobble down before you have the right to wince."

"Oh, yeah?" I said. "Okay, you know best. I have a business proposal for you, though. First you treat me to a big cup of kamra and offer me one free psychoanalysis session. Then you can present me a ceremonial dessert spoon."

"A dessert spoon? What are you talking about, Max?" said Juffin.

I swear he was ready to take his words back. He probably thought he had overestimated the strength of my poor mind.

"You thought I'd agree to 'gobble down' your surprises with my bare hands?" I said. "Please, Juffin, I do have some dignity. Ask your butler."

The joke was below average, but Sir Juffin laughed so loud that the windows trembled. I think he was just glad that I had recovered so quickly. I was pretty glad about it myself: marvelous are thy deeds.

Boomshakalaka!

❖

The courier came in and placed a tray with kamra on the desk. Juffin stuck the huge mug right under my nose. "Now, in return, you're going to tell me everything that happened to you. Be clear, concise, and take it from the top please. Can you manage that?"

"I think I can." And I began telling Juffin about the dreams Shurf and I were having. It was the confession that, as it had turned out, I should have hurried to make from the very start.

I made another amazing discovery, perhaps the most amazing discovery of the entire crazy evening: I could recount my thoughts in a coherent and concise manner if I really wanted to. By the time I finished my improvised lecture on the mysteries of dreams, the kamra in my cup was still hot, and I didn't even need to put it on the burner.

"Quite a story," said Juffin. "Especially the ending. Just like in the good old days. No, I take that back: it's even too much for the Epoch of Orders. I wonder how many lucky stars were shining on you when you were born?"

The door opened and slammed shut. I shivered. Juffin, on the other hand, smiled a broad, friendly smile.

"Oh, come in, Sir Shurf," he said. "I'm dying to interrogate you under torture. I'm under the impression that some bastard has decided to sneak through Xumgat on your back. Am I right, or am I right, eh?"

"You are most certainly right. I have been asking myself why I could not guess what had been happening to me," said Lonli-Lokli. "And I am not the only one in trouble here. I was straddled while I was asleep—or, rather, while I was taking a stroll through Sir Max's dream, which, according to his latest conjecture, is a 'real place' in another World. My Rider had to get there somehow in the first place."

He stopped by my armchair and carefully put down a box covered in faded runes on the desk. Then he cautiously put his hand on my shoulder. I saw that he wasn't wearing either the outer protective gloves or the inner death-dealing ones.

"I never thought you would be able to escape from me, Max. But you did, praise be the Magicians! I can just imagine how disappointed that monster must be. He was so confident in his success."

"I would be, too, if I were him," said Juffin. "By the way, why did you say 'he'?"

"I am not sure," said Shurf, sitting down beside me. "As far as I can trust my own feelings, the creature is most certainly male. I think you should put away this box with my gloves, sir, the sooner the better. My guest might return any moment. You know as well as I do that Riders who have taken a fancy to wandering through Xumgat do not like to leave their steeds for long."

"'Riders'? 'Xumgat'? 'Wandering through'?" I said. "You guys should tone down your metaphors. I don't understand a thing."

"It is actually quite simple," said Juffin. "Xumgat is the ancient name of the Corridor between Worlds. I don't particularly like using that term: it smacks of some ancient mystical posturing. It's much easier to call things by their actual names, right? But then the Corridor between Worlds—it's still an open question who knows more about that place."

"You, naturally," I said. "Sure, I ran around there a bit, but I definitely lack the theoretical background."

"Naturally. But in these matters, you need theory like a buriwok needs an amobiler," said Juffin, laughing. "The question is: Can you get to that place or not? Most people can't, including the powerful ancient Magicians. Among the few who can are our mutual friend Maba Kalox, Sir Loiso Pondoxo (a vampire under his blanket!), and such brilliant fellows as you and me. One either has the gift of practicing Invisible Magic—which is what brings us to that mysterious place—or one doesn't. There's no in between. It's a gift. Some can multiply twelve-digit numbers in their heads and some can't, all their university education notwithstanding."

"True, but an education helps you manage even when you have no talent whatsoever," I said. "One can learn to do long multiplication tables on paper, for instance—or, better yet, to use a calculator."

"Do such things really exist?" said Lonli-Lokli.

"Shurf, you wouldn't believe the magical things in the World," I said. For the first time since he had arrived, I found the courage to look him in the eye. I smiled from an immense sense of relief: it truly was the old Shurf Lonli-Lokli—strong and imperturbable, never passing up the opportunity to add something else to his already huge encyclopedic knowledge. And that meant that life was wonderful. That meant that maybe, just maybe, there would be a tomorrow for you, Sir Max, if you were lucky enough, and if destiny would agree to keep putting up with your silly ass, and if you could learn this lesson well: you can't offload your own heavenly vault onto someone else's shoulders. You can trust anyone you want to, but you can only rely on yourself. Everyone has his own vault to carry; everyone is the Atlas of his own world. It's no one else's fault that you were only beginning to understand the rules of the game after thirty-something years.

Juffin pried me away from my thoughts.

"You know, Max, you yourself just came up with a brilliant metaphor with those calculators of yours. That is approximately what is going on here. When a powerful Magician realizes he cannot enter the Corridor between Worlds by himself, he can turn into what is called a Rider. He finds a person who is capable of traveling between Worlds, and then he captures that person's spirit. For someone who has mastered the higher degrees of Apparent Magic, this is a piece of cake. Ideally, of course, you'd want to capture the spirit of some madman: they are often very talented, and what's more, they have no clue about their own talents or the possible uses thereof. Besides, their spirits don't belong to anyone anyway."

Juffin fell silent and took a good look at Lonli-Lokli. Apparently he liked what he saw, so he continued. "Given enough magical power, one can capture or possess not just someone's spirit but also his body. The body of someone who was born for magical travels. Now, if one really tries, one can also capture all the powers of one's captive. The captive then dies, and the lucky captor keeps a great deal of the victim's talent. People like you or me are of no interest to him: we are too dangerous to deal with since we know what we do, more or less, and can put up resistance."

Another pause. Now the boss was looking at me.

"Although . . . You know, I wasn't going to tell you this so as not to scare you beforehand. Now you know, and this knowledge might come in handy. One such clever fellow already tried to straddle you when you traveled back to your home World. He failed, but you almost lost your memory, thanks to him: the bastard really stunned you. So, how do you like them apples?"

I was shocked and dismayed, but recovered quickly. No doubt I had begun getting used to unpleasant surprises.

"So that's why I couldn't remember anything about my life in Echo! If I were a little weaker, I'd have thought I'd just seen a wonderful dream. But you should have told me sooner, Juffin. I should know such things about myself."

"What's the point? If I'd told you, you might have been too scared to even try traveling between Worlds again," said Juffin. "I was going to look for your fellow traveler, but then I got hooked on your 'cartoons' and thought I could put off looking for the Rider for a while. You weren't in any immediate danger: after such a crushing defeat, the Rider wouldn't have tried to bother you—believe me, I know his kind."

"Fine," I said. "Magicians be with you and that failed tourist." I turned to Lonli-Lokli. "So does this mean you can travel between Worlds, too, Shurf?"

"Not yet. But I will someday. That time has not yet come. In my life, everything happens slowly. It is my destiny."

"I'm afraid you're going to have to get used to the thought that that time has already come," said Juffin. "Don't you get it? It didn't go exactly how you and I had planned it, Sir Shurf. This fidgety fellow"—he nodded in my direction—"stirred you up a bit sooner than he should have and was punished for it."

"Hey! I didn't stir anyone up," I said. "Quit speaking in riddles."

"If there's anything I'm really certain about, it's that I'm tired of speaking in riddles," said Juffin, mocking my earlier line. "Fair enough, I'll explain. You accidentally, one might say out of sheer idiocy, dragged Shurf into your dreams. I believe you both know what I'm talking about. Then there were your joint walks around the outskirts of Kettari. All of this resulted in Sir Shurf being in dangerous—or, I should say, dubious—situations: he is already quite capable of journeying between Worlds, but he is not yet ready to consciously put his talents to good use. Currently, he's no better than some of the inhabitants of the Refuge for the Mad . . . Hold on, boys. That's where we need to sniff around a bit. I have no idea where we will find our client, but we have a pretty good chance of encountering a couple of his victims in the Refuge for the Mad. You're absolutely right, Shurf—there's no way you could have been his first prey. You are way too tough for a novice traveler through Xumgat. What we've got here is a very, very experienced Rider."

"I believe you are correct," said Lonli-Lokli, nodding. "It is unfortunate that I will not be able to take part in the search. The timing could not have been worse."

"Very true," said Juffin. "But there's nothing we can do about it now. Do you want to stay here? I'd rather you stayed here, although, frankly speaking, you'd be much more comfortable in Xolomi."

"Naturally, I shall stay here. Comfort is not the topmost priority at the moment. The small room in your office where we used to keep prisoners is exactly what I need now. It is as isolated from the world as Xolomi is. At the very least, I shall be nearby and you will be able to observe me safely. In addition, I may perhaps bring some benefit without even leaving these premises."

I glanced in perplexity first at Juffin, then at Lonli-Lokli. Shurf noticed my confusion and raised the corners of his mouth in a sympathetic smile. "This Rider might straddle me yet again," he said in a soft voice. "I gave Sir Juffin my gloves, but I am quite a capable Magician even without them. You know, as far as I understand, he feels something akin to personal hatred toward you. I had to be subject to his emotions, so I can assure you that his attempt on your life was born of a passionate desire to kill you, not a necessity. If that creature was afraid of your telling Sir Juffin about my problems, he would have made me silent from the outset: he is powerful enough to do that. When he comes, I have nothing to counter him with—a disgusting feeling. For this reason, I will have to be locked up for the time being—at least until you and Juffin are done with this creature that has straddled me. You know, you were not the only one walking on the edge today. I still cannot fathom the magnanimity you must have had not to spit your venom at me. You had more than one opportunity to do so."

"Nah, it's not magnanimity," I said, embarrassed. "To demonstrate magnanimity, I'd have needed a little time for consideration, and there wasn't any time. No time to decide to spit or not to spit. I just didn't. Why? Magicians only know. Maybe because I was sure that it wouldn't work on you. I thought that the only right thing to do would be to do something completely unexpected, something I'd never done before, something you'd have no idea I'd be capable of doing. Actually, now, in retrospect, it's hard for me to reconstruct how my logic worked back then. Chances are I didn't use any logic at all."

"Allow me to assure you that I had no ready-made antidotes to your poison. I am a living human being, and I would have died from your spit just as any other person would, provided I had not been able to shield myself with my protective glove. The creature that possessed me had no particular reason to value my life. Had I died, my Rider would have found another 'horse' for the joint descent to Xumgat. I believe he has enough of them in his 'stables.' I just wanted you to know that you stood a very good chance of finishing me off."

"Good golly!" I said. "It would've been almost as bad as your finishing me off. Or worse?"

"There is nothing worse than your own death, for when it arrives, everything else collapses. Other events may only destroy a part of your personal universe," said Lonli-Lokli in a didactic tone. He thought for a moment and then added, "Although sometimes even this part may seem disproportionately large. Then, when that part collapses, it takes everything along with it."

"It happens," said Juffin. He looked like someone who knew what he was talking about. "Very well now. I hope you won't have time to get bored in your voluntary incarceration, Sir Shurf. I doubt your Rider will appear in my presence. If he does, he'll regret it. I'm going to let you out from time to time for exemplary behavior. I'd suggest that you refrain from sleeping for the time being, though."

"I think I should, too," said Lonli-Lokli. "I will easily manage to stay awake if you disarm my Rider in three to four days' time. If not—well, you will have to resort to minor violations of the Code of Krember, just like the good old days."

"Oh, don't worry about that," said Juffin. "We won't have to take it to court. That, I promise."

"I have never doubted it, even for a second," said Shurf. "Every cloud has a silver lining: I have quite a few books in my office I have been meaning to read."

"Very well then. Consider this adventure an extended vacation. You can start right now because Sir Max and I need to go to the Refuge for the Mad."

"You think we're that bad?" I said, smiling.

"Even worse: no one can help us," said Juffin, "so we won't stay there long. We'll just visit our fellow comrades in distress and try to find out what sorts of dreams they dream. And that will be it. Now be a good sport and bring Shurf's books to him. I don't want to look into the face of some scared courier."

"Aw, Juffin," I said, shaking my head. "You could've come up with a more convoluted pretext for kicking me out of your office. If you and Shurf need to talk secret stuff behind my back, you could have used Silent Speech."

"How insightful," said Juffin. "Look at the kid: he's a regular genius! 'Secrets.' What secrets? I just wanted to make you run up and down the hallway so you don't feel like you're a great hero and a poor victim all at once."

"Right," I said, walking out of the office.

Whatever Juffin was saying, my wise other heart was positive that they were going to talk secrets. The boss reeked of mystery, and I could smell it a mile away. But I was magnanimous enough to leave the two of them alone. It would be tactless of me, in any case, to gallop up and down the hallway and return a minute later. I decided to give them enough time to talk all the secrets they wanted.

Slowly, very slowly, two-steps-forward-one-step-back slowly, I crossed the Hall of Common Labor, walked backward down the hallway, and went into Lonli-Lokli's spacious office. I picked a stack of books from the white bookshelf over his desk and smiled an involuntary, bewildered smile when I remembered Shurf's recent grumbling about The Pendulum of Immortality, which I had put in the wrong place. The guy was probably my best friend: after all, we even dreamed the same dreams—well, some of the same dreams, anyway.

Funny. I hadn't thought anything of that sort before he tried to kill me.

I returned and put the books on the desk in front of Shurf. He stared at them, thinking.

"Perhaps this will be enough for a while. But not for long. May I ask you, gentlemen, to bring something else from my office?"

"Sure," said Juffin, nodding. "By the way, the old university library has accidentally come into the possession of this soon-to-be-crowned monarch of Fanghaxra. He inherited it along with his residence."

"Hey! That's true," I said, remembering. "You can make a list, and I'll dig through the books tomorrow. Then the next day I'll—"

"Dream on," said Juffin. "Tomorrow you're meeting your subjects, and then it's your official coronation. Have you already forgotten?"

"Gosh, I did forget. All right, I'll rummage through the books right after the coronation. It'll save me a trip to that blasted palace, anyway."

"Will you listen to him?" said Juffin. "'That blasted palace.' Any normal person would be thrilled to live in that luxurious place and wouldn't come out for years."

"Well, you know me," I said. "I love a cold yurt at the outskirts of the Barren Lands, a hard wooden barstool in the Armstrong & Ella, or, if worse comes to worst, the armchair in this office. Luxury items only overload my impoverished intellect."

"Then I hope you're going to love the simple interiors of the Refuge for the Mad," said Juffin. "Sir Shurf, you're under arrest, so off you go to the cell. And if your Rider pops his head in, try to follow my advice. Will you be able to sense the right moment?"

"I have reason to believe that I might be able to accomplish this task," said Lonli-Lokli.

He walked over to the farthest wall of our office, to the Secret Entrance to our "detention cell." The cell was just as good as Xolomi: you couldn't leave, you couldn't perform magic, and you couldn't even send a call to anyone from it. On the upside, however, you could easily hide from someone else's magic in it. Juffin had built this magic room at the dawn of the Code Epoch, right in the very beginning of his present job. A regular prison cell, you understand, couldn't keep even a minor Magician of some worthless Order, and back then the Secret Investigative Force had to deal with much more serious clients on a daily basis.

For as long as I could remember, the detention cell had mostly stood empty. Only once did we have to lock up the dead-but-quick Jiffa Savanxa from the Magaxon Forest there. Even so, as it had turned out, we should've known better.

"Precisely," said Juffin to Shurf as he locked the Secret Door. "I, too, believe that you are capable of accomplishing this task."

"Okay, so we've arrested Lonli-Lokli. Now we can head to the Refuge for the Mad," I said. "Boy, are we having fun!"

"I'm liking it, too," said Juffin. "Let's go, Sir Max."

"Where to?" I said as I was getting behind the lever of the amobiler.

"First to the New City through the Gates of Three Bridges, then straight down parallel to the Xuron. I'll show you the way when we reach the outskirts."

"It's a bit far," I said.

"With you behind the lever, the distance doesn't matter." Juffin was unusually generous with his compliments, but he soon composed himself and added the proverbial fly to the ointment: "Just try not to get us into some silly fatal accident, or instead of doing time, poor Shurf will do life."

"Yeah, I guess the sentence for attempted murder would be too long for Shurf. Well, instead of scaring me, why don't you tell me what we're going to do in the Refuge for the Mad? Or is that another one of your secrets?"

"No, rather a review session for poor students such as yourself. Do you remember what I taught you about finding out about the past of things?"

"Do I? I'm a good learner and almost an A student. How can I forget the very basics of your lectures? You probably won't believe me, but I even practice on occasion."

"Well, I wouldn't think you've had much time for practicing lately," said Juffin. "But maybe it's all for the better and you'll be able to help me tonight. That would be mighty fine."

"Are we going to interrogate furniture again?"

"No, not furniture. My latest lecture on this fascinating topic explains that people can be treated much the same as any inanimate object. The only difference is that an object will tell us about the events that occurred in its surroundings and a person will divulge information about himself. Sometimes he will even reveal things he didn't know he knew. Granted, it's much more difficult to work with people, and sometimes this kind of sorcery will only work on a sleeping person. We're in luck, though. It's close to midnight, and soon most of our potential witnesses will be sleeping like logs. The others will also be sleeping, in fact, just not quite like logs. Not much we can do about that."

I broke into an involuntary smile. "So that's why you had me sleep at your place after each dangerous adventure. And then the next morning, you looked all important and told me you were tired as all get-out and that it was 'all clear to you now.'"

"Did you think I was just crazy about your snoring? Don't try to play the fool, mister. You knew it all along; you just didn't bother to admit it to yourself. Am I right, or am I right?"

"I suppose so," I said, sighing. "You know best. You're the world's greatest expert in the science of knowing me."

"True, that. Now take a right. We're almost there."

About two minutes later I stopped the amobiler by a low decorative fence. Until now, I had thought that the Refuge for the Mad would be guarded as securely as the famous Nunda Royal Prison of Hard Labor in Gugland. It turned out I couldn't have been more wrong; even the gate wasn't locked. Of course, it didn't really matter: a fence like that could only stop someone who preferred crawling around on his stomach.

We left the amobiler by the gate, crossed a grand but very neglected garden, and finally arrived at our destination. Two large windows glowed with a cozy orange light in the middle of the garden, among the thick branches of trees.

"Pick up the pace, Max. They're waiting for us," said Juffin, rushing toward the light like a giant moth.

"How come there's no security?" I said. "Don't tell me it's just one of the things that 'aren't done.'"

The boss's eyebrows flew up. "Of course it isn't done. Why? Who would ever think of attacking these poor fellows?"

"I mean the other way around," I said. "You need the security to keep the loonies in."

"Why would they not want to stay in? They are treated well here—better than in other places, anyway. Our wisemen can ease any torments of the soul. They have even returned many of the inhabitants of this place back to their normal lives. Hold on a minute, Max. Are you saying locking them in is one of the pleasant little customs of your homeland?"

"It is. Did you get a chance to watch *One Flew Over the Cuckoo's Nest*? I highly recommend it. Very educational. It makes the habits of your legendary villain Loiso Pondoxo look like child's play."

I noticed that I was trembling in helpless fury, as though I was the one being tortured and not the defiant brawler McMurphy. Talk about the magic of cinema.

"Don't overdo it," said the boss. "We've come to see a wiseman. He's a scholar. He'll suspect something as soon as he sees you like this. You'll end up with an extraordinary vacation and I with a boatload of troubles. Do me a favor, Sir Max—get a grip on yourself."

I reined in my righteous fury, took a deep breath, and said in a very different tone, "Actually, locking up the loonies isn't a form of mindless torture. It's a necessity. You saw one of my crazy fellow countrymen yourself. Remember how happy he was slitting the throats of those poor women? What would you do with a guy like that? Give him pills and walk him through the garden?"

"Well, I doubt that even our wisemen would've been able to cure that guy," said Juffin. "But at the very least, they would have given him the Crystal of Submission. That would have done the trick."

"That easy?"

"Sure. Piece of cake. If you don't believe it, here's your last chance.

Starting tomorrow, you're going to be treated like royalty. And you know what they call crazy kings—eccentrics. No one will say a word, even if they start dancing naked on the market square. All hail Your Majesty!"

The boss gave me a mocking bow—Sir Melifaro himself would have died of envy—and opened a heavy, ancient door.

The cozy windows we had seen from afar were on the second floor. We ascended a wide staircase covered with a very soft carpet, in case, I guess, one of the crazy inhabitants of this hospitable house decided to count the stairs with his own lower jaw.

"Good night, Sir Hully. I see you as though in a waking dream, Sir Max. The Refuge is honored by your visit. I am happy to say my name: Slobat Katshak, Master Keeper of the Peace of Mind, or Chief Nocturnal Wiseman, to put it simply," said a delicate young man in a light-turquoise looxi.

"Also, the former Junior Magician of the Order of Spiky Berries," said Juffin. "And as much of a night owl as you are, Max."

The little wiseman was about to burst from his enormous hospitality. "Be my guests, gentlemen. My heart will be broken into a million pieces if you decline this humble meal."

"Secret Investigators turning down free food?" said Juffin. "Rest assured, Slobat, Sir Max and I will not leave as much as a crumb of bread on our plates."

Calling it a "humble meal" was, of course, an understatement. The table was densely populated with all manner of trays with food. Still, all Juffin's Rabelaisian bravado notwithstanding, the meal didn't take more than a quarter of an hour: the boss was eager to get down to business.

"Slobat, Sir Max and I must inspect the rooms of the charges in your care," he said. "Perhaps we will need your help, but perhaps not. I think you should come with us and wait in the hallway. This is a classified affair. I am sorry. I know this is not the most entertaining way to spend the night. I guess tonight isn't your lucky night."

"Not the most difficult or unpleasant undertaking, either," said the wiseman. "Where would you like to start?"

"From the most hopeless cases, those whose spirits roam the Universe like waifs and strays during the Troubled Times."

"Sinning Magicians," I said, getting up from the table. "You're a poet, Juffin."

"Nothing to brag about. The premises dispose one to it."

We had to leave the house and walk toward the middle of the garden. Finally, we reached a relatively small one-story building.

"This is the final abode of those who have no hope of ever finding their light half," said the wiseman. "You may inspect the bedrooms. I'll wait outside, if you don't mind."

"Not only do we not mind, we insist," said Juffin, smiling.

We entered a dark hallway. In an effort to economize, the administration of the Refuge hadn't bothered to put up a lamp or even a candle here. This wasn't a problem: I had long ago learned to find my way in darkness, and Juffin, like any other inhabitant of the Unified Kingdom, had had this ability since birth.

"What do I do?" I said in a whisper. "How do I take part in your 'medical exam'? I've never tried it on people before, you know."

"For starters, just watch me. Maybe you'll figure it out on your own. Or maybe we won't have to do anything at all. There's no guarantee that we'll find what we're looking for here. Praise be the Magicians, I only need to enter a bedroom to see if its occupant holds any interest for us."

"By the way, why here? Is this Refuge for the Mad special?"

"You bet it is. It's the only Refuge for the Mad in the Capital. The others are all in distant provinces," said Juffin. "Maybe even this one will move soon. Some respected wisemen believe that staying in the Heart of the World thwarts the healing of mental patients. Now those who've decided to sneak through Xumgat, on the other hand, need all the power of the Heart of the World they can get. I doubt that they'd want to go all the way to somewhere in Uryuland. If our Rider really gains his power from the mentally ill, his victims should be here somewhere."

We entered the first room. The soft part of the floor, which served as a bed, took up almost all the available space. At the farther end of the room, someone was breathing heavily under a pile of blankets.

"Okay, this lady is definitely of no interest to us," said Juffin. "Her poor spirit is wandering Magicians know where, and it has never descended to Xumgat. Of that, I am certain. Let's move on."

"How did you know it was a lady?" I said, carefully closing the door behind me.

"It was a lady—a beautiful one, too. Wait a second, why are you so surprised? I understand that at your age all women seem like mysterious and wonderful creatures, but did you think they never went mad?"

"Of course I know they do. And how," I said. "So we're in the women's ward?"

"You're talking nonsense again. Why would anyone build special wards for men and women? This is a hospital, not a Quarter of Trysts. Another tradition of that homeland of yours?"

"Indeed," I said, blushing. "In our hospitals, women and men are kept separately."

"Are the inhabitants of your world so unrestrained in their passion that they are eager to jump on one another at any opportunity?" said Juffin, surprised. "Even the crippled, the lame, and the sick? I just can't wrap my mind around this. Strange that your behavior is fairly decent. I'm sure you could easily pass for a basket case and end up in one of your horrible and well-guarded Refuges for the Mad back home."

"Spot on, Juffin," I said. "But I deceived them by keeping a low profile."

"Okay, we'll have plenty of time to discuss your ruined youth later," said Juffin. "Now we have pressing business at hand."

We inspected several more bedrooms.

"No, not this one," Juffin would say, and we would move along. We had covered well over half of the hallway when I felt an unpleasant sensation at the threshold of one of the rooms.

Nothing out of the ordinary happened. I just sensed that the person who was sighing deeply underneath a blanket, several paces from where I was standing, felt very cold and lonely. I was all too familiar with that piercing, ice-cold, absolute loneliness—the loneliness without self, without the slightest chance of understanding what was happening to you, without the hope of ever coming back. I had once felt something similar when I fell asleep in the amobiler in the Magaxon Forest and found myself in the Corridor between Worlds. Boy, was I scared then!

"Even if I didn't know anything about such matters, I could easily use your face as an indicator," said Juffin. "It's as crooked as it can be. Looks like we've found what we were looking for, unless the disconcerted spirit of this poor fellow slides back and forth along Xumgat in complete solitude."

"You're definitely on a roll today," I said, letting out a nervous laugh. "I don't remember you ever using such turns of phrase before."

"Indeed. As I said before, the premises dispose one to it," said Juffin, sitting down on the floor. "Pay attention now, and don't distract me. I'm going to ask the poor fellow to tell us his story, so to speak. You sit down beside me and try to tune in. Do what you'd normally do, as if this weren't a person but a regular box or, I don't know, a broom. You use the same principles when working with people; it's just more difficult to establish the connection. Unlike inanimate objects, a person is reticent by nature—any person, mind you, not just a madman."

I sat down next to Juffin and leaned against the wall. The wall was soft and elastic. In this respect, the bedrooms in the Refuge for the Mad on the outskirts of Echo were similar to regular rooms for the violently insane in my "historical homeland."

Then I stared at the shapeless dark hump at the edge of the bed. Our subject seemed to me to be a frail creature. His blanket was pulled over his head. I understood, however, that it didn't really matter. He could just as well be hiding from an X-ray machine under that blanket.

For a few moments, I didn't sense anything special. I just sat on the floor and stared at the sleeping lunatic. If I were interrogating his blanket, I already would have gotten all the information I needed. Then I felt something like a jolt from within. It felt similar to the way your heart pushes against your ribs when a truck turns from around the corner and heads right toward your car.

Following the jolt came a steady stream of mixed visions that seemed to lack any plot or narration. These bright pictures, however, were pitiful inkblots in comparison with the overwhelming loneliness of the creature lost in the Corridor between Worlds, or "sliding back and forth along Xumgat," as Juffin had put it—though this wording sent shivers down my spine.

Juffin shook my shoulder.

"Hey, come back, Max. We've got to hurry. I already found out everything I needed to know. You also felt something at the end, didn't you?"

"I think so."

I shook my head to pull myself together: some part of me was still wandering in that mysterious place—a significant part of me, I should say. My existence without it was hardly complete. Shaking my head didn't help much, so I had to resort to slapping my face. I did it from the bottom of my heart; it even came with a complimentary ringing in the ears.

"Need a hand?" said Juffin.

"Thanks, I think I can manage on my own. What I really need is five minutes and a bucket of cold water."

"Done. This little door leads to the bathroom. But I can't give you more than two minutes. We need to hurry."

I went to the bathroom, took off my turban, and stuck my head under the spigot. The water temperature was ideal: not quite so freezing as to give me another cold, but cool enough to wash off the residue of that poor person's emotions. Juffin stood in the doorway contemplating my suffering with apparent curiosity.

"I've learned some amazing things, Max. I'm sure you've also learned them, but you don't have the experience yet to translate them into a language you understand."

"To transmogrify," I said. I thought the word was very appropriate in this context.

"Another strange word . . . Anyway, we can find more victims of our mysterious Rider in this Refuge for the Mad. A lot more. Many more than I suspected. But let's not waste time: the culprit of this whole ordeal is also in this Refuge. In fact, he has been here for a long, long time. He has kept this last fellow we've interrogated in captivity for eighty years, right from the moment the guy arrived here. I've got to hand it to him, though: the old man is a master of disguise. And who in his right mind—pun definitely intended—would search for the most powerful of the Senior Magicians of the Order of the Staff in the Sand in a Refuge for the Mad? Even I wouldn't think of it. Even I!"

"So, I take it you two know each other," I said, grabbing a towel.

"And how! Magician Gugimagon and I go way back. Back in the Epoch of Orders, he stuck to me like a wet raincoat, hoping that I'd break down and agree to teach him the secret of Invisible Magic. As if it were up to me. The guy had no talent for those things. It was written on his forehead in letters this big."

Juffin stretched his arms like a fisherman boasting to the world of his latest whopper. It seemed as though it was important that I learn, once and for all, how big the letters had been.

"Some friends you've got, Juffin," I said. "Did that poor fellow tell you which room we could find your old buddy in, by any chance?"

"No, he doesn't know. They've never met in reality. Or did you think Gugimagon was the sort to drop by for a cup of kamra?"

"I know nothing about the customs of you evil sorcerers," I said.

"Okay, let's go then, Mr. 'Good Guy' Magic," said Juffin, laughing. "I know you're back in business, so quit your feigning. Great deeds await us. A heart-to-heart talk with Sir Slobat Katshak, for instance."

The boss moved from words to action and gave me a light push in the butt with his knee. He really got carried away.

We went out to the porch and sat down on the stairs next to the wiseman, who had begun to get bored.

"Have you found what you were looking for?" he said.

"Some of it," said Juffin. "Now it's your turn to help us."

"With great pleasure," said Katshak, smiling as though Juffin were about to treat him to some candy.

"We must locate one of your patients here as soon as possible," said Juffin, and fell silent, looking for the right words. "You shouldn't feel any pangs of conscience about it: the man we're looking for isn't really mad. He's just a very talented malingerer. The best malingerer I know. Okay, that takes care of that. Moving right along . . . First, he's been here for quite a while, at least eighty years, but he arrived before the Code Epoch. Last time I saw him was shortly before the Code of Krember was established. Three days before that, to be precise. Second, he's a fairly old man. He's always looked older than me, for as long as I've known him. Very tall, big but not obese. He could have easily changed his appearance but not his stature. Also, he's blind in his left eye."

"Oh, but this is old Kotto Halis you're talking about!" said the wiseman. "We only have one patient who's blind in his left eye. But he couldn't have done anything. If only I could tell you how strong the smell of his madness is! Besides, the old man has never regained consciousness, no matter how many Crystals of Memory we give him."

"Yes, just as I suspected. In a 'conscious state,' he'd have nothing whatsoever to do here. Take us to him. The sooner the better."

"Let's go then." Katshak stood up. He looked stunned. "His room is in the building next to this, among the same poor hopeless cases you've just seen."

Moments later, we were going up the stairs of another one-story building. Sir Juffin Hully had gained such speed that the wiseman and I were clear outsiders in the race. I took it the boss was rushing to give his old friend a bear hug.

This time, Sir Slobat Katshak entered the building with us and walked us to the farthest room in the right wing of the hallway. Juffin stormed into the dark chamber and froze so abruptly that I crashed into his back at a fast clip. The boss withstood the shock and didn't move an inch.

"Blast it," he said. "I knew it."

"Knew what?" I said. And then I saw it. The bed was empty. On its soft surface, dead center, was a single dent. The shape of the dent suggested that the occupant had lain there completely still and then disappeared. Vanished. If he had gotten up from it in the usual manner, there would have been other dents. The material used for floor coverings in bedrooms here in Echo readily takes the shape of the body but is reluctant to return to its original shape. That takes some time—at least a few hours.

"So he did it!" said Juffin, his voice betraying sincere admiration. "He slipped into Xumgat completely—lock, stock, and barrel—and it's not easy for people like him. Slobat, my dear boy, I have bad news for you. You should immediately check how many new dead bodies you have in your Refuge. If I had to guess, I'd say it would be at least a dozen. For his last journey, Gugimagon would have to grab all their strength, without leaving anything to them. Still, I'm surprised he's managed to pull this off!"

"If you say so, I must immediately begin the inspection," said the wiseman. "Will you manage without me, gentlemen?"

"Yes. Moreover, we're leaving. Thank you for your help, Slobat. If someone dares berate you for all the trouble that happened during your shift, please do not hesitate to send me a call. I will be more than willing to give your superiors a lengthy lecture that will undoubtedly restore your reputation. After all, it wasn't you whom sly Gugimagon tricked into thinking he was a madman. But I hope you won't be needing my protection."

"To Magicians with my reputation," said Sir Slobat, sighing. "But I'd give a lot to have stayed home tonight. I hate it when terminal patients die under my care. I feel so sorry for them. I can't help them anyway, so I'd rather I didn't have to see them go. It's nights like this when I consider trying to find another occupation."

"Indeed. This night has left a lot to be desired," said Juffin.

We went out into the garden and headed toward the gate.

"Do you think your friend killed everyone he traveled through the Corridor between Worlds with?" I said. "What about our Sir Shurf? A hole in the heavens above him, we can't even send him a call while he's in that detention cell of yours!"

"Shurf is doing just fine, trust me. He's not going to sleep, and Gugimagon is never going to be able to grab the strength of a person who's awake. I don't think anyone can do that. Besides, I left Sir Shurf a good weapon."

"What is it?" I said. "Or is that a secret?"

"Not much of a secret, really. But it's best not to speak of it before it has done what it's supposed to do. You see, words can sometimes kill one's powers. Just try to be patient a little while longer. I'll tell you everything after I've made sure that Shurf doesn't need my protection anymore."

"And that's why you sent me to fetch the books, so I wouldn't bother you with my questions, right?"

"No, I was afraid you'd sell all of my secrets to the Royal Voice sooner or later," said Juffin. "Especially now, when you and Rogro sing in unison on account of your quarrels with that old grumbler Moxi."

"Yeah, you're right. Speaking of which, I haven't been to the Juffin's Dozen in a long while. I keep getting distracted with this or that. What a life I lead!"

"Don't fret," said the boss, sitting next to me in the amobiler. "You'll have time to catch up on everything soon."

I took hold of the lever and finally decided to ask what was really on my mind. "What are we going to do now? We can't just leave it as is, or can we?"

"Of course not. Now, Sir Max, you and I will have to go to Xumgat and look for the shelter of my old friend there."

"He's probably gone to the World that Shurf and I keep dreaming about. The one with the barren sandy beaches," I said.

"What makes you think so?" said Juffin.

"I have no idea. Except that I don't 'think' so; I know so."

"Excellent," said Juffin, nodding. "We'll look for him there then. First thing tomorrow."

"Tomorrow?" I said. "Why not now?"

"What's with the hurry?" said Juffin, shaking his head in disapproval. "What we really should do now is call Sir Kofa, sit him down in your armchair, and then go hit the sack. Besides, you have a crown fitting tomorrow, remember? It would be a shame if you got lost in Xumgat and missed your own coronation."

"No, it wouldn't," I said.

"Sure it would. His Majesty King Gurig has put so much effort into preparing everything for the event. He even has summoned big shot VIPs from all corners of the Unified Kingdom. If you and I just disappeared, the king wouldn't understand, his respect for our mysterious work notwithstanding. After the ceremony, though, we can disappear for a dozen years at a time—he won't even notice."

"Won't even notice? Right."

"Okay, I'm exaggerating. But even if we wander through a few of those sinning Worlds for a few years, no more than a dozen hours will have passed here. I'll make sure of it."

"Will you?" I said. "Will you teach me how to do that? It seems like such a useful thing to be able to do. Anyway, now I really don't understand why we can't start chasing your ingenious friend right away."

"Because it's a rather risky undertaking, Max. I personally cannot guarantee that nothing bad is going to happen to us. And before you set out for a dangerous journey, you must finish all your business at home, if fate is kind enough to grant you time to do so. If you go out wearing several looxis and their folds are dangling all around you, passersby will step on them, and sooner or later you'll fall on the sidewalk. The first thing to do is to get rid of all the unnecessary stuff, or at least to pull up the dangling folds. Got it?"

"Got it."

"So nice of you to pretend you understand what I'm saying," said the boss. "I'm not quite in the lecturing mood right now."

Despite my boundless trust in Sir Juffin Hully, who assured me that Lonli-Lokli was going to be fine, I remained uneasy until I could see it for myself.

Juffin humored me by opening the Secret Door to the cell. Shurf was sitting on the floor, his legs crossed, his spine perfectly straight, his gaze fixed on the pages of *The Pendulum of Immortality*. He wasn't too enthusiastic about seeing us. He recovered quickly, though, and even expressed a readiness to have a cup of kamra in our company.

Then Shurf returned to his ivory tower, trusty Kimpa came to pick up Juffin, and Sir Kofa Yox sent me a call, saying he would come to the House by the Bridge in a few minutes.

It wasn't necessary for me to wait for Kofa and I could have gone home right away if I had wanted to. The idea didn't really appeal to me, however: I had just tried to send a call to Tekki and found out she was fast asleep. I, on the other hand, was wide awake. Maybe later, when it was almost morning, I would be able to close my eyes and catch a few winks, but not now.

My recent skirmish with Lonli-Lokli had done more damage to me than I had previously thought while I still had my favorite sedative, in the form of the omnipotent Sir Juffin Hully, by my side. I had to admit that I was only eager to go look for that wicked genius Gugimagon because it was not a bad way of distracting myself from my personal problems and anxieties.

"Good night," said Sir Kofa, entering the office. I looked up at him and saw a face with thick, bushy eyebrows rapidly becoming Kofa's own. "You're still here, boy? And what kinds of werewolves, pray tell, are you contemplating at the bottom of your empty cup?"

"I could use a full cup right now—you're spot on—and that's easy enough to fix. Sit down and help yourself to anything you can find. If there's something you can't find, we can take care of it in no time, praise be Dondi Melixis, who has been paying our bills from Madam Zizinda's place."

"I always knew that your working methods were something else," said Sir Kofa.

"Thanks to you. You were the one who taught me that one should spend one's office hours in taverns at the company's expense. Now you can sit back and admire the results of your labors. You have the right."

And we sent a small order to the Glutton Bunba. The capacity of my stomach was staggering. Today I had started munching at dawn and had hardly stopped munching since, except for that brief intermission when I had waged a little war against my friend Lonli-Lokli and flown hither and yon above the spiked roofs of Echo.

I was finally able to appreciate the comic side of my recent adventures —it was about time, too—and laughed in relief. For that reason Sir Kofa was privileged to hear my narration of the evening's events in the genre of black comedy rather than Shakespearian tragedy. Thank goodness at least someone derived some real pleasure from the story.

"Okay," he said when he stopped laughing, "you have convinced me that you had a great deal of fun. Now you only need to convince yourself of the same thing."

"Yeah, that's not as easy as it may sound," I said. "Not to worry, though. Tomorrow I'll be as good as new."

"Tomorrow? Of course. Tomorrow you're having a different kind of adventure. But you like change, don't you?"

"Sometimes," I said. "Usually it takes the form of a rapid change in my decision about which tavern to while away my evening in."

"I think you'll find tomorrow's event more than amusing," said Kofa. "The guests alone will be worth it."

"You mean my subjects? Actually, ever since I taught them to tie their headbands the right way, they haven't looked half bad."

"Well, to each his own, of course, but I didn't mean your subjects. I meant the grandees from our provinces. You're in for a sea of pleasure."

"Are they really funny?" I said.

"Oh, yes. Each in his own way. Besides, His Indefatigable Majesty Gurig VIII has invited almost every foreign ambassador who happens to be in Echo at the moment."

"Hmm," I said. "Why do they 'happen to be' here? Aren't there always ambassadors in the Capital of the Unified Kingdom?"

"No. Why?" said Kofa. "We don't need them here. That's actually not a very good idea, Max. It's bad enough that they bring their backsides to Echo every time they want something from us. Then again, they always want something from us."

"I see. Tell me about our 'grandees,' Kofa," I said. "I don't feel sleepy, and I desire to be entertained."

"Telling won't do them justice. You need to see them. And tomorrow you will. Well, you've already heard about your notorious 'fellow countryman,' I presume?"

"Count Gachillo Vook? Sir Dark Sack? Of course. But frankly, I don't know much about him. I've heard that he got pretty bored in his castle and got all excited when he heard he'd have me as a neighbor. Fortunately, his hopes were all in vain. Oh, and I also heard that he's a fierce warrior. One heck of a miscreant."

"Very true. By the way, the old Count Gachillo taught the art of war to the late father of our king. The Dark Sack can easily take half the credit for the epic hundred-year war, with the Battle for the Code as the grand finale, whatever Grand Magician Nuflin Moni Mak thinks about it."

"Why is he called Dark Sack, by the way?"

"Oh, there's a whole story behind it. Count Gachillo abides by two firm principles. Number one is that he should always travel light. Number two is that it's beneath his dignity to lack the most necessary things when traveling away from home. Since old Gachillo is a decent magician, especially considering that he was born far, far away from Uguland, the count found a simple way of reconciling these two contradictory principles. He simply cast a dozen spells on his old traveling bag. Since then, he's always come to the Capital with no luggage whatsoever except the empty traveling bag strapped to the saddle of his antlered steed. Whatever he needs he can produce from the bag—everything from an outfit for a festive occasion to an army of loyal vassals in full regalia. Hence the name Dark Sack. As far as I know, Count Gachillo is very fond of his nickname."

"How ingenious!" I said. "I should make friends with him. Better yet, I should become his apprentice. I completely and wholeheartedly share his two firm principles. All your stuff in one bag—what could be better than that?"

"See? And you didn't want to become the ruler of the Barren Lands."

"I'd rather Count Gachillo ruled them," I said. "I'm sure he'd feel right in his element."

"You underestimate your own people, Max," said Kofa. "Your subjects would rather die than be subjugated to some 'barbarian,' as they call anyone who wasn't blessed with having produced his first cry in the boundless steppes of the Lands of Fanghaxra. And the 'rather die' part is something Count Gachillo would love to do for them. He's very eager to wield his sword, given the opportunity. Believe me."

"I believe you," I said. Suddenly I yawned, taking myself quite by surprise.

"Are you ready to have some quality time with a pillow?" said Kofa. "Good. Tomorrow's going to be a difficult day for you."

"Not the whole day, though, just the evening, praise be the Magicians. The fun doesn't start until almost dusk. Still, I just realized that my pillow is one in a million. I think I'm going to go cuddle with it. Thank you, Kofa. You've set me up on my feet again."

"Knocked you off your feet, rather. Then again, it was just what you needed, wasn't it?"

"Absolutely," I said, getting up and yawning again. "If there's a hue and cry about an official amobiler being stolen in the morning, know that I'm the culprit. That wicked Lonli-Lokli destroyed mine, and all the stores are already closed. Good night to you, Kofa."

"And good night to you, too," said our Master Eavesdropper.

I sincerely hoped that his words would come true.

And come true they did. As soon as I found myself in Tekki's cozy bedroom, where she was snoozing happily, I got under the blanket and fell fast asleep, and my dreams resembled a documentary on the Garden of Eden. So I slept soundly all the way through to lunch—who could say if there would ever be a rerun?

Waking up was pleasant, too. Tekki was magnanimous enough to leave a small burner with a jug of kamra by the head of the bed. She herself was nowhere to be found. She had probably buried her head in the morning issue of the Echo Hustle and Bustle behind the bar. I sent her a call to thank her.

Don't mention it, baby. I'm just trying to get used to my new role as king's concubine, she replied.

Will you come up?

I'm sorry, I've got customers, and the help is nowhere to be found. It's all my fault: I told her she could come in late today. So make yourself presentable and come down.

Anything you say, ma'am.

And slowly, one step at a time, I made my way to the bathroom, where I dipped myself in each of the eight bathing pools. Then I donned my black-and-gold Mantle of Death and proceeded to the first floor of the house, the Armstrong & Ella tavern.

Indeed, there actually were a few customers there. Their haggard faces discouraged morning chitchat, to put it mildly. But there, on a barstool, sat my old friend Anday Pu. I still hadn't gotten him his longed-for ticket to Tasher. To my utter surprise, he was drinking kamra. For as long as I had studied his habits, he had preferred much stronger beverages at any time of the day.

Tekki greeted me with one of her most beautiful smiles. Then again, I've never known her to smile any other way.

"A hole in the heavens above my coronation," I said. "It's so great being here. Instead, I have to go somewhere else and dabble in international politics and other such nonsense."

Anday Pu jumped on his barstool, perturbed, then turned to me. "Max, you don't catch! It's super cool to be a king! Then you can just tell everyone else to stuff it! If I were you—"

"Yeah. If you were me. That would be something. I'd love to see it. Preferably through a keyhole," I said. "What's going on with you today, buddy? You're suspiciously sober and all dressed up. Wait, don't tell me you're going to the coronation."

"Sir Rogro Jiil, praise be the Magicians, does catch that I'd do a much better job there than some know-it-all writer for the society pages," said Anday. "Because—"

"Because they don't allow journalists in to such events at all," I said. "Now you, on the other hand, as a friend of mine, do stand a chance to gain admission, right? You don't have to answer—I know I'm right. Being my friend is a unique advantage."

"You don't catch, Max," said Anday. "Sometimes you can be so cynical, sound the alarm!"

I laughed to conceal embarrassment. I didn't know what had gotten into me. It's easy enough to offend an artist, not to mention a poet making a living as a reporter. Anday was devastated. It pained me to look at him.

"Hey, stop pouting, Blackbeard Junior," I said, winking at him. "It doesn't matter what I'm blabbing about. What matters is that I'm inviting you to the celebration, seeing that you're all dressed up already."

Anday winced. "I told you my head starts to spin when you call me those strange names. You don't catch, Max. My name is the only thing that keeps me rooted."

"You don't need to be rooted," I said. "You should fly for a change. It's loads of fun, trust me. I tried it myself the other day."

Tekki studied me with candid curiosity, but Anday Pu turned a deaf ear to my inadvertent confession.

"Still, I'm not prepared to be deprived of my only name," he said.

His forced sobriety didn't improve his mood, which even at the best of times was of a somewhat gloomy cast. My ambitious prophecy that living high on the hog and enjoying a brilliant career would one day improve the temper of this hotheaded creature had been no more than wishful thinking.

I gave up, finished my mug of wonderful kamra (I sometimes thought that the daughter of Loiso Pondoxo had been using up all of her sinister inheritance of Magic solely on making this godly beverage), looked out the window, and realized that it was time for me to go.

"Consider yourself lucky," I said to Tekki, "because I'm out of here. First the sinning coronation. Then, later tonight, I'm going to be doing the devil knows what."

"That 'devil' you mention with such regularity, does he really know that much about you?" said Tekki. "By the way, the people I watch sometimes through that magic box of yours also use the word 'devil' a lot. I still don't understand whether this is a spell or just a manner of speaking."

I stopped and contemplated the question for a while; it was worth thinking about. Sir Anday Pu, the descendant of Ukumbian pirates, was so preoccupied with himself, thank goodness, that he wasn't paying any attention to my conversation with Tekki. Giving him access to the secrets of the magic of the cinema was out of the question—the fellow had not been designed for keeping secrets. Not only would he have given it away in the first tavern he visited afterward, he would also have written a dozen articles about it.

Tekki was looking at me, waiting. It seemed as thought she was genuinely interested in the whole devil business.

"I think it originally used to be a spell but has since become a manner of speaking," I said. "That happens when spells lose their power."

"You bet it does," said Tekki in the voice of an expert. "Okay, now I'm beginning to understand. Go ahead and have fun, honey. You know how I spend my evenings nowadays."

"And how. To think that I was the one who brought that damn box here! Well, no one to blame but myself. Anyway, now I really have to go."

I jumped down from the barstool and shook Anday, who had fallen asleep. "Wake up, you wordsmith!" He almost said something rude to me but bit his tongue just in time and trotted along toward the door.

Have a nice trip through Xumgat, Sir Max. And watch your head there. I like you much better with it than without.

Tekki's Silent Speech was so strong that it almost felled me. I stood fast, however, and even had the strength to turn around. She smiled a sad smile and waved.

"Thanks for the advice," I said out loud. "My head is something I'm really very attached to."

All the way to the House by the Bridge, Anday and I were silent. I had a few things to think about—for example, how Tekki had found out about the dangerous trip Juffin and I were about to take. Not that I considered it a big secret, but I hadn't had time to talk about it with her. When I returned home the night before, Tekki had already been asleep. When she got up, I was still snoozing. The only short time we had together, we wasted on mindless chitchat.

It's one of two things, I thought. Either I really talk in my sleep, or . . . Or I have to keep reminding myself who she is. Then again, she is the daughter of Loiso Pondoxo. Clairvoyance is probably the least of her abilities.

I stopped the amobiler by the staff entrance of the House by the Bridge and sighed: I had to admit I didn't know much about her. If anything.

"You can wait for me in the amobiler. I'll be back soon," I said to the journalist.

Funny, but the fellow still lost his peace of mind in the presence of the harmless members of the city police force. At the same time, my Mantle of Death had never made him even remotely timid from day one. Marvelous are thy deeds, indeed.

"I'm okay. I'll wait here. You have things to do there," said Anday, nodding.

The hallway on our side of the Ministry of Perfect Public Order was empty, and so was the Hall of Common Labor. No wonder: the entire Minor Secret Investigative Force was partying in Juffin's office. Even Sir Lonli-Lokli had temporarily left his cell. He was feeding Kurush pastries from the Glutton Bunba and discussing new titles in the city library with Melamori in a low voice. From what I could gather, he was all right. Good, I had one less thing to worry about.

"Lucky you," I said. "You're partying here, and I have to head to the palace. I'm jealous."

"Not yet, you don't," said Juffin. "You're a king, after all. You can arrive last. If His Majesty King Gurig were planning to attend your coronation, then, sure, you'd have had to hurry up. But since politics and etiquette prevent him from appearing at the ceremony, you have the right to a quick glass of something and even one cookie, at the very least."

"'One cookie, at the very least' equals three in my book," I said. "It's the best piece of news I've heard in the past dozen years. What are we celebrating anyway?"

"Your enthronement, of course!" said Melifaro. He tried to guard the tray of pastries with his body. "Hands off! Don't they feed you at the palace?"

"One more word and I'll declare war on this barbarian country," I said, sitting down on the armrest of Melamori's armchair. She put her cold palm on top of my hand.

"Good day, Max." She had the desperate eyes of a person dying from grief.

If you want me to build a raft and take you to Arvarox on it, just give me a holler. I decided to resort to Silent Speech. Some topics should be addressed without delay.

I probably do, but I won't be hollering just yet. Don't pay too much attention to me, Max. My mood is a variable, not a constant. It depends on the weather, among other things, by the way.

Then we need to change the weather.

According to the astrologists' forecasts, it's going to change later today. Thank you, Max, but let's speak out loud now. The prolonged silence looks suspicious.

I submitted. "Don't you guys want to keep me company?" I said to my colleagues. "Without your moral support, that blasted coronation will be the end of me."

"Well, I'm definitely not leaving you alone," said Juffin. "Unlike our king, I am required to be present at this momentous event."

"That's good news," I said. "More volunteers, please?"

"I would love to accept your invitation, but as you know . . ." said Shurf Lonli-Lokli, and made a helpless gesture.

"Yeah," I said. "I know."

"Not only have you gotten yourself into a scrape, you also want to spoil the evening for the rest of us," said Sir Kofa. "No, thanks. I'm staying in the office. Someone has to stay behind and hold down the fort."

"You know, Max," whispered Melamori, "I think I'm going to betray you, too. The very idea of betrayal sounds so attractive. I've wanted to try it since childhood. Plus, I was going to watch a movie tonight."

"I knew it. I know another lady who can't wait until sunset. I'm willing to bet you promised her you'd bring a bottle from the cellars of your uncle Kima, too."

"You are unbearable, Max. You know everything about everyone."

"Well, not everything, but I do know my basic facts," I said, laughing, and turned to Melifaro. "How about you, mister? Will you pass up the chance to rain on my parade?"

"Quit whining, I'm not going to abandon you," my diurnal half said in the tone of a gentleman who has suddenly decided to marry one of the many victims of his masculine charms. "First, this 'parade' basically begs to be rained on. Second, I'd never pass up the chance of seeing an old friend of mine."

"An old friend of yours?"

"Prince Ayonxa Rotri Shimaro, one of the grandees of the County Shimara. He's a great fellow—you're going to like him. His younger brother is also okay, but a bit too fierce for my taste. Prince Ayonxa, on the other hand, is a kind soul and very casual. He also owes me one."

"When our Melifaro had just started his career in the Minor Investigative Force, he managed to pull Prince Shimaro out of a nasty situation," said Juffin. "One of the prince's acquaintances here in Echo was very fond of murder using Forbidden Magic. He liked to think he was avenging some relative who had died in the Battle for the Code. He was smart enough to blame poor Ayonxa, who had just arrived in the Capital for reasons unknown. The prince was looking at doing life in Xolomi. Boy, that was some scandal! His younger brother, Prince Jiffa, turned to me for help. Let me tell you something: on first sight, Jiffa is the one who looks older, yet he is, indeed, the younger one—almost two years younger. Then again, he has been looking after his careless older brother since childhood. Back to the story, though. The esteemed grandee Prince Jiffa had rushed to the Capital incognito, like a simple merchant, and headed straight to me, saying, 'Help me, Sir Venerable Head! Reopen the investigation. We're fellow countrymen, after all.' I was swamped with work at the time—I had to sleep and eat on my feet—so I offloaded it all onto Sir Melifaro, without much hope, I must say. Poor boy was absolutely discombobulated and had no idea which end to begin from.

Imagine my surprise when he brought to me the real murderer the next morning!"

"And then you finally realized how lucky you were to have me in your service," said Melifaro.

"May I suggest that we continue to reminisce about the inimitable exploits of the Ninth Volume of Sir Manga Melifaro's Encyclopedia at the foot of my throne," I said, putting an empty mug on the desk. "Let's go, guys. My subjects have been crying and whining there for half an hour already. Soon the ambassadors will join in."

"You're just jealous and bitter," said Melifaro, laughing. "You hear words of praise, but they're not for you. How sad."

"Have I been praising anyone?" said Juffin. "Okay, let's go, or Sir Max's subjects will indeed start crying. I never thought you'd make such a caring monarch."

For what it's worth, ten minutes later the three of us did manage to get outside. Anday Pu was snoozing on the back seat of the company amobiler. The guy deserved a medal for patience.

"It seems you have brought the press along," said Juffin.

"You know how vain I am. Can't sneeze without my personal biographer knowing about it." I switched to Silent Speech: Don't worry. I'm not inviting him on the trip down Xumgat.

That would have been something.

The boss smiled a conspiratorial smile and sat down next to me.

"Move over, Sir Royal Voice. A hole in the heavens above you, buddy. There's sure a lot of you," said Melifaro, trying to squeeze in.

Anday wasn't so fat as to take up the entire back seat, but he was shameless enough to place his sizable body right in the middle of it.

"Please don't push me, Sir Melifaro," said the descendant of Ukumbian pirates in the tone of the Queen Mother visiting a seaport tavern for the first time in her life.

"The way I see it, the Refuge for the Mad is a much more boring place than our organization," I said, as though reporting my findings from the previous evening.

I grabbed the lever, and we set off to my royal residence. How on earth did I end up being the protagonist of a geopolitical intrigue unleashed by His Sly Majesty? I thought. Not that there was much to think with.

"Look, Juffin," I said. "What is it exactly that I'm supposed to do there? I mean, are there some rules I should play by?"

"Just remember your amusing ruler Caligula and stick to his agenda," said Melifaro.

"Thanks for the advice. The first thing I'm going to do is introduce capital punishment for bad jokes," I said. "So, what about the rules, Juffin? Care to enlighten me?"

"Well, if there are any rules, only the wisest elders of your poor people will know them. Unfortunately, I don't have the pleasure of belonging to that particular level of high society. So you can improvise and do whatever you see fit. The foreign ambassadors have no clue, the grandees from the provinces will think that's just how it's done in the Barren Lands, and your subjects will think you've already picked up our 'barbaric customs.' And I don't think they're going to get friendly enough to try to help you out into the clear."

"I guess I'm in luck then," I said. "Okay, I'll improvise."

"Attaboy," said Melifaro.

I had the hardest time finding a place to park the amobiler and finally parked a whole block away from the Furry House. The sidewalks were crowded with my subjects' antlered steeds, decorated with bric-a-brac. The rest of the street was packed with the amobilers of other visitors.

"Looks like they thought we'd arrive on foot," said Juffin, hopping down to the mosaic sidewalk.

My friend Anday Pu followed us. His habitual brazen impudence had vanished. The poor thing was confused. He looked at me, beseeching, and was about to grab the folds of my Mantle of Death for moral support.

"Stand by, fellow," I said to him. "I'm a king now and have the right to a personal scribe or any other such whim."

"Here we go," said Juffin, and I thrust open the front door of my residence.

The expression on my face morphed into the smile of a hallucinating imbecile: my mind refused to acknowledge the reality of what was going on. Perhaps it was all for the better.

After this momentary and slight lapse of reason, I found myself standing on the threshold of the Grand Reception Hall, formerly the reading hall. The enormous room was filled with people. I tried to find at least one familiar face in the crowd, but all the faces seemed to merge into a single undifferentiated blob. Could it have been panic?

"Can you see where my colleagues are?" I whispered to my "scribe." He nodded. "Good. Go and join them. If you stick close to Sir Melifaro, you won't even get bored."

"I catch!" said Anday, and he disappeared into the crowd somewhere to my right.

I turned my head in the direction he had gone but didn't see either Melifaro or Juffin. What the heck? I looked around and couldn't see anything resembling a throne. Then again, a king that couldn't find the throne in his own palace—exactly the kind of moronic joke that I was known for. I stopped panicking, and my mood improved. I can sit wherever I want to, I thought to myself. Even in the doorway. I'm the boss here.

Then I flung my arms into the air like some impostor prophet about to bestow on an ungrateful humanity his own complete and unabridged collected interpretations of "divine will."

"Words cannot convey the ecstasy I feel at meeting all of you here. I am overcome," I said and sat down in the doorway cross-legged. A murmur of amazement rolled around the hall, so I felt I had to explain my eccentric behavior. "My place will always be here, for the place of a sovereign is always on the threshold between the people and the heavens, separating one from the other and guarding them from each other."

It seemed to me that my first solo number was a success, and it was only good manners that prevented the crowd from applauding me. But no one seemed to breathe.

For a moment, nothing happened. I even began to get annoyed at the sluggishness of my subjects, but then I realized that the poor souls were simply waiting for my command.

"You may approach now and do what must be done," I said.

Turmoil broke out in the middle of the hall. I waited. Most likely there was a throne after all, smack-dab in the middle of the opposite end of the enormous room. All the participants in the ceremony had already taken their places at the foot of the throne and were now forced to relocate.

Now my subjects headed toward me at a solemn pace—perhaps not a particularly majestic sight but passable. Ever since I'd taught them to wear their headbands à la pirates, they looked almost handsome. There were several dozen of these "beach boys," in wide knee-length Bermudas and short soft boots, with huge bags slung over their shoulders.

After approaching me, the fellows gave me a low bow but didn't drop to their knees, praise be the Magicians. Apparently my lecture on the detrimental effect of genuflection had had a positive effect on them.

The procession was led by a robust middle-aged man. His beautiful muscular body was very close to that of a bodybuilder. I'd be willing to bet, though, that this guy could kick the living daylights out of any bodybuilder in the first round: unlike them, he had been gaining his muscle mass in a natural environment—not to show off his muscles on the beach but out of sheer necessity.

"Will you allow me to speak my name, Fanghaxra?" this giant said, his voice trembling with anxiety. I was happy. Huge fellows like him had never before spoken to me in a trembling voice.

"I will," I intoned in the manner of a man who was willing to forgo his principles in the name of the betterment of mankind.

"I am Barxa Bachoy. I have been riding at the head of the warriors of the Xenxa people for forty-three years now."

Oh, so that's the name of this people, I thought. Shame on you, mister, for not bothering to learn it in all this time. That's an F, sir. See me after class.

Barxa Bachoy continued his speech. "Until today, I have been responsible for your people before the heavens, O Fanghaxra, but the heavens have been reluctant to take heed of my voice. Today I ask you to relieve me of this burden."

"Cool," I said. "It's a deal. From now on, everything's going to change. I'm going to take the responsibility for my people before the heavens, and you'll only be responsible for them before me. I promise you that, unlike the heavens, I'm going to take heed of your voice from time to time."

Barxa Bachoy looked as though some inner light had flared up inside him. He was amazed, filled with gratitude. He mumbled something awkward and touching. I think he still didn't understand that nothing had really had changed for him. All his responsibilities still stayed with him. Well, perhaps I relieved him of the need to pursue his fruitless attempts to contact the deaf and dumb heavens.

My new acquaintance, whom I now mentally referred to as the General, stepped aside and gave way to a short, lean old man. He had in his sinewy arms, it seemed, as much power as the muscled biceps that rolled back and forth underneath the tanned skin of the war chief. The grandpa deserves special mention. Something in his stature reminded me of the powerful Magicians of the forbidden Orders of the past epoch. My wise second heart knew very well that the old man could have become just as dangerous and powerful if his life had taken a slightly different turn.

"I greet you, Fanghaxra," said the old man. "I am Fairiba, and wisdom condescends to me sometimes. I have come to call you by your True Name. When its sounds reach your heart, the curse that has followed your people since the day we lost you will be lifted. Ask your venerable guests not to hold a grudge against me for not opening my mouth while pronouncing your name: a king's True Name cannot be pronounced out loud, for it would be against the wishes of the heavens."

"I knew not that my people could use Silent Speech," I said.

"Indeed. Your people do not practice such dangerous magic," said the stern old man. "But I have enough power to reveal to you your True Name."

Frankly, I didn't doubt for a second that this Fairiba could do that and then some. The old man untied the leather straps of his travel bag and shook out its content in front of me. To my surprise, it was just a pile of soil, as though he had decided to do some gardening in my reception hall. Great, I thought. As soon as you get your own palace, this has to happen.

"Our customs demand that the kings of the Xenxa people learn their True Names while standing on their native soil," said Fairiba. "The powerful King of the Unified Kingdom instructed us not to ask you to come with us, for you have responsibilities to him. I ask not the reason. Your people hold secrets sacred. That is why I have brought the soil of your steppes with me. I beg you to step onto it, Fanghaxra."

I got up. Fairiba's request seemed most timely: my legs had begun to grow numb from sitting. For a split second, I was worried that they'd ask me to take off my boots, which would be a tiresome ordeal, but my fears were groundless.

The old man produced from his bosom a small pouch. Out of the pouch he took a small box, and out of the box an even smaller bottle. For some reason, it occurred to me that Fairiba was about to release a genie, wild from millennia of solitude, but that was not what happened.

"Give me your hand, Fanghaxra," said the old man.

I stretched out my left hand. I don't know why I stretched out my left hand and not my right. Maybe because I used my left hand for most of the magic "tricks" I had learned so far.

"It is a sign from the heavens, Fanghaxra!" Fairiba whispered, his voice trembling. "For generations, all Xenxa kings have accepted their names with their right hand. But there lived a sovereign in the days of yore who, as you just did, proffered his left hand to his shaman. He was Droxmor Modillax, who subdued half the lands surrounded by oceans and then disappeared. You will be the greatest of our kings, O Fanghaxra!"

"No kidding," I said.

Fairiba would be in for a deep disappointment. I was planning to abdicate in a couple of years and annex my Barren Lands to the lands of His Majesty Gurig VIII. No "subduing" in my plans, I'm afraid, but "disappearing" is another matter altogether, I thought. I can do that in my sleep, pardon the pun. Maybe this will comfort them somewhat?

The old man opened the bottle and poured onto my palm a few drops of clear liquid. "This water is from the sacred spring of the Lands of Fanghaxra," he said.

He then took out a thin greenish plate from the box. I couldn't determine what sort of material it was made from. Fairiba carefully lowered the plate onto my hand, which was still wet from the sacred water. I thought the smooth plate would slip and fall on the floor, so I clenched my hand.

To my astonishment, the plate felt so cold it burned, like a piece of dry ice from an ice cream vendor. I opened my hand and saw that the plate was gone, and that my left palm was completely smooth: no life line, no fate line, no heart line, no Mercury line (as they were called in a palmistry brochure I had once flipped through). Palmistry aside, this metamorphosis freaked me out big time.

A pictogram began to emerge on the smooth skin of my left palm. I had never seen anything resembling this alphabet in my life. A "simultaneous translation" began sounding in my head, albeit with a slight lag: Ayot Mu-o Limli Niixor, the Sovereign of Fanghaxra.

Fairiba's Silent Speech almost trailed away halfway through, but he stoically went on with it all the way. I could sense that each word required an enormous amount of stamina on his part. I had once gone through the same pain while teaching myself Silent Speech, but my marvelous mentor Sir Juffin Hully—and the power that merely residing in Echo, the magic Heart of the World, bestowed on me—had both been working in my favor.

I found my "True Name" to be a tad on the long side. I had doubts that I'd remember this sumptuous abracadabra even after it had been imprinted on my palm for all eternity, but I decided not to insult my subjects with an untimely suggestion to shorten my precious True Name to at least half the size.

"It is done!" said the old man.

"It is done!" his company echoed.

"It is, isn't it?" I said and sat down in the doorway again. "So how's that old curse doing now? Lifted yet?"

The nomads didn't say a word, but their eyes radiated pure joy and their stern faces assumed a serene expression. From that, I concluded that the curse had indeed been lifted for good—strange, considering I had never been the real Fanghaxra, all the mystical gibberish on my palms notwithstanding.

Meanwhile, the ceremony had reached a lull: everyone was waiting for my commands and I had no idea what to occupy them with. For starters, I decided to wrap up the part where I deal with my long-suffering people: "As you know, business forces me to stay here in Echo. I am happy that Fairiba and Barxa will be with you."

I looked at my newly appointed deputies. They stood with arms akimbo, seeming almost taller now. Their companions also looked happy: despite fears to the contrary, the new boss had confirmed the supreme status of his predecessors—everyone do a jig! Good, good. Hooray for the wise me.

"I want you to make these people happy," I said to my chosen ones. "If you encounter an obstacle while doing so, do not hesitate to inform me by sending a messenger, since you are averse to Silent Speech. I promise to answer you promptly. How long does a good rider need to reach Echo from the Barren Lands?"

"Forty days, if misfortunes do not follow him on his way," said Barxa Bachoy.

"Not too bad," I said. I was happy. It seemed that I wouldn't be burdened by my royal obligations too often.

"We have brought gifts for you, Lord Fanghaxra," said Fairiba. "Our customs demand that we give them to you alone, but if you wish to share your joy with your guests, I dare not impede."

"No need to break the customs. Alone it will be. That makes it even more interesting. But now I need to be with my guests. Take my gifts to the archive: it's a large room to the right down the hallway. Tell my servants to show you the way and bring you some food and refreshments. I'll be with you in a minute."

The nomads picked up their bags and were off. Out of the corner of my eye, I noticed a good dozen servants following them. The generosity of His Majesty King Gurig, who had lent me this band of loafers, knew no bounds, and his notion about my needs was in acute conflict with reality.

Today, however, it was all for the better. I was happy with my own idea of sending my exalted subjects away to another room, giving them their own "children's table" with cookies and candy so they didn't get under the feet of the "grown-ups"—the grandees of the provinces of the Unified Kingdom and foreign ambassadors. I suspected that it wouldn't be easy for them to find common ground and interact with one another. Besides, I doubted that I myself would find much common ground with these important gentlemen—but then again, there wasn't much I could do about that.

When the last bright headband disappeared behind the doors, I stood up and looked around, trying to find my colleagues. Sir Juffin Hully was already walking toward me.

"Good job," he said. "Lean and mean. His Majesty King Gurig will have to take a few lessons in court etiquette from you. And he considers himself to be so democratic. He should've seen you crouching on the threshold. Now that's what I call humility."

"Glad you liked it. But did you see what these guys did to my hand?" I showed the letters on my left palm to Juffin.

"Yes, now your name is the only thing it bears, Max," said Juffin. "Hey, look! It's the ancient alphabet of Xonxona. It was used back in the days when the entire population on our blessed landmass was as nomadic as your subjects are now. It turns out that there are still keepers of ancient knowledge among the people of Xenxa. Funny."

"Is it?" I said. "So, is this writing not going to come off?"

"I'm afraid not. But it's all for the better. One couldn't wish for a better protective amulet than his own True Name written in a forgotten language. You're in luck, my boy."

"Right, but . . . I don't think this inscription can be my True Name. I'm sure this name belongs to the true king of Xenxa, the poor child who once got lost in the steppes, the last of the Fanghaxras. It has nothing to do with me."

"If it weren't your name, it couldn't possibly be imprinted on your paw. Plus, what makes you so sure you're not 'real'? I happen to think that getting lost in the steppes is just the thing you would do," said the boss.

"Oh, come on, Juffin! You know better than anybody where I come from. If there's one thing I'm sure about, it's that I never got lost in the steppes."

"If I were you, I'd try not to think I was too sure about anything," said Juffin, winking at me. "Anything but this one fact: that your True Name is exactly what that esteemed old gentleman said it was."

"Well, I'll be," I said, laughing. "Ayot Mo-a . . . Ma-o . . . There's no way I'm going to remember it."

"You don't have to remember it, nor should you try to say it out loud. It's a mystery, Max, remember? Back in the good old days, you would have had to kill that wise old man personally so that the secret of your True Name belonged to you and you alone. It's only in the past millennium that people have become so frivolous about such things. If you don't remember your name, don't lose sleep over it. When Eternity wants to get acquainted with you, your palm will always be at its service. Eternity, you know, is a highly educated and sophisticated lady. Forgotten languages are her hobby. But I doubt you'll need your True Name under any other circumstances. 'Sir Max' will do just fine."

"Never a dull moment," I muttered. "Just what I need—an introduction to Ms. Eternity. Maybe I should try it out on the ambassadors first. Do you think these gentlemen will live through it if I thrust my mystical palm under their noses and skip the small talk?"

"They'll get over anything as long as they can get out of here as soon as possible," said Juffin. "There's no catering at official ceremonies such as your coronation, and no one wants to hang around here with an empty stomach until midnight."

"So how come they're not running away?" I said. "By the way, I'm already feeling a little peckish myself."

"You can eat—you're home. Okay, here's a good piece of advice for you: go ahead and quickly make the acquaintance of each one of them. These gentlemen have come here with a single purpose in mind: to get introduced to the new king. As soon as they have spoken their inimitable names to you, their missions will be over. Then we can all have dinner here, provided you'll grant me and Melifaro an invitation."

"Dream on. You'll empty my coffers in no time." I made a face that expressed an extreme form of stinginess, bordering on insanity.

"Sometimes you look too much like Grand Magician Nuflin," said Juffin, laughing. "Now I get it: you're not a sovereign of Fanghaxra, you're Moni Mak's illegitimate grandson. What if I told you that all the expenses in this house are on the tab of His Majesty Gurig VIII?"

"Really? Oh, but that's wonderful," I said, smiling a hospitable smile. "How can I pass up the opportunity of sharing my humble royal meal with my friends!"

"How quaint," said Juffin. "Then go ahead and announce to these nice folks that you're dying to learn their names, and make it quick. My belly is as empty as the Corridor between Worlds."

"You mean the Xumgat?" I said, sighing. And then I decided it was indeed time to face my guests.

A little man was already standing behind me. His head barely reached my waist. The midget's attire was an elegant compromise between the fashion of the Capital and the garments of my people. Underneath his classical black looxi, he wore wide pants that reached down to his knees. His tiny torso was clad in chain mail, and on his head he wore a beautiful shawl, the ends of which dangled down and swept the floors.

"I see you as though in a waking dream. I am happy to say my name: Rixxiri Gachillo, Count Vook. I'm sorry we never became neighbors, Sir Max. They say you're one of a kind," said the gnome in a low voice.

"That's what they say about you, too," I said, staring at my new acquaintance.

I had no idea that the infamous Count Dark Sack, the former mentor of the late King Gurig VII and one of the most odious personages in the Unified Kingdom, would be so compact.

"And it is true," said Count Vook. "But let us not despair prematurely. Perhaps we will have the opportunity to entertain each other in the future. Your subjects are a very unreliable people. Well, good night to you, fellow countryman. I have to admit that I've grown weary of this reception: tons of people and nothing to drink."

"Good night," I said, unable to take my eyes off this fellow.

Count Vook nodded, turned around, and headed toward the exit. Watching the retreat of his haughty figure, I found myself wondering whether he was a midget, or whether the rest of us were all just deformed giants.

Then a rather motley crowd surrounded me. First Sir Rep Kibat and Count Kayga Atalo Vulx, ambassadors from Irrashi, one of the few countries that has its own language, introduced themselves to me. I had managed to learn a few Irrashian words in my days as a habitué of the Irrashi Coat of Arms Inn, so I conquered the hearts of the ambassadors once and for all by saying, "Xokota!"—a traditional Irrashian greeting.

Tol Goyoxvi, an amicable representative of Tulan, smiled at me. I remembered how Sir Manga Melifaro reminisced about that distant country with great tenderness. Then there was Verlago Gabayoxi, Prince Gorr, the ambassador from the County Xotta, which bordered with my land. This whole business of my coronation was in fact merely a pretext for annexing that province. He was dressed almost exactly like my unsophisticated subjects but looked as serious as a professor's widow. Next there was Marquis Niiro Uvilguk Van Baunbax from Loxri, wearing something that looked like an extravagant warm evening gown. Then Sir Burik Pepezo from Tarun appeared before me. He was the head of the artists' guild of that distant land. A good half of its inhabitants were artists, so his position, however humble it may have seemed at first glance, gave him power over almost the entire adult population. If I understood correctly, he had come to the Unified Kingdom with the sole purpose of collecting some guild tax from the numerous Tarunian artists who decorated our lives for a living. The ambassador from the distant Kumon Caliphate, Sir Maniva Umonary —who, as chance would have it, was passing through Echo and had dropped by my house—shocked me to the core. He was lying on something that looked like a giant divan. Almost a dozen servants moved the "divan" whenever the man wished to change his location. He looked much more kingly that I did. His obese body reeked of the vulgar luxury of the Arabian Nights.

A tanned pirate's face distracted me from my contemplation of the blissful luxuriance of the Kumonian. My first impression had not deceived me: it was the ambassador from Ukumbia, Sir Chekimba the Beaten Horn. I found out that Beaten Horn wasn't his surname or nickname; it was the name of his ship. It turned out that the right to replace an ancestral name with the name of a ship was a privilege of the eldest and most honored citizens of that pirate state.

Then I was swarmed by the honored citizens of Tasher: Sir Zunakki Chuga Tlax and Sir Chumochi Droxa Vivvi. My head was spinning from the unfamiliar faces and names, but I managed to remember about my friend Anday, who had been dreaming of moving to Tasher, and introduced him to the Tasherian ambassadors—just in case.

Finally my eyes alighted upon a familiar sight: brightly colored tights, short jackets, and oversized fur hats. These attributes belonged to Mr. Ciceric, Mr. Maklasufis, and Mr. Mikusiris, the happy citizens of beautiful Isamon, the very same three people poor Melifaro had once thrown out the window of his living room. They attempted (rather poorly) to pretend we'd never met. They announced their titles to me. Mr. Ciceric was the head of the fur industry tycoons of Isamon, Mr. Maklasufis was Mr. Ciceric's personal Wise Mentor, and Mr. Mikusiris was the Grand Specialist in questions of culture for the Unified Kingdom, something of a technical expert. I had no idea what these Isamonian furriers were doing at my reception—my royal reception—but at the end of the day, I didn't mind. Their silly colorful tights livened up the atmosphere.

I looked around for Melifaro. I thought it would be an interesting experiment for the Isamonians and him to come face to face and look one another in the eye, just to see what would happen. Melifaro was standing nearby in the company of two pleasant-looking gentlemen whose appearance didn't betray anything exotic at first glance. Only when one of them flung back his burdensome hood—a sartorial detail characteristic of the winter looxi of Shimarian highlanders, who still considered our turbans to be too frivolous a form of headgear—did I open my mouth in amazement. And my amazement was justified. The intricate and colorful structure on the stranger's head was truly a masterpiece of the art of hairdressing.

Later I learned that ordinary human hair was completely unsuited for achieving such impressive results. More serious materials were needed: pet hair, bits of wild animal fur, even feathers, not to mention the numerous magic spells that were required to hold together all these foreign materials and to make them take root on the human skull.

I carefully threaded my way through the colorful crowd of foreigners, who had begun to tire me, and approached my colleague.

"This is Sir Ayonxa and Sir Jiffa, the fairy-tale princes of the County Shimara, whose deputy I could have become a dozen years ago if I hadn't been such an idiot," said Melifaro. "Right, guys?"

"It's all right, buddy. I'm sure you'll reconsider," said one of the princes. The other just shrugged. He looked too grown-up and serious to enjoy any prolonged exposure to our Sir Melifaro. It was probably Sir Jiffa, the younger of the princes.

I tried to embellish my official smile with as much charm as possible and gave the sovereigns of the County Shimara a low bow.

"Actually, I was going to reintroduce you to some other old friends of yours," I said to Melifaro. "Remember your Isamonian buddies? The ones you launched out of your window?"

"Whoa! Are they here, too?" he said. "Don't get me wrong, I'm all for repeating the show, but I can't help but feel for the poor fellows. The first time was enough for them, I think."

"Enough is enough," I said. "Do you know that His Majesty and I are going to shell out some funds and feed you and Juffin?" I turned to the Shimara princes and said, "If you truly enjoy the company of this monster, I will be happy to see you at our table."

Prince Ayonxa burst out laughing, and Prince Jiffa looked at me with poorly concealed amazement. He probably had his own notions of how a king should behave. Me, I simply couldn't behave myself when I was standing just three feet away from Melifaro: he would never have forgiven me.

I spent the next half hour being introduced to the grandees of the remaining provinces of the Unified Kingdom. Among them were the Venerable Head of Gugland, Valiba Valibal; Lord Eki Banba Uriux of Uryuland; the Venerable Head of Uguland, Yorix Malivonis; and two burgomasters of the free city of Gazhin, Sir Valda Kunyk and Sir Zebi Xipilosis. Gazhin, one of the wealthiest seaports in the land, is one heck of a place—a single burgomaster just didn't cut it. Valda Kunyk, a big, jolly red-haired guy, was apparently the protégé of the ancient shipbuilding aristocracy, and the lively gray-haired Zebi Xipilosis protected the interests of the town merchants. Or was it the other way around? No idea.

Following the burgomasters was Sir Yoka Yoxtoxop, the sheriff of the Island of Murimak. I remembered Juffin telling me that this man had perfect memory and could see things "the way they were," just like our Lookfi—although, unlike Lookfi, the sheriff of Murimak resembled a warrior rather than a mad scientist. Even the amusing Murimak slang wasn't enough to make him funny.

Just as the reception was ending, Togi Raxva the Golden Eye, Venerable Head of Landaland, approached me. One of his eyes was indeed a bright amber-yellow, just like our Kurush's. The other eye was plain gray. I remembered that it was the wonderful yellow eye that had led to the appointment of Sir Togi Raxva to his position of utmost responsibility: it is a common belief in the Unified Kingdom that one should never disregard such a good sign. By the way, the belief had turned out to be correct. Once an arid country, Landaland had suddenly become the wealthiest agricultural province of the Unified Kingdom. The famous fair in Numban alone was a sight to behold. And if one were to believe the rumors, Togi Raxva was by no means a financial wizard. Rather, under his magical golden eye, the once barren soil of Landaland had become so fruitful that crops could be harvested almost half a dozen times a year.

The official part of the coronation finally reached its last gasp and fizzled out. My honorable guests disappeared one after another through the front door, no doubt to wander around Echo looking for a place to have a good meal. I had worked up a heck of an appetite myself, but I still had to go into seclusion with my subjects and receive my gifts. If only they had baked me some pies—but no, they were sure to start flinging some inedible precious stones at my feet. Drat it.

I approached Juffin, who seemed to be enjoying the social whirlwind. "It would be great if you took the responsibility for the remaining part of the evening into your own hands," I said. "You're good at it. Tell the servants to show you to the pantry and help yourself. I'm going to join you a little later: I have a romantic rendezvous with my people. See, my people want to give me some souvenirs for keepsakes. I'm afraid I'm looking forward to receiving the decaying remnants of my ancestors' throne."

"Receiving gifts is a sacred tradition," said Juffin. "Grab whatever they give you as long as it's free."

"Right. Will you make sure the servants leave me a small crust of bread or something? I've been meaning to learn more about the royal diet, and here's the opportunity."

"A small crust of bread I can guarantee you. If worse comes to worst, I'll break off a piece of my own heart. You'll choke on it and then go around telling stories to naive young women about how kings live on dried crusts of bread alone."

I had to cut short our highly intellectual exchange and go to the former archive. A few dozen representatives of the people of Xenxa were consuming pastries there. The stern-looking nomads were covered in cream from head to toe, just like Kurush, our wise connoisseur of all things sweet.

When they saw me, the fellows tried to swallow whatever they had in their mouths and stand at attention.

"That's all right," I said like a loving grandmother. "Keep on chewing. It makes me happy to see my people eat heartily, so do give me the pleasure of contemplating it."

The subjects dutifully grabbed two pastries each and began consuming them with great relish. They took my token of hospitality for a command. Amazing discipline for a bunch of nomads.

"Barxa! Fairiba! Could you come here for a second?" I said. "I need to talk to you about how we are all going to live from now on. You can stay here until you leave, of course. I sleep at another place anyway. Speaking of which, when did you say you were leaving?"

"Whenever you tell us to leave, sire," said Barxa Bachoy. He looked puzzled, as though surprised that a king would ask such a thing.

"Splendid. Then make it tomorrow," I said. "Tell my people the good news. Okay, now I'm ready for some gifts, if you insist."

I grabbed a pastry from the nearest tray. Normally I wasn't too crazy about honey balls with rainbow cream, but I was starving. I hadn't been king for a day and was already suffering from deprivation.

"May I speak with you first, O Fanghaxra," old Fairiba said diffidently.

"Sure," I said. "You can talk to me anytime. You'll be surprised to learn how easy it is to strike a deal with me."

"It is also easy to strike a deal with Death," said the old man. "Day after day, for centuries, we beg him, 'Not today!' He agrees and retreats. It's a pleasure doing business with him. Only once does he have it his way, but this one time is all it takes."

"Never a truer word spoken, Fairiba," I said, smiling. "What you just said about Death is dead right, if you'll pardon the pun. And it's probably true about me, too."

"Yes, about you, as well," said the old man. "But I wanted to talk about something else. Your people have brought gifts. They know not of your preferences and, if I understand this correctly, you have no need for our gifts. But we merely do as our customs tell us. I wish to ask you to accept our gifts even if you don't like them. When a king rejects gifts from his people, a curse is cast upon them. I know you would never mean to harm your people, but you have grown up among barbarians and do not know all the laws of your land. We have become weary of living with the burden of curses—such a life is not worth much. Please avoid bringing another curse upon us, O Fanghaxra."

"Oh, of course I won't," I said. "No curses, even if you've brought me all the horse manure you've collected over a century."

"We would never do such a thing," said Fairiba, surprised. "What strange things you say!"

He turned to his compatriots, who were still diligently consuming the pastry. That's right, I thought. I haven't ordered them to stop "eating heartily."

"Bring in the gifts! The king is ready to accept them."

And the downpour of gifts began. For starters, there were several baskets of exotic fruit. The one that made me the happiest was a huge melon. I had extensive experience tasting the cuisine of the Unified Kingdom, but I had never seen or tasted a single local melon. I smelled it and realized that it was indeed a real melon, even though its size surpassed my most lavish notions of Mother Nature's generosity.

"Awesome," I said. "You can't imagine how much I like this . . . thing. What's it called again?"

"This is a berry of the steppes. Have you forgotten?" The old man shook his head in disapproval. He looked like a botany teacher who was giving an exam to a bad student.

"A berry, huh?"

I tried to lift the "berry" but failed at the very first attempt. I didn't try anymore after that.

The gifts were not limited to the fruits of nature. I became the happy owner of a whole stack of touching handmade mats and a plethora of colorful kerchiefs, shorts, and other exotic garments. Some things looked brand new, yet others seemed to be secondhand stuff. It looked as though the members of the official delegation had stripped naked everyone at home before setting off on the long journey. I shuddered but didn't say anything. After all, I had promised Grandpa Fairiba to behave myself.

My patience was rewarded: one of the nomads brought a huge furry dog. The dog looked like a grander version of a snowy white Old English sheepdog, a kindly giant sticking out its charcoal-black tongue in ecstasy.

"Sinning Magicians, will you look at this beauty!" I said. "I've always wanted a dog, and here it is. I must have felt it coming."

"This is the best of my sheepdogs," said Barxa Bachoy. "These sheepdogs have always lived in the king's house. We know, sire, that you have no need for several hundred dogs to protect you, so we have brought only one, just to keep up the tradition."

"And you've done exactly the right thing. He's great, but several hundred would've been a bit over the top."

I squatted by the dog and carefully put my left hand on the back of his neck. The dog yelped and turned over on his back, exposing his furry belly.

"Ah, you do still remember how to tame these beasts!" said Fairiba. "Now he will die defending you if you so wish."

"Jeepers!" I said. "That won't be necessary. I can grapple with my own death, thank you very much. I need this dog alive."

"It is very lucky for us, sire, to have guessed your wish," said Barxa Bachoy. "I hope you will also like our final gift."

I looked up and saw three tall, slim, and virtually identical young women standing in front of me, looking scared to death. They had huge black eyes, charming long noses, and short dark hair. (Later I learned that all women in the Barren Lands cut their hair short because they consider the hassle of dealing with long hair to be beneath their dignity.) My goodness! These girls were not just the spitting image of one another: three replicas of the great Liza Minnelli stood before me. Just what a man needed to lose all his marbles quickly and painlessly.

I plopped down on the floor right by my new four-legged friend, who immediately stuck his hairy snout under my hand. I mechanically stroked the dog, much to his visible delight.

"Who are these young ladies?" I said.

"They are your wives, sire," said Fairiba.

"My wives?" I said, horrified. "Oh, boy."

This could only happen to me. That was my special brand of luck. I was about to give these simple folk a short but emotionally charged lecture on the inadmissibility of attempts to ruin their king's personal life, but the imploring look in the eyes of old Fairiba made me shut my mouth. Fine, I thought, we'll set tantrums aside for the time being. It's unlikely that these guys will have the temerity to sneak into my bedroom and verify how my marital life is unfolding. But they've got to explain themselves, drat it!

"Is it customary among the men of my people to have many wives?" I said.

"Sometimes it happens, sire," said Fairiba. "When women deem it necessary."

"I see," I said, although I didn't see anything. "Do these young ladies really deem it necessary to marry me off? All three of them?"

The three peas-in-a-pod copies of Liza Minnelli were silent. I think they were about to faint. I had no idea anyone could be that scared of me.

"This is also part of the tradition," said Fairiba. "These three are not regular women. They are the daughters of Isnouri herself."

"Oh, wow. That explains everything," I said, without trying to conceal my sarcasm.

"Do you wish to banish them, sire?" Fairiba said with trepidation.

"That wouldn't be such a bad idea," I said, angered. "Fine, since I promised not to incur curses, they can stay. But please don't ever bring me any more wives, okay? What I just got should be enough for the rest of my life. Now be a good sport and tell me who that Isnouri is. I must know at least something about my mother-in-law."

The old man's wrinkled faced lit up. "Isnouri is a very old woman of our people," he said. "She is at least three thousand years old, maybe even much older. No one knows for sure, for she does not live among the people. Isnouri rides the steppes alone, without friends or retinue. They say she even sleeps without dismounting her menkal."

"Her what?"

"Her menkal—the animal that we ride. Have you forgotten that, too, sire?"

"I have," I said, mentally making note that it was easy to forget something you never knew in the first place. "Okay, now I know where your legendary Isnouri spends the night. Go on."

"From time to time, Isnouri visits her people to leave one of her daughters with them. We believe Isnouri does not need a man to conceive a daughter. For she lets no one touch her—neither man nor woman. Not even to hold her hand."

"Yet the kids just keep coming, is that it?" I said. "How many has she had so far?"

"Those who taught me the wisdom remembered that Isnouri had left her daughters with us fourteen times. Seventy years ago, she brought us these three sisters. It was a first: never before had she brought us more than one child at a time. We thought they were destined to be alone forever. The daughters of Isnouri had always married the kings of the Xenxa people, and we had no hopes of ever finding you."

"Wait, they married the kings?" I said. "I thought it was the man who decided whom to marry, not to mention the king."

"The man never decides anything," said Fairiba. "Many men have learned to convince themselves that they make the decisions, yet I assure you, sire, it was the daughters of Isnouri who chose to marry your ancestors, and not the other way around."

"Okay, fine. So they did," I said, growing gloomier. Then I turned to the scared triplets. "And you've chosen me. Well, congratulations, girls. A really smart choice, I must say. Can you please tell me your names? I can't marry three strange girls at once."

"Xeilax, Xelvi, Kenlex," whispered the most synchronous trio in the world.

"Marvelous. Now I'm warning you, though, that I'm going to mix you up all the time," I said, "so no offense. You're going to live here for the time being. I'll call for the help; they'll show you the house. Pick any rooms and make yourself at home. You can ask anything you want. You're the king's wives, after all." I gave a nervous chuckle and continued. "Get settled, grow roots. Meanwhile, I'll mull over what to do with you. In a day or two, I'll come visit you here and we'll have a chat. It'll make me very happy if it turns out you can say a few words other than your names."

Then I looked at Fairiba. "That's all, I hope?"

"That is all, sire," said the old man.

"Sweet. I'll ask the servants to accommodate you for tonight, and tomorrow you're heading back home. I'm sure you and Barxa Bachoy know how to rule over my people to make them happy. You can send me messengers sometime in the middle of next winter. If there's an emergency, let me know immediately. Now I'm off."

"We will do as you wish," my newly appointed "prime ministers" said in unison.

"I'm sure you will," I said and sent a call to the butler.

A dozen servants appeared in the doorway. I told them to take care of my subjects and my wives. Who would have thought I'd be giving this command one day? Confusion, which is usual in such situations, arose, and I decided it was time for me to sneak out.

"Let's go, buddy," I said to my furry friend and pulled him gently by his ear. The dog got up and started pacing around me. I thought that the gigantic melon would feel honored to adorn my dinner table and tried to take it out of the basket one more time. This time, I managed to budge it a tad, but it was clear there was no way I could carry it under my arm. It didn't occur to me to call the servants—I was too unaccustomed to them. Instead, I put the melon back on the floor and gave it a gentle kick. The melon rolled in the desired direction. I should probably introduce soccer to this place, I thought. The usual pastime of starving barbarian kings.

The dog ran alongside me and even helped push the melon. Attaboy, I thought.

"I think I'm going to name you Droopy," I said to my four-legged friend. "Your size notwithstanding, what else would I call the dog of a Secret Investigator? I guess I could go with Hound of the Baskervilles, but I'm afraid it would affect your personality in the wrong way. So Droopy it is. Okay?"

He was okay with it, or at least he seemed to be. Unlike the dogs of my home World, he didn't wag his tail. He flapped his ears instead.

When Droopy and I reached the dining hall, the company greeted my new friend with a unanimous Awww! My manner of serving fruit also caused quite a furor. The melon itself, though, didn't make much of an impression.

"It has a weird taste," said Juffin. "Are you sure this 'berry of the steppes' won't make you sick? Because if you get sick tonight, it'll be the most devastating disaster in the history of Magic Chases."

After this remark, Melifaro didn't even want to taste the melon.

The Shimaro princes each took a bite, politely put their pieces back onto their plates, and refrained from commenting.

"Fine, I get to eat it all then," I said, biting into the melon. The boss's ominous prophecies would not stand in the way of this gastronomical orgy. The melon tasted exactly how I'd thought it would. Even better.

"So how do you like your new job so far?" said Melifaro. "Do you like being the barbarian king? I've always wanted expert advice on this matter."

"Well, what can I say? It comes with some benefits. Have you seen my dog? It's a gift from my vassals. What would I do without them? They brought me a whole bunch of useful things. Like a harem, for instance."

"A harem? Dream on," said Melifaro. "What would you do with a harem?"

"That, my friend, is exactly the issue here. The sooner I resolve it, the better."

"Resolve it? Resolve what?"

"The issue. The harem. My harem. They brought me a bunch of these girls, you see. Now I'm going to have to quit investigating because I'll have to be a full-time daddy. I'm going to have to tie their bows, buy ice cream, and so on. I think I'm definitely going to have to jump rope with them, too. First and foremost."

Melifaro blinked in confusion, trying to understand why I was making such absurd jokes.

"Seriously, Melifaro," I said, sighing and sinking my teeth into another piece of melon. "I'm not joking. It's all true."

"Funny," said Juffin. "How many wives did you say you had?"

"Three."

"Ha! Call that a bunch? Look on the bright side. If you were a queen and got three husbands instead, now that would've been a problem. Besides, you need someone to live in this beautiful house, which you are incapable of fully appreciating."

"My thoughts exactly," I said. "That's why I allowed them to stay."

"Well, I'll be darned," said Melifaro, who had just realized that all this talk about my wives wasn't a joke. "How come some people are so darn lucky, huh? A hole in the heavens above you, Nightmare! Why, why is this sinning World so unfair? You get everything, and some good people get nothing!"

"'Good people'? Meaning you? Okay, stop whining. Do you want me to ask my subjects to bring you a dozen wives? I'm not greedy."

"I do!"

"You should get used to the fact that you command your subjects; you don't ask them, Sir Max," said Prince Jiffa. He sounded as though everything we had been saying up until this moment was perfectly logical and fine, and only in this particular instance did I make a tiny mistake.

"But of course," I said. "Thanks for the tip. I'll definitely command them. Our Melifaro will have the largest harem in the Unified Kingdom. Don't fret, my friend."

"Sorry, no go," said Juffin. "You are a king from another land. You can do whatever you please, and then some. Melifaro, on the other hand, is an ordinary citizen, his many immortal exploits notwithstanding. He'll have to do without a harem."

"Oh, I see," I said and turned to Melifaro. "I thought you were a regular person, but in fact you're an 'ordinary citizen.' No harem for you then, I'm afraid."

"Okay, Ayonxa. Now I'm really quitting this job. I'm going to be your deputy," Melifaro said to the older Shimaro. "Nobody appreciates me for what I'm worth here."

"It's high time you quit," said Prince Ayonxa. "Don't worry. You and I, we'll pass a new law, get our own harems, live long and happy lives, and rule wisely and . . . Jiffa, help me out here. How does one rule? Wisely and . . . ?"

Prince Jiffa said nothing but looked at his older brother and Melifaro as if they were his own slow-witted but beloved children.

And that was the end of the dinner.

I told Droopy to keep his spirits up and handed him over to the strangers that thought of themselves as my servants. Then Juffin and I headed to the House by the Bridge, and Melifaro and the Shimaros went elsewhere to "finish up the evening." I was a little worried, but Jiffa's serious face gave me hope that the citizens of the Capital were in no danger.

"It didn't take too long, did it? It went even faster than I thought," said Juffin, getting into the amobiler. "You were great, Max."

"Not me, but whoever first decided not to feed guests at such events. Can you imagine what would have happened if all those ambassadors and grandees had found their way to my dinner table? They would have stayed until the next morning."

"Absolutely. That's why they don't serve food or drinks at official receptions."

"Is that so? How thoughtful of them to take pity on us poor helpless monarchs."

"Well, that's not the only reason, of course. It's considered beneath the ruler's dignity to feed every guest. We usually sit at a table with those we consider to be our equals or those whose company we enjoy, right? Any ruler, including His Majesty King Gurig, has the right to entertain whomever he considers to be his friends. You and I have both had dinner in his palace on more than one occasion. But to feed every single visitor? A royal court is not a tavern. After all, if someone really wants to eat at the expense of His Majesty, he can go to any tavern and ask the proprietor to put his meal on the Crown's tab. The law says that the king must pay for all the poor and starving."

"How quaint!" I said. "And if someone decides to eat at my expense, he can take a ride to the Barren Lands, order a melon-stuffed menkal, and put it on my tab."

"What's a melon-stuffed menkal?" said Juffin.

"Menkals are the antlered steeds of my so-called homeland. And melons are what you thought would make me sick."

"Werewolves forbid, Max," said Juffin. "I think you've overindulged yourself in this suspicious vegetable. Sometimes I even begin to believe you were born in the Barren Lands."

"You're probably going to laugh, Juffin, but those things grow in my World and I've always loved them. Trust me: I used to eat tons of them and nothing's ever happened to me."

"Hmm," said Juffin. "Talk about coincidence."

Our discussion about melons and menkals ended soon after it had started: we had arrived at the House by the Bridge. Juffin jumped out of the amobiler and disappeared behind the door at the speed of bad news. I slapped my forehead: with all this hullabaloo I had completely forgotten about Shurf's books.

What's taking you so long, boy? Juffin showed his impatience by sending me a call.

I forgot to bring books for Sir Shurf. He's going to try to kill me again, and this time he'll have every right to do so. I'm thinking I should probably go back real quick.

It's up to you, though you'll be missing out on your share of kamra.

Ouch, that would be a shame, wouldn't it? Okay. I'll be with you in a second.

I already had a plan. I stuck my hand underneath the seat of the amobiler, trying to probe the Chink between Worlds. It was a great opportunity to keep in shape.

I remembered how I had produced a box of cigars out of thin air for General Boboota. I had had to strain my imagination thinking about the presumed owners of those cigars: coffee cups in their hands, wooden humidor on the desk, and all. Now I tried to use the same method, summoning up in my imagination the bookshelves in a library. It triggered a strange association in my head, and I remembered *The Library Policeman*, a novella by Stephen King. I smirked at myself and thought, Yeah, ransacking that library wouldn't be such a great idea. These thoughts kept me from focusing properly, but a few minutes later a paperback book fell out of my numb fingers onto the floor. I picked it up and read the title: *Our Time Has Gone* by one Ingvar Stefansson. Neither the name of the book nor the author's name rang a bell. No wonder, though. Even though I used to be a voracious reader, there was no way I could have even made a dent in everything my scribbling compatriots had ever written. With my trophy tucked under my arm, I headed to the House by the Bridge.

A courier from the Glutton was bustling about in our office. Sir Juffin had decided to feed the prisoner. Lonli-Lokli, just out of his cell, was playing absentmindedly with a cup of kamra.

"I thought you went to the palace," said Juffin, "to pick up a book and sing a lullaby to your harem."

"You know what? I've had it up to here today with Melifaro's snide little quips," I said. "I sure don't want to hear the same ones from you." I turned to Shurf. "Here's a book for you, buddy. Just one, but it's from another World. I figured no one besides me would bring you a book like this."

"Indeed," said Lonli-Lokli, his usually stony face expressing ordinary surprise. "A book from another World! Who would have thought? Oh, it is so much better than anything one could find in the old university library."

"Well, not necessarily. Actually, I haven't read it, nor have I ever heard of the author, so I can't guarantee you this will be a quality read."

"A quality read? I think that is quite irrelevant. I have never read books written in another World before. To me, this is more than just a book."

"Well, of course."

I imagined how I would react if someone had lent me a book from another World five or six years ago, before I had become Sir Max from Echo or had dared hope that these other Worlds even existed. I doubted I'd be interested in the literary value of such a book. It probably would be "more than just a book" to me, too. Shurf was absolutely right.

"A book from your World?" said Juffin. "Oh, my. You write books there? I thought that movies were enough to entertain you. How do you manage all this in just seventy years, or however long you live there?"

"We're smart and quick," I said. "Can't you tell by looking at me?"

"I sure can. Are you smart and quick enough to descend to Xumgat already?"

"Let's go back to the good old terminology," I said. "Those words you're using now reek of some ancient mystical bunkum, as you yourself admitted the other day. I'm sort of ready for a stroll down the Corridor between Worlds, but to 'descend to Xumgat'? Uh-uh, sir. No way."

"You know, I had a similar reaction when certain allegedly powerful Magicians used such words in my presence," said Juffin. "Maybe that was why I captured so many Magicians—Grand and not so grand—back in the day. I was sick of their manners of expression. The rest was just a pretext."

"Sounds like it could be true," I said, laughing. "So this is the confession of the famous Kettarian Hunter. All the bloodshed could have been avoided, but their highfalutin terminology proved to be the ultimate undoing of the poor little Magicians."

"You sure are in great spirits," said the boss. "Let's go now while you're still in this mood."

"Do we need to go somewhere? I thought you could open the Door between Worlds anywhere."

"I can. Well, not just anywhere: there are places in the World that facilitate such undertakings and places that inhibit them. But today we must use your personal Door. You have only one so far, and it's in your former bedroom."

"Is there a difference between these Doors?" I said. "I thought—"

"Never mind what you thought. When two people travel through Xumgat—I mean the Corridor between Worlds—one of them must be the guide, the other the guest. We need to get to the World from your dreams, so you will be the guide. That's why you and I are going to the Street of Old Coins."

"And kick two beautiful ladies out of the movie theater?" I said. "They're going to scratch my eyes out for this."

"I'm sure they will. Let's go, hero. Sir Shurf, I'm sure you can't wait for us to get out of here so you can be alone with this mystical monument of otherworldly literature, huh?"

Lonli-Lokli didn't contradict him. He sighed and looked at the cover of the book with undisguised tenderness. We locked him up in his detention cell and proceeded to the Street of Old Coins.

I wasn't worried or scared about the upcoming journey. I had never been what you would call brave, but having Sir Juffin Hully at my side was the best calmative I knew: with him I could go to Hades itself. So on our way, I wasn't haunted by premonitions and chatted about inconsequential things with Juffin instead.

"By the way, why were there no women at my reception?" This question had been bothering me all evening. "Neither among the grandees of the provinces, nor among the ambassadors. Looks like women have a hard time climbing up the government ladder in the Unified Kingdom."

"Can you stop thinking about women for a minute?" said Juffin. "Then again, you have a harem now. You're partly right: all the grandees of our provinces are men. And you won't find too many women in the Royal Court, either. But it's not because someone holds them back from occupying higher positions in the government. Usually they don't wish to move up themselves. You see, these jobs normally require being in the public eye and a great deal of fuss and bother. Wise women can't stand that sort of thing, and no one needs stupid women in the government service any more than he needs stupid men. If some eccentric lady does want to try her hand at government affairs, she's usually much better at her job than most of her male colleagues. She quickly becomes far too important to be seen hanging around the residences of foreign kings. You know, women are much more radical than we are: it's all or nothing with them. I already told you this once, when you asked me why there were no women Grand Magicians. If a woman becomes a member of an Order, she won't be interested in such petty things as nominal power over her fellow members. If she gets a government job, she quickly becomes one of the Secret Ministers under almost any government."

"I see," I said, laughing. "In the World where I was born, people still think that, as a rule, women are not good enough to hold a high post. Here you think they're too good for it. But the results are just the same."

"Don't pretend you don't understand it," said Juffin. "The results are radically different, even if it doesn't seem so at first glance. Back in the day, Grand Magician Nuflin turned to seek my help only because our friend Lady Sotofa Xanemer wanted him to. He would have preferred not have me anywhere near Uguland. Better yet, he'd rather have had my head on a platter: back then Nuflin thought everyone would have benefitted from that. And that's just one example."

"Whoa! So someone like Lady Sotofa is behind each pivotal decision made by our government officials?"

"Almost. There are some pleasant exceptions. Take me, for example. I'm an independent guy. Which is for the better. Speaking of women: you'd better start thinking up a way to explain to your girlfriends why we have to pry them away from the TV. We're almost there."

Just as I had suspected, Melamori and Tekki were sitting in my former bedroom, glued to the TV and giggling like tipsy schoolgirls.

The show they were watching—a weightlifting competition—baffled me. Where on earth did this come from? I wondered. I'd never tape something like that in a million years. The tape was probably a humble contribution of the former owner of the collection. So much for knowing someone like the back of your hand.

When they saw us, the ladies were visibly embarrassed. They even blushed. "We're busted. Caught red-handed, right in the middle of some hot stuff," said Tekki. She buried her face in Melamori's shoulder, and they both giggled.

"We're Secret Investigators; it's our job to bust people," I said. "And what, pray tell, is this 'hot stuff' you're referring to?"

"Oh, this?" said Melamori, pointing to the TV. "I've never seen a more vulgar spectacle than these huffing and puffing, half-naked fat guys. Or anything funnier. Is this the usual pastime in your homeland, Max? Have you ever done this?"

"Well, see, I don't exactly have the right constitution," I said. "Besides, this isn't a pastime. It's a way of determining who's the strongest person. Not the smartest way, if you think about it, but still . . ."

Meanwhile, Juffin was staring at the TV. On the screen, a giant in a pink leotard was trying, and failing, to lift a five-hundred-thirty-pound barbell.

"Disgusting," he said. "Ladies, are you really enjoying this?"

"And how," said Tekki. "We've watched it twice already."

"You have, have you? Well, now turn it off and get out of the room. Go have a cup of kamra and get spiffed up. You can come back in thirty minutes and continue your highly intellectual activities since you've grown so fond of these horrible creatures."

"Oh, I see. You need to go somewhere from here," said Melamori.

"No, we want to admire these beauty boys, too. We're just embarrassed when you're around," I said.

"Ah, okay then," said Melamori.

Tekki was already standing in the doorway, smiling at me. It was the kind of desperate smile you would adopt to see off a hero when he's about to embark on a journey down Xumgat, I thought. Jeepers.

"Good night, ladies," said Juffin, bowing to them. "And don't stay here until dawn, or you risk having us land on top of your beautiful heads when we return."

"Not to worry, sir. Our heads are hard enough. But you just might hurt yourselves," said Melamori. Tekki didn't say anything, just shook her head. Then they both walked out of the room.

"Will you look at that?" I said. "They're best friends now. So much for old family feuds."

"Are you joking? Melamori would love to be best friends with Loiso Pondoxo himself, not just with his daughter, just to annoy her daddy. She and Korva have been competing to annoy each other for as long as I can remember. And I think Ms. Melamori is ahead of the game."

"Starting from the fact that she was born a girl, in spite of his dream of having a son."

"Precisely. Now, while we're on the subject, have you noticed that your Tekki is a lot like yourself? You two look different, of course, but the way she talks and walks and—"

"I know. It was the first thing I noticed about her," I said. "And, like any normal narcissistic jackass, I thought it was the best thing that'd ever happened to me. I still do."

"She is a mirror," said Juffin. "Like all Loiso Pondoxo's children, Lady Tekki becomes the reflection of her interlocutor. And their famous daddy was one of the best mirrors around, believe me. It's the most devastating kind of personal charm. Only when she's very scared, sad, or alone does the true Tekki come out, which doesn't happen all that often, right? While you were having a vacation in your World, I dropped by the tavern a few times. Then we often met here in this room to watch movies. Trust me, chatting with Lady Tekki feels like having a split personality, in a nice way. When Tekki spends time with Melamori, she becomes her replica. Disarming, right?

No one can resist. The most logical step is to become best friends."

"You can say that again," I said, perplexed. "Are you . . . sure you know what you're talking about? I mean, I had no idea."

"Of course you didn't. But I know very well what I'm talking about."

"I thought Tekki really was a lot like me," I said in a plaintive voice. "Now it turns out I don't even know the real Tekki."

"Well, you do know the real Tekki a little. The night she poisoned you by mistake, that was the real Lady Shekk. She was very, very scared then. But, as I understand it, that was when you fell in love with her," said Juffin. "Besides, when you look at her, she looks like you for real. This isn't some cheap acting, boy. This is Magic. And what do you care about what's going on with her when you're not around? If you think about it, it's none of your business."

"Right."

"Here's something to ponder. You can't actually know the 'real' anybody. Including yourself. Why should Lady Shekk be a sad exception to this beautiful rule?" said Juffin.

"I guess you're right," I said. "But why are you telling me all this now?"

"Now is as good a time as any. Besides, it might not have occurred to you for the next thousand years."

"Recently the ground seems to keep disappearing from under me," I said. "When it returns, I realize that it's all for the better. It's like a miniature death—the World becomes more beautiful afterward."

"I couldn't have said it better myself," said Juffin. "Now let's get down to business. We just kicked out two beautiful ladies and are sitting here gossiping. As if your bedroom is the only place in the World one can have a good long talk."

"Maybe it is," I said. "So what do we do now?"

"You lie down in your favorite spot and fall asleep, the same way you do when you want to sneak into the Corridor between Worlds. I know it's too early for you and you don't feel tired, but I'll help you. Trust me on this. Now, when you find yourself in the Corridor, look for the Door to the World with sandy beaches that you and Shurf were talking about, and enter it. I'll be right behind you. You're in luck here: I'm an experienced traveler. You won't have to do anything to help me. You'd have a much harder time with a novice. Now go lie down and try to sleep."

I settled in the middle of the soft bedcover. The rack with the video gear was pressing against my back. This inconvenience felt as pacifying as the presence of Juffin himself. Now I really was prepared for anything.

"This is the best way to treat insomnia," said my boss, producing a huge cartoonish hammer out of thin air. "Don't even think of dodging, or it won't work. How do you like my new trick, Max? Much more fun than the old ways."

I was so taken aback that I didn't know how to reply. Things like this didn't happen to me very often. A bright pink hammer smashed down on my poor head.

I didn't feel the hit, of course. Nothing much happened, in fact, except that I felt really sleepy. It didn't resemble general anesthesia: my sleepiness felt very natural, as though I hadn't slept for days and had just now finally reached the bed. I even had the illusion that I could wave off this drowsiness if I wanted to—but I didn't want to . . .

And then I fell asleep. What else could happen to a person when Sir Juffin Hully sang him a lullaby?

And again I was in that improbable place where there was nothing —nothing at all. Even I wasn't there in a sense. I can't explain what the Corridor between Worlds is. Experience isn't a boon here. Rather, the more often you end up in this bizarre place, the more you realize that you'll never be able to explain it to those who haven't been there. Our ancestors, unfortunately, didn't provide us with the necessary vocabulary when they created the languages we must resort to now, for lack of anything better.

I am still surprised that some part of me is fully capable of finding its bearings in this irrational space. Somehow I knew exactly which of the Worlds I had to allow to envelop me, which of the shining dots I had to allow to grow until they obscured all the others so that I could again feel the bright sand crunching under my feet on the empty beaches of my childhood dreams.

I sat down on a warm, red-gray rock and looked around.

Something was amiss with this alien yet so familiar World. A few moments later, I knew what was wrong. There were other people here besides me—far away by the water, but not so far away that I couldn't see them. But I remembered this World as empty and abandoned. That was one of its signature qualities. For this is how we construct a picture of someone we love in our memory: facial features, the voice, a mannerism, a way of responding to an event—all these things make the person predictable, recognizable, and, thus, beloved. When one of these features changes, it unnerves us, for we lack the courage to say goodbye to our old friend and let a stranger into our lives.

Recently I had had to learn to accept such changes without giving way to tantrums. Things had just happened the way they had; I had no choice but to accept them. But the changes that had taken place in the World of sandy beaches I used to love disgusted me right from the start. Even if I could have written that feeling off as a reflex, that emotion was soon replaced by a strong sense of foreboding.

I got up from the warm rock, forgetting that I should probably wait for Juffin, and walked to the sea. To the sea, where there were people who shouldn't have been there at all. They just couldn't be there, period.

A small motley crowd was walking toward me: tattered old gypsy women in colorful skirts and headscarves that glittered with golden threads. One of them carried a scruffy baby in her arms. Another kid, a bit older, was grabbing onto the skirt of a different woman. They began to nag and whimper. Their voices, as piercing as the shrieks of a seagull, were plaintive and brazen. Of course they demanded money, using their dirty babies as an argument. One of the women offered a range of esoteric services by way of bait and lost no time in urging me to "cross her palm with silver."

"I can see your destiny, pretty boy! You'll live a long life. You'll be rich—if you don't die today, that is."

The woman sidled up to me at the speed of a race car. How can she run so fast in the sand? I thought. Then I reminded myself that anything was possible in this World.

And then I lost my mind.

I still can't explain why a bunch of grungy gypsy women made me so furious. Moderate run-of-the-mill irritation would have been an appropriate response to being surrounded by a school of brazen, slatternly beggars. Yet a wave of insane, uncontrollable rage engulfed me and began dragging me away with it.

To my surprise, I liked my rage. I liked letting it take me wherever it wished. I liked riding the crests of its waves. I was ecstatic. Quite physically ecstatic. Each square inch of my body quivered in joy, anticipating a tempest, and the air around me also quivered in the same sweet way, as though the air was an extension of myself. I could no longer sense where my body ended and the surrounding environment began. I had never felt better, however insane that might sound.

The gypsy ladies did not seem to sense any misfortune in the offing. They didn't change their course. They kept coming toward me, mumbling something about my destiny and their starving children.

"So you're a fortune-teller, honey?" I whispered to the loudest of them, surprised at the tender trembling of my own voice. "Too bad you couldn't foretell your own death, sweetheart."

I didn't spit at them, even though my poison would likely have killed them all instantaneously. At that moment, it seemed that I would derive too little pleasure from such a primitive procedure. With the utmost delight, as though stretching my body after a good night's sleep until the joints cracked, I stretched my arms toward her. My forearms were already covered in long dark spikes. I somehow knew that each spike was as poisonous as my spit, but piercing through someone's body with the spikes was infinitely more enjoyable than spitting. I had never felt anything like it in my whole life!

When the spikes pierced her, the woman fell dead on the sand and turned into a heap of dirty, lice-ridden rags. This was no metaphor: her body had indeed disappeared. Only the colorful, tattered fabric was left lying there. The woman—the human—had never existed. I should have guessed sooner. There were no people here, only a series of mirages—each one more disgusting than the next.

The raucous friends of my first victim hesitated, but I didn't wait for them to reach me: I ran after them. The left side of my mouth was smiling a voluptuous smile, but the right side remained senseless and immobile, like after a shot of Novocain. Thank goodness no one offered me a mirror. I doubt that Sir Max from Echo would have liked the spectacle.

Moments later, everything was over: an unattractive heap of assorted colorful rags lay on the sand, and I moved onward. I walked to where the dark silhouettes of other apparitions that desecrated my beautiful once-empty World could be seen against the background of silvery-white water. Frankly speaking, at that moment I wouldn't have been able to forgive real people for such trespassing. I was determined to kill anyone who happened to get in my way, no matter what their damn bodies were made of.

The strangest sensation was the ringing quiver of space around my arms, delightful and tormenting at the same time. The horrendous spikes were gone, but I had no doubt they would appear again as soon as I neared the next victim.

I knew in advance what I would see by the water. Yet when I came close enough to make out the details, I gasped: this was too much! On the bright sand of my beach was all I had once hated—with a helpless, inexplicable but tormenting hatred—about the seaside. Ugly, fat women in bright bathing suits, eating food from plastic bags melting in the heat of the sun, their thin-legged, big-bellied husbands sipping warm beer from burning-hot bottles. Raspberry-pink sunburned girls in bikinis, with disgusting pieces of paper stuck to their peeling noses, and their bow-legged companions in skin-tight swimming trunks. Drunk teenagers, obese men in boxer shorts, loud old hags . . .

I remembered one trip to the beach with my parents. I was around five—a horrible age when you have just begun to realize your absurd but absolute dependence on the will of grown-ups, but you have as yet no strategy for a guerrilla war against them. Nothing particularly memorable had happened to me that day, but when I got home, I snuck into a closet and cried there in the dark, my face buried in the folds of an old coat that smelled of mothballs. "I don't want to grow up! Take me away from here!" I said again and again, addressing no one, fearing that being among those horrible, ugly creatures would turn me into one of them. That I would grow a beer belly, my face would turn purple, and then . . . then I would die, obviously. What else was there to do? Loiso Pondoxo couldn't even begin to imagine the black magic of my home world.

"Oh, what an excellent idea," I whispered. "I don't know who decided to pollute my wonderful World with this human garbage, but letting me kill them all at once was a brilliant plan!"

Then I picked up the familiar sweet mixture of beach smells—perspiration, sunblock, fortified wine, boiled eggs—and lost my human form. Not metaphorically but literally. The creature running around the beach like a hurricane could not have been human. Its (my?) arms turned into something unspeakable and started ripping the pink and chocolate flesh all around into shreds. It was sublime.

"This is my world, get it?" I yelled. "Everything here will be the way I want it to be! And I don't want you here! Get out of here, you bastards! Go to hell, to your resorts, to Golden Sands, to the Florida Keys, to Palm Beach! Just get out!"

Sometimes they died a regular organic death. Sometimes, however,

I noticed that the meat of the flesh turned black and shrank like burned paper. I didn't care.

I regained my senses when it was all over. I found myself sitting on the wet sand. Kind, lazy waves were licking my boots. They had already turned my footwear into a mess that was painful to look at. I felt peaceful and empty inside. The preceding events seemed like a vague but sweet dream. I felt quite emotionless about it.

"Looks like you can lose your temper on occasion after all." I heard Juffin's mocking voice behind my back. "Too bad Sir Dondi Melixis wasn't here to see you. He would have given you a raise. Dear, dear, look at you. You used to be such a nice boy. You should be ashamed of yourself, Sir Max."

"Well, I'm not," I said in an indifferent tone.

"Okay, maybe you shouldn't be," said Juffin, smiling and sitting down next to me. "Maybe it was a trifle. You've learned to fight your mirages. That's a good start. There's just one small thing you still have to learn: how to do the same to the one who sends them."

"Sure thing. Bring him on," I said, still indifferent.

"Ha! 'Bring him on,' he says. You're in no shape for battle, son. I don't think you'd be able to kill a chicken after the performance you've just put on. Which was exactly what our friend Gugimagon was counting on, by the way."

"Was it him?" I didn't feel like I could be bothered to care. I was as imperturbable as Sir Lonli-Lokli, if not more so.

"Wasn't me, for sure." Juffin took the turban off my head and, with the cunning smile of a provincial magician, pulled a clay pitcher out of it. The pitcher was a replica of the pitchers in the Glutton Bunba.

"I think a sip of kamra wouldn't do you any harm. Don't pretend you can't drink it without a cup. I can't be bothered to fetch one for you. Why are you looking at me like that? Did you think you and our precious Maba Kalox were the only ones in the whole World who could do this trick?"

"No," I said and smiled. "Deep down inside I'm sure there isn't any trick you can't do, and that you're the boss of everyone and everything. It's just funny that you pulled a pitcher out of the turban."

"Oh, that's nothing. When old Mackie Ainti taught me the trick of the Chink between Worlds, he posited that for best results one should search the chink just below one's back," said Juffin. "Back then, I was easily shocked by such statements. I even thought of quitting my studies, thinking Magic was a dirty business."

"Hey! This kamra really is from the Glutton," I said.

"Of course. You thought I'd treat you—and me—to some poison?"

Juffin grabbed the pitcher out of my hands and took a few gulps. I put my hand in the pocket of my Mantle of Death for a cigarette. Then I snapped my right fingers to light it. That was a bit too much for me. I was more or less used to performing miracles on demand, but this was almost mechanical. Time out.

"Are we waiting for something in particular, or are you just giving me time to catch my breath?" I said.

"Both. We're waiting for the blissful moment when I'm sure you're fully restored. Then I'll summon that elderly rascal Gugimagon."

"I'm not fully restored?"

"Well, how shall I put this? A half hour ago, you looked pretty bad to me."

"Where were you all the time I was . . . fighting my mirages?"

"I was standing on the Threshold of this World, up to my chin in a sea of pleasure, watching your immortal feats. I decided to keep my distance, though, just in case." Juffin laughed heartily, as if he thought I was the greatest comic of all times and my massacre of the beachgoers was one of my best acts.

"Were they really just mirages?" I said.

"Not 'just' mirages, but . . . Well, sure, they were mirages, all right. You see, I think I managed to trick Gugimagon. Until the very last minute, he was sure you'd come here alone because he thought I'd stay with Sir Shurf, guarding his precious body and his no-less-precious soul."

"Why did he think that?"

"Last night, I gave Shurf a little of my blood and told him to drink a drop of it each time he felt his Rider approaching. A magician who is not too experienced in such matters could easily mix up Shurf's body with mine. My bet was, first, that Gugimagon wasn't very experienced in these matters; and, second, that I still scared the hell out of him. And I was right, which I'm very glad about."

"Was that the secret you didn't want to tell me about yesterday?"

"Indeed. My trick couldn't have worked any better. Gugimagon thought you'd come to fight him alone. He was well prepared for you. Gugimagon calculated that your fit of rage would completely exhaust you, which is what happened. You know, Max, he's scared of you, too. Not scared to death but still scared. And he really, really dislikes you. Shurf was right: it's personal."

I gave Juffin a puzzled look. He shrugged, made a helpless gesture, and even raised his eyebrows, as if to say, yeah, that's just how it is, buddy, nothing more to discuss.

"The first thing he decided to do was to throw everything you hate at you. Things that you least wanted or expected to encounter in your World. And this is, indeed, your World, your very own World," he said.

"What do you mean 'my own World'? I know I've been seeing it in my dreams for a long time, and I've always loved this place. But how can anyone own a whole World?"

"It's simple: without you, this coast wouldn't exist. First you dreamed of fragments of a World that had never before existed. Then a miracle happened—one of the few phenomena that we cannot explain and have traditionally called 'miracles.' This place became real. It materialized. It became real enough to exist even after you die. There are many Worlds that began as someone's dream. Most of them are as unclear and ephemeral as their creators. But you, you have a rare talent that allows you to give your fantasies a long-lasting existence. The beautiful nameless city in the mountains, the predatory enchanted garden that you brought into existence near Kettari, and now this place . . . Strange that Gugimagon took a fancy to it. Perhaps because it's easier to enter a newborn World?"

I kept staring at the boss. What metaphysical nonsense! He must have been mocking me. Oh, whatever. Let him mock me all he wants. I just didn't want to live with this new truth about me and inhabited Worlds. A solipsist wakes up one morning with a terrible hangover and . . . there is nothing around him. What a sad joke.

The ground was disappearing from under my feet again. How many more times was that going to happen this autumn?

"Are you pulling my leg, Juffin?" I said without much hope.

"Why would I? And what are you so worried about? As though this is some groundbreaking news. It's funny how scared you are sometimes of a simple statement of facts."

"Yeah, it's hilarious," I said. "Actually, after all that's happened to me, I could probably do without your last 'statement of facts.'"

"Indeed. But if I were you, I'd be dancing with joy. Or does the thought of your own omnipotence not thrill you?"

I analyzed my feelings and shook my head. "I'm afraid not. I'm sorry. But if you give me back that pitcher of kamra, it'd probably cheer me up a bit. I'm a very primitive creature, you see."

"Fine, here's your slop, you primitive creature. It's almost cold now," said Juffin, handing me the pitcher.

I finished the lukewarm kamra and decided it was time to have some fun. "You know, I feel I've taken a good rest and I'm ready for action. How about you summon Gugimagon real quick, I punch him in the face, and we go home?"

"You won't be 'ready for action' for at least another couple dozen days," said Juffin. "I don't mean your mood or how you feel physically. I mean your potential for repeating your recent exploit. But that's irrelevant. I can handle Gugimagon myself—that's a piece of cake. The problem is that I might hurt you by accident while killing that fellow. You're too weak. I'd love to send you home, but you're in no shape to go anywhere now."

"Is it really all that bad?" I said.

"Bad? No, everything is just fine. Better than fine, even. You can stand up, you can even make fire with your fingers—though you technically shouldn't be able to. We have two options. Option number one: you can take a vacation and stay here for a couple dozen days until you acquire the status of 'conquering hero,' just like you're supposed to. That's an excellent idea in many respects. There's a catch, though. During this time, our friend Gugimagon may pack up his suitcases and head somewhere at the other end of the Universe. At least that's what I would do if I were him."

"And option number two?"

"Oh, that I like even more than option one. I'm going to bury you right now and then summon Gugimagon."

"B-b-bury me?" I said.

"That's right. Earth offers excellent protection from all kinds of things, especially the earth of your own World. I believe it's going to be something special. Now stop making sad eyes at me, Max. Your head is going to be sticking out. You'll be able to breathe all you want, and you'll get to see the battle of the titans. Boy, do I love performing before a live audience!"

"Oh, okay," I said, happy that I wouldn't be buried alive. "But then you're going to have to leave my hands sticking out, too, so I can applaud."

"No way, mister. Right now your hands are your most vulnerable assets, what with all the things you've done with them."

"Suit yourself. You'll get no applause then," I said, stretching out on the warm sand. "Do whatever you want with me, Juffin. I think I'm going to take a quick nap."

"Don't even think about it. No naps while Gugimagon is alive." Juffin produced a small ceramic bottle of Elixir of Kaxar from the pocket of his looxi. "How come you're the one drinking this stuff and I'm the one who remembers to bring it?"

"That's how it's supposed to be. It's called specialization."

I took two bracing gulps of the tastiest tonic in the World—in all the Worlds. It was an overdose, of course, but desperate times called for desperate measures.

"Don't choke on it," said Juffin.

He rose to his feet and moved a few paces away from the water. He hesitated a little and gave an approving nod. He then picked up a small rock from the ground, turned it over and over it in his hands, and hurled it to the ground at his feet. A bright column of sand launched into the sky, quivered, and scattered into millions of shiny grains. It looked like a miniature explosion, except that it was completely noiseless.

"Your little burrow is ready," he said. "It's time to bury you, before you start wanting to brawl after overindulging on your potion."

"Have you ever seen me start a brawl after drinking it?" I said.

"Praise be the Magicians, I haven't. Yet. And I pray to the heavens I won't ever see it," said Juffin, laughing. "Your show today impressed me immensely. I could have sworn that Loiso Pondoxo had risen from the dead. If I didn't know better, I'd think he was your favorite schoolteacher: you emulated his style today. For your information, out of all of my acquaintances, he was the only one who could do those tricks with his hands."

"I'm sure you're trying to flatter me, but your praise doesn't make me feel any better," I said. "That infamous Loiso Pondoxo of yours—he turns up everywhere! He even managed to be the father of my girlfriend, of all things. Are you sure you killed him, Juffin? Recently

I've begun to suspect he's going to swoop down on my head one of these days."

"I did a very good job killing him," said Juffin, though he paused to think about it. "I put him in a rapidly disappearing place. I believe Loiso disappeared along with that place long, long ago. But even if he didn't, I don't think he'll ever 'swoop down on your head.' I locked his personal Door between Worlds after him. And believe me, I locked it very well. Loiso was an unsurpassed master of Apparent Magic—I was no match for him—but in questions of travel between Worlds, he was no better than a novice, much like you are. The trickiest part was to lure him into Xumgat. The rest was easy."

"Will you tell me about it?"

"Some other time, perhaps. I'm kind of busy here. Hop into your hole, Max. We'll look silly if Gugimagon gets away from this World. Naturally, it won't be easy for him. He'd need to find a good 'horse' for that. He probably won't be able to get to Shurf, and those who brought him here are all dead. Still, we shouldn't underestimate him. I wouldn't be surprised if it turns out he has other involuntary helpers besides those unfortunate mental patients and our Sir Shurf. After all, he has been preparing for this journey for no less than a hundred years."

Juffin chattered away while carefully pouring sand between me and the walls of the deep hole. I felt like a root crop, a gigantic carrot. It was funny, and under the influence of the overdose of Elixir of Kaxar, I giggled like a madman.

"Aw, that's so sweet," said Juffin. "I love dealing with you. I'm practically burying you alive in a desert at the edge of the Universe; I'm about to summon Gugimagon, who, by the way, is craving your blood; and there you are, neighing like a drunk horse."

"Why a 'drunk horse'?" I couldn't stop laughing.

"Because sober horses behave themselves, especially under similar circumstances. Fine, you've convinced me. I'm going to have lots of fun, too," said Juffin.

❧

He turned around and walked toward the middle of the beach in quick, long strides. When he was about forty yards away from me, he stopped and yelled, "Gugimagon, you son of a werewolf! Get your backside down here now!"

This impolite summons did more than just thunder above the beach, like a normal human holler. Each word Juffin uttered materialized as it flew out of his mouth. An enormous orange inscription hovered in the air over his head like a speech bubble in a comic book. The letters expanded, and at the same time the color began to fade. A few seconds later, they became pale yellow and covered almost the entire sky. Juffin raised his right hand and made a commanding gesture. The glowing letters flowed like milk out of a pitcher into his outstretched palm. He gave his hand a violent shake, and the transparent fabric of the writing turned into a thin cane, the color of ivory.

"Come here now!" Juffin roared, plunging the cane into the sand. He sounded very compelling. I'd have submitted to his voice myself if he hadn't immobilized me in advance. Then Juffin relaxed, nodded, and returned to me. "He's coming," he said, winking at me. "I've pinned him down. He'll naturally flounder a bit at first, for half an hour or so, until he's exhausted. But he'll come all right."

"That was beautiful, what you just did there," I said.

"Thank you. It was for your benefit," said Juffin. "I could have done the same without resorting to visual effects. I blame your movies for this. I never used to be such a show-off. But, you know, I like it. I have the right to make a routine job enjoyable."

"'Routine job'?"

"Of course. Chasing Gugimagon, that unfortunate talentless romantic and sucker for long journeys, through the remote corners of Xumgat is terribly routine."

"I thought I'd gotten myself into one of the most dangerous adventures of my life," I said.

"You thought right, but one doesn't exclude the other. Besides, you were only in real danger when you were giving a lift home to your friend Shurf Lonli-Lokli. Now if you had been stranded here all by yourself, that would've been something different. I can only imagine what would have happened then."

"Well, I can't. Which is probably a good thing."

"Hey, will you look at that!" said Juffin, pointing to the sea. "It seems Gugimagon has been eavesdropping on us. Now he's offended and wants to prove to me that hunting him will not be as boring as I thought."

I looked in the direction Juffin was pointing and froze in horror: the rippled surface of the sea was no longer a continuation of the level of the beach. The sea stood on end and hung over us like a wall, defeating all the laws of physics, optics, and reason. The angle decreased at a dangerous speed: the wall of water was leaning toward us and was about to come down like the lid of an enormous box.

Juffin sighed, got up, and made a nonchalant gesture. "Back off," he said in the voice of a sleepy dog owner trying to get rid of a pet who has decided he wants to go for a walk at three in the morning. From my own experience, I knew that it could take until morning to reason with a dog. In contrast, calming down the sea was a piece of cake. A moment later, the sea was a smooth surface of lively shimmering turquoise, stretching all the way from the sand to the horizon again.

"Don't pay any attention to that, Max," said Juffin. "That was also a mirage. Who does he think I am, a senile old man? I think I'm about to lose my temper now."

Juffin probably liked his own idea. In any event, he began implementing it without a moment's hesitation.

"Come here!" he said, hitting the knob of the cane. "Come here! Move it! Faster! Faster! NOW!"

He was bellowing so loudly, I thought my nerves would snap. The last howl sounded positively inhuman. People are simply incapable of screaming in such a voice, low and shrill at the same time. I would gladly have burrowed into the sand all the way, so that I wouldn't have to hear Juffin's voice anymore.

Finally, a large tall silhouette reminiscent of a weight lifting champion appeared in front of Juffin. From my vantage point, it looked like a giant. Behind Juffin, I saw another giant looking exactly like the first one. Skinny Juffin didn't look like a match for them. He didn't look much like anything. Thank goodness this wasn't an Olympic event.

"Oh, look who's here! It's Mr. Gugimagon himself. And he's brought his Shadow with him. How nice!" said Juffin in a thin voice, doing an about-face at the speed of lightning.

He grabbed one giant by the haunches without any visible effort and tore the bulky dark body in half, as though it were made out of cardboard. Then he giggled, jumped up like a flea, and grabbed the leg of the other adversary.

"Poor old Sir Gugimagon. He no longer has a Shadow," said Juffin.

He lifted up the giant like a feather and smashed its head into the ground with all his might, exactly like Muscles, Jerry's cousin from the Tom and Jerry cartoons. I'm sure Juffin, a hard-core fan of MGM shorts, reenacted that scene intentionally.

"Did you like it, Max?" said Juffin, smiling one of his most charming smiles. He was still holding his adversary by the leg, waving him nonchalantly in the air. I blinked my eyes, not saying a word. What could I say?

"Sinning Magicians, Max, have I finally made you lose the faculty of speech? Now that's what I call a miracle!" He approached me, dragging along the huge Gugimagon.

"You're not going to kill him?" I said.

"Why are you so bloodthirsty?" said Juffin. "If you had your way, all the Worlds would be as barren as this one. He's as good as dead now, actually. No one can outlive his own Shadow—well, maybe for an hour or two. Enough time for me to have a good heart-to-heart talk with my old buddy."

"Great," I said. "Can you dig me up now?"

"No way! You are completely unshielded. It wouldn't be a good idea for you to walk around the territory where two elderly men just engaged in Magic of the two hundred and twenty-eighth degree."

"Wow!" I said. "Almost the highest degree of Magic!"

"Almost. You know, it turns out it's much easier to perform at that level in a newly created World. A peculiar effect. Now I understand how you managed that wonderful battle scene with the beachgoers. I don't think you'd be able to pull it off at home, which is probably all for the best."

"And I thought I really was that powerful and ferocious. Fine then. If not, so be it."

"All in due time, Max. All in due time."

Juffin sat down beside me—or, rather, beside my head. I had the feeling that I had nothing left but my head. My body seemed to have mixed with the sand and dissolved, and I even liked the feeling.

The boss shook Gugimagon's body like a rag. His victim sat up, his head lolling on the shoulder of his tormentor.

"Sit up straight!" said Juffin.

To my surprise, the body obeyed and straightened up. I could see the face now. Unattractive but impressive, it reminded me of the proud faces of Indian chiefs—not the real ones, of course, but their Hollywood incarnations. His right eye was shut, and his left one stared at me with a heavy, unblinking stare. The iris was dirty white. The pupil, bright as the sun, had the shape of a crescent. I remembered the conversation between Juffin and the wiseman from the Refuge for the Mad: Gugimagon was blind in his left eye. Could've fooled me.

And then I remembered something I couldn't have known or even suspected a second before: This blind white eye had stared at me like this once before, the day I had been stupid enough to decide to visit my home World.

I still shudder when I think about that adventure. From the beginning, everything went wrong: there was no Corridor between Worlds, no search for the right Door, not a single conscious step in the right direction. I fell asleep in my enchanted bedroom on the Street of Old Coins and then woke up under my old checkered blanket in the wretched shack that I once had called home, thinking that the two years of my life in Echo had been a wonderful dream I could already hardly remember.

I had gotten out of that mess, found myself in a worse one, and, for better or for worse, gotten out of that one, as well. After I had returned, I learned to live as though nothing had happened, keeping my memories at bay, not panicking at the sight of checkered blankets. I had even stopped screaming in my sleep. But now, when my eyes met the pale blind eye of Gugimagon, I realized in an instant what had been wrong with my first journey, and why.

Of course I had gone through the Corridor between Worlds. I'd fallen into it as soon as I'd closed my eyes on the Street of Old Coins. But on the border of the invisible and the unthinkable, in the place where a person is left alone with himself—without himself, rather—this very same one-eyed fellow had been waiting for me, wishing to . . . I couldn't quite put into words what it was he wanted to do. But now I knew that I had been in danger that was worse than death—which, allegedly, is as bad as it gets.

"You remembered him now, right?" said Juffin. "Yes, it was he who hunted you when you traveled to your World. Gugimagon stunned you good then. And still you managed to escape from him. Good boy. I wonder how many guys like you weren't so lucky." Juffin gave his captive a light flick on the forehead. "Come on, look alive, buddy. I have a question for you. You, Sir Gugimagon, have gone too far. It was one thing to slaughter those unfortunate madmen—I might have done the same if I were you. If Xumgat doesn't accept you, you must hone your skills and rely on the help of the homeless Shadows that wander there—that would be a noble solution. But why on earth did you think you had the right to use the power of the true minions of Xumgat? Answer the question!"

"You know as well as I do that this bastard isn't human," said Gugimagon. Not only did he say it, he pointed his finger at me in a most rude manner. "And I really needed your other guy. I wouldn't have messed with you and risked everything if I could've done without him."

"They say that one who feasts too much on the powers of the mad becomes mad himself," said Juffin. "Looks like they say right. How quaint. Well, I guess we have nothing more to talk about. Summon the others, Gugimagon, and let's get this over with."

"The others? What 'others'?" said the giant.

"I know there are other minions of Xumgat here—or, rather, the parts of their spirits that you have managed to straddle. I can imagine what happens to the poor remains of those fellows, burning out without their better halves, not realizing what has happened to them. I can summon them myself, but I'm afraid I'll hurt them even more. They're in trouble as it is. Your game is not over yet, Gugimagon. Did you think I'd just kill you and that would be it? No, buddy, we haven't seen each other for ages. You probably don't even know that I can stretch out your death till the end of this World. The two hundred and thirty-third degree of White Magic—just one step short of the Green Fire. You don't remember me fooling around with such tricks back in the day, huh? Would you like to die slowly? Let me tell you, this wonderful World is going to exist for a very, very, very long time. Am I right, Sir Max?"

I nodded, even though I had no idea what they were talking about. The dialogue between the two old Magicians had completely drained me of the ability to think. The only thing that concerned me was this one-eyed fellow's confidence in denying my human nature, not to mention his calling me a bastard. Not that I could be bothered by his opinion of me, but the information was worrying.

"Since when have you paid attention to the delirium of madmen?" said Juffin. "If I'd known you were so sensitive, I'd have buried you up to the top of your head."

"And a minute later you'd have noticed my curious ears peeking out of the sand," I said. "I could have pulled off such an innocent trick, trust me."

"I do," said Juffin, who then turned back to his captive. "Come on, Gugimagon. Move it!"

"I am not going to indulge your whims, Juffin," Gugimagon said. "Do what you want, but those bastards stay here. All of you are brazen, ungrateful, senseless creatures. You were born with a wonderful gift, and you are incapable of understanding what it means to be a man who is doomed to stay where he was born. I paid a very high a price for my journey, and I want everything to stay the way it is now."

"You haven't paid squat!" said Juffin. "It was others who had to pay your fare, and they didn't even get to see the wonders for which you almost put out their Spark. That's what drives me to fury! Summon those who can still return to you, Gugimagon, or else . . . You've known me for a long time. You know I always get what I want."

"Everything will stay the way it is!" said Gugimagon.

"We'll see."

Juffin lifted Gugimagon's body and threw it upward. Instead of one, two bodies fell on the sand. Lightning fast, Juffin tore one of them in half, exactly the way he had done so a few minutes ago.

"A Shadow can resurrect fast, but it can die even faster. Right, Gugimagon? I can go on like this for as long as necessary." Juffin's voice was quiet, almost tender. "I know it hurts, but you leave me no choice. Summon your captives before it's too late. I can get carried away, and then, who knows, maybe Sir Max will want to take a few lessons from me."

"You could let me die a different death," moaned Gugimagon. "You already got your people back. What do you care about the others?"

"You sure do hate those poor souls," said Juffin. "But envy has never set anyone on the right path. Quit fooling around and summon them, Gugimagon."

"All right," said the giant. "But . . . Can you make me die in Xumgat and not here? I know you can. Will you do this for me if I summon those people?"

"Sure, why not?" said Juffin, softening suddenly. "You should have begun with that request. You fully deserve this reward, Gugimagon. After all, you've done the impossible. But first I must release your prisoners. Summon them while you still can."

Now the one-eyed old man looked almost happy. His stubbornness, hatred, and fury were gone.

He is a madman, I thought. What difference does it make where you're going to die? A death is a death. Or not?

Juffin suddenly pulled my ear. His face looked mischievous, but his eyes betrayed seriousness and even sadness—a very untypical combination for him.

"They are here, our comrades in misfortune. Can you feel them, Max?"

"I don't feel a thing. Who are 'they'? You mean those ghosts?"

"What ghosts?" said Juffin.

"Well, those transparent, shimmering shadows by the water. What's wrong?"

"Nothing's wrong. You see them in a peculiar way. I see them completely differently. Rather, I don't see them at all. You and I interpret the same phenomenon in two different ways. Perhaps it's all for the better. How many 'ghosts' do you see?"

"Let me count." I counted. "Seventeen."

"That's correct. Seventeen. Ten definitely can find the way back; the others will have to take their chances. Look, Gugimagon, they treated you with the Crystal of Memory in the Refuge for the Mad. Hand it over. These guys could use some right now."

"Take it," said Gugimagon, handing Juffin a dark, shiny object that looked like a piece of anthracite. "Why do you care so much about them? What difference does it make what's going to happen to those Shadows? They don't belong to your people."

"Of course they don't. They're not even from Echo, not even from the outskirts of the World, except for one woman from Tulan. Magicians only know what they were doing here. Okay, I need to divide the Crystal of Memory into seventeen pieces: ten larger ones and seven smaller ones. Let's see if I can make a good wiseman's apprentice." Juffin began to tap the dark stone rhythmically. "Done. There you go, folks!"

He tossed the dark pieces of crystal into the sea. I saw the glowing transparent figures start to move. Something resembling hands stretched toward the pieces that were slowly sinking to the bottom of the sea.

"Try to get back to your homes, people," said Juffin with surprising tenderness. "And try to remember at least something of this story. The memory of it might help you later, when you enter the Corridor between Worlds of your own accord—if you ever do. Now I'm going to open the Door for you."

He raised his hand and, with visible effort, drew a large rectangle in the air. It looked like he was cutting very thick fabric with a very dull knife: the corners took the greatest amount of effort. At last, he succeeded. I saw the contours of the rectangle glowing with a pale reddish light.

The seventeen ghostly creatures rushed toward Juffin, one after another. They vanished once they touched the glowing outline of the invisible Door. Less than a minute later, everything was finished. Juffin sat down again by the remains of Gugimagon. The giant's game was definitely over: he looked less and less like a living person. But Juffin didn't pay any attention to him. He turned to me and smiled a disarming smile.

"Long, long ago," he said, "when I was a very young lad, the same thing happened to me. Someone like this fellow here"—he nodded in the direction of Gugimagon's immobile body—"stole my spirit. A small part of it—I was lucky. Naturally, back then, I didn't realize what had happened. On the outside, I remained an ordinary boy. No one would have thought of taking me to the Refuge for the Mad. Something was missing, though I didn't realize it. I was very young and didn't know what other people felt. I thought the emptiness I felt inside was a regular human feeling, that life felt empty, stupid, and cheerless for everyone else, too. I couldn't muster a genuine interest in anything. It all seemed pointless: boring and gloomy days that all looked alike, nights without dreams, and a weariness that seemed endless.

"I wandered around, miserable, my eyes dull and unseeing. They saw nothing but my own reflection in a million mirrors, and the reflection made me sick. I'm speaking metaphorically, Max. There are no words to describe just how horrible I felt. The worst part was that there was a piece of me that still remembered it could be otherwise. It pained me, and the pain was unconscious and indescribable. This went on until old Sheriff Mackie Ainti offered me a position as his deputy. Now I realize that the first thing he did when he got to know me a little better was to go to Xumgat, find that little piece of me that was missing, and probably kick someone's butt while he was at it. He released my spirit from captivity. And then I knew the taste of true life again."

Juffin lay on his back, stretched his legs, and put his hands behind his head. He sighed, it seemed, not so much from physical relaxation but from the emotions that filled him.

He continued. "That night I was on the nightshift at the House by the Road. It was my second nightshift—or was it my third one? I dozed off in the armchair and then suddenly woke up. I jumped as though I'd been stung. The wind had opened the window, and I realized that beyond it were beautiful things like raindrops and the smell of wet leaves of the shott tree. It was as magnificent as some purple sunrise at the opposite end of the Universe.

"I jumped out the window and took a walk through the city. I crossed every single bridge—do you remember how many bridges there are in Kettari, Max? I drank some horrible drink in an all-night tavern, amazed at its taste. I touched everything I could get my hands on, just to make sure it was real . . . or that I was real. And it was true: that night I finally became 'real' again and almost went crazy from the sensation. I am still ecstatic about the fact of my own existence and the existence of every single blade of grass under my feet. I have something to compare it to because I can't forget the time that I lived among all of this and felt almost nothing.

"Then I got a grip on myself and returned to work. That sly fox Mackie reprimanded me for hours for my spontaneous leave of absence. Now I realize that he was reprimanding me so I wouldn't go insane from happiness—although I'm not sure he chose the most efficient method."

Juffin smiled dreamily, as though the reprimand from Mackie Ainti, the old sheriff of Kettari, had been the most delightful event in his life. And maybe it had been, in a sense.

"So now you . . . you sort of paid back the debt?" I said.

"You got it!" said Juffin. "I couldn't have put it better myself. You can't imagine how happy I am now, thinking about those poor souls. Maybe some of them have even gone mad with the fullness of sensation, the sudden return of feelings. It's the most charming form of madness, if I do say so myself."

"I think I understand," I said. "When I ended up on the path of the Tipfinger, got lost in my World and forgot myself, and then began to remember again, slowly, step by step . . . It probably wasn't exactly the same, but still . . ."

"Yes," said Juffin, nodding. "All stories about finding yourself are, in essence, one and the same story. Of course you know what I'm talking about. You of all people should know."

He turned to Gugimagon and put his hand on the old man's pale forehead. "I hope you listened carefully. I could have told the story to my colleague later, but I wanted you to know what happened to those you've been stealing strength from. One might say it's pointless to preach to someone who's about to die, but no one really knows what happens to those who die in Xumgat. It may not be real death, but that's what you're counting on, right? If I could choose where to die, that's where I'd choose to die, too."

Gugimagon didn't answer. I couldn't tell if he'd heard anything of what Juffin had been saying. The boss shook his head in disbelief and turned back to me. "This is all fine and dandy, but you and I should get out of here. I'm beginning to feel homesick."

"Me too, but how am I supposed to get out of here if you don't let me dig out of my own grave?"

"Easy. I'll simply open our Door right at the bottom of your grave, as you call it. What a terrible term you've chosen!"

"Comes with the outfit," I said. "It's my Mantle of Death. I have to wear it all the time, and it affects my outlook."

"Well, well," said Juffin, getting up. "It's best for you to close your eyes. It makes it easier for me to open the Door and will protect you from unnecessary stress."

I submitted and closed my eyes, but even through my eyelids I could see the straight lines glowing with the now familiar reddish light. Juffin was probably cutting the fabric of space with the metaphysical counterpart of a blunt knife again.

Then the absolute coldness of the Corridor between Worlds embraced me, and one of the myriad glowing dots was the Door to Echo, right into my bedroom on the Street of Old Coins.

Try to stay here for a moment, Max. This was Juffin's call, no doubt about it. I was surprised. I had thought that there wasn't room for anything in this absolute emptiness, even for Silent Speech. I wanted to reply but couldn't, just like in those distant times when I had only begun to master the basics of Silent Speech.

Don't try to answer. First, you don't yet know how to do it here.

Second, it takes a lot of strength, which you don't have at the moment, Juffin continued. Try staying here until you see me. I think you can do it. If you can't, no big deal. In that case, just allow our World to take you. I just wanted you to see how people die in Xumgat. It's not every day that you see this.

I had no idea how I could "stay" in this place. The Door to my bedroom on the Street of Old Coins was ready to let me in—or, rather, it was ready to take me away from here. Inhabited Worlds usually won't let an inexperienced traveler hang out on their thresholds for long. They are as impatient as angry mothers who pull their disobedient offspring by the scruff of the neck.

"May I wait for Juffin?" I said in an indecisive tone.

I had never tried to speak out loud in this mysterious place, so I was scared of my own voice and the long reverberation, which wasn't so much a sound as a strange sensation in my body. Yet I was positive that this silly monologue might be a good way to bargain with . . . I don't know . . . whomever. I mustered my will and added, "I have to stay here a little longer. I want to."

My wheedling worked, for better or for worse. I was free. The Door to my World still loomed ahead, but its pull had abated.

"Thank you," I said, just in case. I thought a little courtesy wouldn't hurt.

Then I saw Juffin. He was very near, although when you're in the Corridor between Worlds, familiar terms like "near" and "far" are meaningless. Still, it seemed I could touch him if I dared stretch out my hand. Yet . . . Heck, I wasn't sure I even had hands. I couldn't feel my body. All I could do was watch.

Juffin's body seemed huge and shining. The longer I looked at him, the larger and brighter his outlines became. Beside him glimmered some shapeless clump. I realized it was Gugimagon, the formidable traveler between Worlds, the local Freddy Krueger. It occurred to me that he must already be dead: only a dead man could remain so small and dim in this place.

Then something incomprehensible happened. I thought I saw Juffin scoop up his captive with enormous hands that he then rubbed together, grinding the rarified matter of the body. Then he carefully shook the remains off his hands. Mesmerized, I watched how millions of shiny specks of dust poured into the emptiness. They disappeared but were not extinguished. I couldn't explain why, but I knew that these particles continued to exist a strange, indescribable existence.

Juffin was now very close to me—so close, in fact, that he pushed me in the chest so hard that I crashed onto my own bed, just barely missing the rack of video gear.

"Sorry, boy. I think I overdid it a tad. Did you hurt yourself?" said Juffin. He was sitting on the window ledge. His predatory profile stood out against the window—a perfect profile to put on a coin.

"Is that it?" I said, smiling a silly smile. "Are we home? Everything's over?"

"Well, not everything, praise be the Magicians," said Juffin. "Our lives aren't over, for example. They go on, which may call for a little celebration. I suggest we head to the House by the Bridge and free Sir Shurf from his incarceration. He hasn't had a wink of sleep, and he hasn't been having as much fun as we have."

"Of course," I said, jumping up. Then I made a face. "I'd rather change first. I'm all covered in this darn sand."

"You'll change when you get home," said Juffin. "Let's go, Max. You'll need more than just a change. You'll need a bath, and while you're splashing in your four bathing pools, I'll start watching a movie, and poor Shurf will have to stay in his cell until noon, at least. In other words, cleaning up will have to wait. That's an order."

"As you wish. But I'll track sand all over Headquarters."

"That's definitely not going to be my problem," said Juffin. "That's why we keep the junior staff."

"I keep forgetting that we have them," I said. "Some king I am."

"You'll get used to it. It's easy to get used to such things as an army of servants. The problems begin later when you have to get out of the habit."

"Thanks. That really made me feel better," I said.

I had to gallop just to keep up with the indefatigable Sir Venerable Head, who had descended the stairs by sliding down the railing—a favorite sport of primary schoolchildren and mean sorcerers in all Worlds.

"By the way, how did you manage to stay on the Threshold?" he said when I caught up with him on the street. "I didn't dare hope you'd be able to. You're still not in the best shape after the battle."

"Easy. I just asked for permission to wait for you."

"You asked? What do you mean 'asked'?" said Juffin.

"I don't know. I just did. I even said thank you, so it's all right."

"Are you telling me that you just opened your mouth and politely expressed your request?"

"That's right. Why?"

"Well, I'll be! Congratulations, Max. Once again, you've demonstrated that life is an amazing thing. I've never heard of anything like it. You know, it very well may be that you've made a great discovery. So far as I know, no one has ever thought of talking out loud in the Corridor between Worlds. Maybe that's the easiest way to bargain with it?"

"That's exactly what I thought. And you know, I didn't even have to make an effort. Heck, I didn't even know what kind of effort I needed to make."

"I'm going to try it myself next time. Maybe it'll work. You never can tell." Juffin looked at me with candid astonishment. Technically, I was supposed to be suffering a major fit of megalomania, but I wasn't. I had probably been inoculated against it.

The House by the Bridge was quieter than usual. Such massive, porridge-thick silence you can only catch at dawn, and then only if you're lucky.

Our office was empty, but a burner with a pitcher of kamra was already standing on the desk. Sir Juffin, Magicians bless him, had sent a call to the Glutton Bunba beforehand. His order had arrived even before we did. Such promptness could well be tantamount to lifesaving, at least when it came to my life.

I fell into the armchair and grabbed my cup. Meanwhile, the boss began a heroic struggle with his own spells: I wouldn't recommend opening a Secret Door sealed by Sir Juffin Hully himself as a family pastime. He used a great deal of inappropriate language during the procedure. Finally, the evil Door was defeated.

"Am I a great wizard, or what!" said Juffin. "Sir Shurf, you are now free. Consider this to be an amnesty in honor of the coronation of your buddy, His Majesty the King of the Lands of Fanghaxra. As for my old buddy Gugimagon, he's dead as a doornail. And don't you dare tell me it's bad news."

"It is good news, indeed. It took you quite a while, did it not?" said Lonli-Lokli, closing his book. "As for me, I cannot say that I was pleased with last night's events. My Rider kept trying to get at me. I think he was particularly desperate to possess my body after you began destroying his own. It was a good thing that I had your blood, Juffin. Even after he stopped thinking I was you, your blood helped me gain control over the situation. Finally, an hour ago, I was able to relax."

"I'll be damned. That cunning Gugimagon resisted until the very last minute!" said Juffin, shaking his head in amazement. "That's why he was so listless. I think I underestimated my old buddy a little. Do you want to sit and chat with us, Sir Shurf, or do you want do go home?"

"I will stay awhile," said Lonli-Lokli, nodding and sitting next to me. "By the way, you promised to give me a lift home two days ago, Max, yet I am still here. It seems that rumors of the speed at which you drive your amobiler are slightly exaggerated. Perhaps you would care to keep your promise?"

I was stunned at his impudence. If Sir Lonli-Lokli had begun to resort to irony, I should just shut up. I didn't even try to come up with a decent retort.

"Well, if no one's planning another assault on the driver, then why not?" I said.

"And I have your stuff here somewhere, Sir Shurf," said Juffin. He fumbled in the numerous drawers of his desk, most of which, I was sure, opened up to some "fourth dimension"—they were capable of holding too much stuff. After a short search that was spiced up with a few masterpieces of cursing, the boss produced from his desk the magic box with Lonli-Lokli's death-dealing gloves. "There you go. Welcome back to the Royal Service, Sir Shurf. I'm glad that your retirement was temporary."

"Just don't put them on yet, okay?" I said. "Or I'll crash into the nearest lamppost from fear."

"All right, if it makes you feel better," said Lonli-Lokli.

He looked innocent. He scrutinized the box and shook his head.

"Why are you looking at it like that?" said Juffin. "What could possibly have happened to it?"

"Dust," said Shurf.

"Nonsense. Where would it come from in my desk?"

"Nevertheless, the box is dusty," said Lonli-Lokli. He examined the box once again and then wiped it with none other than the black-and-golden fold of my Mantle of Death. I opened my mouth and shut it again because I didn't know how to react to such unprecedented, barefaced impudence. I just stood there, opening and closing my mouth like a fish out of water.

"Unlike mine, your clothes are already dirty," he said in a brazen manner. "A little bit of dust will not make any difference."

Then he took a sip out of his cup. The issue had clearly been settled. Juffin laughed so hard that the windowpanes trembled. Finally, the humor of the situation dawned on me and I joined him. Better late than never.

"You'll make an excellent double act, gentlemen. All venues will be sold out on day one," said Juffin when he stopped laughing. "Okay, all's well that ends well. Go get some sleep, both of you."

"Can't stand looking at us anymore?" I said.

"I can't stand looking at anything. My eyelids are drooping. Plus, Kimpa's already here to take me away from this Refuge for the Mad and deliver me right under my favorite blanket."

Juffin gave a contagious yawn and left the office first.

Since Lonli-Lokli and I had combined our efforts to turn my personal amobiler into a heap of scrap metal, we took one of the official ones.

"So how do you like the book so far?" I said as we pulled off.

"Outstanding. It seems to be a legend or prophecy of some sort—I am not quite sure yet. It talks about the end of humanity."

"Oh, a dystopia," I said, yawning. "It's a popular genre. At least it's not a romance novel."

"What strange terminology," said Shurf.

"Tell me more," I said. "I forget, did I tell you I'd never read the story or heard of the author?"

"You did. Are you genuinely interested?"

"Of course I am. Do you think I'm just trying to keep up the conversation? When was the last time I was so willing to listen rather than talk? You think I can't find a topic for a long, exhausting monologue? I thought you knew me better than that."

"All right, you have convinced me. The story is about the inhabitants of your World, who suddenly begin to die out one after another: the air becomes unsuitable for breathing, or the people become unsuitable for breathing the air of their World. It seems that someone gave them the evil eye, except that the book uses a different term, which I cannot recall at the moment. Only a few hundred people survive. First they wander about by themselves, and then they find one another. It turns out that while the air was fine, they were all deeply involved in some breathing exercises—similar to those you have been too lazy to learn—and these exercises seemed to have helped them to adapt to the new air. They think that the World is coming to an end and wait for the inevitable demise. Then they realize that life goes on: the animals and plants are unaffected; only the humans have suffered. The surviving people decide to settle on an island with a good climate. If I understand it correctly, it is a special place, used for recreation."

"A resort," I said, nodding. "How does the story end?"

"I have not finished reading it, but so far, everything seems to be fine. Several years have passed since the disaster. The survivors manage to start a new life on the island and now realize that they live better than they did before the disaster. I think they stopped growing older, or perhaps the aging process has slowed down. They have almost no children: only one child has been born during the time they have been on the island, and everybody is surprised. One of the main characters decides to circumnavigate the World by means of a flying machine, the principle of operation of which is not entirely clear to me. He discovers that the places where people once lived are now inhabited by birds. A species that used to live only in cities along with people."

"Pigeons," I said. "Or sparrows?"

"Yes, pigeons. The character notices that their behavior suggests that they have become much more intelligent than they used to be. They have somehow restored the things that they found useful and destroyed the rest. The person watching them thinks that the birds have come to replace people. Then he continues his journey and arrives at an island inhabited by turtles. He can communicate with the turtles by means of something similar to our Silent Speech. The turtles tell him that a long time ago a similar disaster had struck their turtle ancestors, who had been replaced by people. And before turtles there were other 'Masters of the World'—that is what they called them.

They were trees. Let me find the exact name—perhaps it will be of importance to you." Shurf opened the book, flipped a few pages, and nodded. "Yes, the trees were called sequoias. Before the trees, there were something else—dragons of some sort, I think. This is where I have gotten to so far. A truly strange book. I have never read anything like it in my life."

"Neither have I. Now show me where to go from here. I still don't know where you live."

"You are on the right course. I will tell you when to make a turn. Max, can you fetch more books from your World? I find them much more fascinating than the movies."

"Okay, just don't tell Juffin. He's unbearable when he gets mad," I said, chuckling. "I'll try to get more books for you, Shurf. Don't get your hopes up, though: I never know beforehand what's going to turn up. What if luck abandons us and I produce an arithmetic textbook for the second grade from the Chink between Worlds? Although, knowing you, you might like it. In other words, I need to keep trying. And I will, as soon as I get some rest after my latest adventure."

"Thank you, Max. Now you should take a left. My house is on the bank of the Xuron. It is sad that you have never visited me there. I should be honored to extend my invitation to you," said Shurf.

"All roads lead to the House by the Bridge," I said, sighing. "That's the problem."

Having said goodbye to Shurf, I thought for a bit and decided it wouldn't be appropriate to barge in on a beautiful girl after my stormy adventures. What I should do, I thought, is go to my house on the Street of Yellow Stones and have a good, honest three-day-long sleep there.

Then I turned the amobiler and drove straight to Tekki's house on the Street of Forgotten Dreams. I'm an expert at making reasonable decisions—but following them through? No sirree, Bob!

Apparently Tekki had also decided to sleep for three days. In any case, she was sound asleep when I got there. Her face looked so stern that

I didn't dare ruin her plans. I got into bed next to her and conked out.

Sinning Magicians, what was I thinking! Not only had I not taken a bath, I hadn't even bothered to undress. For which I paid dearly. Not immediately, but some time later.

※

"I'm trying to find a good reason not to kill you, and I can't. Look at my bed! It's full of sand. Were you dumping sacks of it here all night?"

Tekki was pulling at my nose. Perhaps she thought it was a good idea, but it sure hurt like heck.

"You can't kill me, I'm a king! Without me, everything's going to fall apart here, and my new harem will sink in a sea of tears. Plus, you're hurting me."

"Oh, yeah?" Tekki sounded surprised, as if she had thought she was just tormenting a stone statue.

"Yeah," I said, releasing my poor nose from her tenacious fingers. "Besides, what kinds of werewolves were you looking for under my blanket? I just fell asleep."

"Just fell asleep? It's evening already."

"It is?" I said. I looked around: the windows were dark; a lantern was glowing in the far corner of the room. It was evening all right.

"I wouldn't have woken you up, but Sir Juffin sent me a call and demanded that I commit this travesty. He said he was under the impression that you should be in your office at this time of the day."

"The brute!" I said. "He's 'under the impression,' huh? Wait, has something happened?"

"I don't think so," said Tekki, smiling. "He and Sir Kofa want to watch another movie, and someone has to stay in the office. He told me himself, although he didn't want you to know."

"Oh, I see," I said. "A movie is a very good reason—I can't argue with that."

Moaning, I went downstairs to take a bath. Better late than never.

Five minutes later, I realized I was feeling great, life was great, and Juffin's office at the House by the Bridge was a great place to spend the night. Better late than never, indeed.

The Armstrong & Ella was empty. Praise be the Magicians, it did happen from time to time: the local drunks, like the ocean waters, are subject to the mysterious forces of ebbs and flows. Today they were on the ebb. I was in luck.

"Now open your mouth and tell me everything," said Tekki, putting a pitcher of the best kamra in the Universe in front of me. "I have the right to derive some pleasure from our horrible relationship."

"Yeah, we've really been missing out on the pleasure side recently," I said. "Wait, how about the wonderful show you and Melamori were watching yesterday? The fat men in leotards? You were both glued to the set. That's my doing, if you remember. Who else could have brought you that horrendous entertainment from the other end of the Universe but me?"

"You're right. I forgot about that," said Tekki. "Still, spill it out! I'm sure you've got a dozen or two mind-boggling stories under your tongue."

"Just two. But both are pretty mind-boggling, you're right. One is about the dastardly Magician Gugimagon and his evildoing in the Corridor between Worlds. The other is about my harem. Which do you want to hear first?"

"The one about the harem, of course. All those silly mystical escapades of yours and Juffin's pale in comparison with this romantic drama," said Tekki. "Sir Melifaro, by the way, kept bugging me all day, trying to find out any savory details. I don't remember what I told him just to get rid of him. So I'm warning you, I'm not going take the blame for it."

"Neither will I. He'll have to die of envy," I said. "Okay, so here's the harem story."

And I told her an abridged version of my coronation that culminated in my receiving the most absurd gift of my life. Tekki listened carefully, sometimes nodding in approval but never interrupting me or making a comment. It was a little suspicious. Usually she interrupted me after the second sentence.

"That was a strange story," she said after I finished, and reached for the cookies that I was having for breakfast.

"It is, isn't it?" I said. "And very untimely. I feel like I've suddenly become the father of a very large family. They are just too young, these so-called wives of mine. I guess they need educating and coaching in manners. For starters, someone has to teach them how to wear the looxi and use tableware, like old Kimpa once taught me. But I don't even know where to begin. On the other hand, I could forget all about it and leave everything as it is, but that wouldn't be right, would it? I don't think their careers as my wives will be very long-lasting. In any case, they deserve better. At the very least, they'll have to learn how to stand up on their own two feet."

"Well, I can teach them how to dress and so on. But you'll have to tell them to obey me. I'm sure they'll make good students, given their origins. Their legendary mother, that Isnouri—she's the strangest thing in this whole story, Max. I have heard plenty of stories of the creatures that inhabited the Barren Lands in the old times. You may have ended up with the most wonderful piece of the most remarkable of all the old legends."

"I'd rather have ended up empty-handed," I said. "I don't think I'll make a good guardian. I never even had enough time for Armstrong and Ella. I only played with them every now and then, and then put the burden of taking care of the kittens onto your shoulders. A regular swine is what I am. And these girls are people—they will probably require quite a bit more time than the cats."

"I wouldn't jump to conclusions, if I were you," said Tekki, laughing. "Cats, people . . . If only it were that simple. How do you know what they are, those three sisters, and what they need from you?" She stopped laughing and showed me the door. "Okay, go to the House by the Bridge before your furious boss comes here spitting purple flames out of his fire-breathing mouth. Back during the Troubled Times, he was too lazy to kill me, even after the admonitions of that paranoid old Magician Nuflin. If he now learns that you have been delayed because of me, I'm as good as dead."

"I know. If Juffin can't watch a movie three nights in a row, we all face some truly dire consequences," I said. "But it's completely unfair on his part. I have the right to a personal life."

"Speaking of your personal life, I think I'm going to go straighten things out with your harem," said Tekki, "and admire the palace while I'm at it. I've always wanted to have a dozen servants, and here's my chance. Please send them a call and tell them that they should prostrate themselves as soon as they hear my voice and quiver in anticipation of my orders."

"That's cute," I said. "You should be sitting on that throne, not me."

"Deal," said Tekki. "The next throne is mine."

And I left the Armstrong & Ella.

"Ah, finally!" Juffin was about to fling his arms around my neck. "You should have been here three hours ago. What have you been doing all this time?"

"Believe it or not, I was sleeping," I said.

"With all your wives at once?" That was Melifaro's voice coming from behind me.

I didn't flinch at the remark. I sat down in the armchair, yawned, and smiled a languorous smile.

"With my wives, the wives of my ministers, the wives of their servants, and all the other wives I could get my hands on," I said, winking, and turned to Juffin. "But as soon as I remembered I had a girlfriend, you had to go and spoil everything."

Juffin was inexorable. "I see. You were counting on two extra Days of Freedom. Sorry, you're not getting any. If you've noticed, last night I was just as busy as some other people, but I came to work right after noon."

"You are in a different league altogether. I'm still too young and inexperienced."

I looked over at Melifaro. The poor boy was completely distraught. After Juffin had said he had also been busy last night, Melifaro looked like he might start tearing his hair out.

"Okay, I'm off," said Juffin. He was already in the doorway. "I'm off to witness something much more entertaining than your interrogation under torture, courtesy of this innocent victim of a monogamous society. Listen carefully: if you dare take me away from the TV tonight, I'm going to turn you into the Pink Panther."

"Why the Pink Panther?"

"It would be the easy: you're the spitting image of him already," said Juffin, and he left Melifaro and me alone.

Melifaro was sizing me up, his eyes burning with curiosity. He wasn't a man but a living and breathing question mark.

"If you want me to talk, you must feed me first," I said. "You can imagine my appetite after such a wild night."

"Yes, I can," said Melifaro. "But who's going to stay in the office? Kurush?"

"He's been up for it all along," I said, stroking the buriwok. "They only called me down here so I'd know who's boss. But since I am already here, it makes no sense to leave right away. It would be logical to have the food delivered."

"Absolutely." Melifaro was so interested in my "cooperation with the authorities" that he didn't show off or try to mock my idea of spending the evening in the office. Instead, he immediately sent a call to the Glutton Bunba, and minutes later I was enjoying a hearty breakfast.

"So what's the life of the master of a harem like?" said Melifaro.

"Mmm, it's really something, let me tell you," I said with my mouth full. "The most eventful night of my life. First I slid down Xumgat, then I fell apart in Xumgat, then I stayed in Xumgat, then—"

"Hold on, Max. What are you talking about?"

I decided that a joke that went on too long was a sign of bad taste. "Forget it. I was joking. Look at me: Do you see the 'master of a harem'?"

"Well, Tekki told me that—"

"But of course she did," I said. "You know how she usually is. She was joking, too."

"Darn it," said Melifaro, shaking his head. "That's not a good joke. I didn't believe her at first, but then I thought that with you, one could expect anything."

"One could, indeed," I said. "I have nothing against expectations."

An hour later, I was alone. After the story about my polygamous relationships had turned into a report about the battle with Gugimagon, Melifaro had begun to doze off. I walked him to his amobiler, returned to the office, put my feet up on the messy desk, and realized that my life had returned to normal—although that was a matter of opinion.

The days were flying like butterflies in the wind. Before I knew it, a whole dozen had gone by.

"Max, will it kill you to drop by the Furry House and see the results of my labors?" said Tekki one morning. "Don't pretend you want to sleep now. You do that at work all night long."

"You read me like an open book," I said. "No, I'm not going to sleep now, but that doesn't mean I won't find other pleasant things to do."

Still, two hours later, I had to get up, wash, and get dressed. Even shave. Tekki had taken it into her head that she had to drag me to my royal residence, and she succeeded.

To my surprise, I found the house quite livable—and lived in. Tekki had a talent for turning royal palaces into cozy abodes suitable for ordinary people. My friend Droopy, the huge shaggy dog I hadn't visited in all this time, rushed out to greet us.

"Oh, shame on me! How could I forget about you, buddy?" I said, hugging the dog, who was overcome with joy. "See? Your master is a swine. Why does he still love me?"

"Because he's still not very smart, Max," said Tekki. "He's a puppy."

"A puppy!" I almost fainted. "This thing?"

"The sheepdogs from the Barren Lands are the largest dogs in the World. Didn't you know?"

"I didn't," I said, shaking my head. "I'd better not fall out with him." Although, looking at the dog's good-natured mug, I couldn't imagine I could ever fall out with him.

"Good day, Sir Max," said the cute triplets.

My "wives" had undergone a drastic change in these few days. The elegant looxis that had replaced their short warm jackets suited them perfectly. Only their huge eyes—all three pairs of them—still betrayed a guarded look.

"Very good," I said. "'Sir Max' sounds much better than 'Lord Fanghaxra.' Now, if they could just drop the 'Sir.'"

"They think they should be polite," said Tekki.

"With me? That's nonsense," I said, smiling.

I was a little shy myself, though not as shy as they were. I think Tekki knew that, judging by that playful look she gave me.

"I think you and I should take them for a short walk," she said.

"As you wish, ma'am," I said. "Your wish is my command. I'm just a little barbarian king. You are the ultimate truth. Like Sir Lonli-Lokli, but much more beautiful."

"Now we're talking," said Tekki. "Off you go to start up the amobiler."

After this exchange, the triplets began looking at her as though she were an omnipotent being. I decided to level the final blow. "Everybody talks to me like this here, girls. You're very unfortunate. You were married off to a king with no authority. Next time, you should be more careful."

The sisters blinked in surprise, but one of them giggled quietly, covering her mouth with her hand.

"This is Xelvi," said Tekki. "Xeilax and Kenlex are serious ladies."

"Well, somebody has to be. So where do you ladies want me to drop you off?"

"You don't need to drop them off anywhere. Just show them the Old City. Then we'll see."

I seated the doe-eyed girls in my new amobiler and drove around the Right Bank for two hours at the lowest speed I could manage—no more than thirty miles an hour. I reasoned that the girls' nervous systems were still too weak for faster rides.

Tekki had the natural talent of a first-class guide. The girls listened to her raptly, their mouths agape. I recalled Juffin's strange lecture about how Tekki was a mirror that reflected her interlocutor and thought it would be interesting to see the four of them alone. That might be a surprising sight. I gave it another thought and decided I had had enough surprises for the time being.

Max, are you busy now? Melifaro's call was most timely. My new job as a school bus driver was certainly not the job of a lifetime, and I was tired already.

I am. I'm so busy you wouldn't believe it if I told you. But if you're hinting at dinner for you and me, then I'm free as a bird.

You're clairvoyant. Come then. I haven't decided where to go yet.

How about Moxi's? I haven't been there in a while. It's a quiet place, not too many people.

Oh, the famous Juffin's Dozen? That's a great idea. See you there in fifteen minutes.

"Okay. The tour is over," I told Tekki and the girls. "And no whining. That will get you nowhere with me. Tekki, stop trying to tear off my ear—you didn't let me finish! We're going somewhere for lunch. Thank you, my dear. So nice of you to let me live."

Mr. Moxi Faa was inimitable, as usual. He grumbled a hello, his leather looxi squeaking, sized up my female company with a stern look, gave me a reproachful look, and then slammed a heavy menu down on the table. I thought he was fighting the temptation to smack me in the head with it. But that's Moxi for you.

Soon Melifaro arrived. When he saw the company I was keeping, his jaw fell onto his chest with a loud crack. These are the moments that make life worth living, I thought. All the rest is piffle.

For two minutes, Melifaro was silent. He opened his mouth, thought for a bit, then closed it again. Before this, I wouldn't have thought it possible. He continued to be silent throughout the entire lunch. He did drop a few words, but compared to his usual garrulous self, he was absolutely mute.

The sisters didn't say much, either. They were still very shy, but more than that, the lunch was their first test at using tableware. I could only feel for them. Tekki watched over them like a schoolteacher. The girls turned red, then grew pale and dropped the pie tongs on the floor—just as I had done not so long ago.

As for the table talk, all credit went to Moxi. He used the opportunity to mumble a long lecture on the unique cultures of the peoples of the World whose cuisines we had just dared to sample. I didn't remember a single word of it, but Moxi sure did relieve the tension.

At last our social event came to an end.

"No other client has ever brought so many women with him at one time," said Moxi, handing me the bill. "Congratulations, Sir Max, this is a record. Have a nice day and come again." He said it as though he was forbidding me ever to cross the threshold of Juffin's Dozen again. But that was the zest that made Juffin's fellow countryman the best tavern keeper in Echo. Where else could you get excellent food and a good reprimand thrown into the bargain, and at that price?

Melifaro seemed to have forgotten that he had to go back to work. He sat in the back seat of my amobiler, crowding the triplets, who had grown very quiet. He looked befuddled—a sight to behold.

I drove the sisters back home, and then there were just three of us. Tekki gave Melifaro a searching look and burst into laughter. I couldn't contain myself, either.

"Yeah, yeah, very funny," said Melifaro. But it was too late: we couldn't stop. Then Melifaro said something that almost killed me. "Max, will you get too mad if I lure one of your wives away from you?"

"Which one?" I said and burst out laughing again.

"I . . . don't know," he said. "Is there a difference?"

"Of course there is," said Tekki. "A big difference. First you'll have to guess which one of them stepped onto your heart."

"Oh, that's not a problem," said Melifaro. "If push comes to shove, I can use some magic here. I hope the boss won't throw his best employee in Xolomi for such a trivial breach of the law."

"His what employee?" I said. "I certainly hope he won't throw you in Xolomi, either. There's no way I'd let any of my wives have anything to do with a criminal. So watch your step with the law."

"Are you giving me official permission?" said Melifaro, brightening up.

"As if you need it," I said. "Do what you want, friend. It's your life. Issuing permission is not my area of expertise. I'm a simple barbarian king. I don't decide anything."

"You're so modest, Your Majesty," said Melifaro.

"Yeah, kings have their quirks," said Tekki.

I listened to them with half an ear. I had been meaning to find out whether I could drive the amobiler with my eyes closed, since this mysterious vehicle, as I had once been told, submitted to the will of the driver. And I decided to try it now. Just like that, out of the blue.

Well, whaddya know? It worked.

Curiouser and curiouser, Alice's voice echoed in my head. Yup, curiouser and curiouser. I couldn't have said it better myself.

TWO

ORDINARY MAGICAL THINGS

"JUST WALK BESIDE ME AND DON'T BE AFRAID OF ANYTHING," I SAID to Droopy.

The enormous shaggy creature was clinging to my leg—well, not exactly my leg. The dog's size allowed it to stick its moist noise in my armpit while still standing on all fours, yet the monster was trembling with fear. For the first time, I had decided to break the solitary existence of the honorable guard of my royal residence and take him out for a walk around Echo. The hustle and bustle of midday Old City overwhelmed the "puppy."

"Not exactly what you're used to seeing in the Barren Lands, huh?" I said. "It's not that bad, though. You can't imagine how lucky you are that I'm not walking you down Fifth Avenue in Manhattan."

Alas, Droopy lacked the necessary information (and imagination, for that matter) to realize just how lucky he was. Still, he somehow managed to make his first firm step out into the heart of the terrifying city.

As soon as Droopy climbed into the amobiler, however, things got better: he sprawled on the soft leather of the back seat, relieved, as though he had returned home after a long absence.

"I see now," I said. "We like taking a ride, don't we? Who would've thought."

Naturally, I set off for the House by the Bridge then and there. To show off. I just had to show my wonderful dog to everyone I knew. And where else could I find the maximum concentration of familiar faces at noon if not at the Ministry of Perfect Public Order?

My four-legged friend liked the House by the Bridge at first sight. Apparently, we saw eye-to-eye on certain matters. True, the dog first rushed to the side occupied by the City Police. I ran after him trying to prevent an interdepartmental disaster.

Fortunately, Droopy ran into Lieutenant Apurra Blookey—the best candidate for an introduction to the neighboring organization. By the time I caught up with the dog, the two were already hugging and sniffing each other.

"He didn't scare you, did he, Apurra?" I said.

"Oh, no, Sir Max. How could this beautiful boy scare anyone! He's the friendliest thing in the universe!"

"I completely agree with you, but if this behemoth had sprung out from around a corner, it sure would've scared the bejeezus out of me. Thank goodness it wasn't General Boboota, or we'd all need earplugs."

"Indeed," said the lieutenant. "But I love dogs. Where did you get this one? I've never in my life seen anything like it."

"That's because you're not in the habit of spending your vacation in the Barren Lands," I said.

"Oh, so he's from your homeland?"

"Yes. Technically, I'm supposed to have a few hundred of these for protection—I'm not sure from what, though. Fortunately, my subjects had enough brains to bring me just one monster."

"On the contrary, it's very unfortunate. Trust me, there are plenty of people in the Capital who would love to have a dog like this at any price."

"Bah. Can't believe how stupid I was. I could've sold dogs in between my shifts—better yet, during my shifts, because I'm supposed to sit on my throne in between them. Quite an idea!"

"Certainly. It didn't occur to me that all your time was occupied," said Apurra.

"If you want me to, I can ask my subjects to bring another one for you. They'd be grateful if I asked them for anything at all. Until now, I've only requested one thing: no more gifts. Did you know that those crazy nomads brought me three identical wives?"

"Yes, Lady Kekki Tuotli told me. She and Sir Kofa have taken the girls out to dinner a few times."

"Right," I said, smirking. "Sir Kofa loves taking neophytes out. So nice of him to be the girls' guardian. I can only imagine what they're going to turn into after a year in his company. Well, I'm happy that you and Droopy have become friends, but now I'm going to try to drag this creature back to our side."

"Of course," said Lieutenant Apurra, nodding. "You know, Sir Max, if your subjects can bring another dog, I'll be happy to take it into my care."

"They sure can," I said. "Remind me about it from time to time, though. My head is full of holes as it is. This will be my first stern command. After all, I've got to give them commands every now and then to maintain my reputation as a tyrant."

I grabbed Droopy by the scruff of his shaggy neck, and we marched to the side of the House by the Bridge occupied by the Secret Investigative Force.

My colleagues had just gathered in the Hall of Common Labor for collective consumption of kamra and cookies. Even Lookfi Pence had come down from the Main Archive for this occasion. The only one missing was Sir Kofa Yox. He must have been out lapping up fresh rumors in the city taverns, as he was supposed to do.

"Gotcha!" I said. "Gobbling down delicacies, thinking you can get away with it, huh? Thought I'd never show up? Well, you thought wrong. Here I am. And I brought a sponger with me."

"Who would have thought you'd love your job so much?" said Sir

Juffin. "If I remember correctly, your shift doesn't start for another seven or eight hours."

"You do remember correctly, Juffin, but I thought you'd eat everything up if I didn't show up sooner."

"Sinning Magicians, what's this!" said Melamori, who was already snuggling up to my dog. "I had no idea there were dogs this big!"

"I'm told he's still a puppy," I said. "So he's going to grow even bigger."

"Oh, he's so cute!" Melamori was completely enamored. She squeezed and hugged the dog so vigorously it looked like she was playing an accordion. The rest of the gang was slightly less enthusiastic. Juffin and Melifaro had already seen the dog. Lonli-Lokli maintained his trademark imperturbability, and Sir Lookfi didn't even notice him. He was fumbling with a cookie, probably counting the number of crumbs that comprised it.

"Now you're not the only one who walks the halls of the Department with a furry creature," I said and winked at Melamori. "Speaking of furry creatures, where's yours?"

"He's sleeping in Melifaro's office. These gentlemen think that a hoob has no place at their table, you see," said Melamori.

"You guys don't seem to be very good at loving nature," I said, reproaching my colleagues.

"It's nature that doesn't seem to love us," said Melifaro. "That Arvaroxian spider tried to bite me the other day."

"Liar!" said Melamori. "First, it's not a spider; it's a hoob. Second, Leleo doesn't have any teeth; he has whiskers."

"He doesn't? What was he trying to bite me with, then?" said Melifaro.

"I seem to have become a zookeeper at some point without noticing it," said Juffin with a sigh. "I consider this to be a demotion. What do you think?"

"Well, it depends," I said, sitting down at the table. "Until now, you were the head of a Refuge for the Mad. The smallest in the entire Unified Kingdom—though maybe the most fun."

"How nice of you to call things by their names," said the boss. "All these strange people insist on addressing our organization as the Minor Secret Investigative Force. What nonsense!"

"I have a business proposal for you," I said, turning to Melamori. "You stroke my dog and I finish your cold cup of kamra. Deal?"

"Hmm. The price seems to be about right," she said. "I think I'll accept without haggling."

About an hour later, Juffin decided it was time for him to get some work done, and my presence was not facilitating favorable working conditions. "I have a special mission for you, Melamori," he said in a dramatic tone. "The most difficult of all the missions you've had so far. I'm not even sure you'll manage."

Melamori's pretty face showed absolute concern and concentration. "Has something happened?" she said in a whisper.

"You bet it has! The Secret Force cannot operate: the building is crawling with foreign monarchs and pets. I want you to kick them out one by one and make sure they don't land on my poor head for the next two or three hours."

"Are you telling me that Max and I can go take a walk?" said Melamori. "Just like that, apropos of nothing? Oh, Sir Juffin, you're wonderful!"

"I know I am," said the boss.

"She's going to fail the mission," said Melifaro. "You should give it to me. I'll make sure he stays out for half a year, not just two or three hours."

"No can do," said Juffin. "You're too indispensable. Nothing will induce me to part with you before tonight. You still have that boring case at the Customs hanging over you. Sir Shurf, that means you, too."

"I was just about to ask you how long you were going to ignore that unfortunate incident," said Lonli-Lokli. He got up from the table and carefully straightened out the folds of his snow-white looxi. "May I count on finding you in the Armstrong & Ella when I am finished, Max, or should I look for you elsewhere?"

"Elsewhere be damned, if you are going to pay me an official visit," I said. "In any case, I was going to drop by and see Tekki an hour before dusk, or even earlier."

"Then I will stop by there on my way home," said Shurf.

"I'll wait for you here," said Melifaro. "Recently, our Venerable Head has taken a fancy to the aroma of my toil and sweat, so there's no chance I can sneak out of here for many long hours."

"How sagacious of you," said Juffin. "Sir Max, you're still here? Scram, or I'll find a job for you, too!"

"Ooh, now I'm scared," I said, but made a move to leave, nevertheless.

Droopy was lying in the middle of the room. I grabbed him by his huge ear with one hand, and with the other I grabbed Melamori's sharp elbow. I was so happy I was ready to dole out hugs and kisses to strangers.

"Whose dog is this?" said Lookfi. "Yours, Sir Max?"

Now he was so interested in the dog that he managed to knock someone's empty cup off the table. I had already lost all hope that he'd ever notice my pet.

"Mine and no one else's," I said.

"It's been so long since you and I took a walk together," I said as Melamori and I were getting into the amobiler. "Last time was when we heroically saved poor Moxi from the deadly grip of the greatest poet-cannibal in history—if one can consider that a walk at all."

"Why not? It was a walk, and the moon was full, if I remember right."

"You remember right. So, where to? The sky is the limit, right?"

"Let's go to the former Residence of the Order of the Secret Grass,

Max. Remember, they have that beautiful garden, and they also serve excellent drinks. It's not too cold today. We can sit outside. You liked it there, didn't you?"

"Yes sirree," I said.

Then I realized that a thin veil of vague regret had suddenly fallen upon my good mood. It had all happened a long, long time ago, and I had had very specific plans concerning this wonderful lady. Plans that, as it later turned out, had fallen through. Vain efforts. A pie in the sky. We were "just friends." Oh, well.

"Sorry, Max, this won't do," said Melamori, worried. "If you're going to be all sad about it, who's going to lift the heavy boulder from my silly heart?"

"Droopy. He's born to do that sort of work. Also, what makes you think I'm sad?"

"You know, if you want to control your facial expressions half as well as Sir Lonli-Lokli, you have a long way to go," said Melamori and laughed. "All right, let's pretend that I was wrong about it. Now let's go."

We drove to the New City, found the right street, left the amobiler by the gate, and entered the huge neglected garden. Two years ago, when Melamori had first dragged me into this place, it had been late evening. The garden had been bathed in a bluish light from tiny glass balls filled with glowing gas. Now it was daytime and the transparent glass of the lamps glimmered in the winter sun. The rest was exactly the same. The air of this magnificent place was again cool and crystal clear. The greenery was as fragrant as I remembered. Ideal conditions for an acute resurgence of a case of unfulfilled longing.

We sat down on a bench nestled between the evergreen Kaxxa bushes. Droopy ran off and returned with a stick in his teeth, which he dropped at my feet. Dogs in all Worlds share the very same notions about how to make their masters happy. But I paid no attention to his efforts.

"Well, lady, you're doing a number on me," I said with a sad smile. "Just moments ago I was feeling great, and now I'm again the same guy who sat with you here two years ago. What am I supposed to do with him?"

"Nothing," said Melamori. "When we leave here, that guy from two years ago will vanish of his own accord. Can you suffer for thirty minutes or so?"

"Sure," I said. "There's even something nice about it."

"There sure is. Could you order me something strong? Getting smashed in this garden in your company once every two years—I'm beginning to come up with my very own tradition that anyone can be proud of, huh?"

"What's not to be proud of? A person can be proud of anything if he's determined enough," I said, my mind wandering elsewhere.

Droopy decided he needed more attention and didn't hesitate to show it. He put his huge shaggy legs on my shoulders and licked my nose. The next thing I knew, I was lying on my back on the ground, floundering, my feet in the air, like a giant bug trapped by a gang of young nature lovers. Frightened, the author of my shame sat down on his hind legs. Apparently they didn't give dogs a pat on the back for such behavior in the Barren Lands.

Melamori laughed a tinkling laugh. "You sure can cheer me up when you want to, Max! I should be buying you a drink to reward you for amusing me like that. It was brilliant!"

"I'm taking you up on that," I said, struggling to get up. "And give me a hand, or I'll amuse all the waiters here completely free of charge."

Melamori grabbed my hand and returned me to an upright position without losing a beat. She was a strong lady. She kept her word and ordered us some exotic booze. I'd never met anyone whose tastes were so different from mine. During the tasting, I had to exert a great deal of effort to make it look like I was enjoying the drink. It would have been rude to make expressions of disgust upon imbibing a drink chosen by a beautiful lady.

Things were getting better: my "bug" stunt, combined with a hefty dose of the strange bitter beverage, did a quick job of chasing away the clouds that had started gathering over my mood. I was again the Max of the present, the happy slapdash owner of the Mantle of Death, the experienced sorcerer from the Secret Investigative Force, the novice traveler through Xumgat. The love-struck nutcase I had been two years ago was gone. Good riddance, I thought, to him and other ghosts from the past.

I was so happy about my quick return to my beloved self that Droopy got a much greater share of caresses than he deserved after what he had done. The dog was wagging his long ears: he had no idea he could wag his tail like his fellow dogs in my home World.

"See? I'm totally fine now," I said, smiling at Melamori. "A brazen, complacent son of a gun. Exactly the way I like to be. Does this vacant gaze, the mindless glint of my eyes, suit me? What color are they now, by the way? I'll bet they're blue!"

Melamori grew very serious. She stared into my eyes for a good minute and then said, "No way, Max. They're yellow, like Kurush's. Well, almost—a little darker."

"That's something new," I said. "By the way, it was you who first noticed that my eyes change color. And you reported this phenomenon to me at this very spot, remember?"

"How can I forget it? It had been one of the most stubborn of mysteries to me. I came up with the craziest explanations. I'm ashamed to admit it, but I even wondered whether Loiso Pondoxo's infamous promise to return to life and come back from hell had come true. Stop laughing! I grew up hearing and reading about the mysterious disappearances and returns of great ancient Magicians. They were my bedtime stories. Our house was chock-full of these books. And dinner conversations? I wish you could have heard them, Max! By the way, it's all your fault. You should've just said right away that you had come from another World."

"I don't think so," I said. "'From another World,' you say? Nah. You're all brave now, sure, but back then? I'd like to see how you would've taken it. Plus, Juffin had told me not to tell anyone, though I still don't understand why he pretended that my origin was such a big mystery and why you guys were left in the dark about it all that time."

"It was something of a test," said Melamori with a sigh. "Not for you, for us. We were supposed to solve that little mystery by ourselves. Unfortunately, I turned out to be the dumbest pupil in the entire Secret Investigative Force. But I know why: a personal interest always dulls the mind. Sir Kofa and Shurf had guessed way earlier. Lookfi doesn't count. He can't be bothered with such trivia."

"That's all right," I said, comforting her. "You beat Melifaro, which wasn't too shabby, either."

"Are you kidding, Max?" said Melamori. "Melifaro knew everything the moment you guys met. He just looked at you and knew it. It happens to him sometimes. True, he doesn't like to boast about his abilities, but you might have guessed."

"Ouch," I said. "Don't count on taking away the honorary title of Biggest Dummy of the Secret Investigative Force. That title has already been taken by yours truly. Seriously, until now, I'd been absolutely sure that Melifaro was the only one who still believed the silly story about the Barren Lands that Juffin and I made up. Believed it despite everything, just because it makes things funnier."

"That's partly true. He's so used to playing along that sometimes he forgets which one of your biographies is the real one. Then again, he couldn't care less."

"Instead of this nonsense"—I waved my palm with the ancient letters of my "True Name" written on it in front of Melamori's nose—"instead of this nonsense, this should read, in plain language, 'People are not what they seem.' And I should begin my day with a mandatory mantra of this simple truth. Otherwise I'm going to fall victim to yet another predictable surprise."

"Don't say that! You shouldn't give other people so much credit. If any old person could take you by surprise, we would be living in a completely different, incredible World—terrifying, yet beautiful," said Melamori. "But that's a big 'if.' I don't think you should write any such words on your palm. In any case, I'm not going to be the one to surprise you. That I can promise. I think I'm exactly what I seem. Maybe a little dumber. And maybe far more cowardly."

"Good golly, Melamori," I said. "What's with all the self-criticism all of a sudden? You have a duty to love and cherish yourself. You can't entrust others with such a momentous task."

"I'm not so sure about that," said Melamori. "I've been disgusted with myself recently. I'm tired of dealing with the consequences of my own stupidity and cowardice."

"Are you regretting not having gone to Arvarox with Aloxto?" I finally understood what the whole conversation was about. "But that's exactly one of those rare occasions when you can change everything. He's coming back in a year, give or take a few days."

"Even sooner," said Melamori in a gloomy tone. "You know, I managed to talk Kamshi into giving the Arvaroxians their precious 'filthy Mudlax' this spring. I convinced him that Aloxto's warriors and their encampment by the ferry were spoiling the landscape. Well, that alone wouldn't have been enough to convince him, of course, but it so happened that I was the proud owner of a small piece of information about a minor job violation that could've cost that stubborn warden his career. Yes, Max, I resorted to blackmailing a high-ranking government official: my kin in the Order of the Seven-Leaf Clover would be proud of my performance.

"Anyway, I then sent a call to Aloxto. He's happy, of course. He can manage to live without me, more or less, but he dreams of his long-lost 'filthy Mudlax' every day, nonstop. So our magnificent Sir Allirox has already put his 'two times fifty Sharptooths' on a ship and is bound for Echo, sword in hand. He dreams of beheading that poor, hapless king who lost some stupid war. They should be here come spring—that is, in two or three dozen days, barring any mishaps on the way. Then again, what accident could befall such a horde of herculean studs?" Melamori's voice was full of anger and derision. I couldn't believe my ears.

"Wait, then I totally don't understand why you seem to be growing gloomier and gloomier by the day," I said.

Up until then I was sure that the reason for her permanent depression was the absence of the blond beauty boy Aloxto Allirox. Now that her reunion with him was in the cards, things should have been looking up for her. Or not?

Melamori punched the bench with her little clenched fist. I watched a few splinters fly off in different directions following this careless gesture of my elfin interlocutor.

"Of course you understand it perfectly!" she said, irritated. Then she tempered justice with mercy, and ire with sorrow. "No, I guess you don't. I'm sorry, I didn't mean it like that. It's not going to happen, Max. It will be just like before. I'm going to weigh everything again, and again I'll come to the conclusion that the better is the enemy of the good. My parents would be proud to know how well they've raised me. I used to think I was so brave, strong, and independent. Now I don't think so anymore. My mother's carping that 'a lady shouldn't hang around strange places by herself' doesn't faze me a bit when I'm determined to go out and have some fun. But when I begin to think about leaving everything behind and going to Arvarox, it turns into a powerful mantra. A spell. A curse. Once I close my eyes and imagine how I disembark the ship and step onto an alien shore, I start thinking that Mother was right: a lady shouldn't hang around strange places by herself."

"Well, I can relate," I said. "I don't think I'd have the guts to up and leave for Arvarox myself. You'd have to be some big-time hero to survive there, what with all their crazy customs."

"You wouldn't have the guts?" said Melamori. "That's a bald-faced lie if I've ever heard one, Max! You had the guts to up and leave your own World, the place you were born, and come here. Going to Arvarox is nothing compared to that."

"Trust me, for me the decision to leave was much easier. I was just lucky. I had nothing to lose there, where I was born. Absolutely nothing. Life sucked. But for someone who was about to run away to another World, that was an ideal situation. One couldn't have wished for anything better. You, on the other hand, have something to lose. Am I right?"

"Of course I do," said Melamori. Then she paused and shook her head. "It's only an illusion, Max. In fact, I also have nothing to lose. Of course, I love Echo and love my job. There are a lot of nice people around whom I love to spend time with, but none of that matters. Let me tell you something. Back then, when I refused to go with Aloxto, my main motive wasn't my love and attachment to everything I had to lose. My decision was governed by caution. Cowardice, rather. Panic in the face of the unknown, to call things by their true names."

"Kurush would have said something like 'Humans tend to fear the unknown,' and he would've been right," I said. "Fear is the most fundamental human quality. It's probably even more significant than other anthropological traits."

"And yet I'm sitting next to the person who once decided to set out on a journey between Worlds," said Melamori. She touched my shoulder, as though my material existence could be a forcible argument for her claim. "This means that this 'fundamental human quality,' as you put it, the fear of the unknown, can be overcome. In my case, it's simply a journey to another continent. Nothing out of the ordinary."

"You know, I think it's even simpler." I decided to be blunt. "If you really want to leave with Aloxto, you will. If not, then you won't. Isn't that what it all comes down to?"

"Oh, Max, you're so funny!" said Melamori. "What's Aloxto got to do with any of this?"

I was taken aback. "What do you mean? You had one heck of an affair with him, which shocked all your relatives, certain Secret Investigators, and Echo in its entirety, to boot."

"It doesn't matter what I had with him, or what I will have," she said impatiently. "Aloxto is an unusual creature. He swept me off my feet, I lost my head, whatever—I know, I know. But passion is just passion, Max. You and I both know very well that a person is capable of saying no to his passion, and it doesn't mean that his life goes to rack and ruin. Do you really think that I'm suffering only because, only because—"

"Yes," I said. "Until now, that was exactly what I had thought. Was that silly of me?"

"Silly? No. A bit too romantic for my taste." Melamori's mood had visibly improved. "Maybe I'd even want you to be right," she said. "One true love, broken hearts, they kiss, they die—in the end, everybody cries. But my actual problem lies elsewhere. I only knew what I was really worth when I declined to go with the beautiful blond giant Aloxto. At first, I thought he was offering me a romantic voyage, very much to my taste. I was very excited and almost said yes. But then I got scared, so scared that I couldn't breathe, couldn't sleep, couldn't even budge. I should've realized it sooner, when I felt so scared of you and your strange dreams. I should've asked myself, 'What are you so afraid of? Your own cowardice?' But I hadn't yet learned to uncover the reasons for my own actions, dispassionately and without bias."

She gulped down the rest of her drink, tossed the glass away, and dropped her head onto her arms. Now her voice sounded muffled, as though it came from the depths of her bodily crypt, where under the vault of a happy human life and charming flesh, the real Melamori—a beautiful, weightless creature I had barely known until now—was suffocating.

"The fact is, I'm governed by my banal cowardice and banal attachment to the familiar. True, it won't kill you. In fact, many people live long and happy lives with it. They have families and raise children, future little cowards, much to their loving mothers' joy and satisfaction. I am alive and well and quite attractive. But in light of what I've just said, I find it very difficult to respect myself. I shouldn't have boasted about my one-of-a-kind life. Mom was right: a lady from a good family should live a life of propriety. Get it, Max? Pro-pri-e-ty. I guess propriety is what I opted for. It's who I am now."

For all intents and purposes, Melamori should have burst out crying long before reaching that conclusion. Instead, her rigid gaze was fixed somewhere straight ahead, her eyes completely dry.

"Did you decide to discuss all this with me because you thought I was an expert in radical change of one's place of abode?" I said. "Well, I guess you're right. On the other hand, I couldn't have imagined sitting here with you and trying to persuade you to forsake Echo for the devil knows where. It sends shivers down my spine thinking that I might come to the House by the Bridge one day and you won't be there."

"That isn't going to happen," said Melamori. "Your devil can't possibly know where that 'where' is because I'm not going there. For better or for worse."

"You never know what's going to happen when a good person realizes he has to turn the world upside down just so he can carry on living somehow," I said. "You know, when I was seventeen, I realized that I couldn't—didn't want to—live with my parents. But it took me another year and a half to muster the courage to leave because, just like you, I'm a creature of habit. And deep down inside, I was sure I wouldn't be able to make it on my own, however silly that might sound. I did go through some hard times, but I made it, as you can see. I still think it was the most daring thing I've done in my life. The rest just unraveled on its own once I got the ball rolling. You know, there are two things that can help a lot in this situation."

"What two things?" Melamori stared at me, her mouth agape. My candor had taken her by surprise.

"First, it's your stubbornness. You can't imagine what a person can do in spite of something. Doesn't matter what you do or in spite of what you do it—you just do it. And you have plenty of stubbornness in you. Way more than I do, trust me."

"Maybe I do," said Melamori, cheering up. "What's the second thing?"

"The second thing is fate," I said. "Sounds too bombastic, doesn't it? Yet when fate has plans for us, it finds the means to make us act according to its script. If there is a reason for you to go to Arvarox, fate will keep throwing the opportunity at you over and over again until you do what it wants you to do. That troublemaker fate is also in the habit of making the clouds gather overhead when we resist its persuasion. Only once did you refuse to do what it wanted you to do, and your life has become much worse than it used to be. Fate is very good at persuading us. On those rare occasions that it fails to persuade someone, it kills the poor disobedient hero. Where I come from, there is a saying: 'Fate leads the willing and drags along the reluctant.' This is true. Yet when it drags you along, it drags the lifeless corpse of a fool who had lost his only chance."

"Sinning Magicians, Max! Is this really you?" Melamori was staring at me as though she'd never seen me before. "I had no idea you could speak like that!"

"I can do a lot of things. I'm a jack-of-all-trades," I said. "Unfortunately, I'm also master of none. I used to write poetry, and very lousy poetry it was, let me tell you. I guess it shows occasionally. Like a tic."

"I'm sure you used to write good poetry," said Melamori, smiling. "At any rate, your passionate monologue about fate was just what I needed. You put my mind at ease. Well, you also scared me, but that's even better."

"Really?" I said. "Well, you know best."

"We should go now," she said, getting up from the bench. "Shurf will be dropping by your place soon, and I should probably head back to Headquarters. Life goes on, right?"

"And how!" I stood up and stretched my limbs. "There's one more thing. You've probably forgotten, but I remember it well: I once stopped by your place dressed as Ms. Marilyn Monroe."

"Oh, I remember," said Melamori, laughing. "She was a nice girl. She did manage to trick our clairvoyant Melifaro, by the way. He never figured you out until you told him. It's still my favorite story."

"I'm glad I left a lasting impression," I said. "I wanted to remind you about something else, though. You served some wine that came from the cellars of your uncle Kima. It was called Gulp of Fate, if I remember correctly. When we drank it, we saw little blue sparks playing and glinting in our glasses. You said it was a good sign, that the sparks appeared in the wine only when everything was fine between the people sharing it—wait, not fine but right. That's what you said. So you and I have no reason to be sad. Whatever is happening between us is right. This memory has saved my life on many occasions."

"But that's just a silly sign," said Melamori, shaking her head.

"Right, it's just a silly sign, but it's a good sign," I said. "And one good sign is still better than nothing."

"All right, I'll keep that in mind, too," said Melamori in a serious tone and nodded. Then she grabbed Droopy's shaggy ear and they both raced off, challenging everything that lay in their path. Our heartfelt, soul-searching conversation was over. The score was 1–0, only I had no idea know who was winning.

I dropped her off by the Headquarters and drove home. Nominally, of course, the Armstrong & Ella tavern wasn't my home, yet I was absolutely sure I was driving home. Where else? To compensate for leaving Droopy at my so-called royal residence for three dozen days, I decided to bring Droopy along with me. Moreover, I was hoping to bring him with me to work, even though I suspected that for such folly Sir Juffin Hully might turn me into ashes. Personally.

❖

"Max, now you're really going too far," said Tekki. "First you bring me your cats. Then you offload your numerous wives on me, putting me in charge of their upbringing. Now you're going to make me take care of this beast?"

The aforementioned cats, furry Ella and Armstrong, stared scornfully at their enormous fellow pet from the height of an old cupboard. They were in no hurry to climb down and introduce themselves to Droopy. One could understand that.

"Dream on," I said, climbing onto the bar and pecking Tekki on her nose. "I'm not going to part with him yet."

"It's the 'yet' part that worries me!" she said. "In a dozen days, you're going to leave him here, saying you're attending an audience at the Royal Palace and that dogs aren't allowed in. Then you're going to say that Droopy looks fantastic, and that I'm taking much better care of him than the inhabitants of the Furry House, and that his fur looks great against the color of my hair and the pattern on the carpet in the bedroom, and that means that the dog should stay here. I won't object, you'll kiss me, and by the time I come to my senses, this dog will have taken me for his new master. Max, I know you too well, and I'm freaking out in advance."

"Oh, no. I've had enough today of beautiful ladies who fear looking into their future," I said, sitting down on my favorite barstool. "Trust me, a personal bedroom and a couple dozen servants all longing to fill his food bowl await this beautiful dog back home. They don't have anything else to do anyway. As for my 'wives,' you could have put them to good use. The trio would look fantastic behind the bar, and you and I could go on a well-deserved vacation somewhere. You could also up the prices. As far as I know, the inhabitants of the Capital have never before been waited on by three beautiful identical foreign queens at the same time."

"Great idea, but it reeks of international conflict a mile away," said Tekki. "Besides, they are too serious to fill the glasses of drunken Echoers, if you haven't noticed."

"When would I have the time to notice anything?" I said. "I've seen them three times tops."

"It's your own fault. Also, who's the 'beautiful lady who fears looking into her future'?"

"You have three guesses."

"I see," said Tekki. She smiled, came out from behind the bar, and sat down beside me. "You had the pleasure of listening to Melamori's dramatic reading of the story of the distant and beautiful Arvarox and her alleged cowardice."

"She only covered the latter," I said. "I tried to explain to her that her problems are not unique, and that the inhabitants of all the Worlds—known and unknown to me—face them on a daily basis. I only mentioned in passing, however, the fact that very few of them are actually capable of dealing with and overcoming said problems, and only barely."

"Ah, so you can be wise sometimes, too," said Tekki. Then she buried her nose in my shoulder and added in a quiet voice, "To leave or to stay: I'd give anything to have that kind of problem on my mind."

"How so? Can't imagine your life without wild anxieties?" I said.

"I could do away with wild anxieties, Max. You don't understand. I simply have no choice. And I'll never have one. I can't leave Uguland unless I want to continue my existence as a ghost, you know."

"I don't understand."

"I can't get too far away from the Heart of the World, or I'll die. I'll expire like any other miracle that's been slapped together in a hurry. That's just my nature, honey. Or did you think the children of Loiso Pondoxo were ordinary people?"

"I didn't think about any such thing at all. Plus, I still don't quite understand what you're trying to say. I guess I don't want to understand."

"There isn't much to understand. We—my dead brothers and I—are not ordinary people. I think our prankster of a father simply couldn't have normal children. We are the products of his strange magic and his . . . dark humor. On the one hand, it's not that bad. In a sense, we are immortal. I have no reasons to doubt it since my brothers, after dying during the Troubled Times, became functional beings rather than apparitions. On the other hand, we're not completely free. Forget about traveling between Worlds or to Arvarox—I can't even leave Uguland. My best option is to stay in Echo until the day I die. It's only then that the true life of strange creatures like us really begins. Is this too shocking for you, Max? Maybe I shouldn't have started this conversation. I'm sorry."

"No, no, no. Please don't be sorry. It's good that you've told me. It just makes me a little sad. I had hoped to show you my favorite dreamworld, the little town in the mountains near Kettari. And then maybe some other place worthy of your beautiful eyes. But it's okay. I'll gradually get accustomed to the fact that you're a stay-at-home Tekki and that you're revolted by the thought of someone willingly swapping his favorite bedroom for a room in a cheap inn."

"Well, if I were you, I wouldn't paint it all black. Everything changes. I don't know how, but sometimes 'everything' just up and changes." Tekki laughed. "Who knows, maybe someday you and I will have our chance to take a long walk there."

I had nothing left to do but kiss her. The tavern was still empty, and kissing was much more pleasant than processing the information she had just let loose on me.

I felt someone's heavy stare drilling into the back of my head and turned around. In the doorway stood Sir Shurf Lonli-Lokli. He was absolutely calm. Then again, I'd be surprised to learn that such a trivial spectacle as a kiss could shock this guy. I think that even if Tekki and I had decided to move right along to the next stage he would have simply sat down at the farthest table, taken out some interesting book from the folds of his snow-white looxi, and waited until we were done.

Tekki didn't know Shurf as well as I did, so she hurried to retreat behind the bar. There she gave a big sigh of relief, as though this change of location had invalidated all the actions she had committed on the other side of the bar.

Droopy recognized in our visitor an old friend but restricted his excitement to wagging his ears. He was smart enough to know which of my friends were okay with him jumping on them, and which he should keep a polite distance from.

"I'm always glad to see you, Shurf, especially here," I said. "Why are you standing in the doorway? Come over here."

"I am not standing in the doorway," said Shurf. "I am trying to close the door. It is cold outside. The wind is blowing in from the Xuron. I have read a great deal on the positive effects of conditioning oneself to the cold, but I do not think drafts are a particularly good source of health. Lady Tekki, I believe it is imperative that you have this door handle repaired as soon as possible. I have reason to believe that it will never keep the door latched as it should without a good spell."

"You're right, Shurf," said Tekki. "I've been meaning to take care of it, to call someone to have it fixed, or whatever it is one's supposed to do in such cases. Then I tell myself that it's much easier to cast some spell to keep the damn thing closed. Please don't frown: the second degree of Black Magic does the job nicely. Even your beloved Code of Krember or Magician Nuflin the Terrible himself could have nothing against it."

Lonli-Lokli shook his head and sat down beside me. "I have come to ask you for a favor, Max," he said, taking a sip of the best kamra in Echo.

"Anything," I said.

"You told me you would someday try to obtain another book from your World," he said.

"And completely forgot about it," I said. "No worries, though. I'll get to it right away."

"Right away?" said Lonli-Lokli.

"Sure, why wait? I'll forget again, and then, a couple dozen days from now, you'll remind me about it politely, and I'll be ashamed. Why go through all this?"

"Sometimes you can be very rational," said Lonli-Lokli. I thought I spotted the shadow of a smile in the corners of his mouth.

"First I need to relocate," I said, looking around. "There's no place to hide my hand here."

I walked around behind the bar, where, admittedly, I wasn't supposed to go. Nor was I supposed to crawl on all fours behind it. In this place, however, I could get away with far worse things. Tekki either enjoyed my intruding on her turf or mistook me for the dog—I don't know which. In any event, she patted my head and even scratched behind my ear.

Here I had to rack my brains over where I could hide my hand, which was absolutely necessary. Even experienced magicians, not to mention some novice like me, couldn't fumble in the Chink between Worlds in plain sight. I gave up and just stuck my hand under an old floor mat. I couldn't find anything more appropriate.

My hand got numb right away, as though it had been longing for this job and was now making up for what it had missed. First I got hold of yet another umbrella, a ladies' model: it was yellow with little flowers. The Chink had always been very generous in presenting me with umbrellas. I think it had to do with the fact that people lost umbrellas more often than anything else. But I am not a collector by nature and had no intention of augmenting my collection of multicolored umbrellas with another specimen. Instead, I stuck my hand under the mat again and tried to focus: I thought of a library, its bookshelves filled with hundreds of thousands of good books.

For a few moments, I didn't get anywhere. My head was crammed with unrelated thoughts: about my unfinished kamra, for example. Then it occurred to me that I wouldn't mind smoking a cigarette. Also, Tekki was hanging around all the time, and I couldn't get rid of the idea of grabbing her leg. It took an enormous amount of concentration to shoo away these fragments of useless thoughts and get hold of the only necessary one: The Library.

My hand got numb again. I tried my best to imagine myself climbing a ladder to reach a book with a bright-red cover on the top shelf. The next thing I knew, a red paperback book was falling out of my numb fingers onto the floor. Lonli-Lokli was on a streak with cheap editions. Both the book, Big Earth in Small Space, and its author, Steve Harris, were unknown to me.

"What the heck!" I said. "Why can't I fetch something I know and love? It shouldn't be that hard. I used to be such a bookworm in my day."

"Are you unhappy with the book you got for me?" said Shurf.

"I'm not unhappy. I just got another unknown title by another unknown author, just like before. I think it's our fate, Shurf, to read different books. I'm warning you, though: you're going to have to tell me what it's about again. I doubt I'm ever going to read it, but I might easily die of curiosity."

I gave my haul to Shurf and returned to my spot at the bar. Tekki, true to form, ignored everything that was going on. She was tactful enough to bury herself in yesterday's Echo Hustle and Bustle, though I suspected that she was more interested in the contents of the newspaper than Shurf's and my bibliophile issues anyway.

"Why are you so surprised that you landed an unfamiliar book? Or do you think that during your lifetime you have read everything that has been written?" said Lonli-Lokli.

"Well, not everything, of course," I said, smiling, "but you'd be surprised by how much I have read. I used to be quite a reader, I'll have you know. That was basically all I used to do. It wasn't the worst pastime, frankly."

"It seems you do not read as much now," said Shurf.

"No, not a whole lot," I said. "Basically I don't read at all nowadays. But everything changes, especially when one life ends and a totally new one begins, right?"

"You are quite correct. I should have taken into account the fact that your present life might seem very rich and eventful to you."

"You can say that again," I said.

The door opened, then shut with a bang again.

"You are in high demand today, Max," said Tekki.

I looked at her. She had taken her eyes off the newspaper and was looking at someone behind me. I looked around and shook my head. It was none other than Mr. Anday Pu—practically sober and, therefore, very gloomy.

Droopy lifted one ear and gave a single, indecisive, but very impressive bark. Anday took an instinctive step backward, trying to give the dog a menacing stare in return. It wasn't impressive, but I had to admire the attempt. I can give you a list of people who would rush back outside upon hearing such an unfriendly hello coming from the mouth of such a monster. My name, by the way, would be on the top of that list.

"Wrong tree," I said to Droopy. "He's a friend, silly."

"Thanks, Max. Your dog has the manners of some flea-ridden village mutt. I don't catch why you decided to keep him in the first place. Dogs belong on a farm, not in an urban apartment," said Anday. His French accent was stronger than usual. Was that because he was frightened?

I decided that he deserved the right to show off as compensation for the stress he had endured, so I refrained from lecturing him on

Droopy's numerous virtues. Instead, I slapped a friendly grin on my face. Few people would dare call my bared teeth a smile, but Anday was happy.

Lonli-Lokli put his heavy hand on my shoulder. I jumped up in panic, then broke into a laugh: of course Shurf was wearing his protective gloves. If he hadn't been, there would be no one there to panic in the first place.

Lonli-Lokli shook his head. I mentally prepared for a lecture on the benefits of breathing exercises, which one should practice daily and not once every dozen days—something I totally agree with, in theory—but Shurf was magnanimous enough not to say anything. Perhaps my face expressed a most convincing repentance.

"Thank you for the book, Max," he said. "I hope you will not be offended if I take off for home now. I have great plans for tonight." He waved his present in the air.

"Have you ever seen me take offense?" I said.

"No, I do not recall such an occasion," said Shurf. He bowed to Tekki and then turned to Anday. "Will you be at the Three-Horned Moon tomorrow?"

"Of course," Anday said with a nod.

"Then I will see you there, provided nothing interferes with our plans," said Shurf and left.

I gave Anday a meaningful stare. "What's between you and Sir Shurf, mister? What's the Three-Horned Moon? And how come I don't know anything about it?"

"The Three-Horned Moon is where all great poetry happens here in the part of the Xonxona continent called the Unified Kingdom," said Anday. "It is the only place in this untidy World where respect is given to poets who are still alive, and not just to those for whom the dinner is already over."

"Oh, a poetry club? How come you never told me about it?"

"Are you interested, Max? I figured you didn't give a damn about poets, dead or alive. Now your colleague Sir Lonli-Lokli, he really knows the price of words well aligned and rhymed. Or are you saying I've been looking at you from the wrong window all along?"

"The wrong window? What?" I was confused.

Tekki laughed her tinkling laughter and dropped her newspaper on the floor. "Oh, Max, it's an expression. Anday wanted to say that his opinion of you does not match reality."

"One heck of an expression," I said. "Very graphic. You wouldn't believe me if I told you how many windows you should look at me from, buddy. And at other people, too. I've made the same mistake myself."

"So I didn't catch then," said Anday. "It's all right. It happens. I can take you to the Three-Horned Moon if you're interested."

"I'm interested in everything. A little. Especially poets societies." At this phrase I cut myself short. This was the second time today I had almost admitted I had once been a poet. That was two times too many.

"Just admit that you learned that your friends frequent a tavern you've never heard of and don't invite you," said Tekki. "Now you don't know whether to burst with curiosity or tear everything to pieces. Poor, poor Sir Max."

I laughed, nodding. "Precisely." I then turned to Anday. "Whether you want it or not, I'm going to dog your footsteps tomorrow."

"I didn't catch that. You're going to what me?" he said.

I smiled a wicked smile. The presence of Anday Pu invariably provoked me to dig through the baggage of my passive vocabulary, looking for some odd colloquialisms that would throw off that poor scribe. Tekki also raised her eyebrows in surprise.

"To dog someone's footsteps means to follow someone who thinks he can easily do without me. But, at the same time, it means that no one will dare slap me in the face and say, 'Get away from me!' Now am I making sense?"

They nodded: Tekki with enthusiasm and Anday with a hint of embarrassment, or so it seemed.

"You know, Max, I actually came to you with something . . ."

I never thought Anday was capable of speaking in such a hesitant tone. Maybe I had just never seen him before he got his hands (or, rather, his mouth) full of a pitcher of the local firewater.

"'With something'? Sounds like you mean business. Did you and Sir Rogro have a misunderstanding?"

"No, Sir Rogro has been behaving quite decently," said Anday in an arrogant tone.

I smirked. If only the chief editor of the Royal Voice had heard him, although he probably wouldn't have been surprised. Long before he became the sovereign of the press in the Capital, Sir Rogro Jiil had been an astrologist. So now he had an excellent flashlight with which to peer into the darkest corners of the souls of his numerous subordinates.

"Okay, who's not behaving decently then? One of your colleagues? I'm curious," I said.

"What do I care for those peasants of the paper!" Anday demonstrated to Tekki and me an excellent peevish fold at the corner of his mouth, a contemptuous squint, and an arrogant profile, in that order. Having played with his facial muscles like a bodybuilder plays with his biceps, he continued. "Max, I was robbed eight days ago."

"Robbed?" I said. "Well, that sure is a bummer, but I'm not exactly the person to turn to. Robberies are the problem of our neighbors in the House by the Bridge. That's actually why we keep them there. Oh, hold on a second. You don't take kindly to our friendly policemen, do you? You probably didn't even bother to report this to them. Am I right?"

"Sure I reported this to the rodents," said Anday. "Actually I wanted to talk to you right away, but you weren't here or in the House by the Bridge. I met Melamori there, and she told me exactly what you just did: that you Secret Investigators are too cool for everyday crimes, and that you're not going to investigate some petty burglary. Now if someone were to steal His Majesty's favorite hat from Rulx Castle, that would be a different matter. Then she took me over to the side with the rodents, to another girl. I forget her name, you know, she's all like . . ." Anday's eyes suddenly grew wide, and he ran his hands along the contours of his own tubby body.

I knew he was talking about Lady Kekki Tuotli: I hadn't met any other curvaceous girls in the ranks of the City Police.

"Melamori did the right thing," I said. "What happened then?"

"I told her everything, and she said she'd see what could be done about it," said Anday. "But they still haven't found anything. And I think, Max, that they're not really looking. Who's going to go out of their way looking for some old chest with my granddad's stuff in it? I think they don't catch that—"

"Hold that thought," I said. "Are you telling me that the burglars stole some old chest? Sir Kofa told me that some burglars of the Capital are first-class imbeciles, but I didn't believe him. Silly me. What was in the chest? Your grandpa's pirate outfit?"

"So you know already," said Anday.

"Huh? It was just a guess. Was I close?"

"The dinner is over! You totally catch, Max! That's exactly what was in the chest. Well, maybe a few other things. I kept it in the basement of my house on the Street of Steep Roofs. The last time I opened it was when I was entering the Higher Institute, so I don't remember exactly what was in it. I'm totally blank."

"How did you notice it was gone then?" I said. He didn't strike me as a fellow who does a routine inventory of his own basement.

"It wasn't me. You know that I rent half my house to that pesky Pela family," said Anday, wincing. "I had to give them a twenty-year lease some time ago when I ran out of those shiny round objects without which it's not easy to relax. So they live there now, and I try to avoid going home because those plebeians are very noisy and they're always cooking something."

"Oh, dear," said Tekki.

Anday sensed sincere understanding in Tekki's tone. She had such an abhorrence of kitchen smells that she refused to have a cook in her tavern. In that sense, the Armstrong & Ella was a unique place in Echo: it served only kamra and alcohol, much to the chagrin of Echoers who loved to gobble. It seemed that most of them only came here with one objective: to make sure it still existed.

"You two just don't get it," I said. "It's so nice when the smell of something frying wafts right under your nose."

The two looked at me as though I were the devil. Finally Anday went on. "Eight days ago my tenants' kids were playing in the basement. Those Pelas, they have tons of kids, you know. I can never count how many exactly. And they're always playing!" This time Anday winced so violently it might have seemed the aforementioned children had been playing Kick the Can with their enemy's head for a can. "They were playing hide-and-seek or some such game, and then they saw that there were two strangers in the basement. Two men in plain looxis. The kids got scared and decided to stay put in their hiding spot. They saw how the two men grabbed my grandfather's chest and disappeared."

"Did they go down the Dark Path?" I said.

"Who knows? That's your department. I got an excellent education, but it was after the Epoch of Orders. I don't catch all those 'Dark Paths' or whatever they are," said Anday, "although that has a nice ring to it. The fact is, they took my grandfather's chest with them, and now I figure maybe there was some hidden treasure in it." His almond-shaped eyes shone when he said the word "treasure."

"In any case, guys who can take the Dark Path are rarely complete imbeciles, that's for sure," I said. "You know, Anday, I'm intrigued. I'd like to dig through that old pirate chest myself. Anyway, what exactly do you want me to do about it? Drop everything and step on the trace of those thieves? Lady Kekki Tuotli is a good girl. I think she can handle this case without my help."

"I just want you to remind her about my chest, Max," Anday said. "Maybe the girl didn't catch that she was supposed to find it? I wouldn't bother with something like this if I were her. She probably thinks that the thieves did me a favor by hauling away some useless old junk free of charge."

"No, I don't think so. That 'girl' is not as flippant and frivolous as you might think. But I will remind her. Forgotten treasures of Ukumbian pirates, mysterious thieves going down the Dark Path—a lovely story. I'll help you. Under one condition, though: once the police find your precious chest, you let me rummage around in it. I've always wanted to find some pirate's treasure."

"Thanks," said Anday. "If you tell them it's important, the rodents will turn the city upside down to find it."

"How nice of you not to doubt my omnipotence," I said. "Now, instead of sucking up to me, take me to the Three-Horned Moon. The shortest path to my heart is to drag me to some tavern."

"Can you manage to sneak out from work tomorrow night? We usually gather there about three hours before midnight and stay late. Well, some of us, anyway."

"I think I will. Sometimes my omnipotence knows no bounds. Maybe I will, maybe I won't—you never know. Send me a call before you set out."

"Max, I'm going to say something nasty now," said Tekki.

"Tell me I'm late for work?" I said. She nodded. "Then I'm leaving him with you. As a present. A souvenir. And as my revenge. No one can expel me from a tavern and get away with it."

"It's not revenge, just another client," said Tekki, smiling. "Don't take it personally, Sir Pu. This vicious gentlemen only tyrannizes those he loves."

I jumped off the barstool and shook Droopy, who had dozed off.

"Don't forget about my chest," said Anday.

"I won't. And don't you forget to take me to the Three-Horned Moon, or I'll get furious and find the mysterious chest of Captain Kidd myself. And I'll keep it."

"Who's Captain Kidd? My grandfather's name was Zoxma Pu."

The House by the Bridge wasn't as full as it had been at noon, but it was still a fun place to be. I heard General Boboota's epic roar as soon as I entered the hallway.

"Bull's tits! I've got enough of my own crap in Echo without these crapshooters coming here from the rest of the World! It's high time the Capital was a closed city. You just wait! I'm going to feed your own crap to you until you puke!"

To my surprise, the roaring came from our half of the Headquarters and not from Boboota's natural habitat. I imagined walking into Juffin's office and seeing General Boboota in his armchair. Then I imagined that Boboota was the Venerable Head of the Minor Secret Investigative Force. That's how people go insane, I thought. Out of the blue, without warning—boom!—and the next thing you know is you start thinking some surrealistic thoughts.

For what it was worth, when I opened the door to the Hall of Common Labor, I felt like shutting my eyes and yelling "Geronimo!" like a paratrooper leaping down toward the unknown. I felt like I was diving into another dimension, some parallel universe where General Boboota Box was welcome in the Headquarters of the Minor Secret Investigative Force.

In reality, however, a true interdepartmental idyll reigned in the Hall of Common Labor. Sir Melifaro, dressed in a turquoise looxi, was handing half a dozen frightened criminals over to the open arms of the infuriated General Boboota. Their exotic pantaloons testified to their foreign origin. The general put an enormous amount of effort into making the poor lost souls realize what the score was in the Capital. The door to Juffin's office was ajar. The boss was enjoying the show.

The show, alas, was almost over. When he saw me, Boboota gave a nervous cough, shut up, and tried assuming the most intelligent expression he could pull off—a sight to behold. He should have noticed long time ago that I began spitting venom every time I heard obscenities, but bad habits die hard.

"Good evening, Sir Max," Boboota said, almost whispering. I opened my mouth to return the everyday mantra of courtesy, but Droopy got ahead of me. He gave a single loud, ringing bark. Startled, General Boboota jumped to the ceiling, the arrestees squealed, and Melifaro fell in his chair, moaning: it all was too funny.

"Shush, boy. This is a serious establishment," I said to my dog.

"Serious?" moaned Melifaro.

"Very, very serious," I said with a stony face.

A moment later, we were alone. General Boboota preferred admiring me from afar. That way he felt safer. Melifaro stopped laughing and yawned.

"We were doing their job again," he said. "Wasted a whole day chasing these fellows who had been terrorizing the Customs, along with chief officer Nulli Karif. Turned out they were regular thieves from abroad. It's so not our profile. Had to share our finds with the neighbors, naturally."

"What did they do?" I said.

"Nothing interesting, Max. Trust me."

Sir Juffin finally left his office, sat down next to Melifaro, and began yawning demonstratively. A very convincing duo. I almost believed that they had lived through the most boring day in the entire history of the Secret Investigative Force.

"The fellows came all the way from Kirvaori," said Juffin. "Their extravagant national customs were way too similar to the rituals of one ancient Order, so I thought that something extraordinary had happened. It's my fault—I shouldn't have listened to that chatterbox Nulli. Now all I need is some sleep. Nothing exhausts you more than doing someone else's job well."

"Sleep is good," I said.

"I don't need you to tell me that," said Juffin. "Are you going to drag this beast along with you everywhere you go now? Kurush won't approve. He's used to being the only fauna in my office."

"Actually, I just didn't have time to take him home. I was running late when I realized it. I had a rough day myself. A whole bunch of people stacked their problems upon my muscular back. I even began to like it. Want me to do something for you, too?"

"I don't. Just don't wake me until noon, even if the sky falls, okay?"

"No problem. But if the sky falls, you're going to wake up, what with the racket and all."

"I'm a very sound sleeper," said Juffin, who yawned once more, then left.

"I can take your dog home," said Melifaro. "It's almost on the way."

"'Almost' being the operative word here," I said. "Did it take you long to come up with a pretext to sneak into my royal chambers?"

"Not too long," said Melifaro. "Praise be the Magicians, your house isn't the most well-guarded place in the Unified Kingdom."

"Precisely. Anyone can just walk into any of my houses without overloading his brain coming up with a believable pretext. Why would you even need a pretext, may I ask?"

"You may," said my colleague. "First, it's more fun that way. There must be some sort of storyline. I've always wanted to steal away your wife, and you're turning that exciting undertaking into a mundane task, akin to going to the grocer's."

"Guilty as charged," I said. "And what's second?"

"Second, the upbringing of your beautiful queens from the Barren Lands is radically different from yours, unfortunately. Which is strange, if you think about it: you're supposed to be their countryman. Anyway, unlike you, those ladies don't think anyone can just 'walk into' your house. They'd rather deal with people who can explain what they're doing in not so many words. Besides, they also need to like my explanation."

"You know them so well already. Whenever did you have the time?"

"I didn't," said Melifaro in a sad voice. "Unlike you, those girls are dead serious about their marital status. You should really talk to them about it."

"What exactly do you think I'm supposed to tell them? That you're more handsome? Anyone can see that. Too handsome, I'd go so far as to say."

Melifaro shrugged, paced the room, and sat on the window ledge. "I want them to know that you don't consider yourself to be their legitimate husband," he said. "You've already told this to everyone who's reached puberty in the Unified Kingdom. Don't you think Kenlex, Xeilax, and Xelvi should know, as well? It concerns them, too, after all. They are still under the impression that you'd reprimand them for flirting with other men."

"Hmm. I didn't think about that," I said.

"Didn't you?" said Melifaro. "Or did you think you'd keep them for yourself, for a rainy day, huh?"

"Yeah, when I'm old and nobody needs me. That's when I'm going to remember about them. You're so wise, Melifaro. Thanks for the advice. I wouldn't have thought of it myself."

Melifaro waved me away and laughed.

"You're right," I said. "The girls must know that they can live their lives however they wish. It's only fair. So we're going there together. Do you think people will find it strange that it takes two men to walk such a huge dog home?"

"Shame on you, Your Majesty!" said Melifaro. "Now you're looking for a pretext for a visit to your own home."

"Speak for yourself, mister," I said. "If I'm looking for anything, it's a pretext to shirk work and not feel too guilty about it. The little bureaucrat in me agrees that the House by the Bridge is no place to keep dogs. Now I have to explain to him why I can't send Droopy home with you. Give me a minute and I'll wear him down."

"Are you seriously going to give your beautiful harem a speech?" said Melifaro. "Right now?"

"The sooner I do it, the better. And your presence is mandatory, just to get rid of you once and for all. Besides, I'm going to use your precious body as my armor. I'm a little scared of them, you know."

"That's funny," said Melifaro. "You? Scared? Think of something better."

"Where's your famous clairvoyance now?" I said. "You were insightful enough to crack open the legend about my origin that Juffin and I had concocted on day one. Now you're telling me you fail to see that I don't know what to do with my hands or what to look at when I see those girls."

Melifaro's eyebrows shot up. Then he smiled and dismissed my words. "Oh, I see what you mean. Don't worry about it. It's hard to fool me about something really important, but under ordinary circumstances, I'm as clueless as the next guy. You should've guessed that by now. Remember when you came here with the face of that hot Lady Marilyn? I bought into her curly hair like a fool. Or do you think I was pretending?"

"I'm not sure. Maybe you thought it was more fun that way."

"I could have," said Melifaro.

I poked my head into Juffin's office, where the wisest bird of this World was sitting on the back of the armchair, looking all-important. "Kurush, I'm going to step out for a while. You're in charge."

"Does your 'for a while' mean until morning?" said the buriwok.

"No, no. My 'for a while' means just what it says—for a while. It also means tons of pastry to boot."

"Try not to forget," he said in a sleepy voice.

Thank goodness reaching an agreement with that gluttonous wise guy was a piece of cake.

I motioned at Droopy, and all three of us left the Ministry of Perfect Public Order. Boy, do I love that place! Working there is like one big endless party. Still, I love to sneak out during my working hours from time to time. I guess it fits into my primitive notions of freedom.

My Furry House remained furry in all seasons. To my utter delight, the vines that grew along its walls from top to bottom were evergreen. I was thinking of settling in there for real someday—someday when the dark era of my conceptual reign over the people of Xenxa had come to an end. When no one would prevent me from fulfilling my most cherished desire: to throw out the window most of the bulky junk in the palace and retire the numerous servants—that was the first thing I'd do!

"If I understand it correctly," said Melifaro, "you don't show your face here at all? That's too bad: all this beauty's thrown away on the only barbarian in the city, one who can't even appreciate it."

"On the contrary, I appreciate this place and realize that it's too good for me. Besides, there's too much of it. I'd dissolve here like candy in the mouth. Maybe sometime later . . . You know that I barely spend any time in my place on the Street of Yellow Stones, and it's only got two stories and six bedrooms."

"When was the last time you were there?" said Melifaro. I wrinkled my forehead trying to remember. "Don't answer. The jury has already reached the verdict. You have too much real estate and only one sorry butt, which, by the way, prefers the hard chairs in cheap taverns to luxury." And with that, Melifaro stepped out of the amobiler.

Droopy followed him and jumped down on the sidewalk. He recognized his abode and exploded into enthusiastic barking. Unlike me, he felt at home here.

As soon as I stepped inside, I froze in disbelief: it seemed as though Melifaro and I had made a few circles around and returned to the House by the Bridge. In the doorway of the living room stood Sir Kofa Yox and Lady Kekki Tuotli. Kekki was waving around her thin silvery gloves, anxious to put them on and walk outside.

"Has my humble abode turned into a branch of the Ministry of Perfect Public Order?" I said. "Where's my dog going to live? Droopy needs comfort. He's a royal dog, after all."

"I'm used to seeing Sir Melifaro around here all the time," said

Kofa, "and I'm almost certain I know why. But you, Max? What are you doing here?"

"I kind of thought I lived here," I said.

"If I'm not mistaken, right now you're supposed to be sitting in Juffin's office, your feet propped up on the desk. We've all learned to accept that as part of your job description," said Sir Kofa, smiling.

"I ran off. But for all intents and purposes, you are supposed to be sitting in some tavern, since I've learned to accept that as part of your job description. Am I speaking too fast?"

"No, you're not. I was just going to 'some tavern,'" said our Master Eavesdropper. "See, I've been thinking that engaging in public appearances in the company of just one lady is below my dignity, so I've come to borrow the three of yours."

"And they've already spent three hours dressing up," said Kekki. "Talk about royalty."

"I'm in luck!" said Melifaro. "In fact, I'm going with you. Deal with it. And you, poor thing"—he made a face at me—"you have to get back to work. It's almost nighttime and you haven't killed anyone yet. Not cool."

"My innocent victims can wait," I said. "In any case, I need a meal."

"You should change," said Kofa. "Your Mantle of Death is a dead giveaway for all of us."

"Change into what?" I said. "I don't keep any clothes here."

"You're going to thank me for this," said Melifaro in an avuncular tone. "The Mantle of Death doesn't help digestion." From his pocket, he produced a tiny thingamajig. He then rubbed it between his palms and pitched it to his feet. A moment later, a bright-blue looxi with an intricate fringe lay on the floor.

"I've been meaning to tell you that the color scheme of your wardrobe gives me culture shock," I said, putting on the looxi. "I'm lucky that you haven't brought something pink."

"Are you complaining, or was that your way of saying thank

you?" said Melifaro. "Because if you don't like it, I can take it back and you can wrap yourself in one of your carpets."

"Okay, okay. I give up," I said. "Say, do you always carry a spare set of clothes with you?"

"Sure. In case you come to work in your birthday suit. You know how much I care about you."

"Seriously, though. Why?"

"Well," said Melifaro, "I hate wearing dirty, torn clothes. And given our line of work, clothes become dirty and torn on a regular basis. So it's always a good idea to have a spare looxi on you. Just in case. Got it, Your Majesty?"

My Majesty nodded his head, registering respect for Melifaro's prudence.

Three identical sisters appeared at the far end of the living room. When they saw me, they froze. Soon, though, they recovered and minced toward us. To be frank, they didn't look as identical now. After a few stops in the Capital's fashion boutiques, the girls had undergone a radical change. It turned out they had different tastes. One of them preferred a black-and-white palette, the other combined different shades of green, and the third sister wrapped herself in a bright-yellow looxi worn over a cornflower-blue skaba. I'm sure she's the one Melifaro has fallen in love with, I thought. They'd look terrific together.

❖

Finally, everybody was ready and we left. The triplets desperately tried to fuse together as one: they held hands and clung to one another like three freezing kittens in a cold winter wind. Granted, it was winter and the wind was blowing hard. Thank goodness the temperature rarely falls below freezing in Echo.

"We're not all going to fit into one amobiler, that's for sure," said Kofa. "And I'm not crazy enough to even think of keeping up with your driving. The only thing left to do is to walk to the nearest tavern. The Sated Skeleton is just a stone's throw away, and it's not a bad option."

"And a few more of our crowns will end up in the bottomless pockets of the master of all Skeletons, Goppa Tallaboona," I said.

I had worked up quite an appetite during the day, so for the first fifteen minutes at the tavern, I just moved my jaws in silence and paid no attention to the usual dinner small talk. I did watch the rest of the company, but not too closely. I noticed that the sisters had started to take Sir Kofa for their daddy, which, if one were to believe the legends of the Xenxa people, they'd never really had. Lady Kekki Tuotli had also earned their trust. I wondered how many quiet dinners like this one they had already had together. Melifaro, however, they eyed with a great deal of suspicion, for reasons unknown to me.

I opened my mouth as soon as I had enough energy to put down my fork: I had remained silent for too long. "Thank you, Sir Kofa. It was so nice of you to take care of my family while I was off who-knows-where."

"I'll tell you 'who knows where,'" said Kofa. "I, for one, know very well where you were. But don't mention it, Max. If you have half a dozen more maidens you need taken care of, I'm at your service any time, day or night."

Lady Kekki Tuotli giggled at these words. Apparently, she had nothing against them.

"Oh, Kekki, I just remembered I had something to discuss with you," I said. "A certain man complained to me earlier today that he thinks you didn't pay enough attention to him or his case of the lost treasures of his beloved late grandfather. Ring a bell?"

Kekki stared at me for a moment, then realized what I was talking about and smiled a shy smile. "He's gotten to you, too, now, that funny young man?"

"You bet he has," I said. "My ear is by tradition the long-suffering receptacle of his sob stories. Tell me, are you on his case, or have you decided not to fill your head with trivial nonsense?"

"Frankly, Max," said Kekki with a sigh, "I was going to, but I had absolutely no time. I'm swamped. You know how it is at the police department nowadays: too many incomplete cases and even more complete idiots who don't let me complete the incomplete cases. Besides, I haven't quite reached the period of my life when I want to take my work home because I have nothing else to do, you see. I have quite a bit to do, actually."

Sir Kofa smiled, flattered. My debut as a matchmaker had proven to be a resounding success. The two of them clicked together like two fingers of my own hand. Who would have thought? I could have opened a dating service.

"In other words, the poor fellow was right when he told me you wouldn't consider the disappearance of his chest the biggest case in history," I said. "Well, in that case, I'm just the messenger boy here. Hold on a second." I made a sad face, pressed my hands against my chest, and squeaked, "Kekki, please try to find that sinning chest!"

"Or else you'll die!" said Melifaro in an even thinner voice. I was too surprised to say anything, to his utter delight.

"What sort of a chest is it?" said Kofa.

"No idea," I said. "The fellow didn't even think about it for years. Now he's taken it into his head to think that it's full of some pirate treasure. I think the problem is his lively imagination: he's a great poet, no less, you see. Then again, it may very well be that Kekki and I are two witless fools, and the chest is filled with unimaginable riches. The most interesting part of the story is that the thieves went down the Dark Path, if the testimony of a gang of frightened kids is any indication."

"Precisely my point," said Kekki.

I knew she desperately wanted it to be a most predictable, uninteresting case since she had all but forgotten about it.

"Don't children have eyes?" said Sir Kofa. "I don't see why we

ready to go to work," I said. "Thank goodness I can catch up on some sleep there, what with my tight schedule and all."

Melifaro gave me such an expressive stare that I almost felt the chair underneath me smoking. He was right: I'd gotten sidetracked. I'd left the House by the Bridge with the intention of giving my wives a lecture on freedom in general and their personal freedom in particular. Okay, I thought, it's time I did that. Plus, the atmosphere in the Sated Skeleton favored signing some declaration of independence.

"All right," I said. "I guess a couple of extra cups of kamra wouldn't hurt after all." I winked at Melifaro: buckle up, mister, and enjoy the show.

He was all buckled up already, though, eager to hear what I was going to say to the girls. Heck, I was eager to know that, too. I stared at my cup of kamra and began composing a speech in my head. The composing wasn't quite working out.

"Did a werewolf bite you?" said Sir Kofa. "Has Goppa Tallaboona hired a bad chef? The expression on your face suggests that you're trying to digest a block of wood."

"I'm a primitive being, I'm not denying that, but I'm not that primitive," I said. "This has nothing to do with my digestion. I'm thinking."

"Oh, he's thinking," said Kofa. "Poor boy. And what, pray tell, are you thinking about?"

"About these three beauties," I said, nodding at the sisters. Three pairs of eyes stared back at me.

"Not the worst thing in the world to think about," said Kofa. "And what kinds of thoughts are you thinking about them?"

"Assorted thoughts," I said. I discovered it was much easier for me to address my family-related issues when talking directly to Kofa rather than to the alarmed triplets.

"Imagine if you will, Kofa, three beautiful young ladies growing up far, far away in the Barren Lands. How they lived and what they did there, I have no idea. But, one would imagine, they did live and did do something, and everything was more or less simple for them: the sky was up, the earth was down, menkals had antlers, and so on." I took a deep breath and continued. "Then one day, some wise elders put the girls on antlered menkals and bring them to the house of some stranger and say that he is the new king of the Xenxa people and their new husband to boot. Then the aforementioned wise elders turn around and go back home, leaving the beautiful Kenlex, Xeilax, and Xelvi in a huge foreign house. What's more, the girls probably don't know what to do and how to live now.

"The stranger they consider to be their husband gets rid of them, promising to drop by for a friendly chat someday—something he hasn't yet done, by the way. Well, we all know I'm a regular swine. But, unlike their husband, all kinds of nice folk who claim to be good friends of his do come visit them regularly, praise be the Magicians. It's all fine and dandy, but I doubt it lives up to the young ladies' notion of matrimonial responsibilities." I took my stare off Kofa and turned to the sisters. "Am I describing the situation more or less accurately?"

The girls were smiling. Their smiles were very shy, almost indiscernible, but all three of them were smiling. That was a success. Nay, it was my hour of triumph. I had been waiting all my life for something of this kind. If anything, I was ready to die right then and there since I'd already put on the best show of my life.

"It's good that you're smiling," I said to them. "It's the shortest path to my heart, if that silly muscle is of any interest to you. Plus, you and I have landed in a really awkward situation, so your reaction is most appropriate. Marriage is a funny thing, especially our marriage."

"You don't need us?" said one of the sisters, the one whose bright-yellow looxi had made me laugh. "When Fairiba took us with him, he warned us that this might happen. He told us that you were not like the former kings of the Lands of Fanghaxra, which our elders still remember. From the beginning, we were ready for anything."

"Well, don't lay it on too thick," I said. "I'm sure I need you for something, ladies, since you've appeared in my life. Fate is no fool: she won't bring people together for no reason. I never needed a wife, not to mention three wives, that's true. But that doesn't mean I'm going to kick you out. I want you to stay here at the Furry House and do whatever you want, as long as you're having fun. The only thing I'm going to have to ask you to do is to forget all this nonsense about husband and wives. Let's just agree that you're my guests. Wait. No. That's not exactly right. Guests come and go, and you don't have anywhere to go, nor do you have to. Echo is a wonderful place. You're lucky that fate brought you to the Capital of the Unified Kingdom. I'm still crazy about it, even though one might say I should've gotten used to it by now. Let's say you're something like my nieces. Are you okay with this term?"

One of the sisters smiled and nodded. The other two stared at her in disbelief and then looked at me again.

"I'm sure we'll soon be able to replace the word 'nieces' with the word 'friends,'" I said. "But the process of turning someone you barely know into someone you can call a friend is not something you have much control over. It just happens, so let's not plan anything ahead."

"If I understand you correctly, our lives should somehow change after this conversation. Right?" said the girl in the yellow looxi. She was the most serious of the three, despite her frivolous taste in clothing.

"That's right," I said. "Your lives should change radically. First, I'd be happy if you stopped trembling in my presence. There's no need for that. Listen to Sir Kofa: you should talk to me in the same way he does. I know it's going to be hard in the beginning, but you'll get the hang of it sooner or later. Oh, and the most important thing you should know: you're totally free. You can leave the house and come back whenever you feel like it. You can invite whomever you want. And you should turn to me if you need help or a piece of advice or some other silly thing, like money, but never to ask my permission. If I don't like something, you'll be the first to know. And if someone happens to step all over your heart, as we say here in Echo, just know that your life is your life. I'm not going to stick my nose into it—unless you ask me to, of course." I wiped off my forehead and gave Sir Kofa a sorrowful look. "Do you think I sounded convincing?"

"Very much so. I never knew you were capable of giving such fiery speeches with such a straight face. You had me worried for a second there," said Kofa.

"Well, I'm still worried," said Melifaro. "Very worried, in fact."

"Stuff it, mister," I said.

"Oh, I'd love to," said Melifaro, "but there's nothing in this sinning tavern to stuff it with. Would you mind if I performed this barbarian ritual some other time?"

"Permission granted," I said. "I'm in a very good mood today."

The sisters were still examining me. I thought they looked a little more relaxed now, however. I should've had this conversation a few dozen days sooner, I thought. I have a nasty habit of putting off forever what I should've done a hundred years ago.

"Okay. Now let's move on to the introductions," I said to the sisters. "I'm going to try to tell you apart, if I can."

"I'm Xeilax," said the girl in the bright-yellow looxi. "This is Xelvi," she said, pointing at the giggly sister who had liked my proposition to call them nieces. Then she put her hand on the shoulder of the third sister and said, "And she's Kenlex."

Kenlex was the one dressed in a strict black-and-white outfit. She gave me a sudden heavy, piercing look, sending shivers down my spine. Up until that point, I'd thought she was the harmless goody-goody, the meekest of the three. Then again, I'm such a poor judge of character.

"Okay, let's hope I won't mix you up next time. Now I really must go back to work. Kurush would peck out my eyes if I stayed another minute here, and he would be absolutely right to do so." I gulped the rest of my kamra and got up. "Good night, everyone."

"Take care, buddy," said Melifaro. "Don't get into trouble, and if you do, take my favorite looxi off first."

"Aw, I kind of already set my heart on rolling in the nearest puddle," I said. "What am I supposed to do now? Change my plans because of your whining? Tough luck, mister."

I returned to the House by the Bridge in a superb mood. A good dinner combined with the satisfaction of my "conjugal visit" had affected me in a most invigorating manner. I brought Kurush a dozen pastries. It was clear he'd never eat that many, but in this respect, he and I adhered to the same principle: the more the better.

It turned out I wasn't terribly late. Kurush mumbled something about how it was typical for people to say they were going to step out for just a minute and then come back two hours later. I thought I'd been gone for much longer. It didn't matter anyway because nothing had happened while I'd been out. Which was typical: in this wonderful World, bad things prefer to happen precisely when I'm in.

It didn't seem as though bad things were going to happen today, however. For about an hour and a half, Kurush and I loafed around peacefully. I browsed through yesterday's Royal Voice, and the buriwok ate his pastry. Then I wiped the cream off his beak. Finally Kurush puffed up his feathers and fell asleep. Around midnight, one of the junior staff members of the Headquarters poked his head into the office.

"A visitor for you, Sir Max," he said.

"Let me guess: short, plump, and very brazen?" I thought it must have been Anday Pu, still shocked about the loss of his grandfather's chest. I was sure that his imagination was running wild, coming up with new hypothetical "treasures" that had once been unfairly neglected and were now suddenly gone from his life.

"On the contrary, Sir Max. The visitor is tall, thin, and very polite. He's dressed like an Echoer, but he has a beard down to his waist and braided hair. He also has a Tasherian accent."

"Heh," I said. "When I'm wrong, I can't be more wrong. Well, if he really has a beard that long, show him in. I can't miss a show like that."

The courier nodded, embarrassed, and left. My jokes have the tendency to befuddle and confuse our junior staff, and I'm still trying to be more democratic with them.

A tall bearded man in a dark looxi stood in the doorway.

"Captain Giatta!" I said. "Of course! I should've guessed it was you."

This captain from Tasher had been hanging out in Echo for almost two years, and frankly, it was my fault. I had once saved his life. It was almost an accident: back then I hadn't known what I was doing or why. Captain Giatta, however, took my actions very seriously, however: he had taken it into his head that he must pay me back with something worthy of my feat. As I had never gotten around to coming up with a task for him, he'd had to stay in Echo. He still hoped that sooner or later I'd need his help. I had almost forgotten about his "eternal debt" to me—too many things had happened since then. I'd been through numerous troubles, but they'd required the help of specialists in completely different fields.

"Am I interrupting something, Sir Max?" said Giatta.

"No, of course not. Has something happened?" I said.

"If you mean to ask whether something bad has happened, then no, nothing of that sort," he said, sitting on the edge of the armchair. "I just came to say goodbye."

"Good," I said. "I told you I didn't need anything from you. I'm sure you have been missed at home."

"You've misinterpreted my words, Sir Max," said the captain. "I still hope to pay you back for saving my life someday. I'm not going home. I'm just going on a sea voyage."

"That's excellent," I said. "Where are you going?"

"Frankly, I'm not quite sure myself. The captain of the karuna that hired me hasn't yet told us where we're going. He says, though, that the voyage shouldn't take more than a year. I came to tell you that no later than a year from now I will be at your service again at any time."

"Hold that thought, Giatta," I said. "I don't get it. What captain? Who hired you? You're a captain yourself. Plus, as far as I know, you have your own ship. The entire staff of the Minor Secret Investigative Force went to admire your Old Maid when you arrived in Echo. Has anything happened to it?"

"No, the Old Maid is all right, praise be the heavens," said the Tasherian. He looked perplexed. It seemed he'd just remembered his ship and was happy with his rediscovery.

"Okay, I'm confused," I said. "I think we need a large pitcher of kamra to get to the bottom of this. Or would you like something stronger, Giatta?"

"I think I would," he said.

"Something stronger it is then," I said and sent a call to the Glutton Bunba. I had been going to do it anyway.

"Spit it out," I said, when my desk was crowded with empty dishes. "Because I just don't get it. Instead of going on your own ship, you're hired by some other captain who didn't even bother to tell you where he was going. Is he an old friend?"

"No," said the Tasherian, staring at the ceiling as though he were trying to read the answer there. "Until this morning, I had never heard of him."

"Why then? Is the pay good?"

"Probably . . . I didn't ask." Captain Giatta looked like he had just woken up.

"Well, I'll be," I said, shaking my head. "Now I'm beginning to understand how you ended up working for that scoundrel merchant Agon. I'm sorry, Giatta, but is this how you usually get hired?"

"No. You probably won't believe me, but I'm actually a very cautious man," he said. "I understand you must have a different impression, but when Mr. Agon offered to hire me, I found out every possible detail of the journey and then spent a few days pondering it. I was actually going to decline because I thought he'd been holding something back. I think that was why he put his blasted enchanted belt on me."

"I'd love to believe that," I said. "But your latest venture has surpassed all my notions of human carelessness. All my notions, mind you. Did your new acquaintance put something on you, too?"

"No, no. Nothing of the sort. After the last time, I made a vow not to accept gifts from people I don't know well. The odd part is that I wasn't really looking for a job. I get a good salary at the Customs Service: I transfer large shipments of confiscated goods to warehouses outside town. My Old Maid is excellent for this kind of job. It's a spacious and fairly lightweight banf. I even hired a few people to help me. You have to have other people helping you on a ship even for such short trips. I signed contracts with them until the end of this year. If I leave my job now and go on that voyage, they'll sue me. What was I thinking?"

Captain Giatta gulped down a glass of Jubatic Juice that I had ordered for him and drew a deep sigh. He looked like he had just woken up after an unhealthy midday nap in a poorly ventilated room.

"I take it you've changed your mind about leaving now," I said. "I'm very keen on getting into all sorts of risky ventures, but you've clearly outdone me here."

"Thank goodness I was smart enough to remember my debt and come here to say goodbye to you," said the captain. He took a few more sips from his glass and shook his head. "What was it? It's like a spell. I saw that captain, listened to him telling me about this upcoming 'great voyage,' and got as excited as a kid. I completely lost track of everything. Now I realize I was prepared to go with him to the ends of the earth as a regular sailor if he'd called me."

"Really?" I said. "Talk about charisma."

"I beg your pardon?" The Tasherian blinked.

"Oh, I'm always talking nonsense. Sorry. I just meant that the fellow has an uncanny way of charming others and wrapping them around his little finger."

"I guess you're right," said Giatta, wiping his forehead. "You can't imagine how strong was my sudden urge to go on that accursed voyage! I completely lost my head. I'm so thankful that you started to ask me questions and made me remember so many details. I think I should go home, sleep two dozen hours, and not stick my head out until his Tobindona weighs anchor."

"Tobindona?" I said. "Strange name. Is it a woman's name?"

"No, it's some kind of exotic plant," said the captain.

"A plant you say? Oh, well, to Magicians with that plant. I just repeated the name so as not to forget it. Maybe everything's all right, and you just met a great guy with a great gift of persuasion, and grabbed your first opportunity to get out because you've stayed here too long. That's not impossible. Yet I want to make sure you weren't the victim of some spell because spells are my specialty. I would be sad if I missed my chance to meet this guy. When did you say he was about to set off?"

"He told us to arrive tomorrow at dusk," said Giatta, "and I think he's casting off an hour after that."

"Wait, there were other takers besides yourself, then?"

"Of course. About two dozen more people listened to his speech, and all of them were willing to be employed on the Tobindona."

"All of them? Well, well. And how did you meet him?"

"There's a little square in the Port Quarter. It doesn't even have a name, or perhaps it was forgotten long ago since nobody needs it—everyone knows the place. Sailors come there looking for a job, captains looking for a crew, and plain bored old geezers come there to chat with their younger colleagues. You know how it is."

"More or less."

"Well, I came because I wanted to hire help for the coming year. It's been too much work for me to handle alone recently, so I was looking for a sailor who'd stand in for me on the Old Maid. I saw a group of people gathered around some gentleman, so I approached them to listen to what they were talking about. I ended up signing on to his crew, instead of . . ." Captain Giatta made a helpless gesture and fell silent.

"Okay, put it out of your mind," I said. "If you had come to your senses somewhere around Tuto Islands, despair would have been in order. What's your brilliant orator's name again?"

"I don't know. I didn't even ask him." Captain Giatta was no longer surprised at his own absentmindedness. I think he was beginning to get mad, although I wasn't sure at whom. Not at me, I hoped.

"Captain, go home and get some sleep," I said. "All's well that ends well. And you know what? I don't think you should venture out tomorrow. Just to be on the safe side. What if that was a spell? Wait until the Tobindona casts off—did I get that name right?"

"You did."

"Good. So you are supposed to meet tomorrow at dusk. Where exactly? The port is a large place," I said.

"At the end of the Main Pier of the Right Bank. That's where the Tobindona is docked," said Giatta.

"Thank you, Giatta. I think I'll find it. Well, good night, and don't hesitate to send me a call if your plans suddenly change once again. It's not a good idea to fight spells alone. I know this from personal experience."

Captain Giatta went home, and I fell into deep thought. At first I thought I should go to the port right away and get to the bottom of this Tobindona case, but soon I realized that wasn't the best idea. I doubted I was capable of finding anything quickly in the dark alleyways and nooks of the Capital's port. Worse, I could get lost there. I couldn't tell a karuna from a banf, and I knew next to nothing about anything that had to do with the sea or navigation. True, I thought, that might not be necessary in this case, but . . . Exactly: but.

If I wanted to go to the port, I needed help from Sir Kofa, or even

Melifaro. Besides, I should probably discuss it first with Juffin, who had pleaded with me not to disturb him until noon. Well, at least I had time—not until noon but until breakfast time tomorrow.

I spent the rest of my energy on a feat of a different kind: I called in a courier and demanded that he clean off my desk. To my surprise, the fellow managed this impossible task in almost no time—did he use magic?—and left the office without making a sound. I moved another armchair next to the one I was sitting in, put my legs up on it, and dozed off. Melifaro's warm looxi, which I had forgotten to take off and change for my Mantle of Death, served as a great blanket, its horrific turquoise color notwithstanding.

It was still dark when Sir Kofa woke me up.

"If you like sleeping so much, you can do it at home," he said. "I need to think, so scram."

Of course I didn't have the guts to tell him about Captain Giatta: the word "later" sounds so tempting an hour before dawn. I was so sleepy that I just muttered a thank-you and dragged myself over to a company amobiler, much to the driver's shock: he had never seen me leave Headquarters in the back seat of an amobiler. Usually I try to grab the lever myself no matter what condition I'm in. Today, though, I was really out of shape.

On top of that, the driver unloaded me by my house on the Street of Yellow Stones. Half awake, I realized what had happened only after the amobiler had disappeared around the corner. I wasn't going to submit to fate. Struggling to keep my eyes open, I walked to Tekki's place. Praise be the Magicians, the Armstrong & Ella was just a few blocks away. For someone who's half asleep, though, walking a short distance feels like traveling half the globe.

Good grief, I thought as I opened the bedroom door, I'm being so childish. What difference does it make where I crash? But as soon as I got into bed and pulled the few remaining inches of warm blanket over myself (Tekki had grabbed the rest of the furry cover), I realized there was a difference after all.

Once in bed, I couldn't go to sleep. I started thinking about my most recent conversation with Tekki. She couldn't leave Echo—this was bad news. I had been planning to ask Juffin for a vacation so I could go to Kettari and, of course, take Tekki along with me. I desperately wanted to go back and walk with Tekki through that wonderful place, whose magnificent bridges, empty gardens, and narrow embankments had once made me lose my head. I also had hoped that we'd be able to return to the small nameless town in the mountains that had once been part of my dreams and then became a real place on the edge of the newborn World, a place quite suitable for living. If the words of Mackie Ainti, the old sheriff of Kettari, were to be trusted, I had been solely responsible for that miracle. If only I knew how I'd pulled it off. Until today, I had been positive that I would invite Tekki to go on that trip with me some day, and then—boom!

Maybe I'll be able to share my dream with her, I thought. Once Sir Shurf Lonli-Lokli and I had managed to stroll through my favorite dreams together just by putting our heads on the same pillow. Granted, it was Shurf who was doing the magic—I'd never tried this trick myself. On the other hand, I could sometimes pull off things that I thought I'd never be capable of pulling off. Why not try it now? What if it works? It's an unorthodox way of asking your girlfriend out, sure, but then again, it's me we're talking about.

I laid my head on Tekki's pillow. A silver lock of her hair tickled my ear, and I gently pushed it away. I suppressed the desire to bite the sweet lobe of her ear, relaxed, yawned, and closed my eyes. I took a deep breath, smelling the honey aroma of her hair, and fell asleep.

Sometimes it's as easy as pie to fall into another adventure.

I dreamed I was walking up the gentle slope of a hill. It was hot. Too hot for my taste. Short dry grass, faded in the sun, crackled under my feet. It was hard to walk. After taking a few steps, I noticed the slope wasn't so gentle after all. And yet I kept trudging upward, not knowing how I had suddenly become so adept at mountain climbing.

Now I was on the top of the hill. I wiped off the sweat that covered my face and looked around. From here, a magnificent view opened up onto a nondescript valley among the gentle outlines of hills. Searing heat and shades of golden yellow ruled the landscape here. Dry grass rustled in the hot wind. This was the only vegetation: there were no trees, no bushes, no water, no houses—only the motionless ocean of sunburned grass under a shimmering white sky, with no sun or suns that I could discern.

"You like it here, Max?" The voice came from behind me.

It this hadn't been a dream, I definitely would have jumped three feet in the air and maybe even screamed. But in my dreams, I'm as calm as a boa constrictor. I didn't even turn around. I couldn't take my eyes off the enchanting golden folds of this strange landscape. I answered without bothering to learn who was talking to me. "I'm not sure. This doesn't feel like my dream."

"Of course it doesn't," the voice said. "It's not my dream, either. Actually, it's not even a dream. Just the silly fantasy of one lonely daydreamer. But it's livable, as I've had the chance to find out for myself recently. And why aren't you turning around? I'm not the most disgusting creature in the Universe, whatever Magician Nuflin may think of me."

"I'm sorry. It seems this place inspires a peculiar form laziness," I said. "I am a first-class idler, but until now I never thought one couldn't be bothered to simply turn around."

While I was saying all this, I managed to break the bondage of my gaze at the golden landscape. I felt I could move now, although I didn't feel particularly inclined to do so. Good manners took precedence, though, and I turned to face my interlocutor.

He was sitting motionless on a small flat rock that shimmered and glistened with all shades of honey. The rock looked like a chunk of amber. The man sitting on top of it was of an indeterminate age. He wore loose white pants and a loose collarless shirt. On his feet he wore soft orange leather Uguland boots. His long, skinny arms with their large, strong hands were folded and resting on his knees. His appearance looked a little funny to me. I might have mistaken him for a fashionable beachgoer or a nutty dentist who had decided to open a practice in the middle of a vast desert. I couldn't make out his face because of his long light hair. I took one glance at it and knew it was as coarse as metal wire. His appearance, however, didn't matter. I knew who it was I had come face to face with in this strange place. I don't know how I knew. I just did.

"Sir Loiso Pondoxo?" I said, my heart sinking. "The Grand Magician of the Order of the Watery Crow. Maybe you'll be able to explain to me why your formidable Order had such a silly name. No one I've asked has yet given me an answer. I knew one day you'd appear somewhere right beside me."

"Really? What made you think that?" His surprise seemed genuine.

"Not a day goes by that someone doesn't mention your name to me," I said.

"Well, that doesn't explain anything. People mention lots of names."

I tried to explain to him honestly what I'd always found inexplicable. "I've always had an unusual reaction to people mentioning your name. I'd either laugh like a lunatic or become completely despondent. I mean, it could go either way. Why else would I go from one extreme to the other if I hadn't had this vague premonition?" I surprised myself with my excellent explanation.

"Funny," he said. "See, I didn't ask because I wanted to chat. My only shortcoming is that I'm not clairvoyant. I've never been good at it. This makes life more interesting and less predictable, but sometimes it's a real obstacle. Believe it or not, I've never had a premonition in my entire life. I could never sense what was going to happen or what the outcome of an event would be. I could calculate or make an educated guess, but that's an entirely different process. It's hard for me to imagine how it all happens. You're much luckier in that respect."

He tossed back his long tangled hair and looked at me with bright, attentive eyes. His face looked very familiar, and a moment later I understood why. It was my face—well, almost my face. Sir Loiso Pondoxo looked exactly how I had wanted to look like when I had been young, back when I had believed that a small change in the size of my nose, the outline of my chin, or the shape of my eyes would make my life better.

I was shocked by this discovery, but then I remembered what Juffin had told me about this fellow only three dozen days ago. We had been talking about Tekki. According to Juffin, all Loiso Pondoxo's children were "mirrors"—creatures that reflected their interlocutors. Juffin had said that talking to Tekki was akin to having a split personality. He then had said that Loiso himself had been the best "mirror"—"the most devastating kind of personal charm" had been what Juffin had said. I couldn't agree with him more.

I decided not to tell Loiso that I knew his trick. Let him think that I'm dying to kiss the soles of his boots, I thought. Keeping a little secret had never been against my principles. Besides, I wasn't really interested in his face. I wanted to grab my chance: I had a plethora of questions for this legendary man.

"So you survived?" I said, sitting down on the yellow grass. "Or did you die and this is your personal hell?"

"Both. Are you really interested?" he said.

"Of course I am. It's not every day you get the chance to learn such a great mystery. Besides, I've suddenly got the chance to find out exactly what it is I'm dreaming about. I don't know about anyone else, but this doesn't happen to me too often."

"You're an amazingly frivolous person," said Loiso, grinning. "I can imagine what you've heard about me from the Kettarian. What others say about me, I can't even begin to guess—my imagination has its bounds. And yet you just sat down beside me and began this small talk. Is this bravery? Or is this a new form of madness that just came into fashion in the Capital of the Unified Kingdom?"

"The latter, I think—although, no. You just don't reek of danger. For now, at least," I said honestly.

"Will you look at him? Well, your nose hasn't lied to you. I don't reek of any danger," he said and made a funny, helpless gesture. "But I will, and sooner rather than later."

I smiled. Sir Loiso Pondoxo copied my gestures and intonations in a very cute and cunning fashion—just like his daughter. Juffin was right. I was lucky that the boss had found time to lecture me on this subject. That new information had added fire to the flame of my relationship with Tekki. How could it not, such an exotic little detail? But now I knew better than to melt under the "kind" gaze of her infamous daddy.

I was still in danger of melting, though, but for an altogether different reason: it was roasting hot here. Every minute it was getting hotter and hotter, which only reinforced my crazy hypothesis about this place being Loiso's hell.

"Well, this is all fine and dandy," I said, wiping the sweat from my face again, "but I'd like to wake up now, thank you very much. Just tell me whether I'm your guest or your prisoner. Because if I'm a prisoner, I'm going to have to start fumbling in the Chink between Worlds, hoping to get hold of a fan, or at least an ice cream cone."

"Oh, this isn't hot; it's just very warm," said Loiso mildly. "If you stayed in this World a little longer, you'd know the difference. To wake up, you just need to walk downhill a little. It's very easy to walk away from me, Max. Especially for you. Trust me, the last thing I need is to quarrel with you. After all, you're my first visitor since the day that Kettarian lured me into this trap."

"He says he lured you into a disappearing World," I said, "and that according to his calculations, you should've disappeared along with this place a long time ago. But you didn't. Or did you?"

"No, I did not, as you can see," said Loiso. "You and I find ourselves in that very disappearing World as we speak. It was born out of the dreams of one crazy old hag—an unbearable old bitch, you can take my word for it. There are many Worlds in the Universe that are born out of someone's dreams. When Juffin pulled me in here, that lady was just about to die—very considerate of her. After her death, the World was supposed to disappear, taking me with it, it's true. There was one thing that Juffin didn't take into account, though: the vestiges of my powers were enough to render the old lady virtually immortal. I don't know how long she's going to linger, but it's going to be much longer than people normally do. I can only feel for her heirs: they're not getting anything, not in their lifetime. The funny thing is that the old hag has no idea why Death has been avoiding her. And she never will, I suppose."

"I never thought I'd have to bring such news to Juffin," I said. "I don't know which he's going to like best: the news itself, or the fact that I'm going to be bringing it. Because I'm going to tell him, even if you don't want me to. You know, Sir Loiso, I have this nasty habit of telling him everything. It's like a tic—I can't help it."

"Of course you will tell him," said Loiso. "I wouldn't have let you in this place if that mattered one way or the other. I've become quite used to things here. Adapting to them has been my only pastime and the only way to fill my endless leisure hours. Juffin made sure I couldn't leave this World, and I made sure no one could enter it uninvited. It's not a lot, but it's something. So you can tell Juffin anything you wish. You can even make a few things up—I don't mind. I think he probably knows I'm still kicking, and I suspect he had left this little chance for me to stay alive on purpose: he desperately wanted to watch me try and get out of here. Do you know what they called him when he was sheriff in his hometown?"

"What?" I said.

"They called him a chiffa," said Loiso and gave me a long look. "Right, you probably don't know what a chiffa is. A chiffa is a small silvery fox that lives in the mountains of County Shimara. A very cunning critter. It's so cunning that it's almost impossible to catch him. There is only one way: chiffas are as curious as they are cunning. If a hunter stops behaving like a hunter and begins to do something out of the ordinary, like standing on his head or juggling with his own boots, for example, then there's a chance that a chiffa will leave his hideout to see what's going on. But this will only trick young, inexperienced chiffas. Old chiffas will only buy a real miracle. Back in the old days, there were plenty of good sorcerers among Shimarian hunters. They went to great lengths to get hold of the chiffa's silvery fur."

"I see," I said.

"Well, in that case, you may also see why I don't think the Kettarian will be too surprised to learn that I'm still alive. Deep down, he's probably hoping that I am. It's very much in his character to poke his curious nose out of his burrow and see what I'm going to do in a desperate situation. I actually quite like his attitude."

"So do I," I said. "You know, Loiso, I'm really interested and all that, but I don't think this climate is good for me. So if you don't mind, I'm going to go ahead and take your advice and start walking down this hill. I can only imagine how 'well rested' I'm going to be when I wake up."

"Of course, you should go," he said. "See you."

"Is that an invitation or a warning?" I said. I was on the verge of collapse from the heat. I only managed to stay on my feet because of my inborn stubbornness. The last thing I wanted was to ask Sir Loiso Pondoxo to take me in his arms and carry me where I needed to go. I really liked him, and that meant that I'd be desperate to show off and strut my stuff in front of him—at any cost.

"It's a bit of both, an invitation and a warning," said Loiso. "But I don't think I'll have to go out of my way to have you over here again. You're even more willing to stick your curious nose out of your foxhole than your guardian. You're still a cub."

"True, that," I said. "Next time, though, try to assume the appearance of some beautiful girl from my adolescent dreams. I think there are plenty of wonderful specimens in the corners of my memory. You never know, maybe I'll like you even more." I was beginning to be really brazen—a sure sign that I was feeling really bad.

"There's no need to go that far," said Loiso. "You love yourself more than anyone else."

"Touché," I said, taking my first unsteady step down the hill. "Never mind me, I'm just being a young Turk. I hope you like having my face on yours." My head was spinning, I swayed as if drunk, and my thinking fared no better.

"What's a Turk?" the Grand Magician Loiso Pondoxo shouted to my back.

Funny. His daughter had once asked me the very same question. I couldn't answer: I was laughing and that depleted the rest of my energy. My vision went blank, but I continued to walk down the hill until I tripped over a clump of dry grass and fell, rolling head over heels . . .

. . . and finally sucked in a draft of cool air. Praise be whoever should be praised, I was lying peacefully under the blanket in the semidarkness of Tekki's bedroom. She was lying next to me, sleeping like a baby. All was well.

I looked out the window. The sun had just appeared in the sky. That meant that I had slept for no more than an hour. Who would've thought? Then I looked at my hands and saw fresh scratches on my palms. I had just gotten them in my dream when I clutched at the sharp dry tufts of grass, but the scratches were very real.

Well, what did I expect? That my encounter with Loiso Pondoxo had been one of those dreams one could discuss with a shrink and then painlessly forget? I was mad at myself. I hid the evidence of my romantic journey under the blanket and put my head on the pillow—my pillow this time. After a short but educational walk in the personal hell of the Grand Magician Loiso Pondoxo, I was feeling wretched and needed some real sleep, the kind of deep sleep I usually got when I returned home from a long, hard shift at work. In a sense, that was what had happened.

I fell asleep again, this time without any dreams, which was for the better. I didn't get much sleep, but when I woke up from Tekki's tender and somewhat hesitant touch, I realized I felt great. I also realized that the last thing I wanted was for her to find out that Sir Loiso Pondoxo had invaded my dreams right after I had put my head on her pillow. As if she needed to deal with my stupid problems on top of the consequences of the strange legacy she would have to deal with for the rest of her life. My story was good for Juffin and Juffin alone.

I looked into her calm, still sleepy eyes and listened to my two hearts knocking. The mysterious muscles were pumping blood through their arteries and didn't seem to bother my head with bad premonitions. It was clear that Tekki had no clue about my encounter with Loiso. Good. I had other plans for the morning.

I had kept my promise not to wake up Juffin until noon even if the sky fell. I considered my heart-to-heart talk with Loiso to be an even more serious disaster, but the boss deserved the chance to have a good night's sleep. It was way past noon when I sent him a call.

I desperately need to have lunch with you, Juffin.

Really? You sure go out of your way to save a crown or two.

Guilty as charged. Seriously, though, Juffin, I must talk to you. And you must talk to me. You just don't know it, yet.

I suppose so. Otherwise you wouldn't have troubled yourself with Silent Speech. Fine, come to the Glutton. I've been sitting here for several minutes already.

Uh, actually, my news will require a more intimate setting. I was planning to deliver it in the office. Better yet, in your detention cell with all your magic bolts bolted.

Nonsense, Max. Trust me, the walls of the Glutton Bunba are just as good at absorbing horrible secrets.

"Tekki, I'm off," I said. "I have a feeling this is going to be one heck of a day. I don't know when I'm going to be back. Maybe I'll drop by in a couple of hours—where else can I get some kamra without paying for it? Or maybe I'll come back in a year with a beard down to my belt, apologize, and say I accidentally went on a trip around the world." I smiled, remembering Captain Giatta. Right, I had that case to deal with, too.

"Beards don't grow that fast," said Tekki. "If you want to boast a long beard, you'll have to stay away a dozen years at least. But I don't think it's necessary—the beard, I mean."

"I sure hope so," I said. "Beards only trap food crumbs." I ran outside. Another minute in Tekki's company and I'd think that my talk with Juffin could wait.

Because I had returned home in a company amobiler yesterday, my own amobiler was still on the Street of Copper Pots by the walls of the Ministry of Perfect Public Order. This was no longer a problem, however. After Sir Lonli-Lokli and I had combined our efforts to destroy my first amobiler, I had lived almost a dozen days without any transportation. When I had finally gotten to the place that sold them, the variety of amobilers on the market had made me drunk. Without giving it a second thought, I had bought a few, thinking that I couldn't have too many, given my lifestyle.

Today it turned out that my risky investment had been a far-sighted one. Instead of ripping my hair out and crying, I took one of my spares and drove to the Old City, feeling quite content and somewhat perplexed by my own coolness: I had more or less gotten used to being a powerful sorcerer, but I'd probably never get used to being rich.

Sir Juffin Hully was sitting at our favorite table in the Glutton Bunba. "Sir Max has shown up in double-quick time, as usual," he said to the pitcher in front of him. Then he looked at me and smiled. "Max, your face suggests that you're going to tell me something extraordinary. Something along the lines of Loiso Pondoxo coming back to life."

"So you know?" I said.

"I was joking," said Juffin. "And so were you, I hope." He stopped short and gave me a look that was a mixture of mockery and surprise. "Hold on a second, you're not joking, are you?"

"No, I'm not," I said. "So should I spit it out here, or should I wait until you've finished lunch and returned to the House by the Bridge?"

"Spit it out here. Makes no difference where one hears news like that."

And I told him everything, beginning with the moment I put my silly head on Tekki's pillow and ending with my showing Juffin the scratches on my palms.

"Why were you clutching at the sinning grass to begin with?" Juffin said. "To prove it to me later on?"

"Do you think I'm really that smart?" I said. "I grabbed it mechanically, without really thinking about it. I couldn't think straight by that time. It was real heatstroke. You have no idea how hot it was there."

"Oh, but I do," said Juffin. "I've been there."

"Right," I said. "Well, how do you like the news?"

"Actually, I don't know," said Juffin, staring at me with unconcealed surprise. "In my book, it's too much. I think I'm glad that Loiso is still kicking. I used to think that the Universe had become empty without him. Are you surprised?"

"Probably not," I said. "I . . . liked him, although I do realize that I wasn't dealing with the real Loiso Pondoxo, just my own reflection—idealized, augmented, and corrected in compliance with my own recommendations. You were right: it's the most devastating kind of personal charm. In any case, I bought into it—lock, stock, and barrel. Who could ever resist himself? What does the real Loiso Pondoxo look like, I wonder? Or did you only deal with a nice copy of yourself, too?"

"It depends. Besides, Loiso and I have many mutual acquaintances. Take Maba Kalox, for example—he and Loiso used to be good friends. So I think I know what the real Loiso looks like. He's moody but always aggressive—that's the only thing that never changes in him. He's not evil, but he's definitely aggressive. When you're dealing with the real Loiso, it seems as though he has no choice: he'll either tear everything around into pieces or blow up himself. He's a very charming person, and insufferable at the same time. His old friends in the Xolomi Higher Institute used to tell me that everybody adored Loiso. At the same time, they avoided inviting him to parties. Even back then, there was too much of him for others to be able to relax in his company. He poured bucketfuls of his unpredictability on others. Then again, Loiso was never really fond of parties or other social events. He was a self-contained fellow. Solitude fit him like a glove."

"You seem to be madly in love with your old enemy," I said.

"In a way, you're right," said the boss. "I love strange birds. Loiso Pondoxo was not just an eccentric psychopath; he was a brilliant sorcerer, too. He had an innate talent for Apparent Magic. People used to say that he'd learned to fly before he learned to walk, and I have reasons to believe that legend."

"And yet you beat him," I said.

"Well, looks like I didn't after all," said Juffin. "Still, better than nothing, I suppose. I was lucky that Loiso had begun taking lessons in True Magic much later than I had. Plus, he was more stubborn than talented. This put me at an advantage. It was probably the funniest battle in the entire history of the Troubled Times: two powerful magicians, neither wanting to kill the other yet being compelled to do it. On top of that, both of us were curious to find out how it would end."

"Why did you even engage in that battle of the titans to begin with?" I said. "From the looks of it, you and Loiso could've become buddies."

"It was my job," said Juffin. "I had orders. Also, Loiso was very capable of destroying this World, and he certainly never lacked the desire to do it. It's not a metaphor but a fact. He even had time to do some damage. Kettari, as you know, disappeared from the face of the earth, and for Loiso it was a mere warm-up before the main show. But in any event, we wouldn't have become buddies. Fate has always been very persistent at making our paths diverge, and you can't fool fate."

"Yeah," I said, "that I know. Well, that's all very neat, but what am I supposed to do now, Juffin? I mean with myself, my darn dreams, Loiso, and Tekki, of course? I don't know how to proceed."

"Hold onto your seat, but I don't know either. I don't think you should do anything at all. Live and wait for the situation to unfold. Just make sure your head always stays on your own pillow. Perhaps Loiso can only communicate with you through his daughter. Tekki is his last living offspring, a small reservoir of his powers set aside for a rainy day. She's a 'window' on our World. I suspect that your affair may have been a well-crafted trap from the outset."

"But she has no clue," I said nervously. "That's for sure."

"And that's the dangerous part. If Tekki were capable of controlling the situation in any way, I'd feel much safer. She's a good girl, Max. Don't fret. You don't need to run away from her to the end of the World. Just, to be on the safe side, don't put your crazy head on her pillow, that's all. Can you manage that?"

"It'll be hard, but I'll manage," I said. My good mood had returned to me.

"Maybe it'll be harder than you can imagine," said Juffin. "You don't know what your body is doing while you're running around in your dreams. It tosses and turns, it kicks and mutters. The next thing you know, your head will be on Tekki's pillow."

"Ahem, that's very unlikely," I said, embarrassed. "Tekki and I sleep at different times and often in different places. This morning was an exception rather than a rule."

"Okay, we'll see," said Juffin. "Deep down in my heart, I'm sure these are vain efforts. Loiso is probably powerful enough now to get to you without Tekki's help. He got you once, and now it doesn't matter which pillow your head rests on. On the other hand, who says that visiting Loiso will necessarily harm you? He's a dangerous creature, of course, but you weren't born yesterday, either. I'll bet you're curious as heck."

"I am," I said. "I'm so curious it makes my head spin. Loiso was right about that chiffa fox. You and I are very much alike."

"You bet he was. I'm not sure which of us is more curious. You, probably."

"I'm just younger so it's easier to lure me out of my foxhole simply by standing on your head. And that's exactly what your old friend there is doing."

We both fell silent, each thinking his own thoughts. After a pause, I said, "You know, Juffin, I'm absolutely sure that your great and mighty Loiso Pondoxo poses no danger to me, at least not now. Otherwise, my heart would've warned me."

"And it hasn't?"

"Nope. So I'd love to pay him a couple more visits on my own volition. The only thing that stops me is that the situation might change at some point and there will be no going back."

"There's no going back for you already," said Juffin. "Because there's no going back for anyone. It's just a fairy tale, a pacifier that's as good as a lullaby. Okay, let's consider this conversation about Loiso over. Enough for today. I suspect that you and I will have plenty of time to get sick of this topic. A word of warning, Max: this is a real secret. No one must know about your meeting with Loiso. And I mean no one. Period. Well, except maybe for Tekki, but it's up to you. On the one hand, she has the right to know. On the other hand, who knows what she might do to try to protect you from her daddy?"

"What can she do?" I said.

"She still might try. She holds very dear the chance to touch your body from time to time, you know. Besides, she has her own bone to pick with Loiso. She really hates being in her own shoes, even though I know a lot of people who'd trade with her in a heartbeat."

"Being in one's own shoes is a special thing. There are very few who are lucky enough to be happy about it," I said. "But we always find something attractive about being in someone else's shoes."

"Very wise words, young Max," said Juffin. His lighthearted mockery had a pacifying effect on me. I knew that when Sir Juffin Hully spoke in this tone, the World was safe. It wouldn't disappear or collapse. It would withstand whatever some Loiso Pondoxo or other might do to try to destroy it.

"Speaking of my wisdom," I said. "Something intriguing and peculiar happened last night—" I was going to tell him Captain Giatta's story, but Juffin shook his head and didn't let me finish.

"Talk to Kofa about it."

"How do you know what I was going to say?" I said.

"I don't, but my heart tells me that story is meant for Sir Kofa's ears. Did you think you were the only one with a good adviser sitting in your chest?"

"Fine. Then I'm not lunching with you," I said. "To reach an understanding with Kofa, one must speak with his mouth full."

"Are you saying that you're willing to sacrifice one of the two possible lunches?" said the boss. "Now I see that Loiso cast the evil eye on you after all."

I chuckled and sent Sir Kofa Yox a call.

Kofa, I'm starving. Besides, I'm dying to share a little secret with you and you alone.

Imagine that, I'm also dying to share a little secret with you, or possibly Melifaro. I haven't decided yet. Where are you, by the way?

I'm sitting in the Glutton and staring at Juffin's empty plate.

Good. Bring in Melifaro and start eating. I'll join you in a quarter of an hour.

"Are you done talking with Kofa?" said Juffin, getting up from the table. "Wonderful, let's go."

"I'm not going anywhere with you," I said. "Sir Kofa told me to stay here and expand my circle of companionship, if possible."

"I see. Good luck expanding it then. Kofa doesn't give bad advice. Good day, Max. Maybe we'll run into each other later today."

"It's a small world. And the House by the Bridge is even smaller," I said. "Thank you, Juffin. You set my mind at ease."

"Really? Silly me. I had hoped to scare the living heck out of you instead." He waved goodbye and left. I sent a call to Melifaro.

I've been waiting for you in the Glutton for half an hour already. What's wrong with you?

Nothing's wrong with me, but did you ever stop to think that it's a good idea to invite me somewhere before starting to wait for me there?

I did. Just now. That's why I'm talking to you. Also, if you hurry, you'll have a good chance of getting here before Kofa.

Is this a business meeting or a party?

Does it matter?

Less than a minute later Melifaro rushed into the Glutton Bunba, this time wearing a brand-new fiery red looxi. I cringed but my colleague was quite happy with himself.

"Did I beat Kofa?" he said. "Sweet. Just tell me, has something happened or not? I must know, because if it has, I'll eat twice as much as I usually do so I don't have to waste time on it later."

"I'm not sure. First Kofa will come and tell me his news," I said. "Then I'll decide. But you should eat more, just in case."

"Thanks for the advice. What would I do without you?"

"Mostly stupid things," I said.

"True, that," he said and opened the menu. I noticed that his mood was going off the scale on the "Good" side of the gauge.

"Is everything super?" I said.

"Oh, I don't know. I guess. Yes. It is!" Melifaro wasn't speaking; he was singing, addressing, for the most part, the ceiling. Look at him, mister, and learn, I said to myself. And keep in mind that when you begin an affair, your face assumes the same idiotic expression. Maybe even more idiotic because you just love going overboard with everything.

"What's with the mocking stare?" said Melifaro.

"Don't take it personally," I said. "If anything, I'm mocking myself. Well, maybe you, too. But just a little."

"Oh, I don't mind. Go ahead. It's your right. That's the only thing that husbands who are being cheated on can do, anyway."

"Am I already being cheated on?" I said. "So soon?"

"You will be," said Melifaro. "After your speech yesterday, it could happen any minute now. You took such a load off the girls' poor minds when you said they didn't have to stay in the bedroom with such a monster as you for the rest of their lives. I love you, man!"

"Me? Why me?" I said.

"Why not? Hey, look! Here comes our Master Eavesdropper-Gobbler! And he has his own face, for some reason. Way to blow the cover. Good day, Kofa."

"It's been quite a day, indeed," said Kofa, sitting down next to Melifaro. "How come you're not eating anything?"

"We were too busy talking about women," said Melifaro.

"Really? How very original of you. Still, I suggest we order something to eat and talk about something less exciting so it doesn't interfere with digestion. About work, for example. What kind of news do you have, Max? Is it serious or not?"

"Frankly, I'm not sure," I said. "It may be serious, or it may be nonsense. We need to discuss it."

"Well, I have something really peculiar to tell you, so I'm going to start, if you don't mind."

"I'm all ears," I said.

"Some of you should be all mouth," said Kofa, giving a kind look to the trays of food. He tasted the contents of his pot, nodded, and began his story. "After you and Kekki chatted about that sinning chest for a half hour, I couldn't stop thinking about it. And if I think about something for more than just a few minutes, my feet inevitably bring me to where I can meet the protagonist of a story, or at least where I can find out more about him." Kofa looked at me, smiling. "No, boy, this isn't a metaphor. It's just my little talent—well, one of them, but it's very useful. When I was the General of the Police of the Right Bank, not a day went by that I didn't have to use it. I still do, occasionally. There are hundreds of taverns in Echo, praise be the Magicians, and there's just one me. I'd be worthless at my job if I couldn't come to the right place at the right time."

"Awesome," I said. "Until now, I had a very different idea about your job."

"That's what I thought. That's why I decided to explain it to you while we're at it. In addition, I want you to know why I knew that my story has everything to do with your friend's stolen possessions, Max."

Kofa fell silent and began eating, as though giving me time to process new information. Finally, he went on. "Last night, I took our ladies home and went out, never stopping to think about that sinning chest. I let my legs take me where they thought I should be. I ended up in the Drunken Rain."

"Oh, that's a good place," said Melifaro in a tone of an expert.

"A good place I've never heard of," I said.

"Life is long," said Kofa. "There's still time. Please don't interrupt me."

Melifaro and I felt ashamed and tried to look intelligent. Kofa appreciated our efforts, nodded, and continued. "The Drunken Rain was almost empty, just what a man needs to meet an old friend of his. My old friend's name was Zekka Moddorok. He once was an apprentice at the Order of Green Moons."

"Oh, Anday's father and grandfather used to make a living working for that Order," I said. "They became cooks after they had tired of pirating and settled in Echo. Then they died, when the army of your legendary Gurig VII burned down the Residence of the Order.

But I thought all the members of the Order of Green Moons were killed in the beginning of the Troubled Times. Looks like some of them survived."

"Of course," said Kofa. "A few apprentices and nineteen Junior Magicians—everyone who happened to be elsewhere at the time. The Junior Magicians had to sneak out of the Unified Kingdom, and apprentices weren't prosecuted because no one saw them as a threat.

"I became acquainted with Zekka Moddorok under completely different circumstances. He was a marauder during the Troubled Times and liked it so much he couldn't stop even after the establishment of the Code of Krember. During the first years of the new Epoch, several famous robberies were committed, with and without the use of Forbidden Magic. The police couldn't crack those cases: in the beginning of his career, General Boboota Box was an even dimmer bulb than he is now, and the organization lacked people with the intelligence of Lieutenant Apurra Blookey or the late Shixola.

"Chaos reigned until I put my work in the Secret Investigative Force on hold to catch that sweet young man Zekka personally. I'm not joking about him being sweet. You should have seen his large blue eyes and freckled button of a nose. Back then he was as old as you two are now, yet he looked like a spoiled teenager, much to the chagrin of his numerous victims. He ended up doing time in Xolomi—ninety years, no less. He was convicted of two murders, though most likely those were cases of involuntary manslaughter. But a murder is a murder."

"So he just got out recently?" said Melifaro. "When did you lock him up?"

"In '26. He got out late last year. I had almost forgotten about him—I had other things on my mind—but I recognized him immediately. The same round eyes and innocent, childish smile, as though he's about to ask you if he can have another piece of candy.

"I immediately remembered that Zekka Moddorok had once had a good chance of becoming acquainted with the relatives of your friend, Max. Then I realized that he could be one of the accomplices of the chest thieves. It's just too much of a coincidence. Plus, my premonition led me to the Drunken Rain, and when I looked at the rest of the customers—the three fellows who were dozing off—I felt nothing but boredom.

"Zekka didn't recognize me at first—I had shape-shifted beforehand, naturally—but I wanted to speak with him as myself. There was no need to beat around the bush. By the time I approached his table, I had already taken off the mask. Zekka was taken aback, but I was very polite and lenient. When you want to crack open someone who's not too bright, the best strategy is to let him think you consider him a witness, not a perpetrator. Out of pure relief, he'll start lying so blatantly and profusely that at some point he's going to say something he shouldn't. That's my personal expert advice to you, boys, absolutely free of charge."

"Congratulations, Kofa," said Melifaro. "I've heard this advice from you six thousand six hundred sixty-six times. A neat symmetrical number, isn't it?"

"Very symmetrical, indeed. So nice of you to keep track of my advice rather than make use of it. But why dream of the impossible?"

"Where would I encounter those 'not too bright' fellows?" said Melifaro. "I work solely with geniuses and can't make use of your advice."

"Go on, Kofa," I said. "What did he say that he shouldn't have? Did he complain that Anday's basement was too dusty?"

"Don't rush me. I began by reminding Zekka of his acquaintance with Zoxma Pu. He frowned, pretending he was desperately trying to remember the name, which was already a glaring mistake on his part. No one who has been an apprentice at any Order will ever, ever forget the name of the Order's chef. The kitchen is the coziest place in the Residence of any Order. A novice, baffled by all the magic, can go there and have a rest from the madness transpiring around him. It's like coming home and pressing your face into your mother's apron, if you know what I mean.

"Then I told Zekka that there was some unbelievable mystery connected with their late chef, which I was investigating as part of my job, and that I'd be grateful if he could remember any little detail. I didn't mention the chest, of course. Instead, I said that there was a reward for any assistance in this case. Almost immediately, Zekka 'remembered' and began pouring out the details of his distant youth. He was on a roll, so I could afford to relax a little and even ordered some Fire in the Dragon's Throat—the house specialty—for both of us.

"Zekka thanked me, then complained that he felt a little chilly, pulled an old looxi from the back of his chair, and began wrapping himself in it. I was even about to ask him why on earth he was wearing these old rags. He comes from a very well-to-do family, and I've never heard any rumors about the Moddoroks rejecting their misguided son. His mother is still crazy about the blue eyes of her little baby boy.

"I had just opened my mouth to ask Zekka about his financial and family affairs when he mumbled something about the door not being closed and sitting right in the draft. With these words, he got up and headed to the door. And then something unfathomable happened."

"You lost your appetite?" said Melifaro.

"Worse. I lost my suspect. I never took my eyes off him, yet he disappeared in the middle of a well-lit room and I didn't even see it happen. The needle of the gauge in my pipe didn't budge, which means that he didn't use Forbidden Magic."

"So he went down the Dark Path then," I said.

"Oh, no, he didn't," said Kofa. "Trust me, if something as extraordinary as that had happened, I would have sensed it."

"Hold on, Kofa," said Melifaro. "Let me get this straight. Are you saying that Zekka Moddorok just vanished, evaporated right in front of your eyes?"

"Not really. At some point I just couldn't focus my vision on him. I know it sounds insane, but my sight just went all blurry. Then I started seeing circles, and everything went a little wonky, like when you're about to faint. It only lasted for a couple of seconds, no longer. I blinked a few times and it passed, but when I stared at the space between the table and the door, Zekka Moddorok wasn't there. He was nowhere in the tavern. I ran outside, but he wasn't on the street, either."

"Should I listen to the end of your story, or should I go look for this invisible man right away?" said Melifaro, getting up.

"No need to go look for him," said Kofa. "And let me tell you why. Sit down."

"Fine," said Melifaro, sitting back down. "If you say so."

"If I told you that this had never happened to me before, I wouldn't be exaggerating," said Kofa. "It made me furious. I decided I'd turn this World inside out as many times as it would take me to find this fellow, and no later than right after dawn."

"I see now," said Melifaro. "If I understand you correctly, Mr. Zekka Moddorok has already made himself comfortable in our detention cell in the House by the Bridge. I know you!"

"In a sense, he has indeed made himself comfortable in the House by the Bridge—but not quite the way you think he has," said Kofa. "But let me go on. I like to tell things in an orderly fashion."

"Of course, of course," said Melifaro.

"I returned to my table and focused on my desire to find Zekka. But I couldn't even do that! Which was something almost unheard of. Then I tried a different approach. Instead of thinking about where Zekka was at that moment, I thought about what he had done. I didn't doubt for a second that he had done something already. I went out, and some time later, I found myself on the Left Bank—more specifically, by the villa of old Sir Chaffi Ranvara. And I had a very distinct feeling that Zekka had been there not long ago. I didn't want to bother Sir Ranvara or his servants—it was after midnight—so instead, I sent a call to Kekki and asked her if anything bad had happened at Ranvara's villa recently.

"Kekki replied that just four days ago the villa had been robbed. The burglars had taken money and a great deal of valuables—all under very mysterious circumstances. The villa had been full of servants all day, and the room where most of the valuables had been stored had been locked with a very strong, intricate lock—the work of an old craftsman. The lock would scream if anyone tried to pick it, and Sir Ranvara always carried the only key in the pocket of his looxi. The door showed no signs of a break-in, and there were no windows in that room. In any event, there had been so many people in the villa that it was unimaginable that no one had noticed anything. Of course the police suspected every servant since they didn't know better.

"I then asked Kekki if there had been similar cases around that time, and what do you think? Seven days ago, a large sum of money had been stolen under similar circumstances—and not just from any place but from the Chancellory of Big Sums of Money!"

"Whoa!" said Melifaro. "How come they never turned to us?"

"Well, the loss of a 'large sum of money' wasn't a good enough reason to pass the case to the Secret Investigative Force," said Kofa. "Now, if they had stolen all the money . . . But that would've required an army of very muscular thieves. Anyway, that's irrelevant. With this news, I set out to pay a visit to Lady Moddorok, Zekka's mother. I had to get her out of bed. It's not in my nature to do such a thing, but desperate times call for desperate measures. Besides, what was she thinking, giving birth to such a rogue? So I told her that her son was in trouble. I said his old enemies from ninety years ago were following him, and that I needed to know where he was staying or else those horrible people might find him before dawn, and I was the only person who could save her poor baby. It was utter nonsense, but it worked like a charm on the old lady."

"He told his mother where he was staying?" I said. "Some criminal."

"Exactly," said Kofa. "But you have to know this fellow really well to understand why I wasted my time chatting with his old lady.

He visits her almost every day because, you see, that old ex-con just can't live without his mommy's sweet, sweet love."

"I'll be darned," I said.

"People often make blunders like that. Even criminals much tougher than Zekka," said Kofa. "Here's an interesting one. About two hundred years ago, I was chasing after a murderer who couldn't live a day without a cream puff pastry. Instead of lying low somewhere in the suburbs, he would come to Echo daily for his favorite treat. I busted him right here in the Glutton, except that back then Mr. Bunba himself was behind the bar." Kofa gave a soft sentimental sigh and began filling his pipe. "The odd part was that Zekka Moddorok wasn't at the address his mother gave me. I found a little Secret Door in his bedroom, and behind it a closet filled with Chaffi Ranvara's valuables, as well as a great deal of money, fresh from the mint. Only an imbecile couldn't guess the origin of the coins.

"I called the police and made them happy with my find. Then I went to the House by the Bridge and sat in your chair, Max, because I was going to give the situation a lot of thought. The policemen had stayed behind to ambush Zekka in his own bedroom, but I had doubts that the fellow would be so stupid as to come home. He was either increasing the distance between himself and Echo at a very high speed or waiting for the morning to look for another place. I was almost positive that he'd prefer the latter: he loves the Capital and his mother. What's more, Zekka apparently had very good reason to consider himself impossible to catch, and a head stupid enough to believe that it would last forever.

"I thought I should probably stick to the protocol and call Melamori. She could stand on Zekka Moddorok's trace, and that would be it. But I didn't want to wake Melamori up an hour before dawn. I told myself we could catch Zekka a couple of hours later—no hurry. I dozed off in the armchair, then sent a call to the Glutton and demanded some semblance of a breakfast. Yet when I was about to take my first sip of kamra, my feet took me outside. I suddenly felt I was about to find Zekka. After all, I had promised myself to find him before dawn.

"I walked out of Headquarters, got into the amobiler, and drove off not knowing where I was going. I couldn't get rid of the feeling that I was about to grab Zekka Moddorok by his hair. It was like looking blindfolded for a piece of smelly cheese: you can't miss it. I didn't even notice when my amobiler swerved from the pavement to the sidewalk. It all happened in a matter of seconds. The sidewalk looked empty, although I was having a hard time focusing my eyes again, just like earlier in the Drunken Rain. Then I felt a hard jolt and heard a scream. Trust me, boys, I've heard plenty of screams in my long, long life, but that scream was one of a kind. I still have a ringing in my ears.

"My amobiler skidded to the side, and I crashed into the wall of a house. I was fine, except for some bruises. I got out of the wrecked amobiler and saw lying dead on the sidewalk the object of my investigation, wrapped in the same raggedy old looxi. Zekka Moddorok was truly very unfortunate. My luck had led me to him like a magnet, so I had swerved onto the sidewalk. But I hadn't noticed him, nor had he noticed me or my amobiler, the quietest amobiler in the Capital. I had run over him. And I did it as skillfully as an executioner at the court of some bloodthirsty emperor obsessed with newfangled forms of torture and death.

"But if you think my story ends with me bringing the body of the unfortunate Zekka Moddorok to the House by the Bridge, delivering him to the morgue, and calling Sir Skalduar Van Dufunbux so he could officially determine the cause of death, you are mistaken."

"We don't think that," said Melifaro. "You wouldn't have wasted that much time just to tell us this weepy story. It's clear you want something from us, and the story of the late Zekka Moddorok is to be continued."

"Precisely. It was clear to me that the poor fellow couldn't have done all those things on his own. All those mysterious robberies in front of so many witnesses in broad daylight! And the way he slipped away from me in the Drunken Rain? Besides, I never forgot for a minute that I had met Zekka when I was trying to find the thieves that had stolen the old pirate chest. Old chests usually have old things in them, so while Skalduar was busy with the dead body, I was examining the dead body's clothes and belongings. First I looked for some amulets or charms, but Zekka didn't have anything of that sort. Then I turned to his clothes—and look what I found!"

Kofa produced a small parcel from his looxi. It was another looxi—or, rather, it looked like an old gray cloak. Kofa put the cloak around his shoulders, but nothing happened. I thought he would disappear like in a fairy tale.

"It's all right, boys," said Kofa, smiling. "Nothing's going to happen while I'm sitting here at the table with you. But watch what happens as I'm leaving. Watch me closely, though."

Melifaro and I stared at Kofa. He got up and walked toward the door. I felt very disinclined to watch his back and wait for a miracle that wasn't going to happen. It would probably turn out—again—that I was a genius and those tricks didn't work on me. Plus, there was something in my eye, and I couldn't focus on the large silhouette of my older colleague.

"Max, I think I just went insane," said Melifaro. "Where'd Kofa go? Do you see him?"

"No," I said, realizing "those tricks" worked very well on me, too. I had also lost sight of Kofa, even though I had been staring at him the best I could.

"How do you like them apples?" said Kofa. It turned out he had been standing by our table all the time. "Isn't this something? Just what I need in my line of work. Our wise Kurush says this cloak belongs to the category of 'ordinary magical things.' I like the way he puts it. This is a catch-all term for the various sorts of charms made far away from Uguland. Usually, they are not very powerful objects, which is understandable: only the lowest degrees of Apparent Magic are used when making them. But when such things turn up in immediate proximity to the Heart of the World—here in Echo, that is—their magical powers intensify. Back when this cloak belonged to the grandfather of your friend, Max, it probably could only distract an attacker and make the aiming harder, nothing fancier than that. Here in Echo, it makes whoever wears it invisible. More than that, no one pays the slightest attention to him. At the same time, magic indicators don't register a thing! What a neat little rag."

"It sure is," said Melifaro. "The best part is that you got hold of it so quickly. Otherwise we'd still be running around chasing it. Besides, this garment from overseas suits you. All the beggars at the port will envy you."

"Indeed," said Kofa. "This is all fine and dandy, but we're going to have to put our brains to work now. We're going to have to imagine where that chest might be, along with its mysterious contents. There could have been something else in it besides the cloak. Plus, there were two burglars hauling it off, and that second burglar could be anyone. We should get down to it right away."

"Before we put our brains to work, I suggest we listen to my story," I said. "It's a lot shorter than yours, and you'll have just enough time to polish off your dessert to the accompaniment of my soporific mumbling. I'm done with mine."

"Order another one," said Melifaro. "Maybe then you'll finally burst, and I'll have to comfort your numerous widows."

"Not at all," said Kofa. "If he bursts, you'll be busy doing his job in addition to your own. Get on with your story, Max."

And I told them the strange story of Captain Giatta. All the time I was telling the story, I hadn't been able to get rid of the feeling that the captain had come to the House by the Bridge not last night but at least two years ago. Something weird was happening to my sense of time.

"So there you have it," I said when I finished. Now I was more convinced than ever that the story was as nonsensical as it was insignificant. I didn't know why I'd bothered to tell it at all.

To my surprise, Kofa's eyes lit up. "You're so incredibly lucky, Max!" he said. "Did you ever stop to think that what you have in your hands is the other end of the tangle of yarn that I was trying to unravel last night?"

"Uh, no." I said. "Why? I mean, what makes you think so? Intuition?"

"This has nothing to do with intuition, my boy. Pure academic knowledge. I didn't waste a minute this morning. I was gathering information about the traditional magic of the islands of the Ukumbian Sea," Kofa said, turning to Melifaro with a wink. "Your father must be cursing me left and right. I sent him the first call three hours before noon, and only just now left him in peace."

The offspring of the great encyclopedist smiled from ear to ear. "Cursing you? Please, Kofa! Sir Manga loves to chat, especially if during said chat he can demonstrate that he's the one and only true know-it-all in the World."

"All right then," said Kofa. "I hope Sir Manga got some pleasure out of the long, long, oh so incredibly long lecture I demanded from him. And his efforts were not in vain. Imagine this, boys: among the numerous Ukumbian amulets and charms, pirates attach most value to those that give you some power over other people—that increase your powers of persuasion or your personal charisma, as it were. It's understandable: such things come in handy when you need to keep in check a whole gang of muscular drinking men who have not the faintest idea about discipline. Imagine what such a thing might be capable of once it turns up here, in the Heart of the World."

"Are you suggesting that the mysterious captain who was hiring a crew for his around-the-world trip had an amulet like that?" said Melifaro. "And as soon as he opened his mouth, everyone around him was simply at the mercy of his oratory skills?"

"Let's go to the port," I said. "We'll look for that Tobindona. The sooner we find it, the better."

Melifaro jumped up. No flies on him, that's for sure.

"In a minute," said Kofa. "We still need to discuss one little detail. Did it occur to you that whoever he is, he is capable of persuading us to think whatever he wishes, too?"

"We're not that stupid!" I said.

"No, we're not," said Kofa. "And we're not that blind, either. Yet none of us could see a person wearing this cape, no matter how close we were. Not one of us. What makes you think the other talisman from that chest is going to be any less powerful?"

"Hmm. I guess you're right. But you have this magic dust rag. That means no one will see you. He'll be addressing his passionate speeches to Melifaro and me, and you'll be standing at a safe distance," I said.

"Not so safe that I won't hear his 'passionate speeches,' as you put it. I'm not so sure that he must see everyone he's addressing. It's enough that they can hear him."

"Then just plug your ears!" I said. Odysseus could protect his whole crew from the enchanting choir of the Sirens. It should be much easier to resist the sweet voice of one single trickster, I thought.

"Good idea," said Kofa. "That's what we're going to do. I'll plug my ears and watch you succumb to the spell of one of the ordinary magical things. I'm dying to see how it's going to work on you."

"Aren't you afraid he's going to suggest to us that we get rid of you?" said Melifaro. "Then we'll go on his around-the-world journey with him. My father will be happy to learn that his son is following to the family tradition."

"He may persuade you to try to get rid of me, but you won't be able to find me," said Kofa. "I'll be wearing the cloak."

"Darn it," said Melifaro. "There goes my dream of circumnavigating the earth. You'll get us out of the holds of any ship. Let's go then. Time is short."

On the way to the port, Kofa was trying to make earplugs from whatever materials he had at hand.

"Drat it!" he said. "It's not working. I still can hear fairly well."

"Plug your ears with beeswax," I said. "Let's stop by some store where they sell candles. Show me the way. Beeswax is a versatile material." I decided to stick to the classical canon: what was good for Odysseus should be good for us.

"How do you know so much?" said Melifaro.

"Comes with the territory," I said.

"There's a place where they sell candles and slabs of soft beeswax around the corner there," said Kofa. "Just what we need."

When he came out of the shop, he was in the greatest of moods.

"So?" said Melifaro. "Just don't tell me this monster was right for once. This will break my heart."

"I can't hear a word you're saying!" said Kofa. He was yelling, like many people who are hard of hearing.

"See?" I said. I was very glad that my years of reading had begun to pay off.

❦

I still think of the port in Echo as a labyrinth that only the initiated know their way around. Well, maybe a couple of geniuses like Sir Kofa can find their way in it, too. Unfortunately, as soon as we climbed out of the amobiler, he put on the old pirate cloak, so I could only hope he was somewhere close by. Nevertheless, Melifaro was also one of those few geniuses: he was navigating the motley sea of people here so effortlessly that it made me envious.

"Where did you say that sinning karuna was docked?" he said.

"At the very end of the Main Pier of the Right Bank," I said.

"Really? I should've asked sooner. We could've parked the amobiler much closer," he said. "Kofa, you should've known better, too! You know that to this barbarian a port is just a port. He doesn't care which gate he arrives at."

Melifaro was talking into empty space, as if he were praying. I'd never seen a more moronic dialogue: Melifaro couldn't see Kofa, and Kofa couldn't hear Melifaro.

"Quit grumbling, Sir Melifaro!" Kofa's yelling came from behind me and slightly to the left. "It's a five-minute walk; you won't even break a sweat."

"So you can hear everything?" I said.

There was no answer.

"He just noticed my indignation," said Melifaro. "You could have guessed that yourself."

A few minutes later, I began thinking we were bound to wander around huge barrels, tarred planks, and gloomy, broad-shouldered men forever. Melifaro was sending my confused face a look out of the corner of his eyes as he jumped over the numerous sacks that were blocking our way.

"Don't fret, buddy. We're almost there. There's the Tobindona now, see?" he said as we were covering the final leg before the finishing line.

"Yes, I see," I said. "She's a real beauty!"

"Yeah, yeah," said Melifaro. "They all seem like beauties to you, as long as they can float. A very ordinary karuna. Nothing special."

"You, sir, are a snob," I said.

"No, I'm not a snob. I'm almost an expert. When you have someone like Anchifa for a relative, you're bound to become an expert in those matters."

"Right. Your pirate brother probably let you on board his old one-mast tub once and let you take the helm for a few seconds. I'm sure it was at least a hundred years ago, and he never again repeated that experiment. I can just imagine what his poor vessel looked like after your brief visit."

"You're one heck of a clairvoyant, Max! Believe it or not, that's almost exactly what happened—only not a hundred but eighty-something years ago. He still won't let me on board his Filo. It sounds like a joke, but I've honestly never been on board since!"

"Your Anchifa is a very wise man," I said. "Hey, look, we're here. What do we do now? Do you have a plan?"

"Absolutely. A great plan, too. We get on board and then take it from there," said Melifaro. Well, what else would you have expected from him?

Without waiting for an invitation, we went up to the deck of this beautiful—whatever that snob Melifaro said—two-mast ship.

"Hey! Captain!" yelled Melifaro. "Anybody here? We've got to talk to you!"

"No need to shout, sir. I'm right here."

A very tall, stooping man approached us. Neither his looxi of thin black leather nor his jauntily tied multihued headband made him look like a sailor. Even I looked like an old salt of the sea compared to this Jacques Paganel.

"My name is Kao Anlox," said the captain. "At your service, gentlemen. Would you be so kind as to introduce yourselves?"

I almost burst out laughing. This wannabe traveler had the manners of a provincial intellectual. Melifaro was enjoying it, too, apparently. Nevertheless, he managed to compose himself enough to continue.

"We are from the Secret Investigative Force, Mr. Anlox. Do you know why we're here, or must we explain?"

"Of course I know," said the captain, smiling a disarming smile. "You've come to claim the chest that used to belong to old Zoxma Pu. I'm sure my dissolute acquaintance Zekka Moddorok took up his old bad habits and was caught like a fool. Well, that is his problem now. As for the chest, you see, Zekka and I simply took what belonged to us."

"How interesting," said Melifaro, shaking his head. "Are you saying that some of your belongings were in that chest?"

"Indeed. You see, in his day, Zoxma meant to give those things to us as gifts. We were good friends. When Zekka and I became apprentices at the Order of Green Moons, we were sent to work in the kitchen. Those were the rules: each apprentice was to do household duties for several years. Old Zoxma and I were almost on the same footing. He was an apprentice, too—to his son, Sir Chorko. It was humiliating for him, but the old man had blown all his money, and the pay at the Order was good. Zoxma hardly talked to his son at all but readily conversed with us. At first, he did it demonstratively, out of spite toward his son, but we soon became friends. Of course he talked a great deal about his past, being a pirate and all that. I think that was when Zekka decided to become a burglar. He thought it was very romantic. I, on the other hand, lost my head over the old man's stories about faraway lands. For many years, I tried to become a sailor but failed for various reasons. And now I have this beauty, my Tobindona."

"Very nice, but you were talking about the chest," said Melifaro.

"Of course. Zoxma was about to give us his old talismans as gifts. According to him, he kept them in a red chest in the basement of his house on the Street of Steep Roofs. He talked about it all the time! I'm willing to believe that the old man only mentioned it in the beginning to aggravate Sir Chorko, but Sir Chorko couldn't have cared less about what his father planned to do with his old junk. In any case, Zekka and I had gotten used to the idea that the things belonged to us. At the beginning of '83—I mean the year 3183 of the Epoch of Orders—Zoxma told us that he would give us the things on the Last Day of the Year. We were so excited! We thought that the old man's talismans would turn our lives around. Perhaps that would have been the case, but at the end of the year, the Residence of the Order of Green Moons was burned to the ground and all our friends perished.

"Zekka and I were spared by pure chance: we had been sent to the marketplace to get groceries the day before. We had gotten a little carried away and stayed in a tavern until late—it wasn't often that we had the chance to walk outside the Residence—and by the time we returned, the Royal Guard had already surrounded the place. We had to flee.

"Then we each took our own path and met again, for the first time since then, less than a dozen days ago, again by chance. I went to have something to eat at the Drunken Rain, and Zekka was already sitting there. We recognized each other and started talking. It turned out we didn't have much to brag about—neither of us. Poor Zekka had just gotten out of Xolomi and was living on his mother's generous allowance—not a healthy situation for a grown man, don't you think? My situation was better. At least I'd never been to jail and I had a decent job. But that isn't enough to make you really happy with your life, is it?"

I nodded without even thinking about it: I couldn't have agreed with him more. I was beginning to like this pleasant, awkward Mr. Kao Anlox more and more. I also began to realize why Captain Giatta had decided to drop everything and journey to the ends of the earth with this fellow. He had the crazy eyes of an eternal teenager—another devastating kind of personal charm. Besides, there were other charms —the "ordinary magical things"—that intensified his personal charisma. I should be keeping that in mind. I did, but the more Kao Anlox talked, the less important that information seemed.

"Zekka and I stayed in the Drunken Rain all night. We talked and talked, and then we talked some more. At some point, we remembered old Zoxma Pu. The times when we helped him in the kitchen were good times, probably the best times of my and Zekka's lives. We were very young, and we thought an incredible future lay before us—well, different from everybody else's, at least. It turned out we couldn't have been more wrong. Perhaps many people can say the same about themselves, and it's very sad."

The captain sighed and seemed to be holding back tears, but soon he composed himself and continued. "Of course, we also remembered about the mysterious pirate charms that the old man had been meaning to give us. It may sound silly, but we thought that had we gotten them back then, our lives would have turned out differently. Then we decided to try to get hold of them anyway, just like that, for good luck.

"We didn't have much faith in the success of our undertaking. We were sure that the new owners of the house had long ago gotten rid of the chest, or peeked inside it and appropriated whatever they found. Yet we decided to take a chance. What if? we thought. What if this was our last chance to change our fates? These things are hard to explain, but we really thought the old pirate's charms would help us change our lives, for better or for worse. Any change seemed better than no change.

"The next day Zekka and I used the Dark Path. We had learned a thing or two at the Order, even though we'd only spent a few years in it. We were happy beyond what words can describe, gentlemen, when we saw the old red chest! We took it and returned to Zekka's living room, where our Dark Path had begun. Each of us chose the charm we thought belonged to us: we had agreed upon it years ago. Then we both realized we had nothing else to talk about, so I said goodbye to Zekka and left. It's hard to explain, but we both realized that we had met only to finally get hold of the charms that had been promised to us a long, long time ago. Once we had gotten what we wanted, we lost interest in each other. It was as though someone had flipped a switch."

"So what did you do after you left Zekka's?" said Melifaro.

"Why, this, of course," said Kao Anlox, making a gesture, as though he was trying to embrace everything around him. "I went straight to my boss at the Chancellory of Concerns of Worldly Affairs and told him I was quitting. I was so happy I then I went to the Old Thorn to have at least half a dozen bowls of the Soup of Repose. Poor Chemparkaroke almost had a heart attack. For the past forty years, he had been used to my coming once every two dozen days and ordering exactly one bowl of his wonderful soup. I think I managed to shock that old Murimak fox.

"The next morning, it was someone else who woke up in my bed.

He had the courage to go to the port and rent the Tobindona and hire a crew. It was unbelievable how many people dreamed to go on an around-the-world journey with me! And none of them even asked me about the pay, which was the one thing I had been dreading most. Renting the Tobindona made quite a dent in my pocket, although the owner—bless his kind soul—agreed to rent it out to me for a quarter of the price. I'm afraid I hired more people than I needed, but I just couldn't stop.

"Tonight I'll have to pay for my carelessness. I'll have to tell all those people that I simply cannot take them all. They might have to draw straws. You know, gentlemen, I think it's Zoxma Pu's charm that's been helping me. Everything has been going oh so well for me ever since I got hold of it."

"Are you saying you're not completely sure that your charm is responsible for all your recent success?" I said.

"Well, to be frank with you, I took it just for good luck, or even as something to remember my youth and my friend by, as I told you already. I didn't believe that Ukumbian pirates could do real magic. But now I'm beginning to think that old Zoxma's charm does help me somehow—I mean really help me."

"Do you have it on you?" said Melifaro.

"Yes, of course. Here," said Kao Anlox, tugging at the end of his colorful headband.

"Would you be so kind as to take it off for a moment?" said Melifaro. "We need to get a closer look at this thing."

"Here you go," said the captain, untying the headband and handing it to Melifaro. "Will you give it back to me? I know it sounds silly, but without old Zoxma's charm, I'll lose all confidence in myself, and I'm leaving tonight. Oh, wait a minute, maybe I'm not going anywhere at all? You've come to arrest me, and I have no proof that Zoxma Pu promised to give Zekka and me his possessions. No matter how you slice it, it looks like a regular burglary."

"We'll see," said Melifaro. He was waving the colorful headband in the air, trying to attract Kofa's attention since he couldn't hear a word of our conversation.

"I get it, I get it," said Sir Kofa from somewhere behind my back. He approached us, taking off his magic cloak. Then he took out the beeswax plugs from his ears. "Hand over the rag, son. Let's have a look."

"Oh, I didn't see you," said Kao Anlox. "When did you arrive?"

"Just now," said Kofa airily.

He took the headband out of Melifaro's hand. First he raised it up to his pipe and looked at the gauge, which displayed the precise degree of magic that had been used for making the object. He nodded and looked at the headband again. "I think we all need to have a cup of kamra, captain," he said. "And we need to talk. I . . . don't quite know what to do with you."

"Maybe you shouldn't do anything with me?" said Kao Anlox. "I didn't mean any harm to anyone. I just wanted to go on a sea voyage. Maybe I would've even written an addendum to Sir Manga Melifaro's Encyclopedia—the ninth volume, so to speak. There's no harm in that!"

"You're a bit too late, I'm afraid," I said. "The ninth volume is standing before you."

Melifaro shook his head. "Never mind him, Mr. Anlox," he said. "But my father would be flattered to know that his erudite madness still has the power to agitate human minds."

"Are you the son of Sir Manga?"

"The youngest," said Melifaro.

The captain was on cloud nine. He all but forgot about his looming arrest and the consequences thereof and stared at Melifaro as though he were a pop star. I could have sworn he was going to ask for Melifaro's autograph.

"If you don't invite us for a cup of kamra this instant, I'm going to arrest you," said Kofa. "This is your only chance to bribe us, captain."

"Oh, I do beg your pardon," said Kao Anlox, blushing. "I'm just so taken aback."

He took us down to his cabin, which looked more like the cozy living room of a girl than an abode of an old sea dog. Then he sat us down on some soft chairs that were bolted to the floor, muttered some apologies, and disappeared behind the door. He probably went to make kamra himself: there was no one else on the ship, not even a cook.

"Well, gentlemen, what do you propose we should do with him?" said Sir Kofa.

"Let him go, maybe?" said Melifaro. "If Dad finds out I arrested one of his fans who was about to go on an around-the-world trip, he won't ever speak to me again. It's the only surefire way to fall out with him that I know of."

"Yes, I think that would be only fair," I said. "Since one of the accomplices suffered such a harsh punishment, the other may get off with only a scare. The arithmetic mean would be approximately the right sentence."

"So you both liked him after all, huh?" said Kofa. "Now that's what I call a charm."

"You like him, too," I said. "It's written on your forehead, even though you didn't listen to him. I wonder why our captain didn't just ask us to leave and forget about him forever? It should've worked in theory."

"True," said Melifaro. "He didn't try to persuade us, yet I had the hardest time trying to ask him questions. Drat that personal charm of his!"

"The truth is that this young fellow honestly doesn't realize the immense power of the thing he got hold of," said Kofa. "That much is obvious."

"That's right, he did say he'd taken the headband 'just for good luck,'" said Melifaro. "And only now has he begun to suspect—suspect, I say—that the charm was helping him."

"And he's convinced that he was able to hire all these folks for free because Echo is full of people who dream of around-the-world trips," I said. "I don't know if I should laugh or cry at such gullibility."

"It's definitely not worth crying over," said Kofa.

"No, no. Please cry," said Melifaro. "You'll look terrific with your eyes all red and a swollen nose. All the girls are going to throw themselves at you."

"I hope I've prepared some good kamra, gentlemen," said Kao Anlox, coming in and putting down the tray with a pitcher and mugs on the table. "I'm usually pretty good at it."

"Judging by the aroma, you are, indeed," said Kofa with the air of an expert. Well, he was the greatest expert in these matters.

For a while, we drank our kamra without saying a word. I even went so far as to light up a cigarette. The captain seemed to be as absentminded as our Lookfi Pence. I'd have to wave the cigarette in front of his nose for a few minutes for him to notice I was smoking something not of this World.

"This is what I think, captain," said Kofa. "On the one hand, you're very lucky: neither I nor my colleagues are eager to arrest you, although that's what we should do. I don't know what Zoxma Pu promised you a hundred and fifty years ago, but that's no reason for breaking into his grandson's house and taking things, even such things as an old, useless chest. Where is it, by the way? And the rest of its contents? There must have been something else in it."

"Actually, no," said Kao Anlox. "I realize you have no reason to believe me, but I have no other proof. As for the chest itself, we burned it. Zekka said we should get rid of the evidence, and I thought he knew better, considering his occupation."

"Indeed," said Kofa.

"He's not lying," said Melifaro. "He hasn't once lied to us, in fact. I haven't had occasion to meet such an honest person in a long while. Maybe you have something stronger than kamra, captain? I'm feeling all sentimental now, and I desperately need a drink. I can't stand being sentimental."

"I'm awfully sorry, but I'm afraid I don't have anything of that sort," said Kao Anlox. "It simply didn't occur to me that one should keep strong liquors on a ship."

"Unbelievable!" said Melifaro. "How, pray tell, were you going to go on your journey then? Stinking sober? The crew certainly won't appreciate it."

The captain sighed and stared at the floor.

"Well, my boy, your arrest, as you might have guessed by now, is not going to happen," said Kofa. "But I have another piece of news that you might like far less. We must confiscate this charm." He waved the headband about. "Not because we are cruel bastards who wish to ruin your life and rob you of your luck, but because this is a truly magical thing. It is too powerful to be in the possession of any citizen of the Unified Kingdom. Even Mr. Zoxma Pu's heir."

"I knew it," said the captain. "I'm never going to go on an around-the-world journey! Not with my luck, I'm not."

"You don't understand how incredibly lucky you are that we're taking this headband away from you," said Kofa. "You still don't understand that the people that you hired were eager to go with you not because they were desperate romantics wanting to sail around the world but because the poor souls simply couldn't resist the magic powers of your charm. Now imagine this: you sail away from Echo, the charm loses its powers, and you find yourself among several dozen very angry men who demand explanations and money for their service."

"Are you telling me that—" Kao Anlox shook his head. "Oh, dear. Old Zoxma mentioned that this headband helps you become a more charming person and a good interlocutor, but . . . I had no idea!"

"Zoxma himself didn't know what his charm was capable of once it reached the Heart of the World," said Kofa. "He probably never put it on after he moved to Echo. The fashions were different. Your friend

Zekka Moddorok, on the other hand, quickly figured out what happens to ordinary magical things in the Capital of the Unified Kingdom. It's odd that you didn't get it."

"It must be the many years of working at the Chancellory of Concerns of Worldly Affairs," said Kao Anlox. "I was one of the junior staff for a long time there. Among us, it was customary to look down upon all foreigners without exception. We thought they knew no magic, and their sciences were at a very low stage of development. I got so used to this notion that I learned to take it for granted, never giving it another thought. When Zekka got so excited about our find, I thought it was pure superstition on his part. But I really believed that the charm that had belonged to such an amazing old man would bring me good luck. Now I realize what a fool I was: to possess a magical thing and not guess the extent of its magical powers! That's too naive, even for me."

"It's the price you've paid for your snobbery," said Kofa. "You're just like the junior staff of any organization. Well, captain, all's well that ends well. Want a piece of advice? Buy the fellows that are coming here tonight a drink and tell them honestly what happened. Maybe they'll laugh, maybe they'll direct a few strong words at you, but they won't hold a grudge for long. In my experience, sailors are a jolly bunch."

"Just make sure you buy a lot of booze," said Melifaro. "In my experience, that jolly bunch have cast-iron throats and bottomless pits for stomachs."

"Of course, I'll do that," said Kao Anlox.

"And after you explain yourself to your crew," I said, "you should repeat your offer about the journey. Who knows . . ." I had no idea why I said this. My colleagues raised their eyebrows but didn't say anything.

"Thank you, sir," said Kao Anlox, "but I don't think this is going to work. If I had Zoxma Pu's headband, even without its magical powers, I might have tried. But I don't have it, and without it I don't have the luck, which old Zoxma had once wanted to share with me. And I've never had any luck of my own, even in much simpler matters."

"Oh, that I can fix for you," I said. From the pocket of my Mantle of Death, I took out a small dagger. Until now, I had only used the small gauge that was built into its handle. I had hoped that someday I would use its blade. I sliced the fold of my Mantle of Death, cutting out a large triangular piece of black-and-gold fabric. "Here," I said. "There are plenty of people in this World who say that I'm the luckiest guy in the Universe. I can afford to share some of my luck with you. I've got plenty left where that came from."

Kao Anlox grabbed the piece of fabric and stared at me. My colleagues also gave me puzzled looks. Sir Kofa was the first to recover.

"Well, I'll be!" he said. "Sir Max is set to revive the best traditions of the Epoch of Orders. He's sharing his luck! Only the Grand Magicians used to do that, and then only a few of them. Well, captain, now you can consider yourself really lucky, trust me. Put this thing on. One headband in exchange for another. Who knows, perhaps this charm will serve you even better than the old one. As for us, we've done all we could, and then some. Let's go, boys."

"I'm going to cry," said Melifaro, getting up. "I'm going to flood this karuna with my tears, and it'll sink right here and now before it even gets a chance to sink somewhere in the vicious Sea of Ukli at the end of the World!"

We left Kao Anlox, who was completely baffled, in his cabin. As we were walking out, he began to fold the piece of my looxi into a headband. I must admit, black suited him.

"It's not fair that you share your luck with strangers," said Melifaro. "You could have given me a piece of your magic rag."

"You? What would you want with it?" said Kofa.

"Nothing. I'd just have it in my possession," said Melifaro. "I'm a very greedy guy, like all farmers' children."

"Do you want to know why I did it?" I said. My colleagues

stopped and stared at me. "Now I'm going to have to go home and change. I can't keep this on until tomorrow morning." I demonstrated the damaged fold of my Mantle of Death. "This is my only good pretext for going straight to the Armstrong & Ella and spending an hour or two there. It's a very long and deliberate procedure, you know, to undress and then dress again. Not to mention all the possibilities in between."

"You're one passionate fellow, I must say," said Melifaro.

"Do I detect a hint envy?" I said and tripped over a bale that lay in the middle of a passageway. I hurt myself badly, so the incident smacked a bit of retribution. I yelled, "Are we ever going to get out of this mess!"

"This isn't a mess. This is the port of the Capital of the Unified Kingdom," said Kofa, his patriotism on display. "I can tell you've never been in the port of the free city of Gazhin. Now, that's a mess. Plus, we're almost out. Do you recognize this amobiler?"

"Now I do," I said and got in the driver's seat. "By the way, I'm not as passionate as you think. I mean, you can come with me. We have the right to loaf for half an hour."

"That we do," said Kofa. "Lady Tekki's kamra is something to die for, which is another testimony to your incredible good luck, boy."

"I'm really happy for both of you, but I'd better go back to work," said Melifaro. "It's a widely held belief that without me the House by the Bridge is going to fall apart."

"Are you sure that's where you're going?" I said.

"Where else would I be going?" said Melifaro. Then he laughed and added, "A hole in the heavens above you, Max! You could've pretended that you believed me. I need to derive some pleasure from making you a cuckold."

"No, I need to derive some pleasure from your feeble attempts at it. But fine. There's a bunch of my amobilers parked by the Armstrong & Ella. You can steal whichever one you like. I'll tell Boboota, he'll issue a warrant for your arrest, and then we'll all sit back and have fun watching the situation unfold."

"What a brilliant idea," said Melifaro. "Just turn away when I'm stealing it. It's so much more adventurous that way."

"If you want adventures, go back and take that ship for an around-the-world trip," said Kofa. "It'll be for a great cause, too. The poor fellow will have at least one volunteer."

"You'll see, he'll have as many volunteers as he needs," I said. "Not in one day, of course, but he will. I'm just not sure what kind of adventure he's going to get once he's out at sea. My so-called luck is a very interesting thing."

"In any event, we have the opportunity to test it now," said Kofa.

I stopped the amobiler by the Armstrong & Ella. The door was still flapping in the wind—Tekki had never gotten around to having it fixed. In this regard she and I were two of a kind: it would've taken me a year to get around to it, too.

"Call that a bunch? Just two poor excuses for an amobiler," said Melifaro, getting behind the lever of one of them. "Where do you want me to leave it?"

"There's already one by Headquarters, so leave this one at the Furry House. My amobilers should be evenly spread around the city," I said.

Tekki greeted Sir Kofa and me with a warm smile. "I knew you'd pop up," she said to me. "I put kamra on the burner, even though no one had ordered it. It's not often that I can guess when you'll be coming."

"It's hereditary," I said. "Clairvoyance has never been the strong point of your infamous ancestor—" I cut myself short because I was going in a dangerous direction. I hastened to add, "Someone once told me that."

"There are plenty of amateur historians in Echo who have devoted their lives to studying the life of my legendary daddy," said Tekki. "It's too bad he's never going to know that. There's something unfair about posthumous fame, don't you think, gentlemen?"

"Certainly," said Kofa. "You go out of your way, stick your neck out, bend over backward to get something done—and then someone else ends up having all the fun. I've been meaning to ask you, Tekki, was it Loiso who taught you to make kamra, by any chance? You're suspiciously good at it."

"Is this an interrogation?" said Tekki, laughing. "The Secret Investigative Force has already stepped on my trace? Kofa, please! Can you imagine Loiso Pondoxo in the kitchen among pots and pans?"

"Why not? I can imagine all sorts of people in the kitchen, including your friend Sir Max. In my imagination, though, he keeps fumbling around the top shelf and pulling down a jar of cookies. But imagining him bending over a pan? No, even I can't do that."

"Oh, I'm sure he could steal something out of a pan, too!" said Tekki. And then they both went on and on for another half hour until a company amobiler drove by to pick up Kofa.

"I need to meet with Juffin," he said, "if only to tell him how the story of the ordinary magical things ended. You, on the other hand, have no need to hurry. You're not supposed to show up at work for another two hours."

"Another three hours," I said.

"Another three hours. You can go ahead and carry out that 'lengthy procedure' of changing your clothes that you were dreaming about on the way here."

"What did he mean by that?" said Tekki after Kofa left.

"I think he was hinting at something a real man should do once left alone with a beautiful lady," I said.

"Demand food?" said Tekki.

"Say, your clairvoyance is in top shape, bad inheritance notwithstanding," I said, laughing.

I had to hand it to myself: I was on time for work. By the time I got to the House by the Bridge, everybody had left except Juffin.

"Where's your dog?" he said.

"Droopy wouldn't hear of going to work when they don't pay him," I said. "Besides, who am I to drag a royal dog to our pitiful excuse for an office?"

"I guess you're right," said Juffin. "Okay, take my seat and do what you please with your life. I'm off to watch a movie. Don't you wish you were me right now?"

"Believe it or not, I don't," I said. "I must be a saint. Plus, I already have thought of a way to entertain myself tonight."

"Playing a game of Krak with your new friend Loiso, I presume?"

"No, no. It's a common form of social entertainment," I said. "I'm going to sneak out for a couple of hours and visit the Three-Horned Moon."

"You're a poetry lover now, too?" said Juffin. "Sir Lonli-Lokli I can understand. The guy had quite an adolescence: empty aquariums, dead Magicians, icy hands, and yours truly to boot. I'm prepared to forgive him for such eccentricities."

"I'm going to make sure no one picks on him there," I said, laughing.

"Echo poets picking on Sir Shurf Lonli-Lokli? It's too bad Mr. Galza Illana died fifty years ago. His hand is the only one that could do justice at committing that battle scene to canvas."

Juffin's remark only added fuel to my laughter. I had once had the chance of contemplating one of the horrendous paintings by the painter of the court of Gurig VII. It was the portrait of General Boboota Box in full regalia against the background of some epic battle. The "masterpiece" was utterly revolting.

Juffin left. Watching a movie from my collection wasn't among the things he could put off for very long. I relaxed in his armchair and spent a couple of hours reading yesterday's newspapers. Then I read the newspapers from the day before yesterday, which were even more boring. But boredom was exactly what I needed to make my life a little less monotonous.

❖

Three hours before midnight, Anday Pu sent me a call as promised. I told Kurush that he would have to keep a solitary watch over our half of the Ministry of Perfect Public Order for a while, changed my Mantle of Death for a neutral dark-lilac looxi I had brought from home, and walked outside.

Anday was standing by my amobiler, shuffling his feet.

"Thanks for remembering to invite me," I said. "Get in and show me the way."

"It's easy," said Anday. "It's by the Square of Spectacles and Entertainment."

"Interesting," I said. "It's right by the Furry House, and I've never even been there."

"The Three-Horned Moon is not easy to see. You must know which corner to turn," Anday said in the tone of some ancient Grand Magician divulging one of his most cherished secrets.

"By the way, we've already found the burglars who stole your chest," I said.

I thought Anday had the right to know the story. After all, he was the legitimate owner of the "ordinary magical things" that were now in the Royal (that is, our, to call a spade a spade) possession. I had to give him the short version: the trip to the Square of Spectacles and Entertainment took only ten minutes, even though I drove as slowly as I could. In the evening, the roads of the Old City were jammed with amobilers. I wish I knew where they were all going.

"I'm sorry, but we can't return the things to you, Anday," I said. "It's strictly forbidden, and you don't want any trouble with the law. In a few days, you'll receive your monetary compensation. That's the rule. It's a substantial sum of money, as far as I know."

"I catch," said Anday, nodding. "I don't need grandfather's old charms. I'd rather take those little round things. At least I can spend them easily. It'd be even better if instead of them you gave me a ticket to Tasher."

"Here we go again," I said. "What's this with Tasher? You're going to bore yourself to death there and then beg us to let you return here."

"You think it'll kill me?" said Anday. "You don't catch! Even if I want to come back to Echo, I'll be coming back to live where I want to come and live. Now I live where I was born. There's a difference."

"Darn it, you're right. Very well put, my friend," I said. "Here's the square. Where to now?"

Anday showed me where to park and dove into one of the numerous narrow passages between houses. I followed him. I couldn't imagine that there could be a tavern somewhere around here. The narrow passage became wider, and soon we found ourselves in a cozy round courtyard, lit by orange and blue lights coming from square windows.

"Here it is, the Three-Horned Moon." Anday pointed to a tiny sign hanging over a massive old door. There was no inscription on the sign, only an intricate engraving depicting a crescent moon with the top horn splitting into two.

The Three-Horned Moon belonged to the category of pleasant inexpensive taverns that were abundant in Echo. A long bar, wooden tables of assorted sizes to accommodate any number of revelers, a traditionally mixed crowd of customers—nothing out of the ordinary.

On second glance, however, I noticed that the crowd was far from ordinary. I had never witnessed such a high concentration of beaming eyes per square unit of area of a tavern. I was used to being surrounded by the amiable but drowsy and sated faces of the run-of-the-mill inhabitants of the Capital. Well, maybe grumpy Moxi attracted a special clientele in his Juffin's Dozen, but there were too few tables there to produce the desired effect.

"Sinning Magicians, Max! How did you end up here?" For the

first time in my life, I was witnessing a genuine expression of surprise on the normally imperturbable face of Lonli-Lokli.

"See, Shurf, you've surprised me so many times that I decided to give you a taste of your own medicine," I said. "Did I succeed?"

"You did," said Lonli-Lokli. His face had already recovered its usual dispassionate expression. If I hadn't known him as well as I did, I'd have thought I was seeing things.

"Nice place," I said. "I especially like the faces. Say, Anday, are all these people poets?"

"Almost," said Anday. "Including some of the best. Not just your everyday rhymesters and peasant scribblers. We've also got true poetry connoisseurs, like Lonli-Lokli here."

"And this kind of contingent comes here every day?" I said.

"Not just this kind! Usually it's not this crowded, though. Today we're having a lot of readings, a sort of poetry contest. It happens whenever there's a new moon. It's a tradition here, so you're in luck."

"A contest? What are the rules?" I said.

"Well, actually, anyone can volunteer to recite some new poetry, and the so-called contest happens later when everybody gets drunk and starts beating each other up," said Lonli-Lokli. "It is a natural phenomenon: at a certain level of intoxication talented people find it particularly hard to come to an understanding."

I shook my head. Sir Shurf was definitely in his element here. Or maybe the place had a special inspirational charm.

While I was chatting with my friends, someone had already come to the bar and begun reciting something. The tavern was so noisy I couldn't make out a single word.

"Maybe we should move a little closer," I said. "I can't hear a thing. Can you?"

"There's nothing to hear," said Anday nonchalantly. "At the beginning of the evening, it's just random people. You know, kids who first managed to rhyme three and a half words with the help of a bottle of Jubatic Juice the night before. When one of the masters gets up there, everyone goes quiet. It's a very delicate moment: you need to catch when to stop talking and start listening. Usually everybody catches, though."

"Holy moly! Another familiar face," I said when I saw Sir Skalduar Van Dufunbux, our "coroner," walk in the Three-Horned Moon.

"Ah, yes. Sir Skalduar is a regular," said Anday in a respectful tone. "When I came here for the first time about thirty years ago, he already had his own table. The old man doesn't write anything, but boy does he catch! The dinner is over! How do you know him, Max?"

"What do you mean? He works in the House by the Bridge."

"Are you saying that gentlemen is a regular rodent?" Poor Anday was dismayed.

"Well, he's anything but regular," I said. "He is the Master of Escorting the Dead. The old man examines the dead bodies that end up in our organization."

"So he's an expert in stiffs that the rodents find?" Anday reinterpreted the new information. "Not too shabby!"

"It's time you dropped the phobias of your youth, pal," I said. "I'm sick and tired of telling you that there are decent fellows among the Capital's police force."

"Time I dropped the what?" said Anday. "I don't catch."

I had to laugh. My conversations with Anday resulted in the most peculiar combinations of colloquialisms of the two Worlds.

Meanwhile, Sir Skalduar Van Dufunbux paraded across the crowded tavern to a table next to ours, sat down, and greeted us.

"It looks like Sir Anday is not just one of the best poets of our time but also a great proselytizer," said Van Dufunbux. "Soon the entire staff of the Secret Investigative Force will be gathering here in the Three-Horned Moon. Only the infallible Sir Juffin Hully will be sitting in the Glutton in solitude."

"You don't know Juffin," I said. "He'll make a timetable, and we'll be forced to take shifts sitting with him there. He's a tyrant."

I made the joke almost mechanically. I was shocked by the fact that Sir Skalduar had called Anday "one of the best poets of our time" without a hint of irony. I had been under the impression that Anday had been exaggerating his literary talent, to put it mildly. I had never bothered to listen to his drunken mutterings. (Anday only had the courage to recite poetry when he got himself besotted.) Somewhere deep down inside, I held the moronic, naive conviction that a brilliant poet had to be tall and handsome, with a fiery gaze, covered in a veil of mystery—oh, and preferably cold sober, too. Stupid, I know.

Then the tavern fell silent, as though an invisible director had taken it into his head to press a button and mute the sound in this speck of the Universe. A pleasant, gray-bearded man was shuffling his feet by the bar. His appearance, by the way, was very close to my deeply harbored ideal: tall, slender, handsome. Except he was a far cry from being covered in a "veil of mystery," and his "fiery gaze," if there was one to speak of, was hidden behind his eyeglasses.

His poetry, however, was magical. The last thing I could have imagined was that one could hear something of that caliber in a crowded tavern a stone's throw away from the Square of Spectacles and Entertainment—or, indeed, anywhere in this World. Maybe somewhere in a very special heaven for poetry lovers.

During the rest of the evening, the reverential silence that attended recitals worthy of note fell a few more times, but the poetry of other masters did not strike any special chords in my body. Perhaps I had no chords left in me, having spent them all on the first poet. That mild-mannered, gray-bearded bard had stolen my heart and soul.

"Max, you have not been yourself for the past half hour," said Lonli-Lokli. "Has something happened?"

"Something horrible has happened," I said. "I heard good poetry and was impressed. Now I'm going to walk around in a waking dream and demonstrate signs of inborn imbecility for three days running. I'm rarely impressed by something, but if I am, it's very deep. Does anyone know the name of that bearded fellow?"

"Which one?" said Anday. "There are many bearded fellows here."

"Are there? The one with a gray beard and glasses. When he came to the bar, it was the first time this evening that silence fell."

"Oh, that was Kiba Kimar himself!" said Anday. "Did you really like his poem, Max?" He sounded unconvinced.

"Does it show?" I said. It's not easy for me to admit such things. Stripping naked in public is easy for me, but admitting that good poetry touches my funny soul in a special way is too much.

"Man, you catch big time!" said Anday, shaking his head. "They say his poetry is intended for the best connoisseurs only! Frankly, I don't always catch myself why there's all this fuss about Kiba. Sometimes I catch, too, but not before I eat at least three bowls of the thickest broth from the Old Thorn."

"I also believe that Sir Kiba Kimar is the best of the best," said Shurf. "He somehow manages to write only about the things that really matter. And he holds back exactly as much as is necessary. So the reader—that is the audience in our case—has to supply what he is holding back. Usually we do not realize that we create our own extension of the poem. If you have not noticed, one can never memorize a single stanza of his poetry. I have tried to many times. In this regard Kiba Kimar's poems are akin to the powerful spells of ancient times, some of which took hundreds upon hundreds of years of daily recital to be memorized."

I listened to Lonli-Lokli but refrained from commentary. For the first time in a very long while, I felt I needed to be silent. More than that—I couldn't say a word. I had thought that the phrase "enchanted by poetry" was a cheap metaphor. As it turned out, in some cases, it was a cold, hard fact.

Closer to midnight, my friend Anday Pu also got up and went to the bar. I prepared to listen to him attentively.

His poetry would have been as good as my own might have been, a long time ago, if something incredible had actually been there, behind the intricate interweaving of semitransparent hints. But underneath a thin veneer of nimble word juggling lay nothing but endless loneliness and almost childish bewilderment: How come, nobody likes me, darn it, wonderful fellow that I am?

"It gives me immense pleasure to look at you when you listen to poetry," said Lonli-Lokli. "You should see the guilty expression on your face. One would have thought that you had asked Anday to recite some of your own poetry and then realized that you did not like it."

"Do you like it?" I said.

"Of course. It is absolutely clear that Anday Pu is a very talented young man," said Shurf.

"Right," I said, sighing. "It is absolutely clear." I was in no mood for arguing, not to mention arguing with Sir Lonli-Lokli—an absolute waste of time and effort.

Anday Pu finished amid dead silence. As I had come to understand, this was a sign of absolute recognition. The fellow was beaming like a freshly minted coin. In his joy, he ordered a pitcher of spicy Ukumbian bomborokka: the blood of his pirate ancestors was bubbling in the veins of this tubby little man.

"Did you like it, Max?" he said. To my surprise, I realized he wasn't boasting but honestly wanted to know my opinion. He looked at me with a timidity that I hadn't noticed in him before.

"Well, I did and I didn't," I said. "You'd probably be surprised to learn that when I was a poet I used to write similar stuff. It's hard for me to be objective."

"You used to write similar stuff?" said Anday. "The dinner is over! Why haven't you ever read it to me? Did you think I wouldn't catch?"

"No," I said, smiling. "It's just been a long time since I got myself that drunk. See, I only remember my poetry at a particular stage of drunkenness: after I begin to throw up but before my face hits the plate. In any other state, I'm incapable of such feats."

"And so we learn not only that can Sir Max write poetry, which in itself is outside the frame of my mind's picture of him, but also that he can get himself sozzled," said Shurf. "Are you really full of surprises, or do you just enjoy pretending you are?" The question might have seemed rude if it hadn't been accompanied by a hint of irony.

"Is there a difference?" I said. "In that case, I don't know. Both, I suppose. It's not all that bad, though. Those feats are in the past. A long, long forgotten past. You should know, if anyone does, that people do change, sometimes radically."

The former Mad Fishmonger nodded. He could hardly disagree.

"Why aren't you writing now?" said Anday. "Or are you? Do I catch?"

"I once realized that you should write poetry on napkins while you're waiting for your order in a small café. Reading is unnecessary: it only spoils good poetry. Once you've written all over the napkin, you should crumple it—better yet, put it in an ashtray and burn it. Not the most ingenious habit, of course, but one I adhered to so adamantly that I became really good at it. Then I thought that, instead of wasting perfectly good napkins, it'd be just as good if I simply looked at them and told myself that the words I wanted to write on them didn't exist in any language. It turned out all right in the end. The last thing this World needed was my poetry."

"I don't catch," said Anday. "It's too complicated."

"Yeah, I don't catch myself," I said. "The atmosphere in this place doesn't do me any good. I think I should go back to the House by the Bridge before that clueless young man in me wakes up. And we'll all be better off if he remains sleeping."

"I must be going, too," said Lonli-Lokli, folding his snow-white looxi around himself. "I was going to leave sooner, but I wanted to stay and listen to your poetry, Anday."

"Thank you, sir," said Anday. He had already recovered from my confession. A healthy portion of bomborokka can make any problem seem insignificant.

"Want me to give you a lift, Shurf?" I said. "I hope the streets are almost empty now. That means that you'll be home in a quarter of an hour."

"Thank you, Max. It is very kind of you," he said. "And most timely."

Silence fell in the Three-Horned Moon. Another master was reciting his verses. We whispered our thanks to Anday, bade goodnight to Sir Skalduar, and left.

⁂

"I sometimes think that you are much older than you seem to be," said Shurf. "You have known bad times, you have been a poet, and you have been a drunkard. When did you have time to do all that, Max? Or is this a secret?"

"A hole in the heavens above you, Shurf!" I said, laughing. "This is no secret. First, I'm very quick. Second, I did it all at the same time. Plus, I exaggerated the 'face in the plate' part for Anday's benefit so he could feel he had something in common with me. It's my way of sucking up to the master. I didn't really do much carousing. As for my age— Well, that will have to remain my little secret."

"From the pictures that you call movies and the books you fetched from your World, I have inferred that your lives are much shorter than ours," said Shurf. "Do you grow up faster?"

"It's not just the growing up part that we do faster," I said.

"Does it affect you, too?"

"It did while I lived there. Now I live here, and Juffin says I have every chance of living as long as any of you. I sure want to believe that."

"So you're not older but younger that you seem to be?" Shurf was too much of a pedant to let it go without nailing it down.

"That's correct," I said. "I've only lived a little over thirty years.

Oh, but please don't tell Melifaro. He'll immediately try to adopt me and send me to preschool."

"I am not in the habit of exposing someone else's secrets," said Shurf. "Nor have I ever been. I think you know that. How odd: you have surprised me so many times tonight that it is almost beyond my capacity to be surprised. Are you doing this on purpose? And if so, what is the purpose?"

"Are you kidding, Shurf? On purpose? What nonsense! Today's just been that kind of day. New moon, the Three-Horned Moon, poetry contests, sentimental reminiscences, and so on. Let's change the subject. Have you finished the book I fetched for you yesterday?"

"Not yet. I am going through it very slowly. I have to keep going back and rereading parts that I do not understand. It talks about very odd things. People from another World visit yours. They are very powerful, as far as I can tell. They have rather peculiar ideas about how the Universe works. They believe that all living creatures can be classified according to a principle I do not quite follow. In light of this notion, they are going to exterminate humanity, sparing only a select few, which are somehow different from their fellow humans and are thus entitled to be left alive. I am afraid I cannot tell you much about it. One should have some understanding of the contents of a book in order to retell its plot."

"I think you got another sci-fi book," I said, sighing. "Another dystopian novel. You're just lucky with this genre from the looks of it."

"Both of the books you obtained for me belong to a particular genre?"

"Heh. 'Particular' is the word here," I said. "In your case, it's particularly ironic: to get introduced to a strange world by reading stories that were deliberately created to represent a universe as different as possible from the author's reality."

"It is ironic indeed," said Shurf. "Yet I have managed to pick up some valuable information—your life expectancy, for example. There were other details, as well, such as elements of culture, everyday life, and a few other things that are vastly different from what I am used to. This is an excellent mind game, to paint an accurate picture of an unknown World using only bits and pieces of information that cannot always be distinguished from fiction. Yet however fascinating and educational this may be, Max, we have arrived at my house. To my utter regret, we will have to continue our conversation tomorrow. Good night."

"Good night," I said, watching Lonli-Lokli's white silhouette dissolve in the darkness of the garden, as though he were a beautiful ghost from an old movie.

I wish I knew what kind of picture of my World he had painted in his own mind. I was sure any science fiction writer would be dying to know that, too.

❖

Kurush wasn't the only one waiting for me in the House by the Bridge. Sir Kofa Yox had decided to keep him company.

"I should've brought more pastries," I said, smiling.

"Why?" said Kofa. "There's nothing worse than eating pastry on an empty stomach. On the other hand, the Glutton is entirely empty now, and you and I can have a late dinner there and talk, of course."

"Kurush, will you be okay here all by yourself?" I said.

"Some time later, I will need you to clean my beak," said the buriwok. "So please try to come back in an hour."

"Will do," I said. "Sir Kofa, will you kindly remind me?"

"I will, I will," said Kofa. "So much fuss about this."

"Where are today's trophies?" I said, opening the Secret Door of our staff-only entrance.

"The headband is in Juffin's safe—we won't be needing it any time soon. As for the cloak, I've already broken it in. I'm not parting with it now. So much better than changing my appearance all the time. Oh, thanks for reminding me. I left it in the office. I'll go fetch it now. I was planning to take a walk in town later tonight."

"It's bad luck to go back," I said.

"Did you say something?" said Kofa, turning around.

"Never mind me. It's silly. When I was a kid, many people believed in it. I hope it doesn't pertain to other Worlds."

Kofa didn't listen. By the time I was through, he'd already returned, holding the cloak under his arm. "It would be rude of me to put this on now," he said. "You'd have to drill a hole in me with your eyes just to keep me in sight."

We didn't disappoint Kurush: we were so hungry the dinner only lasted forty minutes. The service at this late hour had been very prompt so as to get rid of customers as quickly as possible.

We parted in the doorway. I had to go back to the House by the Bridge to clean the sticky sweet cream from Kurush's beak, and our Master Eavesdropper had other plans. He was going to hunt for new secrets and rumors in Echo's all-night taverns.

Kofa put the old magic cloak over his looxi—he was excited about his new toy. Then he waved goodbye to me and dove into the orange misty light of the street lamps. I couldn't resist experiencing the magic again, so I watched Sir Kofa's silhouette going away. He should have disappeared by now, but I could still see him—no otherworldly powers tried to prevent me from contemplating Kofa's back. One of my hearts kicked against my ribs, followed by the other one. They had been lying low for a while, and now—boom!

"Kofa!" I said and ran to him.

"Huh?" he said, turning around. "Forget something?"

"No, Kofa, but I can see you!"

"Really? Well, you must be the most extraordinary creature in the World," he said, "and no charms work against you."

"Yes, but earlier today . . . Never mind. Let's do this: I'll put on the cloak and walk a few yards up and down the street. If you can't see me, I'll give it back to you and go back to the Headquarters, relieved. What I need now is a peaceful heart. At least one."

"You think so? No, that's impossible. But all right, put it on," said Kofa, handing me the cloak.

I put it on and started walking down the street. I honestly tried to become invisible. I did everything I could. That primarily consisted of saying to myself, Goodness me! I so want to hide from that horrible Kofa! It was unnecessary, of course. As far as we understood how ordinary magical things worked, the Ukumbian cloak required no effort on the part of its owner to blind the eyes of others.

"Max, you were right," said Kofa in a defeated tone. "I can see you, too. The thing doesn't work. I wish I knew why. It's great that you noticed it. Can you imagine what might have happened to me?"

"Let's go back to Headquarters, I said. "We need to look into your wardrobe. Why would it stop working all of a sudden?"

Kofa took the cloak, examined it, and shrugged, and we both went back to the House by the Bridge.

❧

I didn't have the slightest idea how we were supposed to "look into" the cloak or where to start, but Kofa didn't need a kick start in these matters.

"It's a different cloak, Max," he said after he had examined the old gray fabric. "It looks almost identical, but it's a different one. Ours had a torn lining sewn up with red thread in one place. Just two little stitches. I noticed it when I was studying it in the morning."

"A different cloak? How can that be?" I said.

"My thoughts exactly," said Kofa. "When I put it on earlier tonight, it was the original cloak. No one could see me—even our colleagues, including Juffin himself. I took it off in this office, and no one has been here except you and Kurush. That means that it was you who swapped it. I'll arrest you, and the case will be closed."

"Of course it was me," I said. "Who else would have done such a thing?" I pondered a little and said, "What about the junior staff? Janitors, couriers? They come and go at will, and we don't even notice them half the time."

"I'll be darned, boy, you're right!" said Kofa. "While I was waiting for you, I saw a janitor whirling around here. I didn't pay much attention, of course."

"Those guys don't even need a magic cloak while they're doing their job," I said. "They are the most invisible people. Looks like he was the one who stole the cloak—swapped, rather. I wonder why."

"I don't think he was a regular janitor," said Kofa. "I would have understood if someone had just stolen it—although who would want an old rag like this unless he knew what it was? But to switch it for another one just like it, this guy not only knew what he had come for, he came prepared."

"Yikes," I said. "A conspiracy!"

"Exactly," said Kofa. "It didn't occur to me until now how much sense job protocols make. Heck, I've written a few thousand job protocols myself during my career, and this experience doesn't predispose one to adhering to them too closely. If I hadn't left the cloak on the back of the chair but locked it in the safe as I was supposed to, our conspirators would have been given a run for their money!"

"What do we do now?" I said.

"We? We get mad. Angry. That's what. It's the best mood for going hunting. And I'm very angry now."

"Should we wake up Melamori, or do you want me to step on the thief's trace? Mind you, though, he may not survive the experience."

"The last thing I'm worried about now is the thief's health. Now that isn't in my job description."

"Excellent. Let's hop to it then."

I paced the room, paying attention to the sensation in my feet. Finally I found what I had been looking for: a trace that didn't belong to any of my colleagues, I was sure of it. And then I felt as though an impenetrable but transparent cone had dropped on me. I could see the world around me virtually undistorted, but the air underneath the cone was poisoned. I could see very clearly that the evening I had enjoyed at the Three-Horned Moon, Kofa's and my current investigation, my sweet plans for the next morning, and everything that had been, was, and would be—all of that was not only pure nonsense but the helpless cramps of a living piece of meat, the agony of an insect. My body realized that it would die one day and was rehearsing it. Giving it a first reading, so to speak.

I composed myself promptly: I knew the feeling. I was the one and only lucky fellow who had a talent for stepping on traces of dead people, drat it!

"Kofa, this man is already dead. It's a dead man's trace," I said.

"Dead? Wow, that didn't take long," said Kofa. "You can step off the trace and recover now. Yes, that was an excellent idea: to send an accomplice to fetch the cloak and then kill him so no one could step on his trace. The new owner of our trophy is a smart fellow—not so smart as to know that you can follow the trace of a dead man, but then again, it's not his fault. Before you showed up in Echo, that had been considered impossible. And praise be the Magicians, we haven't yet announced your achievements on the first page of the Royal Voice."

While Kofa was talking, I rummaged through Juffin's desk for the ceramic bottle of Elixir of Kaxar. "The only panacea I know of," I said after taking a hefty gulp of the liquid, "that can cure the effects of walking down traces of dead people. What would I do without it?"

"It's unpleasant, isn't it?" said Kofa. "Poor thing. Everyone else has normal talents."

"I know. Mother Nature must have been drunk when she made me. But anyway, I might as well just stop whining now. What we need to do is follow that darned trace. If all goes well, where this trace ends, the trace of the murderer begins, still warm. I'm ready whenever you are."

"I'm ready. Let's go," said Kofa, getting up from the chair. "I can run very fast if necessary, so don't make allowances for my age or constitution."

"I wouldn't think of allowances when it comes to you," I said, smiling.

I put the bottle of Elixir in the pocket of the Mantle of Death, stepped on the trace of the dead man, and rushed across the hallway of Headquarters out into the street. Kofa was indeed following right behind me.

❖

That short walk down the streets of Echo at night was one of the nastiest undertakings in my life. More than anything, I wanted to get down on all fours and howl at the thin new moon. But I managed to contain myself.

"Here," I said, hesitating at a corner. "Something happened here. Kofa, this fellow went down the Dark Path! I should try to follow him. I've never attempted to follow a dead man's trace down the Dark Path before. I hope it's possible, at least in theory."

"In theory, what you're doing now is impossible," said Kofa, "but you're doing it. In other words, I'm sure you can do it. Impossible things are your specialty."

"Are you coming with me?"

"Of course I am. If you end up in hell, rest assured I'll keep you company."

"And I'll bet you'll find a nice tavern with good cuisine even there." I tried to force a smile. I had to do it for someone who was about to follow me into hell.

I let the disgusting dead trace lead me and take me away to the devil knows where. For this to happen, I had to throw away the thought that I was still alive, which, under the circumstances, wasn't too far-fetched. Finally I felt firm ground under my feet and made a mind-boggling jump to the side—the most effective way to get off the trace you're standing on. I had to get off it, simply because I wasn't made out of steel, even though I wished I were.

I looked around. I was relieved to see Kofa standing just two feet away from me. From the looks of it, we weren't in hell. We were in a dark and empty room. On the floor I saw a motionless body. I was happy to see it! I sure hoped that it was the dead man whose trace had almost killed me.

"You must immediately take a gulp from your precious bottle, boy," said Kofa in the tone of a family doctor. "You look like a person who's about to faint any second now."

"Like heck I am," I said. "No swooning for me. Your advice, however, is much appreciated."

"I don't give bad advice very often." Kofa made sure I was capable of opening the bottle of Elixir of Kaxar myself, nodded, and approached the dead body. "Well, well, well, what have we here? Oh, nothing original, praise be the Magicians. Stabbed to death. I think he's the one we were looking for. He wears the uniform of our junior staff. Ah, he is one of our junior staff. I don't remember his name, but I recognize him. A hole in the heavens above him! A janitor who could go down the Dark Path was working in our organization, and no one bothered to find out what he had been doing before the War for the Code. I want to look the fellow who hired him right in the eye. But it's all for the better. I'll run a check on the rest of them tomorrow. Max, are you ready to look for another trace? The one who killed this lousy creature is the most interesting character in this nasty story. I'm very eager to meet him."

"So am I," I said. "Give me another minute, and we'll be off."

"No hurry if you haven't recovered yet. I'll look around this place. I don't think it's important, but who knows? Only please lean against the wall. It's a simple rule, but it helps avoid unpleasant surprises in unfamiliar surroundings.

"I used to have a colleague, Sir Jura Feella, the General of the Left Bank Police. He was a very eccentric old man, even for the Epoch of Orders. Jura was an adamant adherent to this rule. Whenever he had to rest somewhere beyond the city limits, he would always erect a tall wall behind him. By the way, it wasn't a simple trick. It required Black Magic of the ninety-second degree. It all ended in a very funny way: one of General Feella's numerous enemies shot him with a regular Baboom. That fellow was a pretty good magician himself. He managed to climb to the top of Feela's famous wall. Shooting from there was much easier than from any cover."

"So nice of you to give me practical advice and then make sure I don't follow it," I said.

Sir Kofa left to search the house. Fifteen minutes later, he returned with an expression of utmost boredom on his face.

"Nothing interesting, huh?" I said.

"A house is a house is a house, boy. A place where people live, or don't live. It's not often that you encounter a truly interesting one. As for this one, its occupant has been living a long, ordinary, and quite lonely life. Are you ready to take me for a walk now?"

"I am, as long as the subject of our next pursuit hasn't died yet. That would be too much for me!"

I had anticipated finding the trace of the murderer somewhere near the dead body, and I was right. Moments later, Kofa and I walked outside.

"Our murderer took an amobiler from here, and we have no means of transportation at hand," I said, somewhat perplexed.

"You asked Melifaro to leave one of your amobilers by the Furry House," said Kofa. "It's just two blocks away. Don't you recognize the place?"

"I don't. The city changes at night, as though there are two different Echos—Echo at night and Echo during the day. I sometimes think that even the layout changes."

"Really?" said Kofa. "I didn't know you'd noticed. Okay, I'll go get your amobiler."

"But please hurry," I said. "This fellow could kick the bucket any second now, what with me standing on his trace."

"Good riddance, I say," said Kofa.

"Another dead man's trace? That would be an overload. Besides, it would be a good idea to ask him a few questions first. Granted, Juffin can revive any dead person for a short while, and I'm pretty sure I can make him talk, but can you imagine how much time we'd waste? What if there's someone else behind all this?"

"Someone else?" said Kofa, wincing. "That would be an overload. Although you just might be right."

Kofa left and returned a few minutes later in my amobiler. I took his place at the steering lever and tore off at a speed that exceeded even my own notions of reckless driving. Moments later, we were at the western outskirts of the Old City, somewhere near the Skauba Cemetery, in the only neighborhood of Echo that one might call the slums. It consisted mostly of old one-story houses that weren't in good repair—compared to other neighborhoods, of course.

"He's still alive!" I said, jumping out of the amobiler. "A tough guy. Who would have thought?" I hit my elbow hard against another amobiler—a plain-looking old jalopy—but at that time I didn't pay any attention to it. There will be enough time later for wound licking, I thought.

"We're in luck," said Kofa.

I shot like a bullet through the front door of the nearest house. The paint was peeling, and the door swung in the cold winter wind exactly like the door of the Armstrong & Ella. If I were a locksmith rather than a Secret Investigator, I would have had my work cut out for me today.

I was approaching the end of the trace. At moments like this, any Master of Pursuit experiences something akin to the trancelike fury of an ancient berserker. My victim lay motionless on a sofa in the dark living room, having no strength to put up any resistance or run away. If I had come just a moment later, we'd have ended up with another useless dead body on our hands. But I jumped off the trace just in time. Now we were both free from each other, my victim and me.

"Good evening, Lady Misa," said Kofa. "I'll take your knife, if you don't mind. Aw, look at you. So tired you can't move your arms? Poor thing, how are you going to kill your dear guests then? You know, I think I'll relieve you of this nice little dagger, too. Thank you. You won't be needing it now."

"Don't tell me I almost killed your ex-girlfriend," I said.

"That's exactly what you almost did," said Kofa, chuckling. "Allow me to introduce you to Misa Luddis, alias No-Nose Misa. The first lady among the elderly connoisseurs of blatant violence. Some two hundred years ago, she was a celebrity: none of her colleagues could do what she could with cold weapons. I'll never forget our walks at night: I helped this lady to get to Xolomi about five times. I had to make sure she didn't hurt anyone on the way. Are you still breathing, my love?"

"Dream on, you accursed old rodent!" said the "celebrity." Her voice was very weak but full of rage. "You're going to die before me anyway! What did you come up with this time? Who's the darned werewolf that stepped on my trace? Back in our day, we drowned people in the Great Gugland Mire for this!"

"That's a great idea," said Kofa, smiling. "For you, my love, I'm prepared to revive this noble tradition. You'll be the first. We'll go to the Great Gugland Mire alone—only you and me. It will be so romantic." He turned to me and continued. "I've known this old witch for a very long time, boy. She won't say a word to us without a good spell, even if we call in Melifaro and make him kiss her. I wonder which one of us can make her talk sooner. I'll need about a half hour—I know this from many years of experience. But I've heard something about your Lethal Spheres. They say you can make anyone do whatever you want him to, if I understand correctly."

"Let's see. I have no desire to kill your girlfriend, so I can try to make her talk," I said. I snapped the fingers of my left hand—a unique, almost imperceptible gesture. I'll never cease to be amazed at Sir Shurf's mentoring talents, for he had taught me this incredible trick in a matter of minutes.

One could say, however, that I was a disappointment as a student. When performed by Shurf, the trick inevitably leads to a lethal outcome. When I do it, the result is usually "I am with you, Master!" and so on and so forth. In order for my Lethal Sphere to murder someone, I must genuinely want to kill that person, and that's not as simple as it seems. Funny, despite my venomous spit and the Mantle of Death that I had to wear for the benefit of the public peace, I was still a lousy killer.

My "interview" with No-Nose Misa was no different from my previous experiments. After a semitransparent ball, glowing with green, came out of the tips of my fingers and touched the woman's chest, she moaned, "I am with you, Master." The variety of the lexicon of my victims left a lot to be desired.

"Good," I said. "While you're at it, tell us where the cloak is," I said, yawning and perching on the edge of a lonely chair in the middle of the living room. My work shift could be a little less eventful, not to mention shorter—we had started right after noon. Plus, my elbow had begun to hurt. However had I managed to hit it?

Despite the pain and exhaustion, I finally got a good look at the lady. Tall and skinny, the old woman had so many wrinkles that one would think she was the oldest living person in this World, which was full of people remarkable for their longevity. Her nickname notwithstanding, Misa had a nose—a very short flat one, which did not add to her charm. Nor did she look frail. In spite of her button nose, she looked like an actual old witch fresh down from the Witches' Sabbath.

"I gave the cloak to the pretty boy who hired me," said Misa. "That was our agreement."

"Bingo, Kofa! A third one," I said.

"What are you so happy about?" said Kofa.

"That I was right. I love being right. I guess there's nothing else to be happy about." I turned back to the old woman. "Care to elaborate? Who's that 'pretty boy'? What did he hire you for?"

"I don't know who he is, Master," said Misa. "At first I thought he was some rich fop. The son of a gun was wearing a colorful looxi. Not even every slut in the Quarter of Trysts can afford to wear such fancy duds." I giggled, recalling Melifaro's extensive collection of clothes. He could be suspect number one. My "slave" continued: "He leeched onto me at the Jubatic Fountain about three hours before midnight. You don't normally find such sleazy ass-lickers in the Fountain, but there he was. When he opened his yapper, I figured he was the real deal, even though he was wearing women's clothes. He said he'd pay me six hundred crowns if I sliced a certain fellow. Then he put down a hundred and I said yes. I hadn't done such a kind deed for such good money in a long while.

"He named the address and told me to be there at midnight and wait in the living room. He said the fellow that needed slicing and dicing would appear out of nowhere but I shouldn't be afraid. Pfft, as if I was scared. I dealt with all sorts of bastards in the good old days."

"Fine, fine," I said. "But the cloak? The old gray cloak? What happened to it?"

"I took the cloak that the little bastard was holding and brought it here. The pretty boy wouldn't come here himself. He sent a kid just about an hour ago. The kid picked up the cloak and brought me my money—all of it. I haven't been that lucky in a long time. Yeah, then I felt dizzy and had to lie down."

"It's all clear to me now," said Kofa. He was smiling like a cat after a good meal. "No point in looking for the kid. Either he doesn't know anything, or we'll waste a great deal of time on him, even if he does. Let's just go straight to the Jubatic Fountain and find the trace of that pretty boy of hers. I hope this is going to be our last trip for today."

"It's not that easy," I said. "You're overestimating my talents, Kofa. Imagine how many traces there will be in the tavern. Dozens upon dozens." I turned to Misa again. "Can you show us where your employer was sitting?"

"I can, Master."

"Sweet. Come with me then."

The old woman slipped down from the sofa and plodded along. Kofa moved to the back seat because No-Nose Misa just had to sit in the front next to me. All creatures that were touched by my Lethal Spheres had the irresistible urge to be close to my precious body. Against the orange fog of the street lights, the old woman's head looked like a beautiful skull that any horror movie would be honored to feature.

"In my homeland, death is often depicted having no nose," I said to Kofa. "A cute coincidence, huh?"

"Wonderful," he said. "One would think our Misa had been getting around."

"Where's that Jubatic Fountain?" I said. "I've never been there."

"Magicians forbid!" said Kofa, laughing. "Turn left here. The place is not exactly your style. The dirtiest den in the city. Poor Boboota can't wait to get it closed down, but Juffin and I won't let him—for his own good, by the way. It's very convenient to have the cream of the crop of the underworld, such as our beautiful Ms. Misa here—turn left again—gather together in one place instead of spreading out around town. There's a reason for that, too. The Jubatic Fountain is the most democratic tavern in the Capital. You pay a couple of handfuls as an entrance fee and drink as much as you can. In the middle of the tavern, there's an actual fountain of Jubatic Juice. Food costs extra, of course, but people don't go there for a nice dinner. Okay, now turn right. The Jubatic Fountain is at the end of the block. You'll see it in a minute in all its glory."

"Yuck," I said.

We stopped across from a big one-story house. The windows were blazing, suggesting that despite the late hour the place was still open. The large hall, however, was almost empty. A few indistinguishable figures were sitting at a table at the farthest end. They paid no attention to us. Even my Mantle of Death didn't impress them. The fellows were already beyond good and evil, apparently.

In the center of the hall stood a drinking fountain. Living up to its name, it reeked heavily of the Jubatic Juice.

"Show us where you sat," I said to the old woman.

"Right here, Master." She led us to a table by the fountain. "I sat here, and the pretty boy's butt was rubbing against this." She patted an old wooden chair that was painted a touching pink.

"Good girl," I said. She sounded very sincere. I was happy that she wasn't senile. Then again, people of her occupation were much less prone to senility than decent folks. I sat in the pink chair, shuffled my feet on the floor, and paused in anticipation. And then the sensation came. It hit me like a mallet. "Oh, this is a tough one!" I said to Kofa. "Some powerful Magician from the old days, I swear. It feels like someone's grabbing my heels. I've never felt anything like it before."

"Really? Interesting. But the hunt will have to wait. First we need to take this beauty to the House by the Bridge. I enjoy the company of a lady, but not to the degree that I want to bring Misa along everywhere we go."

"Agreed," I said. "Only we don't need to take her anywhere. She can go on her own."

"Oh, I forgot," said Kofa. "You can make her do whatever you want!"

"Precisely." I turned to the old woman. "Be a good sport, sweetheart, and go to the House by the Bridge. Then ask the policemen to lock you up good and tight. Then you can rest. You've had a long, hard day."

"Thank you, Master," said Ms. Misa, and she walked obediently toward the exit. Sir Kofa watched her with rapt attention.

"Who would have thought there would be a day when No-Nose Misa would show up in the Ministry of Perfect Public Order and ask to be put away! You've made me a great present, boy. I should send a call to the policemen on duty now so they don't swoon. It's not every day you see such a marvel."

"Okay, but let's do it on our way," I said. "I can't stand hanging around here anymore."

"Of course, of course. Let's go. I never knew you'd make such a zealous Master of Pursuit."

"I'm a little embarrassed," I said, rushing headlong to the front door. "I sometimes think I can't do anything and I'm just pretending. I've seen Melamori do it, so I know approximately how to act."

The few customers of the Jubatic Fountain had never paid us any attention, and I was pretty sure I liked it that way.

My next victim was fond of long walks, so I couldn't drive. A Master of Pursuit must mimic the actions of his victim.

"Someone will see your amobiler parked by that old dive," said Kofa, laughing. "Can you imagine what it will do to your reputation?"

"It's not the first time," I said. "I've had a 'reputation' all my life and never did anything worthy of mention to deserve it. Boy, am I pissed at that pretty boy! My feet are almost numb from all this running around today, and the bastard just had to take it into his head to go for a stroll."

While I was grumbling, we ended up by the Grave of Kukonin, a pleasant little tavern. Kofa and I had been there once before on business. Several policemen were ambling about and shuffling their feet around the Grave. Inside Lieutenant Chekta Jax was pacing back and forth, exercising his muscles. He was, as usual, burdened with a sense of the utter importance of everything that was happening to him and, thus, was very gloomy.

"I'm afraid we'll have to make a pit stop here," said Kofa, throwing me a compassionate glance. "Will you manage?"

"I'm going to have to," I said. "I'll try grinding my teeth. Maybe it'll help."

"What happened here, Chekta?" said Kofa. "Tell me, and make it quick."

"According to my job description, I have no right to report the situation to anyone before my superior has read my official report," said Chekta Jax.

"I personally wrote that job description about two hundred years ago," said Kofa. "I'll have you know that the Secret Investigative Force didn't even exist back then. Now the Third Amendment to the Code of Krember states that any human being in the territory of the Unified Kingdom must cooperate with the officials of the Minor Secret Investigative Force to the best of his abilities. You, boy, are in the territory of the Unified Kingdom and are a human being, to a certain extent. So cooperate, and on the double."

"I am not quite sure what happened here, sir," said the lieutenant. "I was called to investigate a murder." He looked like he wished the earth would swallow him up.

"Well, a hole in the heavens above you, mister!" I said. "Couldn't you have said so right away? Mind you, I've never wanted to kill someone more in my life than I do now. And I could do it with impunity! Sir Kofa is my witness: you've breached the Third Amendment."

Lieutenant Chekta Jax gave me a look full of genuine hatred. He really wanted to smash my face in, but the poor thing couldn't afford such a luxury—not now, not the next day, not the next year, not ever—and that made him really, really sad.

Sir Kofa was already talking to the overexcited proprietor of the place and nodding. "Thank you, my friend," he said to the proprietor.

"Good job. Concise and to the point. Max, one minute. I need to look at the body. So should you, actually."

"Admiring dead bodies is my favorite pastime," I said. "But I'll do it only on the condition that the trace drags me in the right direction."

"That's where it should be dragging you. To kill someone, you have to come close to him, don't you think?"

I made a strange zigzag around the dining hall and couldn't resist the temptation to sit at one of the tables. I had to make a stop.

"Looks like my pretty boy rubbed his skaba against this stool for a long time," I said.

"That's correct," said Kofa. "That's where he sat waiting for his delivery boy who brought him the cloak. The proprietor remembered a well-dressed man and a little boy carrying a parcel—except that he's sure that the man then went out, leaving the money on the table. Figures."

I finally felt I could get up from the table. I walked around the tavern and stopped by the bar. On the floor at my feet lay the dead body of an elderly man in a warm brown looxi.

"I'm not feeling the urge to move along now," I said. "He stood here for several minutes."

"Exactly," said Kofa. He bent down to examine the body. "I see. A regular knife wound, but right in the heart. Nice job. Today's a cold weapon day for us, it seems. Killed by our client, I'm sure. It couldn't be anyone else. We can go now, boy. Your suffering is almost over."

"Phew!" I said, heading for the exit. I had nothing to complain about. Kofa had done a quick and excellent job with this case. I couldn't have wished for it to finish any sooner.

"You can go back to the Headquarters," Kofa said to Chekta Jax. "This murder falls under the jurisdiction of the Secret Investigative Force now. Consider yourself lucky that we got here so soon. You won't be doing our job, which is a plus. Good night, gentlemen."

The gloomy face of Lieutenant Chekta Jax depicted an epic battle between relief and disappointment. Alas, I had no time to admire the evidence of that psychological conundrum.

"So, our pretty boy immediately used the cloak to settle an old score," I said. "That's too shallow. I thought he was the 'real deal,' as No-Nose Misa put it."

"Who knows? But I don't think he was settling any old scores," said Kofa. "I don't think he even knew the victim."

"Why kill him then?" I said. "Just for kicks?"

"Almost. I suspect he did it to test how well his new acquisition worked."

"To test it?" I said. "Makes sense, of course, but he could've tried a less violent experiment. Steal something, for example."

"I believe he was aware that the cloak worked fine for stealing. Looks like our client knew poor Zekka Moddorok well, or at least had been following his adventures. He was well prepared. How else would he have known about the cloak and where to find it? This fellow had been following Zekka's trail for a long time."

"Okay, that I can understand," I said. "But what exactly happened in the Grave of Kukonin? I mean, how did it all happen, and when?"

"Less than an hour ago. We're all but stepping on the heels of our pretty boy, whoever he may be. As to what happened in the tavern, it's very simple. The victim stood by the bar, waiting for the barman to finish washing up the glasses and take his money. Then he moaned, touched his chest, and fell. The barman thought he had had a heart attack and was going to call for a wiseman, but then he saw the wound and the blood. Of course he didn't see anyone besides the victim. The tavern was empty—everybody had left.

"I'm almost sure that our pretty boy was standing by the dead body the whole time. He wanted to make sure that nobody could see him. There wasn't much risk in that. If anything went wrong, he could just run off. The barman is an old fellow and doesn't strike me as someone who could try to detain our killer. There was no one else in the Grave, so it all worked out nicely for him. Can you tell how long before we catch up with him?"

"I can only tell you that he's not hiding just around the corner, unfortunately," I said. "I hate him already. Why oh why didn't he take an amobiler? Echo's a big city."

"I wholeheartedly share your indignation," said Kofa.

"At least he's got stamina," I grumbled. "Nothing could induce me to follow a trace like this if it belonged to another dead man."

"Don't be so sure," said Kofa, shaking his head. "If even half of what I've heard about you is true, the fellow may give up the ghost any second."

"I hope he doesn't. No-Nose Misa survived, and I was on her trace for a long time while you were going to fetch my amobiler."

"Women in general are much tougher than we men, and Misa is tougher than all other women put together, despite her age. Hey, look, Max! Do you know where we are?"

"I'm not really paying attention. I've been focusing on trying not to trip."

"This is the Bridge of Kuluga Menonchi," said Kofa.

"And that means that we're headed to Jafax," I said. "Holy moly! Looks like you and I are going to save the mighty Order of the Seven-Leaf Clover from all known disasters at one go. No wonder I feel so exhausted."

"Oy vey, Max. Magician Nuflin will owe us a little for this night, he will," said Kofa. He was so good at impersonating the Grand Magician Nuflin Moni Mak that I couldn't contain a smile. Kofa also smiled and winked at me. "Exhausted, you say? Why not take a sip of your Elixir of Kaxar?"

"Oh, thanks for reminding me," I said, taking the bottle out of my pocket. "My head is full of holes. Maybe you want a sip yourself?"

"Maybe I do want a sip myself," said Kofa. "Sometimes brilliant ideas do visit your head, holes notwithstanding."

"Thanks. Ah, now we're very close."

We were walking alongside the tall wall surrounding the Main Residence of the Order of the Seven-Leaf Clover. Juffin had once told me that climbing over this wall would be impossible even if you had the best mountain climbing equipment in the World. You'd be climbing forever because the wall disappeared into some unknown but allegedly unpleasant infinity.

"Of course we must be close," said Kofa. "There's no place for him to go now. The Transparent Gates of Jafax open only at sunrise and sunset, and no cloak will help him find or pass through the Secret Gates. He'd need a spell, but that would be too much for him. He's already missed the sunset and is probably waiting for the sunrise. That's just plain silly. If I were him, I would be hiding away in some cozy place until morning."

"So would I," I said. "And yet he's still hanging around here somewhere."

"Now that is simply stupid," said Kofa. "If you're foolish enough to engage in a felony, you should at least try to enjoy it. What's to enjoy here, shivering in the cold winter wind—with you already sniffing around the end of his trace to boot?"

"On top of all that, the fellow is still alive," I said. "Or maybe I'm just out of shape."

"We'll know very soon." Kofa grabbed me by my shoulders and forged ahead. "You're losing your concentration, boy. If your client is alive, he could be biding his time looking for some amusement, like shooting a Baboom or throwing daggers. Some people have very unusual hobbies."

"But he's supposed to be lying unconscious somewhere by now," I said.

"There are people, and there are people," said Kofa. "Oh, crap!"

The next thing I knew my colleague was lying on the ground and cursing. The primary topic of his tirade was fecal matter, which was mentioned in a number of very intricate combinations with other words. The bad influence of General Boboota was unmistakable. Prolonged exposure to his personality left no one untouched.

I couldn't stop running even if I had wanted to. The trace was pulling me so hard it felt like I was rolling downhill, not running. As a result, I crashed into Kofa, who was already pulling himself up off the ground.

Now we both ended up on the ground. Of course, I couldn't miss the opportunity to crush my long-suffering elbow again. It hurt so bad my arm felt like it had exploded. It was now my turn in this contest for the best expletive of the season. Baffled, Kofa fell silent and listened.

"How do you spell that?" he said. "And the one just before it?"

"Ask Lonli-Lokli," I said, embarrassed. The pain subsided a little, and I cheered up. "During our mission in Kettari, he drew up a list of profanities from my distant homeland. I had to get pretty drunk to muster enough courage to explain some of them to him."

"Oh, dear," said Kofa. "Well, I guess I'll have to bother Sir Shurf about it some day. In any case, thanks for taking my mind off the pain in my foot that I just dislocated. It worked like a charm."

"We're having the time of our life today, you and I," I said. "On top of that, I lost the trace when we were all topsy-turvy."

"What's 'sitturvy'?" he said absently. "And what do you need that trace for now?"

"Life goes on," I said. "I mean, I also hurt myself when I fell, but it's not the end of the world. Let's get cracking!"

"Haven't you figured out what I tripped over yet?" said Kofa. "Or did you think I went temporarily blind?"

"I'll be darned!" I said, laughing. "You tripped over our pretty boy? But of course, he's wearing the sinning cloak! Still, I don't see him. Do you?"

"I don't need to see him. I can feel him. The fellow is indeed unconscious, just as you suspected. I think if you stood on his trace a little longer, he'd be dead all right. He's lucky that you and I are such fast runners. Let me take the cloak off him. Behold!" said Kofa, now waving Anday's grandfather's gray cloak in front of my nose.

"Not much to behold," I said. "He's lying facedown, and his ass doesn't look that much different from any other ass, especially considering the amount of clothing he's wearing."

"You're the expert," said Kofa. "Now we can finally go back to Headquarters. I already sent them a call. An amobiler is on the way and should be here in a quarter of an hour."

"That's an outrage!" I said. "I would've gotten here in less than three minutes."

"You are an unbelievable boaster, Sir Max. Your driving skills are indisputable, but do we have to hear you brag about it at every turn?"

"True," I said. "But if I didn't blow my own horn, I'd be a disgustingly perfect human being. This way I have one harmless shortcoming, and everyone's happy . . . Wait a second, my foot is hurting now, too. The right one. Strange, because I only remember hitting my elbow."

"I think it's still mine," said Kofa. "You took my pain because my foot almost has stopped hurting. It's very kind of you, but I suspect you did it without realizing it."

"I did?" I said. "You can take your pain back anytime. I didn't mean to take yours. I've got my own."

The company amobiler arrived very quickly. I looked at the driver with appreciation: I liked guys who drove fast, plus I was getting cold. Echo has very mild winters, but when you are sitting on the ground on the bank of a river with streams of hard-earned sweat trickling down your back, your body starts to protest.

We loaded our still immobile quarry into the back seat, squeezed ourselves into the amobiler, and headed off to the House by the Bridge. At last.

I was sitting in the back seat next to the captive, an old man with an utterly unexceptional face.

"Do you know him, Kofa?" I said.

"No. But it makes no difference. Sooner or later he'll come to and tell us everything. If not us, then Juffin. Although you can always resort to one of the Lethal Spheres."

"I can try," I said. "But first I need to do something about my elbow and sit in an armchair with a cup of hot kamra—get warm, relax, and recall that life is great. Because now I'm afraid one of my Lethal Spheres would actually kill this fellow. He really ruined a perfectly good night for us."

When we were pulling up to Headquarters, something hard and cold poked me in the side. I groped around trying to catch hold of the object and . . . cut myself. I jumped out of my seat in a flash, and the next thing I knew, I was sitting on top of my captive, holding his wrists in a deadly grip. I had no idea I was capable of such a lightning-quick reaction. Fortunately, the fellow was an even worse fighter than I was, and he wasn't in his best form now. As a result, the knife, with its long thin blade, ended up in my possession.

"What's going on back there?" said Kofa, turning around.

"Nothing now," I said, "But a second ago he tried to stab me." I gave my captive a stern look. "What's with the showing off, buddy? You can hardly lift a finger, and I could've spat venom at you out of fear. Or are you okay with that?"

He closed his eyes and didn't say anything. I couldn't tell whether he was too exhausted to talk or just despised me—the human heart is a mystery, at least some of the time.

I moved my left hand along the side of his body—another trick from the arsenal of Shurf Lonli-Lokli, who had been coaching me in Applied Magic. Our prisoner disappeared in between my left thumb and index finger—a much safer place for someone with his temperament.

"You should have done that long time ago," said Kofa.

"Yes, but sensible thoughts come to me with the sluggish gait characteristic of a royal persona," I said. "Want me to help you to the office?"

"Don't push it, boy. You think I can't cross the hallway on my own? Someone would have to tear off my head, at the very least, before I was that incapacitated."

Kofa was limping, but that didn't affect the speed at which he moved. He was the first to run into the office and fall into my favorite armchair. The silent struggle for the right to plant our backsides in it had been going on between us almost since my first day here. I must admit that Kofa was leading with a huge advantage in this sport.

"I already sent a call to the Glutton," he said in the tone of a magnanimous victor. "Madam Zizinda's cook on duty is much worse than Madam Zizinda herself, but much better than the others. Shouldn't we lock up our prisoner?"

"Nah, let's leave him where he is, in my palm. He doesn't bother me, and actually it makes me feel better this way. What if he has some unknown methods of escape up his sleeve? Just thinking about trying to stand on his trace again makes me sick. Besides, I'm going to interrogate him soon."

"Just admit that you've forgotten all about him, and now you're too lazy to unstick your backside from the chair to go anywhere . . . Then again, you have every right to be."

When the long-awaited tray from the Glutton appeared on the desk, I fell upon the food with gusto. Ten minutes later, I was feeling great. I was warm, a scrumptious cookie was melting in my mouth, and even the dull pain in my elbow seemed almost pleasant. The ache didn't bother me so much as it testified to the fact that I was alive. It added a new note to the symphony of familiar sensations. I poured myself more kamra, pulled out a cigarette from where I had stashed it in the Mantle of Death, and noticed with satisfaction that Kofa was also in a benign good humor.

"Now I can commence the interrogation," I said, yawning. "I can't get any more good-humored than this. I feel like I could pour him some kamra—if he behaves himself, that is. You're probably also curious to know what he has to say."

"Well," said Kofa, yawning even wider, "frankly, the case is as clear as it can be to me, save a few details."

"Is it?" I said. "Care to enlighten me? Because to me nothing is clear."

"Here's what I think. This pretty boy has something to do with the glorious Order of Green Moons, as did the gentlemen who stole the chest from the basement of your friend's house. Our late janitor, who, as it turned out, could go down the Dark Path, was likely their former colleague, as well. The Order of Green Moons was the only Order that taught its apprentices the art of the Dark Path. Their Grand Magician, Mener Gusot, was crazy about that trick." Kofa yawned again and began filling his pipe. I gave him a pleading look. The cruel sadist didn't say a word for another three minutes. Then, when he lit up his pipe, he continued. "As I understand it, our hero had a personal score to settle with Magician Nuflin himself, or the entire Order of the Seven-Leaf Clover. He was doomed to fail from the start, though. The Ukumbian cloak is a neat little thing, but it's only good for tricking regular folks. Perhaps it's even good enough for tricking us Secret Investigators, but he didn't manage to pull that off, either.

"His plan was solid. First a thief appears in this office, someone no one pays any attention to. Then he doesn't just steal the cloak outright; he switches it for another one just like it, which gives our conspirators a great deal of extra time. The poor fellow then takes the cloak to the meeting point, where he meets with No-Nose Misa's dagger.

"Technically, this is where we are supposed to lose all the leads, but we're lucky, because you can follow the trace of a dead man. Still, the man who's sitting in your palm now was cautious enough to send a kid to Misa instead of coming for the cloak himself."

"Speaking of the kid," I said, "I'd feel much better if we found him, too."

"You think so?" said Kofa. "I think you're being overzealous, but if it'll help you sleep better, in the morning I can send Melamori to the house of No-Nose Misa. She can step on the kid's trace and bring him over here. I don't think he's so evil that I should let you step on his trace."

"Right. But I still don't understand how he knew that we had the cloak. And when did he have the time to make an exact replica of it? You'd need to have—or at least look at—the original, right?"

"Right," said Kofa. "I'm sure he knew Zekka Moddorok very well. To find out about what happened to Zekka was as easy as pie: he only had to visit Zekka's inconsolable mother or even just spot a policeman's face in the window—this would tell any smart person that the magic cloak had been repossessed by the people in the House by the Bridge—and then take measures. I personally think that the copy had been produced a few days prior and was intended to fool Zekka. I could be wrong, but we can always ask. Weren't you going to interrogate him?"

"Didn't someone just say everything was clear to him and that he wasn't interested?" I said.

"No, you must have misheard," said Kofa, batting his eyelids.

I didn't make a fuss and accepted his excuse. I gave my fist a vigorous shake, and the body of my prisoner crashed onto the floor. I still hadn't learned to do this trick with due finesse.

The old gentleman, in a splendid colorful looxi and bright-red turban, tried to get up. The expression that he made was . . . Well, you should've been there, as they say. I could feel for the guy. He already had enough reasons to hate me for the rest of his life, and this fall might have been the last straw. I hastened to snap the fingers of my left hand. A ball of bright-green light headed toward the wrinkled forehead of the old man. To my surprise, he flung both his hands in front of him and mumbled something. The little fireball slowed down, as though apologizing, before his invisible shield. It looked as though it hesitated to enter his body without a formal invitation from him.

I was puzzled. "Oh, come on!" I shouted at my Lethal Sphere. And it worked. The green blob of light sped forward, hit the palms of the prisoner, and disappeared. Then the fellow gave himself a slap in the face with one hand. With the other hand, he gave himself the finger. His hands seemed to have a mind of their own that was not in accordance with the rest of his body.

Kofa burst out laughing. I couldn't say I wasn't enjoying the show myself. Nevertheless, I had to launch another Lethal Sphere. This time, praise be the Magicians, the victim relaxed and muttered "I am with you, Master"—the usual deal. I relaxed as well and reached into the pocket of my Mantle of Death for another cigarette. Kofa could laugh all he wanted, but the first misfire sure made me nervous.

"Let's hear your name, for starters," I said.

"How wonderfully original," said Kofa, laughing. "Don't be offended. If you only knew how many thousands of times I have begun an interrogation with this question."

Our arrestee composed himself and began to speak. "My name is Nennurex Kiexla."

"Have you heard this name before, Kofa?" I said, looking at him with hope.

"Vaguely," said Kofa. "I seem to remember there was someone by the name of Kiexla among the members of the Order of Green Moons, but I never met him personally."

"Okay, Sir Nennurex Kiexla. Get up from the floor and sit down in this chair," I said. Then I pushed a cup toward him. "Have some hot kamra. You're blue from the cold."

"Sometimes you're so good at playing nice, Sir Max, that I even begin to believe that you are," said Kofa.

"What do you mean?" I said. "I am a very nice fellow." To my surprise, Kofa only shook his head. Well, I'll be, I thought. What did he think of me then?

Sir Nennurex Kiexla drained the hot kamra in one gulp and put the cup down timidly on the desk.

"Pour yourself more, and you can have something to eat if you're hungry," I said. Then I turned to my colleague. "Kofa, let me just order him to answer your questions. My head is too empty now."

"Not too empty for a single sober thought," said Kofa.

"Sir Nennurex, I will appreciate it if you answer all the questions put to you by this gentleman here," I said to my "loyal servant."

"As you wish, Master," he said, and Kofa took over the interrogation.

"I'm primarily interested in one junior staff member of the Ministry of Perfect Public Order. Your accomplice. The police picked up the body. They say it was Itlox Bouba, but this name doesn't ring a bell. Who was he?"

"That wasn't his real name. His name is . . . was Sir Unboni Marixva."

"Oh, boy. Yes, you did take some measures," said Kofa. He looked very displeased. He turned to me and said, "Would you believe it, boy, that the most famous Junior Magician of the Order of Green Moons has been hanging around the Ministry of Perfect Public Order for a year and a half? He's been dusting our desks, and we didn't even know it. I'll have to personally run extensive checks on every new hire from now on. Come to think of it, we got off cheap this time. Tell me, Sir Nennurex, weren't you a Junior Magician of the Order, too?"

"I was an apprentice," said Nennurex. "I entered the Order late. Besides, Magician Mener didn't deem me a talented student. He was probably right: I have never even learned to go down the Dark Path. But by the time I joined the Order, it needed good warriors more than talented magicians. The old man realized it too late."

"You got that right," said Kofa. "This is very interesting. What did Sir Unboni Marixva do here in the Ministry of Perfect Public Order? As far as I know, until last night he was harmless. Had he reformed and decided to make an honest living?"

"He told me he was just waiting for his chance," said Nennurex. "Marixva had a warped sense of humor. He found it hilarious that he was scrubbing the floors in the office of the Kettarian, who had no clue who he was. I think that was why Marixva didn't do anything. He was much happier knowing that he was fooling you than actually doing you any harm. He had no aversion to you or Nuflin. He was a very dispassionate person."

"Max, I was a fool when I told you I wasn't interested," said Kofa. "I'm more curious now than ever. Go on, Sir Nennurex. Tell me how it all happened. How did it all begin? Who learned about the cloak and what were you going to do with it?"

"I learned about the cloak. Zekka Moddorok told me. We got together often in the past few months. He found me almost half a year ago, right after I had arrived in the Capital. Zekka wanted me to be in his gang like when we were young. During the Troubled Times, he and I used to murder and rob a little here and there. Then I left for County Xotta: staying in Echo was too dangerous, and I didn't want to risk my life before I could take my vengeance."

"Take vengeance? On whom? For what?" said Kofa. "For old Magician Mener? As far as I know, even his favorite students couldn't stand him."

"Not for him—for the Order. It's a matter of honor, not favoritism," said Nennurex Kiexla.

"He talks like an Arvaroxian," I said.

"Indeed," said Kofa. "Out of all the survivors of the members of the Order of Green Moons, the only one who cares about its honor is the least talented of its apprentices. Juffin's going to love this. Moving right along, Sir Nennurex, how does Unboni Marixva come into the story, and why did you decide to kill him?"

"I told Marixva about the cloak after I found out that the Secret Investigative Force was on Zekka's case. While Zekka had the cloak, I could take my time making a replica and waiting for the opportunity. But only Marixva could steal the cloak from the House by the Bridge. I lied to him about the cloak so that he didn't try to flee with it. I knew that he wouldn't help me if he found out that I was going to sneak into Jafax."

"What did you tell him exactly?" I said. Kofa looked at me with an unfavorable eye. Judging from his expression, I was asking an irrelevant question.

"I told him the cloak made you healthier and even younger if you wore it long enough. I knew that Unboni Marixva cared about his health. Such magical things do exist, so he believed me right away. I also told him that for its effects to manifest themselves, the cloak must be worn at dawn, just so he wouldn't try to put it on."

"Very clever," said Kofa. "So he thought I was mending my health or even trying to rejuvenate myself. He would be in on all the rumors in the Department."

"But why kill him?" I said. "You could've just taken the cloak and disappeared."

"I had to kill him so you wouldn't step on his trace. A human life is worth nothing when it comes to the matters of justice, especially the life of a man indifferent to the laws of honor."

"I'll bet he has some Arvaroxian blood in his veins," I said. "Okay, I'll shut up now and not interfere."

"You're not interfering," said Kofa. "On the contrary, you're helping me. But we're done now, I think."

"Maybe," I said. "But— Hold on a second. We can ask him about the boy so that Lady Melamori doesn't have to step on the poor child's trace. Who's the boy you sent to No-Nose Misa's house, Nennurex?"

"He was my son."

"Oh, this is neat," I said. "In a hundred years or so when he grows up, he'll come to the House by the Bridge to avenge his father. Well, at least I don't have to worry about my future. A hundred years from now, I won't get bored. Where is he now?"

"I sent him home to his mother. Yesterday I arranged for a merchant who was going to County Xotta to take them both away with him. I didn't think I would get out of Jafax alive."

"Did your son know about your plans? Has he been helping you?" I said. "Don't lie to me."

"He knows nothing, Master. Why would I tell him anything? Last night I just asked him to go to the old hag's house, give her the money, and take the cloak. I raised my son well—he didn't even think of asking questions."

I shook my head. I could hear the tone of a classic abusive parent in his voice. I wanted to cover him top to bottom with my venomous spit. I hate coercion, and talking to bastards like him makes me furious, even when they have no way of coercing me personally. It was good that I had recently learned to contain myself.

The child is very lucky, I thought to myself. For the next couple hundred years, his abusive daddy won't be able to practice his perverted parenting methods. If I were him, I'd run away. I could hardly stand my own parents, who had been much more normal. But then again, people get used to everything.

"Right, then the boy can go home," said Kofa. "The last thing we want is to arrest a child. Max, I'm afraid you'll have to move your backside after all. Take Sir Nennurex to some vacant cell. We'll call the guys from Xolomi later. Juffin won't forgive us if we deprive him of his favorite pastime."

I took the great avenger to the doors of one of the small detention cells. Instead of walking inside, he shuffled his feet in the doorway, boring a hole in me with the look of a martyr. Of course, I thought. He can't stand parting with me without getting a command, and letting him go would be dangerous—Sir Nennurex is a slyboots. Who knows what's on his mind?

"You must be without me now," I said. "I want you to feel good and behave yourself. Actually, why don't you just go to sleep, Sir Nennurex? Go to bed and sleep until somebody wakes you up."

He obediently got into bed, closed his eyes, and fell asleep. The submissive indifference of this iron-willed man was something so abnormal that I shuddered. I found my own ability to make normal people stare at me with a devoted look and prattle "I am with you, Master" somewhat revolting.

But by the end of my journey back to the office through the long hallways and corridors of the Department, I had put this silly problem out of my head. It certainly wasn't worth jumping off a bridge into the Xuron over.

While I was gone, Kofa hadn't been wasting any time. He had put the pitcher with kamra on the burner and heated it up. I sank into the armchair and stretched my legs. There's nothing better than a hard-earned break.

"You can go home now if you want to," said Kofa. "I don't know how many gallons of Elixir of Kaxar you've consumed today, but you don't look all that chipper to me."

"I'm just malingering so that you'll feel sorry for me," I said. "And it looks like I'm really good at it."

"You're so good at it I'm about to cry," said Kofa. "Finish your kamra and scram. I'm going to stay here and wait for Juffin. He'd better fix my foot if he doesn't want me to stay home in bed until the Last Day of the Year. Also, if I were you, I'd start collecting your amobilers now. You'll have all but forgotten where you left them by morning."

"You're absolutely right," I said. "At the very least I should pick up the one I left by the Jubatic Fountain, or the locals will strip it for parts. Which would be sad: it's a good amobiler. Not cheap, either." I poured the contents of the cup down my throat and got up—not without regret—from the cozy armchair. "Good night, Kofa. And thank you for sending me home."

"In some sense, I owe you one," said Kofa, smiling. "You helped me hush up the consequences of breaching my job protocol. Good night, boy."

"Speaking of hushing up," I said, "I'm willing to keep my mouth shut about it if you buy me a good dinner. And something else maybe. I'll have to think about it."

"How quaint, Sir Max," said Kofa. "You have a natural bent for professional blackmail."

The guy who had driven us away from the inhospitable walls of Jafax was still behind the steering lever. To his utter surprise, I told him to move over but to stay in the amobiler. Then I took the driver's seat and drove off at a suicidal speed through the orange light of the street lamps, contemplating with a great pleasure the reverential horror in the eyes of my passenger.

A few moments later, I stopped by the Jubatic Fountain and got into my own amobiler.

"Did you enjoy the ride?" I asked the young driver. He just nodded. The poor thing was lost for words. I felt great. It was as if I had been awarded the Nobel Prize in spite of my relatives, former classmates, and ex-girlfriends—everyone who had once given me up for lost. A moronic feeling. I shook my head, ridding it of the excess of stupidity, then smiled at the driver. "Remember this ride next time you get behind the lever. You're pretty good at driving this thing, and if you really want to, you'll be able to drive as fast as I do. Or even faster. There are no special skills involved. You just have to stop fearing high speeds. You should dream of it."

I spoke in the tone of a newly minted guru, but I couldn't resist the desire to pass on my "great knowledge" to a potential pupil. In addition, I was guided by practicality. I wanted to have at least one speed demon among the staff drivers of the Ministry of Perfect Public Order. Occasionally, I needed their services.

The only way I could account for the fact that I had enough energy left to undress when I walked into the small bedroom on the second floor of the Armstrong & Ella fifteen minutes later was the amount of Elixir of Kaxar I had consumed during this long, long night.

Perhaps it was an overdose of that tonic that pushed me into committing another rash action. After a few moments of pondering, I put my head down onto Tekki's pillow, in dangerous proximity to her silver curls. I thought that one more meeting with the "great and mighty" Magician Loiso Pondoxo wasn't going to hurt. If he really wanted to hurt me, he would have done it last night.

On the contrary, I thought, I have a good chance to get answers to a whole lot of questions. Loiso was a very sociable fellow. I don't know about Juffin, but I sure look a lot like a chiffa, the Kettarian fox. Loiso was spot on there.

I closed my eyes, and the coming dream swirled me into its delightful and merciless whirlpool.

Sometimes, before I fall asleep, I experience a short but very intense bout of panic. It is during that unique and brief moment that I realize why sleep is often called a little death. I'm scared that when I fall asleep I will disappear, and that tomorrow a completely different creature will wake up in my place. It will call itself Max, but only by coincidence. Even so, that new Max will last only until the next night.

This time, the panic was so strong that I screamed and jumped out from under the blanket, not even considering that I might have woken up Tekki. I forgot that she even existed, let alone slept right next to me.

I looked around and shuddered: instead of the pile of the rug, pale blades of dry grass were moving in the hot wind around me. I was standing at the foot of the familiar gently sloping hill and not in the bedroom.

I'd been known for having extravagant dreams, but never before had I fallen asleep while jumping out of bed and screaming. Woken up screaming? Yes, but fortunately not very often.

"Loiso! Are you here?" I shouted. Clearly I was losing my mind.

If you want to see me, come up. I can't go down this side of the hill. It's too great a luxury for such an honorable prisoner of this place.

Strange as it might seem, Loiso Pondoxo's Silent Speech had a soothing effect on me. I composed myself and began climbing uphill. A few minutes later, I was at the top—sweating, panting, but absolutely calm. Sometimes all it takes to recover from a shock are a few kind words and exercise.

Loiso was sitting on the same amber rock in the same posture: strong hands folded on his knees, his face hidden by his long blond hair.

"Back so soon?" he said. "Even sooner that I expected."

"You're so good at standing on your head that I simply can't stay in my foxhole," I said, laughing, as I realized that I had been caught in the snares of his metaphor for good.

"Perhaps that's what I've been doing, in some sense. Not just now, though, but all my life," said Loiso, turning to look at me.

"I came to ask you a ton of questions," I said, sitting down next to him. "I thought that since you hadn't had the opportunity to chat in so long, I might have a chance to get answers to a couple of them."

"I might," he said, nodding. "Ask me whatever you want. If you need a talkative interlocutor, you've come to the right place."

"Thanks. Well, the first thing I want to understand is this: to get to this place here, I have to fall asleep with my head on your daughter's pillow. No traveling through the Corridor between Worlds, nothing of that sort. The whole thing seems a lot like a regular dream. But yesterday I scratched my hands on some grass here, and when I woke up, the scratches were still there. Real, ordinary scratches." I gave Loiso a puzzled look and even showed him my palms.

"Indeed," he said. "Very ordinary scratches. What was the question again?"

"Is this what's happening to me here for real?" I said. I seemed to have lost all the clever words I had prepared for the occasion. These things happen to me all the time, and at the most inappropriate moments.

"Is this 'for real'?" said Loiso. "One could say it is. The odd thing is that we never have any guarantee that what happens to us happens 'for real.' When you're sitting on the toilet at home, you simply have no reason for asking yourself, 'Is this for real?' But essentially, that situation is no different from this one here. It is possible that you are a vegetable and you have been gobbled up by some herbivore beast whose gastric juice is capable of inducing realistic hallucinations in the food it's digesting. You are simply enjoying a mind-boggling illusion of an interesting and eventful life right before it's time to go. Do you like your hallucination, Sir Max?"

"It's all right, I suppose," I said. There was something simultaneously horrifying and comforting in his words. They could be true, which would mean that I was in a pickle (or was a pickle?), but fortunately I had no way of verifying them.

"You shouldn't pay so much attention to my words," he said. "It makes no difference. In any event, we have nothing but our senses. Why should we care about the monster that is digesting us if all of our senses are telling us we are sitting on top of a hill under this white sky and chatting, because you think you need to have this chat and I don't mind indulging my guest's wishes? Do you have more questions for me?"

"No, thanks. You know, Loiso, I'm a very impressionable fellow, even though nobody believes me when I say it. So I think I'm going to call it a day for now."

"I don't believe it, either," said Loiso. "Not for a second."

"Oh, great. You too, huh? Fine, suit yourself. But why?"

"See? Now you're ready for my 'horrifying' answers again."

"Hmm, you've got me there," I said. "But this is something I really need to know. Why did you let me in here? Or did you invite me?"

"It just happened," said Loiso. "Forgive me for saying such a trivial thing, but it's your fate. And mine. Nothing we can do about it. According to my calculations, some day you'll be able to take me away from here. I'm just not sure how. You have this crazy personal trait, you know, the ability to set free anyone you come across. You were born that way, and there's nothing that can be done about it, either. See? I'm not even trying to keep my plans a secret from you."

"I'd love to take you away from here this instant, if I only knew how. But . . . Juffin says you were going to bring the World to an end and I don't like that idea one bit. I just fell in love with your World."

"That's because you were born in another place. A different World always has an irresistible charm, however good or bad it might be. But one's own homeland, on the other hand, often induces painful revulsion, much of it absolutely groundless. If you want my opinion, the World I used to live in could have been ideal if it hadn't been populated by humans. For the most part, people are completely unsuited to the Worlds they inhabit. Their dull, eternally gobbling faces, clothes flapping in the wind for the sole purpose of hiding from the heavens the flabby, flaccid bodies of the lazy gluttons. Once I simply walked into a tavern in Echo, and an extreme, indescribable fury engulfed me.

"Don't look at me like a girl who has just seen a spider. Have you forgotten what you felt when you tore to pieces the useless human beings on your beloved sand beach in another World? Don't try to tell me you weren't enjoying it. You were as happy as you could be. But fret not. I no longer desire to destroy the World I was born in. It's silly to repeat a failed experiment. That isn't my way. There are plenty of Worlds in the Universe, I'll have you know."

I didn't try to object. The heat had turned me into the aforementioned semi-digested vegetable. "What do you really look like?" I said. "You still have my face. Why? I told you there was no need to flirt with me. I'm already—"

"Believe it or not, this is what I 'really' look like. Aren't you disillusioned with your silly term? Was I wasting my time entertaining you with my ominous metaphors?"

"No, you weren't. I just haven't yet found a substitute for that phrase," I said. "Does your face . . . really . . . look like mine?"

"It has recently. What it looked like when I entered the Xolomi Higher Institute or a hundred years after I graduated, I don't remember myself. Guess when was the last time I looked in the mirror?"

"About five centuries ago?"

"Something like that. You have to go now, Max. I am a wearisome interlocutor, if you haven't noticed, and you don't yet have the guts to withstand the local climate. The last thing I want to do now is dig you a grave. I can't tell you how hard the soil is here. Mind you, you don't need to put your head on my daughter's pillow. It's enough to say 'I want to see Loiso' before you go to sleep. I needed Tekki to arrange for our first meeting, but we won't be needing her help anymore. It's a good thing you didn't tell her about us. You guessed right: she wouldn't like it. The girl hardly knows me, yet she dislikes me a great deal. Still, it's understandable."

"Can Tekki interfere?" I said.

"Yes, she can. She can do a lot of things. She'll definitely try," said Loiso, smirking. "I don't care, but I don't think you're going to like her interference. Well, never mind. There's no call for alarm—scare tactics don't work on you. Nothing works on you. You'll still do whatever you feel is right."

"Thanks for the compliment," I said.

"You think it was a compliment?" said Loiso, surprised. My head began to spin, but I tried to continue our conversation.

"Loiso, I'm leaving you as curious and puzzled as I was before I came. You didn't really tell me anything. Like this apocalypse of yours—what's your stake in it? Are you just angry? Sure, I remember what I did on the beach, and I understand why you brought it up, but I think that blind fury in and of itself doesn't cut it. It doesn't explain anything. You're not that shallow."

"I'm not saying it's just blind fury. It's a mystery that I have been trying to unveil. The greatest mystery of all of them. He who witnesses the end of a World has a microscopic chance of consuming all the power, all the strength of a dying speck of the Universe. It's almost impossible, yet it's worth risking everything you have."

"And then what?" I said.

"I don't know. In order to answer that question, one must destroy at least one World and see what happens. I haven't had any luck with that so far. But you really must go now, Max. You look like a dead man who's beginning to disintegrate. You shouldn't overindulge yourself in talking to evil sorcerers."

He laughed, got up from the rock, stretched his hand as if to help me get up, and suddenly jabbed me in the side—quite painfully, in fact. That jab was enough to send me rolling down the hill. Sharp blades of grass scratched my face and hands, but I barely felt them. The damn heat had nearly killed me. It looked like I wasn't that tough to kill after all.

I opened my eyes in the familiar, cozy darkness of the bedroom and closed them again. I was exhausted. He never told me why such a powerful Order had such a ridiculous name, I thought when I was falling asleep. Why a "Watery Crow"? The answer to that question was what lured me into that devilish heat in the first place. And I still didn't know.

I woke up after the timid winter sun had already made its noon announcement to anyone interested. I lay in bed another half hour enjoying the unique combination of a great mood, extreme laziness, and a complete absence of thought in my head.

I was feeling tired: tired of miracles, of poetry, of mysteries, of Loiso Pondoxo, and of myself, first and foremost. Surprisingly enough, I liked being in this state of exhaustion—though not for too long, of course.

Eventually I managed to drag myself to the bathroom and then to the bar in the Armstrong & Ella. Tekki was already there, and Armstrong and Ella themselves were purring by her feet. I felt like lying on the floor and dying from an overload of tenderness and cuteness. To survive, I opted for a more toned-down expression of emotion.

"Have you looked at your face?" said Tekki. "Did you get into a fight with all the poets in Echo?" I grabbed a tray made out of polished metal from the nearest table and looked at the poor semblance of a reflection in it. "Not quite what you were hoping for, huh?" said Tekki, handing me a small mirror. "Here, have a good look."

"Pfft. A couple of scratches," I said, heaving a sigh of relief. My nose and chin were covered in the thick web of superficial scratches that I had received when I was rolling downhill. That wicked Loiso didn't have to push me, I thought. I could have walked down by myself.

"Enough for one night, I suppose," said Tekki, covering my face in some transparent stinky gel. "In thirty minutes, you can go outside. What happened to you?"

"A lot of things," I said, sighing. I was in no mood for making up believable excuses, lying, or—Magicians forbid!—telling the truth. But Tekki seemed to have been satisfied with my answer.

"Get ready for receiving your numerous friends any minute now," she said. "Our rotund poet just sent me a call. He wanted to know if you had opened your pretty eyes yet. I think it's just the beginning."

"Gosh, I have no personal life," I said. "How can you still stand me?"

"I wish I knew myself," she said. "Maybe I'm just very patient."

The door slammed behind me. I turned around and saw my friend Anday Pu, a brilliant poet and a most unhappy person. His appearance was very timely. I was just about to stick my scratched nose into his business. After all, he had been asking me to do it for a long time.

The descendant of Ukumbian pirates said hello, climbed atop a barstool, and began chatting with Tekki. He must have decided that after his performance in the Three-Horned Moon his status had grown in my eyes and he could do anything now.

"You know, Blackbeard Junior, if you really want to move to Tasher, I think I can arrange that," I said. "Go to the Port Quarter right now. Find the house of Captain Giatta and tell him I sent you. Also tell him . . . No, don't tell him anything—I'll tell him myself.

Just ask him when he's going back home to Tasher. He'll take you with him and help you settle there—that is, unless you've changed your mind."

"Changed my mind! Are you joking? How can I change my mind! Now you catch, Max. That's so great! Thank you so much. I'm going to see the captain right now," said Anday like a machine gun. "Why did you decide to help me? Was it my poetry? Did you catch?"

"Exactly," I said. "It was your poetry."

Of course the poetry of this haughty wordsmith—which sounded so much like my own youthful experiments, full of open self-admiration and melancholy—didn't have anything to do with it. At least not directly. I had the opportunity to let Captain Giatta go home and to prove to Anday, using his own example, that a dream fulfilled didn't always equal happiness. That hypocrite Loiso Pondoxo could see right through me. I did like to "set free anyone I came across." Maybe just so they didn't get in the way.

Fortunately, Anday couldn't read my mind. He said goodbye and rushed out of the tavern to the Port Quarter, his feet barely touching the ground. I followed his figure with my eyes and sent a call to Captain Giatta.

I finally thought of a way you can pay me back, Giatta. A really funny fellow is on his way to see you. He's my old friend, and he's been dreaming of moving to Tasher. If you take him there and help him settle in the new place, consider your debt to me paid. But don't rush with your departure this time. First finish up your business here.

Sir Max, is this really what you want? Or are you just trying to get rid of me after such a long wait?

I really want this, I said very sincerely. I don't quite know why, but I desperately want this.

All right, I'll do it for you. Can your friend wait until the Last Day of the Year? I need to pay my assistants and get a new crew. This will take time.

Of course. There's no rush. In any case, he won't be waiting long.

The winter is coming to an end, and the Last Day of the Year is just around the corner. He will wait all right. He has no choice—you're his only chance.

I said goodbye and, relieved, poured myself another cup of kamra.

"What's going on, honey?" said Tekki. "Are you into settling other people's lives now? It's a thankless business, and not the most original one."

"I know," I said, smiling. "But that pretty boy Anday was flirting with you so openly that I thought it would be better to send him off someplace far way before it's too late."

"Phew!" said Tekki. "What a relief. I was afraid he'd sweep me off my feet with his poetry. He's really sweet. And those almond-shaped eyes of his . . ."

I made a face and shook my fist at her. Tekki took my fist into her hands, pulled it close to her face, admired it for a few seconds, and then laughed.

We spent two more hours of our lives in the greatest of spirits, but then I felt a desire to go to the House by the Bridge that was stronger than I was. As the years went by, the fire under my backside wasn't getting any cooler.

"If you were going to pour out the story of Kofa's and your adventures, I have to tell you that I already saw Kofa himself, as well as the great avenger Nennurex Kiexla—and No-Nose Misa, to top it off," said Juffin. He tried to assume an air of suffering but failed miserably.

"All right then, I'll pretend that I've already told you everything and shut up," I said. "How's our Master Eavesdropper-Gobbler feeling?"

"Great, as usual, I think. Oh, you mean his foot? He's already forgotten that anything ever happened to it. By the way, you should lift off the spell from your victims. I've been trying to send them to Xolomi since morning, but they're so enchanted that it pains me to look at them," said Juffin.

"I'll get right down to it," I said. "In theory, I'm supposed to feel immense pleasure when I do. A mutual friend of ours believes that I have a hypertrophied desire to set people free. He doesn't put it as eloquently as I just did, though."

I looked into the detention cells housing the victims of my Lethal Spheres and issued them my last command: to rid themselves of the irresistible desire to follow my commands. I didn't feel any "immense pleasure" doing this, of course. Perhaps a sense of mild relief, akin to what you feel when you bid good riddance to bad rubbish.

"Beautiful," said Juffin when I returned. "Baguda Maldaxan's people will come pick them up in a few minutes. Then I'm going to abuse my exalted position as boss and go to the Street of Old Coins."

"Will you take my girlfriend to the movies?" I said. "I have a feeling she's too shy to bother you. From time to time, she thinks my former bedroom has turned into an extension of your office."

"And she's right," said Juffin. "Okay, I'll send her an invitation since she's so tactful and all. I hope you won't ask me to invite her daddy, too?"

"And all her sixteen ghost brothers to boot," I said. "By the way, what did you watch last night? More cartoons?"

"More cartoons and a pretty good movie about some crazy Magician. After he died, he got into the habit of visiting people in their dreams. And he didn't just scare people; he actually murdered them—just like that Phetan that almost spoiled your housewarming party a little over two years ago. Do you remember him?"

"Do I!" I said.

"See? Our worlds are not that dissimilar," said Juffin. I realized that Juffin thought *A Nightmare on Elm Street* belonged to the genre of neorealism, but I wasn't in the mood to disabuse him of the notion. Then again, who knows where screenwriters get their stories from?

❖

Lonli-Lokli appeared in my office an hour later. He looked like a man who was beset by sudden and urgent personal problems.

"Max, I finished your book," he said, sitting down across from me.

"And judging by your tone, you're dissatisfied with it. Mind you, though: I didn't write it."

"'Dissatisfied' is not the term I would use here," he said. "But I am confused and do not understand the World you were born in. Answer me this: Are all your compatriots so hopelessly horrible?"

"Well . . ." I grinned crookedly as I remembered my new friend Loiso Pondoxo, the charming misanthrope, as well as my own recent adventures on a certain sandy beach. Sir Shurf couldn't have found a better person to turn to. "There were times in my life when that was exactly what I thought," I said finally. "Then there were times when I thought the opposite. I think my feelings toward humanity depended solely on the state of my personal affairs. Don't lose any sleep over the book, though. I told you it was science fiction, which means the contents of the book have very little to do with the way things really are. How did it end, by the way? Yesterday you only told me the beginning."

"I am afraid I have not understood much myself. I do not know where to begin. You see, the powerful beings from another World, which I told you about yesterday, gave a few select people the ability to save the rest. They gave their chosen ones time and almost unlimited strength so they could help the rest of the people become perfect and occupy a higher rank in that strange classification of living beings that the aliens had come up with. Granted, their system of values is mostly in line with my own."

"Sounds great," I said. "Maybe I should read this strange book myself, just to familiarize myself with that value system. So how did it end?"

"Initially, the chosen ones were happy with the outcome," said Shurf. "They tried numerous ways of changing their compatriots. In particular, they established a system of birth control that was somehow connected with your horoscopes. As far as I can judge, they achieved impressive results. Then they got bored with it. Well, not bored, but they were disappointed in their fellow earthlings. And they destroyed everyone before their powerful masters from another World got the chance. The aliens, however, approved of their decision. The book left a bad taste in my mouth. There is something shatteringly hopeless in it. I should very much like to look the person who wrote it in the eye and ask him how he can live with it."

"Aw, Shurf. It's just another dystopia. Forget about it. The author would be surprised to know that someone took his story so much to heart. In my World, people read this nonsense when they're bored and then forget it as soon as they close the book. I highly recommend that you do the same."

"Your people have nerves of steel," said Shurf. "Or they have no imagination whatsoever."

"Perhaps. But I tend to think we were just brought up differently. It's simply unpleasant to get so emotional about a book. I suspect I owe you a good dinner. If one of my compatriots ruined your day, I simply must put things right."

Lonli-Lokli didn't mind. Our dinner at the Juffin's Dozen marked another period that I put at the end of the apocalyptic chapter that my life had been opening up over and over again recently. Enough is enough, I told myself.

The remaining two dozen days before the Last Day of the Year went by quickly and pleasantly. I felt no urge to have another meeting with Sir Loiso Pondoxo. I put off this social visit until some indeterminate "later." Occasionally my life enters phases of wonderful, sweet laziness, which, unfortunately, don't last long.

I spent the First Night of the New Year in my office, as I was supposed to. My colleagues were sleeping after the mind-boggling frenzy that engulfed all living creatures on the eve of that notorious event. Only Sir Juffin Hully went to the Street of Old Coins. He finally had time to relax and watch a movie. I could have afforded the luxury of keeping him company—the city was dead calm—but I preferred to nap in the armchair because the activities of the night before had worn me out.

Soon after midnight, I was awoken by the soft creaking of the door.

"Max, will it kill you to open your eyes if I come in?" said the descendant of Ukumbian pirates, also known as a would-be citizen of sunny Tasher.

"How nice," I said. "Finally you've come without announcing your presence to a dozen junior employees."

"That's because I didn't see a single rodent downstairs or in the hallway," said Anday. He produced a dusty clay bottle from under his looxi and put it on the desk. "It's from grandpa's old stock," he said. "Not some sickly sweet potion that they make in local taverns, but a real two-hundred-year-old Ukumbian bomborokka. I came to say goodbye. Your Tasherian friend Giatta says we're casting off at dawn."

"Are you happy?" I said, fumbling for the bottle of Elixir of Kaxar in the drawer. Without it, I would've been lousy company.

"Me? Uh, sure. I suppose." He said it in such a sad voice that I got worried.

"If you don't want to go, don't," I said. "You don't have to do it, buddy."

"No, no, no. I do want to go! Really. I'm just scared, Max. Sound the alarm."

"Well, that's normal. Of course it's scary to leave everything behind and set off for who-knows-where, even if there isn't much to leave behind," I said.

"Max, I don't catch. What am I going to do there?" said Anday.

"Publish a newspaper," I said, laughing. "You've got the experience. I'm sure in Tasher they have no clue that people need to read newspapers."

"A newspaper? That's great, but your friend says his fellow countrymen mostly don't know how to read," said Anday.

And then it dawned on me. "You know what?" I said. "If they can't read, you can publish comic books. You know, stories in pictures! They can have short captions that even half-literate people can make out."

"In pictures?" said Anday, cheering up. "Well, I'll be, Max!"

The night flew by. I tried to explain to Anday (and to myself) what a newspaper for illiterate Tasherians might look like. Anday, praise be the Magicians, had artistic talent. Excited, I overindulged in "real two-hundred-year-old Ukumbian bomborokka," which I hadn't done in a long time. I ended up dozing off in the armchair. Anday realized that his farewell party was over and began intoning his sad goodbyes.

"Don't make such a doleful face, buddy," I said in a sleepy voice. "Or I'll think that I'm sending you into exile rather than to the wonderful country of your dreams. You can send me a call anytime you want, several times a day. Plus, you're not going away forever. You can come back whenever you want to. 'Abandon all hope, ye who enter here' is a stupid motto. No door in the world closes forever."

"You don't catch, Max," said Anday. "I'm leaving forever. Everyone always leaves forever. You can't come back. Whoever comes back is not us. It's someone else, but nobody catches that. How did you say it, 'Abandon all hope, ye who enter here'? Is this from a poem?"

"It is," I said. "A very old one. And not mine."

"It's very good," said Anday and left.

I was still sitting in my armchair, stunned. That funny fellow managed to really nail it. What did he say? "Whoever comes back is not us; it's someone else"? Oh, boy.

I got up and left the office. I was wide-awake and needed to go for a walk. The soft orange light of the street lamps; the piercing, cold wind from the Xuron; the colorful cobblestones of the streets; and the greenish disk of the moon in the velvety black night—they were all lucky charms protecting me from the desperation of loneliness. In a sense, they, too, were "ordinary magical things."

Maybe it was someone else who returned to the House by the Bridge an hour later, but whoever he was, that guy, he was calm and happy. At least for a while.